Two innocent ladies need to bestow their
hearts and their hands in marriage wisely…

But in the drawing rooms and ballrooms of
Victorian high society or amid the revelry
and intrigue of Queen Elizabeth's court,
it can be hard to decide if a man is really a
rogue, rake, hero or husband-to-be!

Christmas
BETROTHALS

**Two brand-new, fabulous Christmas
historical romances**

**Christmas festivities and romantic
dilemmas from exciting, talented writers
Sophia James and Amanda McCabe**

D1381489

Christmas BETROTHALS

Sophia James
Amanda McCabe

M&B™ and M&B™ with the Rose Device
are trademarks of the publisher.
Harlequin Mills & Boon Limited, Eton House,
18-24 Paradise Road, Richmond, Surrey TW9 1SR

CHRISTMAS BETROTHALS
© Harlequin Enterprises II B.V./S.à.r.l. 2009

Mistletoe Magic © Sophia James 2009
The Winter Queen © Ammanda McCabe 2009

ISBN: 978 0 263 87699 4

011-1109

Harlequin Mills & Boon policy is to use papers that are
natural, renewable and recyclable products and made from
wood grown in sustainable forests. The logging and
manufacturing processes conform to the legal environmental
regulations of the country of origin.

Printed and bound in Spain
by Litografia Rosés S.A., Barcelona

Mistletoe Magic

SOPHIA JAMES

Sophia James lives in Chelsea Bay on Auckland, New Zealand's North Shore, with her husband, who is an artist, and three children. She spends her morning teaching adults English at the local migrant school and writes in the afternoon. Sophia has a degree in English and history from Auckland University and believes her love of writing was formed reading Georgette Heyer with her twin sister at her grandmother's house.

Look out for Sophia James's latest exciting novel, *One Unashamed Night*, available in March 2010 from Mills & Boon® Historical romance.

Author Note

Christmas is a time of family and laughter and joyousness, a time when all the good things in the world seem to come together in a crescendo of happiness.

But what happens when people have no family left or the secrets that bind them to their kin preclude the simple ability to embrace the haphazard chaos that is often Christmas?

In this story I wanted to draw in two people on the edge of loneliness and add children, pets, colour and carols. I wanted to see whether the magic of the season had its own power and whether a kiss bought under a sprig of mistletoe could change two lives forever.

I'd like to dedicate this book to my friend Jane, whose sense of style inspired Lillian.

Prologue

Richmond, Virginia—July 1853

Lucas Clairmont found the letter by chance, wrapped in velvet and hidden in the space beneath the font in the Clairmont family chapel.

A love letter to his wife from a man he had little knowledge of and coined in a language that had him reaching for the pew behind him and sitting down.

Heavily.

He knew their marriage had been, at best, an unexceptional union, but it was the betrayal in the last few lines of the missive that was unexpected. His uncle's land was mentioned in connection with the Baltimore Gaslight Company's intention of developing their lines. Luc shook his head—he knew Stuart Clairmont had had no notion of such a scheme and the land, bought cheaply by Elizabeth's lover, had been sold for a fortune only a few months later.

Loss and guilt punctuated the harder emotion of anger. Jesus! Stuart had died a broken man and a vengeful one.

'Find the bastard, Luc,' he had uttered in the last few hours of his life, 'and kill him.'

At the time Luc had thought the command extreme, but now with the evidence of another truth in hand…

Screwing up the parchment, he let it slip through his fingers on to the cold stone floor, the written words still teasing him, even from a distance.

His marriage had been as much of a sham as his childhood, all show and no substance, but the love of his uncle had never wavered.

Shaking his head, he felt the sharp stab of sobriety, the taste of last night's whisky and the few bought hours of oblivion paid for dearly this morning, as his demons whispered vengeance.

Here in the chapel though, there lay the sort of silence that only God's dwelling could offer with the light streaming in through the stained glass window.

Jesus on the cross!

Luc's fingers squeezed against the hard smooth wood of oak benches, thinking that his own crown of thorns was far less visible.

'Lord, help me,' he enunciated, catching sight of the pale blue eyes of a painted cupid, hair a strange shade of silver blonde, and white clothes falling in folds on to the skin of a nearby sinner, dazzling him with light.

A sinner just like him, Luc thought, as the last effects of moonshine wore off and a headache he'd have until tomorrow started to pound.

Elizabeth. His wife.

He'd been away too much to be the sort of husband he should have been, but the truth of her liaison was as unexpected as her death six months ago. His thoughts of grief unravelled into a sort of bone-hard wrath that shocked him. Deceit and lies were written into every word of these outpourings.

He should not care. He should consign the evidence of his wife's infidelity to a fire, but he found that he couldn't because a certain truth was percolating.

Revenge! One of the seven deadly sins. Today, however, it was not so damning and the ennui that had consumed him lifted slightly.

It would mean going back to England. Again.

His home once.

Perhaps he could claim it back for a while, for apart from the land there was nothing left to hold him here. Besides, Hawk and Nathaniel had asked him to come back to London repeatedly, and he felt a sudden need for the company of his two closest friends.

'Ahhh, Stuart,' he whispered the name and liked the echo of it. The bastard who had swindled his uncle was in London, living on the profit of his ill-gotten gains no doubt.

Daniel Davenport. The name was engraved in his mind like a brand, seared into flesh.

But to kill him? The dying glances of others he had consigned to the hereafter rose from memory.

Not again! He leaned back on the pew and breathed in, trying to determine only the exact amount of force necessary to make Elizabeth's lover sorry.

Chapter One

London—November 1853

'Miss Davenport is a young woman any mother would be proud of, would you not say, Sybil?'

'Indeed, I would, for she countenances no scandal whatsoever. A reputation unsullied in each corner of her life, and a paragon of good sense, good taste and good comportment.'

Lillian Davenport listened to the compliments from her place in the little room, deciding that the two older women hadn't a notion of her being there. To alert them of her overhearing such a private matter would now cause them only embarrassment and so she stayed silent, letting the heavy petticoats in her hands fall to her side and ironing out the creases in white shot silk with her fingers.

'If only my Jane had the sort of grace that she has, I often say to Gerald. If only we had drilled in the importance of the social codes as Ernest Davenport did, we might have been blessed with a very different daughter.'

'Sometimes I think you are too hard on your girl, Sybil. She has her own virtue after all and…'

They were moving away now and out of the ladies' retiring room. Lillian heard the door close and tilted her head, the last of the sentence lost into nothingness.

One minute. She would give them that before she opened the door and took her leave.

A paragon of good sense, good taste and good comportment.

A smile began to form on her face, though she squashed it down. Pride was a sin in its own right and she had no desire to be thought of as boastful.

Still…it was hard not to be pleased with such unexpected praise and, although she frequently detected a general commendation on her manners, it was not often that the words were so direct or honest.

Washing her hands, she shook off the excess, noting how the white gold in her new birthday bracelet caught the light from above. Twenty-five yesterday. Her euphoria died a little, though she pushed the unsettled feeling down as she walked out into a salon of the Lenningtons' townhouse and straight into some sort of fight.

'I think you cheated, you blackguard.' Her cousin Daniel's tones were hardly civil and came from a very close quarter.

'Then call me out. I am equally at home with swords or pistols.' Another voice. Laconic. The drawl of a man new from the former colonies, the laughter in it unexpected.

'And have you kill me?'

'Life or death, Lord Davenport, take your choice or stop your whining.'

There was the sound of pushing and shoving and the two assailants came suddenly into view, Daniel's head now locked in the bent elbow of a tall, dark-haired man, her cousin's eyes bulging from the pressure and his fair hair plastered wet across his forehead.

Lillian was speechless as her glance drew upwards into the face of the assailant. Jacket unbuttoned and with cravat askew, the stranger's jaw was heavily shadowed by dark stubble and she was transfixed by two golden eyes brushed in humour that stared now straight at her. Unrepentant. Unapologetic. Pure and raw man with blood on his lip and danger imprinted in every line of his body.

It seemed that her own throat choked with the contact, her heart slamming full into the ribs of her breast in one heavy blow, leaving her with no breath. A warmth that she had never before felt slid easily from her stomach, fusing even the tips of her fingers with heat, and with it came some other nameless thing, echoing on the edge of a knowledge as old as time. Shocking. Dreadful. She pulled her eyes from his and turned on her heels, but not before she had seen him tip his head at her, the wink he delivered licentious and un- trammelled.

Mannerless, she decided, and American, and with more than a dozen other men and women looking on she knew the gossip about the fight would spread with an unstoppable haste.

Pulling the door to the retiring room open again, she

returned to the same place she had left not more than a few minutes prior.

Anger consumed her.

And dread.

Who was he? She held out one hand and watched it shake before laying it down on her lap and shutting her eyes. A headache had begun to form and behind the pain came a wilder and more unwieldy longing.

'Stop it,' she whispered to herself, placing cold fingers across her lips to soften the sound as the door opened and other women came in, giggling this time and young.

'I love these balls. I love the music and the colour and the gowns…'

'And of all the gowns I love Lillian Davenport's best. Where does she get her clothes from, I wonder? Ester Hamilton says from London, but I would wager France—a modiste from Paris, perhaps, and a milliner from Florence? With all her money she could have them brought from anywhere.'

'Did you see her exquisite bracelet? Her father gave it to her for her birthday. Her twenty-fifth birthday!'

'Twenty-five! Poor Lillian,' the other espoused, 'and no husband or children either! My God, if she does not find a groom soon…'

'Oh, I would not go that far, Harriet. Some women like to live alone.'

'No woman wants to live alone, you peagoose. Besides Lord Wilcox-Rice has been paying her a lot of attention tonight. Perhaps she will fall in love with him and have the wedding of the year in the spring.'

The other girl tittered as they departed, leaving Lillian speechless.

Poor Lillian!

Poor Lillian?

Paragon to poor in all of five minutes, and a stranger outside who made her heart beat in a way that worried her.

'Mama?' The sound came in a prayer. 'Please, Lord, do not let me be anything like Mama.' She pushed the thought away. She would not see this colonial ruffian again; furthermore, if his behaviour tonight was anything to go by, she doubted he would be invited into any house of repute in the future. The thought relaxed her—after all, they were the only sort of homes that she frequented!

Wiping her brow, she stood, feeling better for the thought and much more like herself. She was seldom flustered and almost never blushed and the heartbeat that had raced in her breast was an unheard-of occurrence. Perhaps it was the fight that had made her unsettled and uncertain, for she could not remember a time when she had ever heard a voice raised in such fury or men hitting out at each other. Certainly she had never seen a man in a state of such undress.

Ridiculously she hoped the stranger would have had the sense to adjust his cravat and his jacket before he entered the main salons.

No! Her rational mind rejected such a thought. Let him be thrown out into the street and away from the city. She wondered what had happened to arouse such strong emotion in the first place. Cards, probably, and drink! She had smelt it on their clothes and her cousin's behaviour of late had been increasingly erratic, his sense of honour tarnished with a wilder anger ever since returning home to England.

Poor Lillian!

She would not think about it again. Those silly young girls had no notion of what they spoke of and she was more than happy with her life.

Lucas Clairmont draped his legs across the stool and looked into the fire burning in the grate of Nathaniel Lindsay's town house in Mayfair.

'My face will feel better come the morrow,' Lucas said, raising his glass to swallow the chilled water, the bottle nestling in an ice-bucket beside him.

'Davenport has always had a hot temper, so I'd watch your back on dark nights as you wend your way home. Especially if you are on a winning streak at the tables.'

Luc laughed. Loudly. 'I'd like to see him try it.'

'He is no lightweight, Luc. His family name affords him a position here that is…secure.'

'I'll deal with it, Nat,' he countered, glad when his friend nodded.

'His cousin, Miss Lillian Davenport, on the other hand is formidably scrupulous.'

'She's the woman I saw in the white dress?' He had already asked Nat her name as they had walked to the waiting coach and now seemed the time to find out more, her pale blue eyes and blonde hair reminding him of the lily flowers that grew in profusion near the riverbeds in Richmond, Virginia.

'Is she married?'

'No. She is famous not only for her innate good manners but also for her ability to say no to marriage proposals and, believe me, there have been many.'

Luc gingerly touched his bottom lip, which was still hurting.

'Society here is under the impression that you are a reprobate and a wild cannon, Luc. Many more tussles like tonight and you may find yourself on the outskirts of even the card games.'

Lucas shook his head. 'I barely touched him and he only got in a punch because I wasn't expecting it. Where does Lillian Davenport live, by the way?'

'We're back to her again. My God, she is as dangerous to you as her cousin and many times over more clever. A woman who all men would like to possess and who in the end wants none of them.'

Cassandra bustled into the drawing room, a steaming hot chocolate in hand.

'Take no notice of my husband, Lucas. He speaks from his own poor experience.'

'You were lining up, Nat, at one time?'

'A good seven years back now. Her first coming out it was, and long before I ever set eyes upon my Cassie.'

'And she refused you?'

'Unconditionally. She waited until I had sent her the one and only love letter I have ever written and then gave it back.'

'Better than keeping it, I should imagine.'

He nodded. 'And those famous manners relegate anything personal to the "never to be discussed again" box, which one must find encouraging.'

'So she's not a gossip?'

'Oh, far from it,' Cassie took up the conversation. 'She is the very end word in innate good breeding and perfect bearing. Every young girl who is presented at Court is reminded of her comportment and conduct and encouraged to emulate it.'

'She sounds formidable.'

Cassandra giggled and Nathaniel interrupted his wife as she went to say more. 'Lord, Cassie, enough.' He caught her arm and pulled her down on to his knee. 'Luc is only here in London until the end of December and we have much to reminisce about.'

'I'll drink to that, Nat.' Raising his glass, Luc swallowed the lot, already planning his second foray into discovering the exact character of Daniel Davenport.

Lillian pulled up the sheets on her bed and lay down with a sigh. She had left her curtains slightly open and the moon shone brightly in the space between. A full moon tonight, and the beams covered her room in silver.

She felt…excited, and could not explain the feeling even to herself, the sleep she would have liked so far, far away. Her hand slid across her stomach beneath the gossamer-thin silk nightdress.

John Wilcox-Rice had been most attentive tonight, but it was another face she sought. A darker, more dangerous countenance with laughing golden eyes and a voice from another land. Her fingers traced across her skin soft and gentle, like the path of a feather.

Bringing her hands together when she realised where they lingered, she closed her eyes and summoned sleep.

But the urgency was not dimmed, rather it flared in the silver moon and in the pull of something she had no control over. A single tear ran down her temple and into her hair. Wet. Real. She was twenty-five and waiting for…what?

The stranger had tipped his head to her, night-black hair caught long in the sort of leather strap that a man from past centuries would have worn. Careless of fashion!

His hands had been forceful and brown, work imbued into the very form of them. What must it be like to have a hand like that touch her body? Not soft, not smooth. Fingers that had worked the earth hard or loved a woman well!

She smiled at such a thought, but could not quite dismiss it.

'Please…' she whispered into the night, but the entreaty itself made her pause.

'Let me find someone to love, someone to care for, someone to love me back.' Not for her money or for her clothes or for the colour of her hair, which men always admired. Not those things, she thought.

'For me. For just me.' Words diffusing into the silence of the night as the winds of winter buffeted the house and the almost full moon disappeared behind thick rain-filled clouds.

Chapter Two

Her father was at breakfast the next morning, an occurrence that was becoming more and more rare these days with the time he spent at his clubs and his new interest in horseflesh pulling him away from London for longer and longer time-spans.

'Good morning, Lillian,' he said with a lilt in his voice and her puzzlement grew. 'I have it on good authority that you had a splendid time at the Lenningtons' last night?'

A splendid time? She could not for the life of her quite fathom his meaning.

'Lord Wilcox-Rice called to see me yesterday afternoon to ask if he might court you with an eye to a betrothal later in the month and I had heard from Patrick that you spent much of the night at his side.'

Lillian grimaced at her youngest cousin's penchant for telling a tale. 'I was there as a friend.'

The words were wrung out in anger and her father's brows lifted in astonishment.

'Wilcox-Rice has not said anything to you yet? Perhaps the boy is shy or perhaps you did not encourage him as it may have been prudent to.'

'I do not wish for his advances. I could not even imagine…'

'All the best marriages begin with just that. A friendship that develops into love and lasts a lifetime.'

The unspoken words hung between them.

Like your marriage did not. Mama. A quick dalliance with an unsuitable man and then her death. Repenting it all, and an absolution never given.

'Lord Wilcox-Rice wishes for you to become better acquainted. He wants you to spend some time with him at his estate in Kent. Chaperoned, of course, but well away from London and it may give you the chance to—'

'No, Papa.'

Her father was still. The knife he held in his hand was carefully set down on his plate, the jam upon it as yet to be spread. 'I think, Lillian, we have come to an impasse, you and I. You are a girl with a strong mind, but your years are mounting and the chances you may have for a family and a home of your own are diminishing with each passing birthday.'

Lillian hated this argument. Twenty-five had pounced upon her with all the weight of expectations and conjecture; an iniquitous year when women were no longer young and could not fall back upon the easy excuse of choice.

'John Wilcox-Rice is from a good family with all the advantages of upbringing that you yourself have had. He would not wish to change you, and he would make an admirable father, something that you must be now at least thinking about.'

'But I don't have any feelings for him. Not ones that would naturally lead to marriage.'

With a quick flick of his fingers her father dismissed the servants gathered behind them. Left alone, Lillian could hear the ticking of the grandfather clock in the corner of the room, time marked by mounting seconds of silence.

Finally her father began. 'I am nearing fifty, Lillian, and my health is not as it once was. I need to know that you are settled before I am too much older. I need grandchildren and the chance of an heir for Fairley Manor.'

'You speak as if I am over thirty, Father, and I can see little wrong with the state of your health.' She did not care for the harshness she heard in her voice.

'Then if you cannot understand the gist of my words, I worry about you even more.'

His tone had risen, no longer the measured evenness of logic and sense, and Lillian walked across to the window to look out over Hyde Park where a few people rode their horses on the pathways. Everything was just as it should be, whereas in here....

'I will give you till Christmas.'

'I beg your pardon?' She turned to face him.

'I will give you until Christmas to find a man of your choice to marry, and if you have no other candidate by then you must promise me to consider Wilcox-Rice and without prejudice.'

His face was blotched with redness, the weight he

had put on since last year somehow more worrying than before. Was he ailing? He had seen the physician last week. Perhaps he had learnt something was not right?

Regret and remorse surged simultaneously, but she did not question him. He was a man who held his secrets and seldom divulged his thoughts. Like her, she supposed, and that made her sad.

She was cornered, by parental authority and by the part in her heart that wanted to make her ageing father happy, no matter what.

'It is not so very easy to find a man who is everything that I want.'

'Then find one who is enough, Lillian.' His retort came quickly. 'With children great happiness can follow and Wilcox-Rice is a good fellow. At least give me the benefit of the wisdom old age brings.'

'Very well, then. I will promise to consider your advice.' When she held out her hand to his, she liked the way he did not break the contact, but kept her close.

Half an hour later she was in the morning room to one side of the town house having a cup of tea with Anne Weatherby, an old friend, and trying to feign interest in the topic of her children and family, a subject that usually took up nearly all the hours of her visit. Today, however, she had other issues to discuss.

'There was a contretemps last night at Lenningtons'. Did you hear of it?'

Lillian's attention was immediately caught.

'It seems that your cousin Daniel and a stranger from America were in a scuffle of sorts. I saw him as he

walked from the salon afterwards. He barely looked
English, the savage ways of the backwaters imprinted on
his clothes and hands and face. So dangerous and unciv-
ilised.' She began to smile. 'And yet wildly good-looking.'

'I saw nothing.'

'Rumour has it that you did.'

'Well, perhaps I saw the very end of it all as I came
from the retiring room. It was but a trifle.' She tried to
look bored with the whole subject in the hope that Anne
might change the topic, but was to have no such luck.

'It is said that he has a reputation in America that is
hardly savoury. A Virginian, I am told, whose wife died
in a way that was…suspicious at the very least.'

'Suspicious?'

'Alice, the Countess of Horsham, would say no
more on the matter, but her tone of voice indicated that
the fellow might have had a hand in her demise.' She
shook her head before continuing. 'Although the gossip
is all about town, the young girls seem much enamoured by his looks and are setting their caps at him in
the hopes of even a smile. He has a dimple on his right
cheek, something I always found attractive in a man.'
She placed her hands across her mouth and smiled
through them. 'Lord, but I am running on, and at thirty
I should have a lot more sense than to be swayed by a
handsome face.'

Lillian poured another cup of tea for herself, while
Anne had barely sipped at hers. She hoped that her
friend did not see the way the liquid slopped across the
side of the cup of its own accord and dribbled on to the

white-lace linen cloth beneath it. How easy it was to be tipped from this place to that one. His wife. Dead!

Her imaginings in a bed bathed in moonlight took on a less savoury feel and she pushed down disappointment.

No man had ever swept her off her feet in all the seven years she had been out and to imagine that this one had even the propensity to do so suddenly seemed silly. Of course a man who looked like this American would not be a fit companion for her with his raw and rough manner and his dangerous eyes. The promise she had made her father less than an hour ago surfaced and she shook away the ridiculous yearnings.

Betrothed by Christmas! Ah well, she thought as she guided the conversation to a more general one, if worst came to the worst, John Wilcox-Rice was at least biddable and she *was* past twenty-five.

She met John at a party that evening in Belgrave Square and she knew that she was in trouble as soon as she saw his face. He looked excited and nervous at the same time, his smile both protective and concerned. When he took her fingers in his own she was glad for her gloves and glad too for the ornamental shrubbery placed beside the orchestra. It gave her a chance to escape the prying eyes of others while she tried to explain it all to him.

When the cornet, violin and cello proved too much to speak over she pulled him out on to the balcony a little further away from the room, where the light was dimmer, the shadow of the shrubs throwing a kinder glow on both their faces.

'You had my message from your father, then, about my interest—' he began, but she allowed him no further discourse.

'I certainly did and I thank you for the compliment, but I do not think we could possibly—'

'Your father thinks differently,' he returned, and a sneaking suspicion started to well in Lillian's breast.

'You have seen my father today?' she began, stopping as he nodded.

'Indeed I have and he was at pains to tell me you had agreed to at least consider my proposal.'

'But I do not hold the sort of feelings for you that you would want, and there would be no guarantee that I ever could.'

'I know.' He took her hand again, this time peeling back the fine silk of her right glove, and pressing his lips to her wrist. Without meaning to she dragged her hand away, wiping it on the generous fabric of her skirt and thinking that this meeting place might not have been the wisest one after all.

'I just want you to at least try. I want the chance to make you happy and I think that we would rub along together rather nicely.'

'Well,' she returned briskly, 'I certainly value your friendship and I would indeed be very loath to lose it, but as for the rest....'

He bowed before her. 'I understand and I am ready to give you more time to ponder over it, Lillian, for as like-minded people of a similar birth I am convinced such a union would benefit us both.'

She nodded and watched as he clicked his heels

together and took his leave, a tall, thin man who was passably good looking and infinitely suitable. A husband she could indeed grow old with in a fairly satisfying relationship.

Sighing, she made her way to the edge of the balcony, the same moon as the night before mocking her in her movements, remembering.

'Stop it!' she admonished herself out loud.

'Stop what?' Another voice answered and the American walked out from the shrubs behind her, the red tip of a cheroot the only thing standing out from the black of his silhouette.

'How long have you been there?'

'Long enough.'

'A gentleman would have walked away.'

He pointedly looked across the balustrade. 'The fifteen-foot drop is somewhat of a deterrent.'

'Or stayed quiet until I had left.' The beat of her heart was worrying, erratic, hard. 'Why, most Englishmen would be mortified to find themselves in this situation…' She didn't finish, owing to a loud laugh that rang rich in the night air.

'Mortified?' he repeated. 'It has been a long while since I last felt that.' His accent was measured tonight and at times barely heard, a different voice from the one he had affected at the Lenningtons' with its broad Virginian drawl. She was glad she could not catch his eyes, still shaded by the greenery, though in the position she stood she knew her own to be well on show.

Perhaps he had orchestrated it so? The gold band on the ring finger of his left hand jolted her. His marriage finger! She tried not to let him see where she looked.

'We have not even been introduced, sir. None of this can be in any way proper. You must repair inside this instant.'

Still he did not move, the dimple that Anne Weatherby had spoken of dancing in his cheek.

'I am Lucas Clairmont from Richmond in Virginia,' he said finally. 'And you are Miss Davenport, a woman of manners and good taste, though I wonder at the wisdom of Wilcox-Rice as a groom?'

'He is not that. You just heard me tell him so.'

'He and your father seem to believe otherwise.' Now he walked straight into the light and the golden eyes that had haunted her dreams made her pause. She swallowed heavily and held her hands hard against her thighs to stop them from shaking, though when he picked a slender stem from a pyracanthus bush behind him and handed it to her she leant forwards to take it.

'Thank you.' She could think of nothing else at all to say. The thorn on the stem pricked the base of her thumb.

'I am glad I have this chance to apologise for frightening you yesterday at the Lenningtons'.'

'Apology accepted.' For the first time some of her tension dissipated with the simple reasoning that a criminal mind would not run to seeking any sort of amnesty. 'I realise that my cousin can be rather trying at times.'

His teeth were white against the brown of his face and Lillian was jolted back to reality as his eyes darkened and she saw for a moment a man she barely recognised.

A dangerous man. A man who would not be moulded or conditioned by the society in which he found himself.

So unlike her. She stepped back, afraid now of a thing that she had no name for, and wondered what her cousin had done to cause such enmity.

'Have no fear, Miss Davenport. I would not kill him because he's not worth being hanged at Newgate for.'

Kill him? My God. To even think that he might consider it and then qualify any lack of action with a personal consequence.

I would if I could get away with it.

John Wilcox-Rice's gentle mediocrity began to look far more appealing until Luc Clairmont reached out for her hand and took it in his own. The shock of contact left her mute, but against her will she was drawn to him.

Against her will? She could not even say that!

His finger traced the lines on her palm and then the veins that showed through in the pale skin of her wrist.

'An old Indian woman read my hand once in Richmond. She told me that life was like a river and that we are taken by the currents to a place we are meant to be.'

His amber eyes ran across hers, the humour once again back. 'Is this that place, Miss Davenport?'

Time seemed to stop, frozen into moonlight and want and warmth. When she snatched her hand away and almost ran inside, she could have sworn it was laughter she heard, following her from a balcony drenched in silver.

She stopped walking quite so briskly once she was back amongst others, finding a certain safety in numbers that she had never felt the need of before. Would he come again and speak to her? Would he create a fuss? The very thought had her hauling her fan from her reticule, to waft it to and fro, the breeze engendered calming her a little. She stuffed the sprig of orange berries into her velvet bag, glad to have them out of her fingers where someone might comment upon them.

'Your colour is rather high, Lillian,' her aunt Jean said as she joined her. 'I do hope you are not sickening for something so close to the Yuletide season. Why, Mrs Haugh was saying to me just the other day how her daughter has contracted a bronchial complaint that just cannot be shaken and…'

But Lillian was listening no more, for Lucas Clairmont had just walked in from the balcony, a tall broad-shouldered man who made the other gentlemen here look…mealy, precious and dandified. No, she must not think like that! Concentrating instead on the mark around his bottom lip that suggested another fight, she tried to ignore the way all the women in his path watched him beneath covert hooded glances.

He was leaving with the Earl of St Auburn and a man she knew to be Lord Stephen Hawkhurst. Well-placed men with the same air of menace that he had. The fact interested her and she wondered just how it was they knew each other.

As they reached the door, however, Lucas Clairmont looked straight into her eyes, tipping his head as she had seen him do at the Lenningtons' ball. Hating the way her heartbeat flared, Lillian spread her fan wide and hid her face from his, a breathless wonder overcoming caution as a game, of which she had no notion of the rules, was begun.

Once home herself she placed the crumpled orange pyracanthus in a single bloom vase and stood it on the small table by her bed. Both the colour and the shape clashed with everything else in her bedroom. As out of place in her life as Lucas Clairmont was, a vibrant interloper who conformed to neither position nor venue. Her finger reached out to carefully touch the hard nubs of thorn that marched down its stem. Forbidding. Protective. Unexpected in the riot of colour above it!

She wished she had left it on the balcony, discarded and cast aside, as she should be doing with the thoughts of the man who had picked it. But she had not and here it was with pride of place in a room that looked as if it held its breath with nervousness. Her eyes ran over the sheer lawn drapes about her bed, the petit-point bedcover upon it in limed cream and the lamp next to her, its chalky base topped by a faded and expensive seventeenth-century tapestry. The décor in her room was nothing like the fashion of the day with its emphasis on stripes and paisleys and the busy tones of purple and red. But she enjoyed the difference.

All had been carefully chosen and were eminently suitable, like the clothes she wore and the friends she fostered. Her life. Not haphazard or risky, neither arbitrary nor disorganised.

Once it had been, once when her mother had come

home to tell them that she was leaving that very afternoon *'to find excitement and adventure in the arms of a man who was thrilling'*. The very words used still managed to make her feel slightly sick, as she remembered a young girl who had idolised her mother. She was not *thrilling* and so she had been left behind, an only child whose recourse to making her father happy was to be exactly the daughter he wanted. She had excelled in her lessons and in her deportment, and later still when she came out at eighteen she had been daubed an 'original', her sense of style and quiet stillness copied by all the younger ladies at Court.

Usually she liked that. Usually she felt a certain pride in the way she handled everything with such easy acumen. But today with the berries waving their overblown and unrestrained shapes in her room, a sense of disquiet also lingered.

Poor Lillian.

John Wilcox-Rice and his eminently sensible proposal.

Her father's advancing age.

The pieces of her life were not quite adding up to a cohesive whole any longer, and she could pin the feeling directly to Lucas Clairmont with his easy smile and his dangerous predatory eyes.

Standing by the window, she saw an outline of herself reflected in the glass. As pale as the colours in her room, perhaps, and fading. Was she her mother's daughter right down to the fact of finding her own 'thrilling and unsuitable man'? She laid her palm against the glass and, on removing it, wrote her mother's initials in the misted print

Rebecca Davenport had returned in the autumn, a thinner and sadder version of the woman who had left them, and although her father had taken her back into his house he had never taken her back into his heart. No one had known of her infidelity. The extended holiday to the Davenports' northern estate of Fairley Manor was never explained and, although people had their suspicions, the steely correctness of Ernest Davenport had meant that they were never even whispered.

Perhaps that had made things even harder, Lillian thought. The constant charade and pretence as her mother lay dying with an ague of the soul and she, a child who went between her parents with the necessary messages, seeing any respect that they had once had for each other wither with the onset of winter.

Even the funeral had been a sham, her mother's body laid in the crypt of the Davenports with all the ceremony expected, and then left unvisited.

No, the path Rebecca had taken had alienated her from everybody and should her daughter be so foolish as to follow in those footsteps she could well see the consequences of 'thrilling'.

John Wilcox-Rice was a man who would never break her heart. A constant man of sound morals and even sounder political persuasions. One hand threaded through her hair and she smiled unwillingly at the excitement that coursed through her. Everything seemed different. More tumultuous. Brighter. She walked across to the bed and ran a finger across the smooth orange berries, liking the fact that Lucas Clairmont had touched them just as she was now.

Silly thoughts. Girlish thoughts.

She was twenty-five, for goodness' sake, and a woman who had always looked askance at those highly strung débutantes whose emotions seemed to rule them. The invitation to the Cholmondeley ball on the sill caught her attention and she lifted it up. Would the American be attending this tomorrow? Perhaps he might ask her to dance? Perhaps he might lift up her hand to his again?

She shook her head and turned away as a maid came to help her get ready for bed.

Chapter Three

Luc spent the morning with a lawyer from the City signing documents and hating every single signature he marked the many pages with.

The estate of Woodruff Abbey in Bedfordshire was a place he neither wanted nor deserved and his wife's cries as she lay dying in Charlottesville, Virginia, were louder here than they had been in all the months since he had killed her.

He did not wish for the house or the chattels. He wanted to walk away and let the memories lie because recollection had the propensity to rekindle all that was gone.

Shaking away introspection, he made himself smile, a last armour against the ghosts that dragged him down.

'Will you be going up to look the old place over, Sir?'

'Perhaps.' Non-committal. Evasive.

'It is just if you wish me to accompany you, I would need to make plans.'

'No. That will not be necessary.' If he went, he would go alone.

'The servants, of course, still take retainers paid for by the rental of the farming land, though in truth the place has been let go badly.'

'I see.' He wanted just to leave. Just to take the papers and leave.

'Your wife's sister's daughters are installed in the house. Their mother died late last year and I wrote to you—'

Luc looked up. 'I did not have any such missive.'

The lawyer rifled through a sheath of sheets and, producing a paper, handed it across to him. 'Is this not your handwriting, sir?' A frown covered his brow.

With his signature staring up at him, Luc could do nothing else but nod.

'How old are these children?'

'Eight and ten, sir, and both girls.'

'Where is their father?'

'He left England a good while back and never returned. He was a violent man and, if I were to guess, I would say he lies in a pauper's grave somewhere, unmarked and uncared for. Charity and Hope are, however, the sort of girls their names suggest, and as soon as they gain their majority they will have no more claim to any favours from the Woodruff Abbey funds.'

Luc placed the paper down on the table before him. So poor-spirited, he thought, to do your duty up to a certain point and then decline further association. He had seen it time and time again in his own father, the action of being seen to have done one's duty more important than any benefit to those actively involved.

Unexpectedly he thought of Lillian Davenport. Would she be the same? he wondered, and hoped not. Last night when he had run his fingers across the pale skin on her wrist he had felt her heartbeat accelerate markedly and seen the flush that covered her cheeks before she had turned and run from him.

Not all the ice queen then, her high moral standards twisted against his baser want. Because he *had* wanted her, wanted to bring his hands along the contours of her face and her breasts and her hips hidden beneath her fancy clothing and distance.

Lord, was he stupid?

He should not have made his presence known. Should not have sparred with her or held her fingers and read her palm, for Lillian Davenport was the self-styled keeper of worthiness and he needed to stay away from her.

Yet she pierced a place in him that he had long thought of as dead, the parts of himself that he used to like, the parts that the past weeks of sobriety had begun to thaw against the bone-cold guilt that had torn at his soul.

The law books lined up against the far wall dusty in today's thin sun called him back. Horatio Thackeray was now detailing the process of the transfer of title.

Woodruff Abbey was his! He turned the gold ring on his wedding finger and pressed down hard.

Lillian enjoyed the afternoon taking tea in Regent Street with Anne Weatherby and her husband Allen.

His brother Alistair had joined them, too, a tall and pleasant man.

'I have lived in Edinburgh for a good few years now,' he explained when she asked him why she had not met him before. 'I have land there and prefer the quieter pace of life.' Catching sight of a shopkeeper trying to prop up a Christmas tree in his window, he laughed. 'Queen Victoria has certainly made the season fashionable. Do you decorate a tree, Miss Davenport?'

'Oh, more than one, Mr Weatherby. I often have three or four in the town house.'

'And I am certain that you would do so with great aplomb if my sister-in-law's comments on your sense of style are to be taken into consideration.' He smiled and moved closer. 'If I could even be so bold as to ask for permission to accompany Anne to see these Yuletide trees next time she visits, I would be most grateful.'

The man was flirting with her, Lillian suddenly thought, and averted her eyes. Catching the glance of Anne at her side, she realised immediately that her friend was in on the plot.

Another man thrust beneath her nose. Another suitor who wanted a better acquaintance. All of a sudden she wished that it could have been just this easy. An instant attraction to a man who was suitable. The very thought made her tired. Perhaps she was never destined to be a wife or a mother.

'You're very quiet, Lillian?' Anne took her hand as they walked towards the waiting coach.

'I have a lot to think about.'

'I hope that Alistair is one of those thoughts?' she

whispered back wickedly, laughing as Lillian made absolutely no answer. 'Would he not do just as well as Wilcox-Rice? His holdings are substantial and Scotland is a beautiful place.'

The tree in the window was suddenly hoisted into position with the sound of cheering, a small reminder of her father's ultimatum of choosing a groom before Christmas. Lillian placed a tight smile across her face.

'I am not so desperate as to throw myself on a stranger, Anne, no matter how nice he is and I would prefer it if you would not meddle.'

The joy had quite gone out of the afternoon and she hated the answering annoyance in her oldest friend's eyes. But today she could not help it. She had not been sleeping well, dreams of Virginia and the dark-haired American haunting her slumber, the remembered feel of his thumb tracing the beat on her wrist and the last sight of him tipping his head as he had left the room in the company of his friends.

To compare Lucas Clairmont to these other men was like equating the light made by tiny fireflies to that of the full-blown sun, a man whom she had never met the measure of before in making her aware that she was a woman. Breathing out heavily, she held on to her composure and answered a question Alistair asked her with all the eagerness that she could muster.

Chapter Four

The gown Lillian wore to the Cholmondeley ball was one of her favourites, a white satin dress with wide petticoats looped with tulle flowers. The train was of glacé and moiré silk, the festoons on the edge plain but beautiful. Her hair was entwined with a single strand of diamonds and these were mirrored in the quiet beading on her bodice. She seldom wore much ornamentation, preferring an understated elegance, and virtually always favoured white.

The ball was in full swing when she arrived with her father and aunt after ten; the suites of rooms on the first floor of the town house were opened up to each other and the floor in the long drawing room was polished until it shone. At the top of the chamber sat a substantial orchestra, and within it a group of guests that would have numbered well over four hundred.

'James Cholmondeley is harking for the renommée of a crush,' her father murmured as they made their way inside. 'Let us hope that the champagne, at least, is of good quality.'

'He must be of the persuasion that it is of benefit to be remembered in London, whether good or ill.' Her aunt Jean's voice was louder than Lillian would have liked it. 'And I do hope that your dress is not hopelessly wrecked in such a crowd, my dear, and that the floor does not mark your satin slippers.' She looked up as she spoke. 'At least they have replaced the candles in the chandeliers with globe lamps so we are not to be burned.'

Lillian was not listening to her aunt's seemingly endless list of complaints. To her the chamber looked beautiful, with its long pale-yellow banners and fresh flowers. The late-blooming roses were particularly lovely, she thought, as she scanned the room.

Was Lucas Clairmont here already? He was taller than a great deal of the other gentlemen present so he might not be too hard to find.

John Wilcox-Rice's arm on hers made her start. 'I have been waiting for you to come, Lillian. I thought indeed that you might have been at the MacLay ball in Mayfair.'

'No, we went to the Manners's place in Belgrave Square.'

'I had toyed with the idea of going there myself, but Andrew MacLay is a special friend of mine and I had promised him my patronage.' A burst of music from the orchestra caught his attention as the instruments were tuned. 'The quadrille should be beginning soon. May I have the pleasure of escorting you through it?'

Her heart sank at his request, but manners forced her

to smile. 'Of course,' she said, marking her dance card with his name.

The lead-off dance might give her the chance to look more closely at the patrons of this ball, as the pace of the thing was seldom faster than a walk and Lucas Clairmont as an untitled stranger would not be able to take his place at the top of the ballroom without offending everyone.

Her heart began to beat faster. Would he know of those rules? Would he be aware of such social ostracism should he try to invade a higher set? Lord, the things that had until tonight never worried her began to eat at her composure.

Still as yet she had not seen him, though she supposed a card room to be set up somewhere. She unfurled her fan, enjoying the cool air around her face and hoped that he would not surprise her with his presence.

The quadrille was called almost immediately and Lillian walked to the top of the room, using up some of the small talk that was the first necessity for dancing it as she went.

Holding her skirt out a little, she began the *chasser*, the sedate tempo of the steps allowing conversation.

'Are you in London for the whole of the Yule season?' Wilcox-Rice asked her, and she shook her head.

'No, we will repair to Fairley in the first week of January and stay down till February. Papa is keen to see how his new horses race and has employed the services of a well-thought-of jockey in his quest to be included in next year's Derby Day at Epsom. And you?' Feeling it only polite, she asked him the same question back.

'Your father asked me down after Twelfth Night. Did he not tell you?'

Lillian shook her head.

'If you would rather I declined, you just need to say the word.'

She was saved answering by the complicated steps of the dance spiriting her away from him. The elderly gentleman she now faced smiled, but remained silent; taking her lead from him she was glad for the respite.

Luc watched Lillian Davenport from his place behind a colonnade at the foot of the room. He had seen her enter, seen the rush of men surround her asking for a dance and Wilcox-Rice placing his hand across hers to draw her away from them. Her father was there, too; Nat had pointed him out and an older woman whom he presumed was a family member. She seemed to be grumbling about something above her and Luc supposed it must be the lighting. Lillian looked as she always did, unapproachable and elegant. He noticed how the women around her covertly looked over her dress, a shining assortment of shades of white material cascading across a lacy petticoat.

She had worn white every single time he had seen her and the colour mirrored the paleness of her skin and hair. He smiled at his own ruminations. Lord, when had he ever noticed what a woman had worn before? The mirth died a little as he thought about the ramifications of such awareness. With determination he turned away, the quadrille and its ridiculous rules taking up the whole of the upper ballroom. British aristocracy took itself so seriously; in Virginia such unwritten social codes would be laughed about and ignored. Here, however, he did not wish for the bother of making his point. In less than two months he would be on a ship sailing back to America where the nonsensical and exclusive dances of the upper classes in London would be only a memory.

The chatter of voices around him made him turn and Nathaniel introduced two very pretty sisters to him, the elder laying her hand across his arm and showing him a card that she had, the dances named on one side and a few blank spaces that were not filled in with pencil upon the other.

'I have a polka free still, sir. If you should like to ask me…'

Nat laughed beside him. 'I have been fending off interested ladies since you arrived, Luc. Do me at least the courtesy of filling your night so that I have no further need of mediation and diplomacy.'

Cornered, Luc assented though it had been a long time since he had learned the steps to the thing. A complicated dance, he remembered, though not as fast as the galop. He wished he had taken better heed of his teacher's instructions when he had been a lad, and wished also that it might have been Lillian Davenport that he partnered.

The girl's younger sister thrust her own card at him and he was glad when they finally turned to leave.

Lord, time was beginning to run short and he did not want to be in England any longer than he had to be.

A flash of Lillian caught his eye as she finished with the quadrille and bowed to her partner. Finally it looked as though Wilcox-Rice might depart of his own accord and that he could get at least a little conversation with the most beautiful woman in the room.

But when another man claimed her for the waltz he admitted defeat and moved into the next salon to see what could be had in the way of supper.

The dancing programme was almost halfway through and Lillian was quite exhausted. She had deliberately pencilled in two waltzes with made-up initials just in case Luc Clairmont should show, but by midnight was giving up the hope of seeing him here.

Sir Richard Graham, a man who had pursued her several years earlier and one she had never warmed to, had asked her for the third galop and she had just taken her place in the circle when she felt a strange tingle along the back of her neck.

He was here, she was sure of it, the shock of connection as vivid as it had been on first seeing him outside the retiring room at the Lenningtons'.

Gritting her teeth, she took four steps forwards as her partner took her left hand in his, and when she moved back again she casually looked across her shoulder.

He was three or four couples behind them, partnering a pretty girl whom she knew to be the younger one of the Parker sisters and he looked for all the world as if he might actually be enjoying the dance. Certainly the Parker girl was, her colour high and her eyes flashing, the dimples in her cheeks easily on show.

Perhaps he had been here all night and made no effort to single her out. Perhaps this sharp knowledge she felt when he was near her was not reciprocated. Stepping forwards, she gained in ground on the couple in front of her and Graham's hand closed upon her own, slowing her down. Concentrate, she admonished herself. Concentrate and pretend that Lucas Clairmont is not there, that you do not care for him, this reckless colonial who can only do your reputation harm.

For the next few figures in the dance she felt her confidence return, then drain away altogether as he winked at her when she caught his eyes across the small space between them. She turned away quickly, not deigning any reply, and listened to some inconsequential thing her partner was relaying to her, trying to give the impression of the free-and-fancy woman she did not feel at all. When the dance ended she curtsied and allowed Graham to take her hand and lead her back to the shelter of her aunt, a courtesy she rarely took part in.

'You look flushed, my dear,' Jean said as she finished off a sizeable glass of lemonade, followed by a strawberry bonbon. The first strains of a waltz filled the air and Lillian looked at her card. The initials she had written there stared back at her.

'Your partner for this next dance is rather tardy.' Aunt Jean looked around expectantly. 'Ahh, here he is now.'

Lillian's head whipped upwards as Luc Clairmont strode into view beside them, and again she was mesmerised by his reckless golden eyes.

'Miss Davenport,' he said before turning to her companion. 'Ma'am.'

Her aunt's mouth had dropped open, the red of the strawberry bonbon strangely marking her tongue.

'Aunt Jean, let me introduce you to Mr Lucas Clairmont, from America. Mr Clairmont this is my aunt, Lady Taylor-Reid.'

Again Luc bowed his head. 'Pleased to meet you, ma'am.'

Her aunt flushed strangely. 'How long have you been in England, Mr Clairmont?'

'Only a few weeks'

'Do you like it?'

'Indeed I do.' He looked straight at her, the dimple in his cheek deeper than she had seen it, the gold of his eyes glinting in mirth.

The music had now begun in earnest, the dance getting underway and, excusing herself, she allowed Lucas to guide her through the throngs of people.

On the floor his hand laced around her waist and she felt the warmth of it like a burn. In England it was proper for couples to stand a good foot apart, but the American way seemed different as he brought her close, his free hand taking her fingers and clasping them tight.

'I had thought I would have no chance for a waltz with you, Lillian. How is it that your card is empty on the best dance of them all?'

She ignored his familiar use of her name, reasoning that as no one else had heard him use it, it could do no harm.

'It was a mix-up,' she replied as they swirled effortlessly around the room. He was a good dancer! No wonder the Parker sister had looked so thrilled.

'Are there other mix-ups on your card?'

She laughed, surprised by his candour. 'Actually, I have the last waltz free…'

'Pencil me in,' he replied, sweeping her around the top corner of the room, her petticoat swirling to one side with the movement of it, an elation building that she had never before felt in dancing.

Safe. Strong. The outline of his muscles could be seen against the black of his jacket and felt in the hard power of his thighs. A man who had not grown up in the salons of courtly life but in a tougher place of work and need. Even his clothes mirrored a disregard for the height of fashion, his jacket not the best of cuts and his shoes a dull matt black. Just a 'little dressed,' she thought, his apparel of a make that held no pretension to arrogance or ornament. She saw that he had tied his neckcloth simply and that his gloves were removed.

She wished she had done the same and then she might feel the touch of his skin against her own, but the thought withered with the onslaught of his next words.

'I am bound for Virginia before too much longer. I have passage on a ship in late December and, if the seas are kind, I may see Hampton by the middle of February.'

'Hampton is your home?' She tried to keep the question light and her disappointment hidden.

'No. My place is up on the James River, near Richmond.'

'And your family?'

When he did not answer and the light in his eyes dimmed with her words, she tried another tack. 'I had a friend once who left London for a home in Philadelphia. Is that somewhere near?'

'Somewhere…' he answered, whirling her around

one last time before the music stopped. Bowing to her as their hands dropped away from each other, he asked, 'May I escort you back to your aunt? Your father does not look too happy with my dancing style.'

Lillian smiled and did not look over at her father for fear that he might beckon her back. 'No. I have not supped yet and find myself hungry.'

The break in the music allowed him the luxury of choice. If he wanted to slip away he could, and if he wanted to accompany her to the supper room he had only to take her arm. She was pleased when he did that, allowing herself to be manoeuvred towards the refreshment room.

Once there she was at a loss as to what to say next, his admission of travelling home so soon having taken the wind from her sails. She saw the Parker girls and their friends behind him some little distance away and noticed that they watched her intently.

When he handed her a plate she thanked him, though he did not take one, helping himself to a generous drink of lemonade instead.

'Are you in London over Christmas?' His question was one she had been asked all the night, a conversation topic of little real value and, when compared to the communion they had enjoyed the last time of meeting, disappointing.

She nodded. 'We usually repair to Fairley Manor, our country seat in Hertfordshire, in the first week of January.' When he smiled all of the magic returned in a flood.

'Nathaniel Lindsay is to give a house party at his country estate in Kent on the weekend of November the twentieth. Will you be there?'

'The Earl of St Auburn? I do not know if I have an invite…'

'I could send you one.'

Shock mixed with delight and ran straight through into the chambers of her heart.

'It is not proper.'

'But you will come anyway?'

He did not move closer or raise his voice, he did not reach out for her hand or brush his arm against her own as he so easily could here at this crowded refreshment table, and because of it, the invite was even the more clandestine. Real. A measure taken to transport her from this place to another one.

An interruption by the Countess of Horsham meant that she could not answer him, and when he excused himself from their company she let him go, fixing her glance upon the tasteless biscuit on her plate.

Alice watched him, however, and the smile on her lips was unwelcome. 'I had heard you witnessed the fellow in a contretemps the other evening? Do you know him, Lillian, know anything of his family and his living?'

'Just a little. He is a good friend of the Earl of St Auburn.'

'Indeed. There are other rumours that I have heard, too. It seems he may have inherited a substantial property on the death of his wife. Some say he is here to collect that inheritance and leave again, more gold for his gambling habit and the fracas with your cousin still unresolved. Less kind folks would say that he killed the woman to get the property and that his many children out of wedlock are installed in the place.'

'Are you warning me, Countess?

'Do I need to, Lillian?'

'No.' She bit down on the lemon biscuit and washed away the dryness with chilled tea, the taste combined as bitter as the realisation that she was being watched. And watched carefully.

Of course she could not go to Kent even if she had wanted to. Pretending a headache, she excused herself from the Countess's company, and went to find her aunt.

Luc saw her leave, the ball still having at least an hour left and the promised last dance turning to dust. The Countess of Horsham's husband was a man he had met at the card tables and a gossip of the first order. Lord, the tale of his own poor reputation had probably reached Lillian and he doubted that she would countenance such a lack of morals. Perhaps it was for the best. Perhaps the 'very good' had a God-given inbuilt mechanism of protection that fended off people like him, a celestial safeguard that separated the chaff from the wheat.

When the oldest Parker sister obstructed his passage on the pretext of claiming him in the next dance, he made himself smile as he escorted the girl on to the floor.

Once home Lillian checked the week's invitations scattered on the hall table. When she found none from the Earl of St Auburn, she relaxed. No problem to mull over and dither about, no temptation to answer in the affirmative and have her heart broken completely. She remembered her last sight of Lucas Clairmont flirting with the pretty Parker heiress she had seen him with earlier in the evening, the same smile he had bequeathed her wide across his face.

On gaining her room, she snatched the stupid orange pyracanthus from the vase near her bed and threw it into the fire burning brightly in the grate. A few of the berries fell off in their flight, and she picked them up, squeezing them angrily and liking the way the juice of blushed red stained her hand.

She would invite Wilcox-Rice to call on her tomorrow and make an effort to show some kindness. Such an act would please her father and allay the fears of her aunt who had regaled her all the way home on the ills of marrying improperly and the ruin that could follow.

Lillian wondered how much her father had told his only sister about the downfall of his wife and was glad, at least, that Aunt Jean had had the sense not to mention any such knowledge to her. Indeed, she needed to regain her balance, her equanimity and her tranquil demeanour and to do that she needed to stay well away from Lucas Clairmont.

Chapter Five

Woodruff Abbey, in Bedfordshire, was old, a house constructed in the days when the classical lines of architecture had been in their heyday, early seventeenth century or late sixteenth. Now it just looked tired, the colonnades in the portico chipped and rough and numerous windows boarded in places, as though the glass had been broken and was not able to be repaired. The thought puzzled him—the income of this place was well able to cover expenses towards the upkeep and day-to-day running, according to Thackeray, his lawyer. Why then had it been left to look so rundown?

At the front door he stopped and looked at the garden stretching from the house to the parkland below and the polluted business of London seemed far away. Breathing in, he smiled, and the tense anger of the past few years seemed to recede a bit, the faded elegance of the Abbey soothing in its dishevelled beauty.

The door was suddenly pulled open and a man stood

there. An old man, whose hat was placed low upon his head and whose eyes held the rheumy glare of one who could in truth barely see.

'May I be of assistance, sir?' His cultured voice was surprising.

'I am Lucas Clairmont. I hope that Mr Thackeray has sent you word of my coming.'

'The lawyer? Clairmont? Lord! You are here already?'

'I am.' Luc waited. The man did not move from his place in the middle of the doorway, his knuckles clutching white at the lintel as though he might fall.

'The Mr Clairmont from America?'

'Indeed.' He bit back a smile. Was he going to be invited into his own house or not?

'Who is there, Jack? Who is at the door? Tell them that we need nothing.'

A woman appeared behind him, a woman every bit as old as he was, her shawl wrapped tightly across a thin frame, spectacles balancing on her nose.

'It is Mr Clairmont, Lizzie. Mr Clairmont, this is my wife, Mrs Poole'

Her eyes widened behind the glasses and the frown that had been there when he first saw her thickened.

'We had word, of course, but we had not thought…'

Her words petered out as she stood beside her husband, both of them now looking across at his person as if they could not quite believe he was there.

'May I come in?'

The request sent them into a whirl of activity and as the door was thrown wide open they stepped back.

The wide central portico was open to the roof, and the oversized windows let in a generous amount of light. He noticed that the floors were well scrubbed and that the banisters and woodwork had been polished until they shone. Not an unloved house, then, but one strapped by the lack of cash.

'We are Jack and Lizzie Poole, sir,' the woman said once the door was again fastened, 'and we have served this estate for nigh on a century between us.'

Luc nodded, easily believing the length of time stated.

'And where are the other servants who help you?'

'Other servants, sir?' Puzzlement showed on their brows.

'The cook and the governess, the maids and the grooms. Where are they?'

'It's only us, sir, and it has been for a very long time.'

'But there are children here?'

Both their eyes lit up. 'Indeed there are. Miss Charity and Miss Hope and good girls they are at that.'

'Who teaches them, then? Who sees to their lessons?'

'There is nobody else.'

'So I am to understand that it is just you and the two girls who live here and have done so for some months?'

'Almost twelve months, sir, since the money stopped coming and they all up and left! Not us though, we could not stand around and see the wee ones homeless.'

Luc took in a breath and he swore he would visit Thackeray the instant he returned to town in order to get to the bottom of just where the funds had gone.

'Where are the children? Could they be brought down?'

'Down, sir?'

'From the nursery?'

'Oh, goodness gracious, they are seldom there. If it is a fine day they will be down by the lake, and if it is a wet one in their hut near the trees.'

This time he did laugh. Two little girls without the weight of the English society rules upon them promised to be interesting indeed. His own childhood had been much the same, a violent father whom he saw only intermittently and a mother who was never well. Perhaps these old people would have been an improvement!

A noise from one end of the hall had them turning and a child stood there. A thin pale child with the shortest hair he had ever seen on a girl of her age and large blue eyes.

'Charity,' Mrs Poole said as she walked forwards. 'You are back early. Come and meet Mr Clairmont, dear, for he is just come from London.'

The girl's teeth worried her bottom lip and her light glance was full of anxiety, but she allowed the woman to shuffle her forwards.

'She does not speak as such since the passing of her mother, sir, but she will certainly know you.'

Did not speak? He had had little to do with children in his life and was at a loss as to how to deal with this one. Still he tried his best. 'I would like to see your tree house one day.'

She nodded. At least she understood him without lip reading, her eyes trained upon the floor.

'Her sister, Hope, will not be in till after dark. Will you be staying, sir?'

He wondered what Hope did for all of the hours of daylight, but with the lack of concern on all the faces before him refrained from asking the question.

'I have not booked passage back to London until the morrow and I think there is much to discuss about this situation.'

Lizzie Poole looked at her husband and Charity clutched the old lady's hand tighter, Luc calculating in a second that although there was not a lot here in the way of material richness, love was apparent. For that at least he was glad.

'Jack here will see you to your room, Mr Lucas, and I will go to the kitchen to prepare some dinner. Charity love, will you give me a hand?'

When the child smiled the sun came out, her deep dimples etched into her cheeks and blue eyes dancing with laughter. A beauty, he thought suddenly, and Lillian Davenport came to mind. This girl had her sort of timeless elegance, even dressed as she was in a gown about two sizes too small and patched everywhere. He wondered what the sister would look like as he followed Jack Poole up the solid oak staircase.

Dinner consisted of two tiny cooked carcases he presumed to be wild fowl, a bowl full of boiled potatoes and a handful of greenery that looked like the watercress farmers in Virginia grew by the James.

'The land provideth and the Lord taketh away,' Mrs Poole told him sagely as they sat at a table in the kitchen, the fire in the oven behind a welcome asset to keep out the cold.

Hope was still outside, he presumed, as her place was empty. Charity sat next to him, her hands folded in her lap as she waited for grace to be said. A long and complex prayer of thanks it turned out to be too, a good five minutes having passed as Lizzie Poole gave acknowledgement for all the things that God had sent them, for their health and hearth and laughter, for the fuel which fed the fire and the earth which supported them. To Luc's mind she seemed a trifle generous in her praise, the fowl in particular looking like they had seen but three months of life and barely eaten anything in that time. Still, it was refreshing to see gratefulness in small blessings and he wondered what she might say of the overladen London tables should she ever see them.

Just as they had finished the kitchen door banged open and an older child walked in. She looked nothing like her sister, except for her thin build, her hair a wild tangle of long deep brown curls and her skin darkened by the sun.

'I am sorry to be so late, Lizzie,' she said, stopping as bright emerald eyes met his own. Another beauty, but of a different mould.

'This is Mr Lucas Clairmont, Hope. He has come from London today to see you and your sister.'

Hope's eyes went to Charity's and a communication passed between them. A silent language of perception and accord.

'Very pleased to meet you, sir.' She curtsied in a way reminiscent of another age.

'Mrs Poole tells me you spend a lot of time outdoors. What things do you do there?'

'We fish sometimes for the dinner table, and collect this cress. If we are lucky, we bag hares or wild birds and in the spring we steal the eggs from the nests that are low in the hedgerows.'

'So this bounty is your doing?' he replied, gesturing to the food on the table.

'Some of it is, sir. Winter is the most difficult time to gather, but come spring we can find all sorts of berries and mushrooms and even wild tomatoes.'

'So your sister helps you?'

'Of course.' She flashed a smile and the other nodded. Tonight Charity appeared a lot more worried than she had a few hours ago but Hope picked up quickly on her fright, settling herself on the other side of the girl and again that wordless communication that excluded everyone in the room.

'They are very close, sir. If anyone were to split them up…'

'I have not come here to do that.'

'This house is the only home they have ever known and were they to be thrown out…'

'I have not come to do that, either.'

'Their mother was perhaps a trifle wild, I realise that, but Charity and Hope have never caused us even a moment's worry.'

Luc placed his eating utensils down and laid his hands on the table. 'Thackeray led me to believe the girls were being looked after in the manner my late wife would have wished them to be. If I had had any notion of the lack of finance you have put up with for the last God knows how many months—' he stopped as the old lady winced at his profanity '—for the last months,' he repeated, 'then I would have been up here a lot sooner.'

'So we can stay?' Hope asked the question, the same emotion as her name easily heard in her voice.

'Indeed you can, and I will see to it as soon as I return to London.'

He left Woodruff Abbey with all of its inhabitants waving him goodbye and a handful of warm potatoes wrapped in cloth that Charity had given him.

The first thing he did when he arrived in the city was to tell the elderly Horatio Thackeray that his services as his lawyer were no longer needed, and set an investigator on to the trail of finding where the money had gone. In his stead he hired a younger and more compassionate man whose reputation had been steadily rising in the city.

'So you wish for Woodruff Abbey to be kept in trust for the children?' David Kennedy's voice contained a tone in it that could most succinctly be described as incredulous.

'That is correct.'

'You realise of course that once the deed is filed it is binding and you would have no hope of seeing your property back should you change your mind at a later date?'

'I do.'

'You also wish for the monies from the estate to be placed in a fund to see to the running of the Abbey, and for a specified number of servants to be hired to help the older couple?'

'That is right.'

'Then if you are certain that that is what you want and you have understood the finality of such a generous gesture, you must sign here. To begin the process, you understand. I shall get back to you within the month when the deeds are written.'

A quick scrawl and it was done. Luc replaced the ink pen in its pot and gathered his hat.

'There is one proviso, Mr Kennedy.'

The lawyer looked startled.

'The proviso is that you tell no one of this.'

'You do not wish others to know of your generosity?'

'I do not.'

'Very well, sir. Will that be all today?'

'No, there is another thing. I am transferring funds from an account I hold here in London, which shall stay in place in case of any shortfall. Under no circumstance at all do I wish for the inhabitants of the Abbey to go without again. If indeed there is any problem at all, I expect to be contacted with as much haste as you could muster to remedy the matter.'

'That shall be done, sir. Might I also say how pleased I am to have the chance to do business with you—'

'Thank you,' Luc cut him short. He had a card game he could not miss that was due to start in just over two hours and he needed to take the omnibus to Piccadilly.

Lillian tucked her diary away in the small console by her bed and told herself that she should not write of her thoughts of Lucas Clairmont.

She had heard that he had been away from London

for the past five days, travelling according to Nathaniel Lindsay's wife, Cassandra, who was the sister of Anne Weatherby. Where, she had no clue, though according to Anne he had left his lodgings and given no idea of when he expected to return.

Presumably it would be before the house party on Friday. She wondered who he knew in England to take him away for such a period and remembered the Countess of Horsham's scandalous gossip. Lillian shook her head. Surely a man of little means and newly come from the Americas would not have the wherewithal to house any children, let alone those born out of wedlock?

Lucas Clairmont was a mystery, she thought, his accent changing each time she saw him and some dark menace in his golden eyes. Not a man to be trifled with, she decided, and not a man whom others might persuade to take any course he did not wish to, either.

She made her way down to the library on the first floor of the town house and dislodged a book on the Americas that her father had bought a few years earlier. Virginia and Hampton and the wide ragged outline of Chesapeake Bay was easily traced by her fingers and there along a blue line signifying the James River lay Richmond, surrounded by green and at the edge of long tongues of water that wound their way up towards it. What hills and dales did he know? What towns to the east and west had he visited? Charlottesville. Arlington. Williamsburg and Hopewell. All names that she had no knowledge of and only the propensity to imagine.

A knock on the door brought her from her reveries and she called an entry.

'Lord Wilcox-Rice is here, ma'am, with his sister, Lady Eleanor. He said something of a shopping expedition.'

'What time is it?' Lillian asked the question in trepidation.

'Half past three, miss. Just turned.'

Rising quickly, she was glad that her day dress was one that would not need changing and pleased, too, for the bright sky she could now see outside.

'Of course. Would you show them through to the blue salon and let them know that I shall be but a moment whilst I fetch my bonnet and coat.'

Ellie Wilcox-Rice was one of Lillian's favourite acquaintances; in fact, it was probably due to her influence that Lillian had allowed even the talk of an engagement to her friend's brother to be mooted.

As they walked along Park Lane she laughed at Ellie's rendition of her Saturday evening at a ball in Kensington, a wearying sort of affair, it seemed.

'I should have much rather been at the crush of James Cholmondely's ball.' Ellie sighed. 'Jennifer Parker said she had the most wonderful time and that she had danced with an American with whom she fell in love on the spot.'

'Probably Mr Lucas Clairmont,' John said, waiting as the girls looked at a shop window, beautifully decorated for the approaching Christmas season. 'He has all the ladies' hearts a-racing, I hear, and no one has any idea of who exactly he is.'

'Does he have your heart a-racing, Lillian?' Ellie's laughter was shrill.

'Of course he doesn't,' John answered for her. 'Lillian is far too sensible to be swayed by the man.'

'Jennifer thinks he is rich. She thinks he has land in the Americas that rival that of the Ancaster estate. Hundreds and thousands of acres.'

'Did he say so to her?' Lillian was intrigued by this new development.

'No. It is just she has a penchant for Mr Darcy in *Pride and Prejudice* and imagines Lucas Clairmont in much the same mould.'

'A peagoose, then, and more stupid than I had imagined her.' John's outburst was unexpected. Usually he saw the best in all people.

'Jennifer also said that you had a waltz with this man, Lillian.'

'Indeed I did, and he is a competent dancer, if I recall.'

'But he made no impression upon you?'

Looking away, Lillian hated her breathlessness and her racing heart. To even talk of him here…

'Why, speaking of the devil, I do believe that is him coming towards us now. With Lord Hawkhurst, is it not?'

His sister laid her hand upon his. 'John, you absolutely must introduce me to him and let me make up my own mind.'

The two men walked towards them, both tall and dark, though today it appeared as though Luc Clairmont laboured in his gait and when they came up close Lillian could well see why. Today he looked little like he had last time she had met him, his left eye swollen shut and a cut across the bridge of his nose. When her glance flickered to his hands she saw that he wore gloves. To cover the damage to his knuckles, she supposed, and frowned.

'Wilcox-Rice.' Lord Hawkhurst bowed his head and the exchanges of names were made. When it was her turn for introduction, however, Luc Clairmont made no mention of the intimacy of their meetings so far, tipping his hat in much the same way as he did for Eleanor.

Today the light in his one good eye was dulled considerably, his glance almost bashful as she looked upon him. He barely spoke, waiting until Hawkhurst had finished and then moving along with him.

'Well,' said Eleanor as they went out of earshot, 'it looks as if Jennifer's prince has had an accident.'

'Been in another fight, more like it,' John interjected. 'There was talk of a scuffle at the Lenningtons' the other week.'

'Really.' Ellie turned to look back and Lillian wished that she would not.

'Who would he fight?'

'The gambling tables have their own complications.' John was quick to answer his sister's question. 'Your cousin, by the way, Lillian, is numbered amongst those who have had more than a light dab at the faces of others.'

'Daniel?' Ellie questioned, grimacing at the name. 'But he dresses far too well to fight.'

Despite herself Lillian laughed at the sheer absurdity of her friend's statement as they made their way into Oxford Street.

'I can well see why Jennifer Parker is so besotted.

Have you ever seen a more dangerous-looking man than Lucas Clairmont?'

When John frowned heavily, they decided that it was prudent to drop the subject altogether.

Christmas decorations were beginning to appear in more of the shops and a child and an elderly woman stood by the roadside selling bunches of mistletoe from a barrow.

Ellie rushed over dragging Lillian with her, carefully separating the foliage until she found a piece that she wanted.

'They say if you kiss a man under mistletoe you will find your one true love. Wouldn't that be wonderful? Perhaps you might kiss my brother? Here, Lillian, I will buy a sprig for you.'

Eleanor gave the woman some money and was handed two brown parcels, the greenery contained in thick paper and string. As they went to leave a young couple came up to the barrow. They were not well-to-do or dressed in anything near the latest of fashion, but when the man held the mistletoe up to the woman there was something in their eyes that simply transfixed Lillian.

Laughter and warmth and a shining intensity that was bewitching! She saw love in the way their hands brushed close as he handed her the packet and in the breathless smile the woman gave back to him as she received her gift. Only them in the world, only the small circle of their joy and happiness, for the bliss between them was tangible to everyone that watched.

Yearning overcame Lillian. Yearning for what she had just seen, the mistletoe a reminder of what she had never found and would probably never have. She glanced at John, who was castigating his sister for wasting her money on such frippery and a heavy sadness settled over her.

Christmas with its hope and promise had a way of undermining rationality and logic, replacing it with this mistletoe magic and a great dollop of hunger for something completely untenable.

'I do hope you are not swayed by my sister's nonsense, too?' John said, and with the shake of her head Lillian placed the brown packet in her bag and averted her eyes from the couple now walking on the other side of the street.

Chapter Six

Her cousin Daniel was in the library the next morning when she went down to find again the book on the Americas and he did not look pleased.

'Lillian. It has been a while since we have talked.' His face was marked by the underlying anger she had got used to seeing there.

For the past few years Daniel had been away from England and the ease of conversation that they had at one time had was now replaced by distance. Some other more nebulous wildness was also evident.

'Does my father know that you are here?'

'Yes. He is just retrieving a document that my mother has asked me to find for her.'

'I see.'

He flipped at the pages of the book on America as it lay open on the table next to him. 'It's a big land. I was there on the east coast. Washington, mainly, and New York.'

'Is that where you met Mr Clairmont?'

He frowned and then realisation dawned. 'Ah, you saw us the other night at the Lenningtons'.'

'I met him in the street yesterday with Hawkhurst. He had the appearance of being in another fight and I thought perhaps—' But he did not let her finish!

'Stay away from him, Lillian, for he is trouble.'

She nodded, and, pleased to hear her father's footsteps in the hall, excused herself.

John Wilcox-Rice arrived alone in the afternoon and he had brought her a bunch of winter cheer. Blooms that would sit well in her room and she thanked him.

Today he was dressed in a dark blue frock coat, brown trousers and a waistcoat of lighter blue. His taste was impeccable, she thought, his Hessians well polished and fashionable.

After her talk with her cousin that morning she was in a mood to just let life take her where it would. Thoughts of children and a home of her own were becoming more formed. Perhaps a life with John would be a lot more than tolerable? Her father liked him, her aunt liked him and she liked his sister very much. The young couple from yesterday came briefly to mind, but the time between then and now had dulled her sense of yearning, her more normal sensibleness taking precedence.

So when he took her hand in his she did not pull away, but savoured the feeling of gentle warmth.

'We have known each other for a passably long time, Lillian, and I think that if we gave it the chance…'

When she nodded, he looked heartened.

'I have asked your father if I could court you and he has given his permission. Now I need the same permission from you.'

The warning from Daniel and the Countess of Horsham's gossip welled in her mind.

Stay away from Lucas Clairmont. Stay away from trouble.

'It is six weeks until Christmas. Perhaps we could use this time to see if…?' She could not finish. To see what? To see if she felt passion or fervour or frenzy?

When he drew her up with him in response she stood, and when his lips glided across her own she did try to answer him back, did attempt to summon the hope of joy and benefit.

But she felt nothing!

The shock of it hit her and she pulled away, amazed at the singular smile of ardour on John's face.

'I will consider that as a troth, my love, and I will treasure the beauty of it for ever.'

The sound of a maid coming with tea had him moving away and taking his place on a chair opposite her. Yet still he grinned.

A gentleman, a nice man, a good man. And a man whose kisses made her feel nothing.

She lay in bed that night and cried. Cried for her mother and her father and for herself, trapped as she was by rules and rituals and etiquette.

John's fragrant flowers were on the table beside her bed, but she missed the ugly single orange bloom. Missed its vigour and its irreverence and its unapologetic raw colour. Missed the company of the man who had given it to her.

He had had a wife who had died quite recently according to the gossip. Lord, how had he dealt with that? Badly, by all accounts, as she thought of his gambling and his obvious lack of funds.

Closing her eyes, she brought her hand to her mouth and kissed the back of it as John Wilcox-Rice had kissed her lips today. There was something wrong with the way that he had not moved, the static stillness of the action negating all the emotion that should have been within it.

Lord, she had never in her life been kissed before and so she was hardly an expert, but a part of her brain refused to believe that that was all that it was, all that was whispered about and written of. No, there had to be more to it than what she had felt today, but with Christmas on its way and the honouring of a promise to find a spouse, she was running out of time to be able to truly discover just what it was.

A new and more daring thought struck her suddenly.

Perhaps she could find out? Perhaps if she invited Lucas Clairmont to call and offered him a sum of money for both his service and his silence, she might discover what she did not now know.

To buy a single kiss!

She smiled, imagining such a wild and dangerous scheme. Of course she could not do that! Lucas Clairmont was hardly a man to bargain with and any trust she might give him would be sorely misplaced. Or would it? He had melted into the background at the Lennington ball and she had heard no gossip of her conversation on the Belgrave Square balcony. Indeed, when she had seen him in the street yesterday he had barely acknowledged her. But was that from carefulness or just plain indifference?

She moved her hand and slanted her lips, increasing the pressure in a way that felt right. A bloom of want wound thin in her stomach, the warm promise of it bringing to mind the dangerous American.

Quickly she sat up, hard against the backboard of the bed, pulling the bedding about her shoulders to try to keep the cold at bay.

This was her only chance to find out. She had been in society for nearly eight years and not once in all that time had she lain here imagining the things she did now about any man.

Forty-two days until she would give a promise of eternal obedience and chastity to a man whose kisses left her with…nothing.

Her teeth worried her top lip as she tried to imagine the conversation preceding the experiment. It hardly seemed loyal to tell him of her reaction to John's kiss and her need to see if others would be the same, and yet if she did not he might think her wanton. A new thought struck her. Could men kiss well if they thought that they were being compared in some way? Would it not dampen a natural tendency?

And how much should she pay him? Would he be offended by fifty pounds or thankful for it? Would he want a hundred if he kissed her twice?

The hours closed in on her, as did the fact that Luc Clairmont would be gone after Christmas. A useful knowledge that, for he would be a temporary embarrassment only, should her whole scheme founder!

The thought of Christmas turned her thoughts in another direction.

Mistletoe!

That was it. If she hung the mistletoe Ellie had bought her yesterday above the doorway and angled herself so that she stood beneath the lintel in front of him... Just an accident, a pleasant interlude that would mean nothing should his kiss rouse as little feeling in her as John's had.

She sat up further.

Would he know of the traditions here in England? Would he even see it?

Could she mention the custom if he did not? Her brain turned this way and that, and the clock in the corner struck the hour of two. Outside the echo of the other clocks lingered.

Did Luc Clairmont hear them too? Was he awake with his swollen eye and wounded leg?

She slipped from her bed and walked to the window, pulling back her heavy cream curtains and looking out into the darkness.

Park Lane was quiet and the trees across the way were bleak against a sodden sky. Tonight the moon did not show its face, but was hidden behind low clouds of rolling greyness, gathering in the west.

A nothing kiss in a rain-filled night and the weight of twenty-five years upon her shoulders.

If she did not take this one chance, she might never know, but always wonder...

Sitting at her desk, she pulled out a piece of paper and an envelope and, dipping her pen in ink, began to write.

The letter had come a few minutes ago and Luc could make no sense of it. Lillian Davenport had something of importance to ask him and would like his company at three o'clock. The servant who had brought the message was one of Stephen's so he presumed it to have gone to the Hawkhurst town house first. The lad also seemed to be waiting for a reply.

Scrawling an answer on a separate sheet of parchment, he reached for his seal. Out of habit, he was to think as he placed it back down, for of course he could not use it here. 'Could you deliver this to Miss Davenport?'

The young servant nodded and hurried away, and when he had gone Luc lifted Lillian's missive into the light and read it again.

She wanted to speak to him about something important. She hoped he would come alone. She wondered about the Christmas traditions in America and whether mistletoe and holly were plants he was familiar with.

He frowned. Though he grew trees for timber in Virginia, the subject of botany had never been his strongpoint. Holly he knew as a prickly red-berried plant but mistletoe… Was that not the sprig that young ladies liked to hang in the Yuletide salons to catch kisses? A different thought struck him. What would it be like to kiss Lillian Davenport?

He chastised himself at the very idea. Lord, she

seemed to be very familiar with Wilcox-Rice and he was leaving in little more than a month.

But the thought lingered, a tantalising conjecture that lay in the memory of holding her fingers in his own and feeling the hurried beat of her heart. He guessed that Lillian Davenport was a warm and responsive woman beneath the outward composure, a lady who would be pleasantly surprised by the wonders of the flesh.

Raking his hand through his hair, he stood, wincing at the lump on the back of his head. Four men had jumped him on returning to his lodgings three nights ago and it was only his training in the army that had allowed him the ability to fend them off until help arrived.

He wished that Hawk had not persuaded him to take a walk the other day, the same walk that had brought him face to face with Lillian and her friends. Damn, he had seen in her eyes the censure he had noticed in every single one of their meetings and who could blame her?

The charade of his visit here began to press in. He would have liked to tell Lillian that he was not a bad man, that he had been a soldier and that he held great tracks of virgin land in Virginia filled with timber. But he couldn't because there were other things about him that she would not countenance.

Still, for the first time in a long while he felt alive and excited, the inertia in Richmond replaced by a new vigour.

He came through into the small yellow downstairs salon like one of the sleek black panthers she had once seen as a statue in an antique shop in Regent Street, all restless energy and barely harnessed menace, but she also saw he limped.

'Miss Davenport!' Today his injured eye looked darker, the bruising worsened by time, though he neither alluded to it nor hid it from her. Her letter was in his hand, she could see her tidy neat writing from where she stood and there was a question in his stance.

'Mr Clairmont.'

Silence stretched until she gestured him to sit, the absurdity of all she had planned, now that he was here, screaming in her consciousness. How did she begin? How did one broach such a situation with any degree of modesty and honour?

'Thank you very much for coming. I know that you must be busy—'

'Card games happen mostly at night,' he interrupted and she swore she saw a glimmer of amusement in his velvet eyes.

'And your leg is obviously painful,' she hurried on. To that he stayed wordless.

Her eyes strayed to the door. Did she risk broaching the subject before the parlourmaid brought in the refreshments or after? Relaxing, she decided on after, reasoning she could then instruct the girl to leave them alone for the few moments it would take to conduct her…experiment.

Lord, she hated to call it that, but was at a loss as to what else to name it.

'I hope London is treating you well…' As soon as she said it she knew her error.

'A few cuts and bruises, but what is that between a man and a beautiful city?'

'Was it a fall?'

He frowned at that and grated out a 'yes'.

'I had an accident last year at Fairley, our family seat in Hertfordshire.'

'Indeed?' His brows rose significantly.

'I fell from a horse whilst racing across the park.'

'I trust nothing was broken?'

'Only my pride! It was a village fair, you see, and I had entered the race on a whim.'

'Pride is a fragile thing,' he returned in his American drawl, and her cheeks reddened. She shifted in her seat, hating the heat that followed and fretful that her letter had indeed told him far too much. Her eyes flickered to the mistletoe she had hung secretly, a sad reminder of a plot that was quickly unravelling, and then back to his hands lying palm up in his lap.

Suddenly she knew just how to handle her request. 'You told me once of a woman who had read your hand in the town of Richmond?'

She waited till he nodded.

'You said that she told you life was like a river and that you are taken by it to the place that you were meant to be.' The tone of her voice rose and she fought to keep it back.

'The thing is, Mr Clairmont, I would hope at this moment that the place you are meant to be is here in my salon because I am going to ask you a question that might, without some sense of belief in fate, sound strange.'

'I know very little about the properties of mistletoe

or holly,' he interrupted. 'If it is botany that you wish to quiz me on?'

'I beg your pardon?'

'Your letter. You mention something of particular plants.'

Unexpectedly she began to smile and then caught the mirth back with a strong will as she shook her head.

'No, it is not that. I had heard from…others that the state of your finances is somewhat precarious and wanted to offer you a boon to alleviate the problem.' She knew that she had taken the wrong turn as soon as he stood, the polite façade of a moment ago submerged beneath anger.

Panic made her careless. 'I want to buy a kiss from you.' Blurted out with all the finesse of a ten-year-old.

'You what…?'

'Buy a kiss from you…' Her hands shook as she rummaged through her bag, trying to extricate the notes she had got from the bank that very morning.

When she finally managed it he swore, and not quietly.

'Shh, they might hear.'

'Who might hear? Your father? Your cousin? Someone has already had one go at me this week and I would be loathe to let them have another one.'

'Someone did that to you?' Goodness, she had lost hold of the whole conversation and could not even think how to retrieve it.

With honesty!

Taking a breath, she buried vanity. 'I am a twenty-five-year-old spinster, Mr Clairmont, and a woman who has been kissed only once, yesterday, by Lord Wilcox-Rice. And I need to know if what I felt was…normal.'

'What the hell did you feel?'

She drew herself up to her tallest height, a feat that was not so intimidating given that she stood at merely five foot two, even in her shoes.

'I felt nothing!'

The words reverberated in the ensuing silence, his anger evaporating in an instant to be replaced by laughter.

'I realise to you that the whole thing may seem like a joke, but…'

He breathed out. Hard.

'Nay, it is not that, Lilly, it is not that.' She felt his hand against her cheek, a single finger stroking down the bone, a careful feather-touch with all the weight of air.

A touch that made her shiver and want, a touch that made her move towards this thing she wished for, and then vanishing as a sound came from outside in the corridor.

Luc Clairmont moved back too, towards the window, his body faced away from hers and his hand adjusting the fit of his trousers. Perhaps he was angry again? Perhaps on reflection he saw the complete and utter disregard of convention that her request had subjected him to?

She smiled wanly as a young maid entered the room and bade her leave the tea for them to pour. Question shadowed the girl's eyes and Lillian knew that she was fast running out of minutes. It was simply not done for an unmarried lady to be sequestered alone for any length of time with a man.

At twenty-five some leeway might have been allowed, but she knew that he would need to leave before too many more seconds had passed.

Consequently when the door shut behind the servant she walked across to him.

'I do not wish to hurry you, but—'

He did not let her finish. The hard ardour of his lips slanted across her own, opening her mouth. Rough hands framed her cheeks as the length of his body pressed against hers, asking, needing, allowing no mealy response, but the one given from the place she had hidden for so, so long.

Feeling exploded, the sharp beat of her heart, the growing warmth in her stomach, the throb of lust that ached in a region lower. As she pressed closer her hands threaded through his hair, and into the nape of his neck, moving without her volition, with a complete lack of control.

He was not gentle, not careful, the feel of his lips on her mouth, on her cheek and on the sensitive skin at her neck unrestrained.

And then stopped!

She tried to keep it going, tipping her mouth to his, but he pulled her head against his chest and held her there, against a heartbeat that sped in heavy rhythm.

'This is not the place, Lilly…'

Reality returned, the yellow salon once again around her, the sound of servants outside, the tea on the table with its small plume of steam waiting to be drunk.

She pushed away, a new danger now in the room and much more potent than the one that had bothered her before.

Before she had been worried about his actions and now she was worried about her own, for in that kiss something had been unleashed, some wild freedom that could now not be contained.

Lucas Clairmont placed her letter on the table and gathered his hat. 'Miss Davenport,' he said and walked from the room.

Lord, he thought on the journey between Pall Mall and his lodgings. He should not have kissed her, not allowed her confession of feeling 'nothing' with Wilcox-Rice to sway his resolve.

And now where did it leave him? With a hankering for more and a woman who would hate him.

He should have stayed, should have reassured her, should have at least had the decency to admit the whole thing as his fault before he had walked out.

But she had captivated him with her pale elegance and honesty and with the fumbled bank notes pushed uncertainly at him.

To even think that she would pay him?

Absolute incredulity replaced irritation and that in turn was replaced by something…more akin to respect.

She was the one all others aspired to be like, the pinnacle of manners and deportment and it could not have been easy for her to have even asked him what she did. Hell, she had a hundred times more to lose than he, with his passage to Virginia looming near and a reputation that no amount of bad behaviour could lower.

Why on earth, then, had she picked him? She must

have weighed up the odds as to what he could do with such information, the pressures of society here like a sledgehammer against any deviation from the strict codes of manners.

Why had she risked it?

The answer came easily. She did so because she was desperate, desperate to discover if what she felt for Wilcox-Rice was normal and hopeful that it was not.

Well, he thought, with the first glimmer of humour coming back. At least she had found out that!

Lillian threw herself on her bed and took the breath she had hardly taken since Lucas Clairmont had left the house.

He had been angry, the notes she had tried to give him in her fist, a coarse message of intent and failure. She rolled over and peeled each one away from the other.

Two hundred pounds! And if he had taken them it would have been worth every single penny. Turning, she looked at the ceiling, reliving each second of that kiss, her fingers reaching for the places his had been and then falling lower.

What if he had not stopped? What if he had not pulled back when he did? Would she have come to her senses? Honesty forced her to admit she would not have and the admission cost her much.

'If you aren't careful you will be your mother all over again, Lillian.' Her father's voice from the past, a warning to her as her mother lay dying, the words uttered in a despair of melancholy and sorrow. She had been thirteen and the fashions of the day had begun to be appealing, the chance to experiment and change. She blinked.

Had such advice altered the person she might have become? Was she changing back?

She shook her head and lay still, closing her eyes against the light.

The knock on the door woke her and for a second she could not work out quite where she was, for seldom did she doze in the afternoon.

Her bedroom. Lucas Clairmont. The kiss. Reality surfaced and with it a rising dread.

'You have some flowers, Miss.'

A maid came in with a large unruly bunch of orange flowers and her breath was caught. 'Is there a card?'

'Indeed, miss, there is.' The maid broke the envelope away from a string that kept it joined to the bouquet, speculation unhidden in the lines of her face.

'That will be all, thank you,' Lillian said, waiting until the door was shut before she slit open the card.

I FELT SOMETHING

The words were in bold capitals with no name attached.

Without meaning to, Lillian began to cry—in those three words Luc Clairmont had given her back the one thing she had not thought it possible to regain.

Her pride.

Holding the flowers close to her breast, her tears fell freely across the fragrant orange petals.

Chapter Seven

'Mr Clairmont from America was at the club as a guest of Hawkhurst today.' The tone in her father's voice told her that he was not pleased. 'The man is a scoundrel and a gambler. Why he even continues to receive invitation from people we know confounds me.'

'And yet he seemed such a nice young man when he came to ask you to dance, Lillian, at the Cholmondely ball. How very misleading first impressions can be,' her aunt said.

'You have danced with this American?' Her father's heavy frown made her heart sink.

Danced. Touched. Kissed.

'I have, Father. He asked for my hand in a waltz.'

'And you did not turn him down? Surely you could see what sort of a fellow he was.'

'Men like him pounce quickly on the unsuspecting, Ernest. It is no point in chastising Lillian, for she is blameless in it all.'

Blameless?

The bunch of orange blooms still stood by her bed, carefully tended and watered daily, but she had not seen him again, not in the park, not at the parties, not in the streets as she walked each day.

'St Auburn is a particular friend of Clairmont's, is he not?'

Jean shrugged her shoulders. 'I do not know the man personally. Daniel could probably tell you much more about him.'

Lillian looked more closely at her aunt, trying to ascertain whether she knew of the wayward pursuits of her son and deciding in the smile she returned her that she probably did not.

'I ask the question,' her father continued, 'because an invitation came for you yesterday, Lillian, to attend a country party of the Earl and Lady St Auburn in Kent and I should not wish for you to go should the American be there.' He sipped at his tea, fiddling with a pair of spectacles he held in his right hand.

'When would the party be held, Father?' She tried to keep her voice as neutral as she could.

'It would run from this Friday to Sunday. If you were interested, perhaps Wilcox-Rice could take you?'

'Indeed.' She bit into her toast and honey.

'So you are saying that you would go?'

'Lady St Auburn is a friend of mine. I should like to catch up with her news.'

'Would you be able to travel down too, Jean? Lillian can hardly go unchaperoned.'

Her aunt sighed heavily, but accepted the responsibility, giving the impression of a woman who would have preferred to be saying no.

The house was beautiful, a six-columned Georgian mansion, the grounds as well manicured and fine as she had visited anywhere.

They were late. She could see that as they swept up the circular driveway, a crowd of people in a glass conservatory to the left of the house. From this distance she could not be sure that Lucas Clairmont was amongst them, but John Wilcox-Rice at her side did not look happy.

'I cannot imagine why you should want to come to this party, Lillian. The set St Auburn hangs with are a little wild and if he did not have so much in the way of property and gold I doubt he would be so feted. Besides, the man always seems slightly unrestrained to me.'

'Cassandra is Mrs Weatherby's youngest sister, John, and I have a lot of fondness for her.'

'Then you should have seen her in the city.'

'But Kent is lovely at this time of the year. Surely you would at least say that?'

Jean stretched suddenly, waking as the carriage slowed and stopped.

'Goodness. Are we here already? The roads south get quicker and quicker. Perhaps we should persuade your father to acquire a property here rather than in Hertfordshire, Lillian, for it is so much more convenient for London.' She looked out of the window at the sky. 'Have you ever seen such a clear horizon, none of the yellow smog on show?'

A group of servants milled around the coach, waiting for the party to alight, the younger boys already hauling the luggage off and listening for instructions as to where it should be taken.

The Davenport family seat of Fairley Manor came to Lillian's mind as she saw the precision and order that accompanied their arrival. The housekeeper bowed and presented herself and the head butler was most attentive to any needs that the small group might have.

Wilcox-Rice in particular was rather grumpy, barely acknowledging the efforts of the St Auburn servants to please. He did not even want to be here, he mumbled under his breath, and Lilly wondered why she had not seen this rather irritating trait in his nature before.

But with the sun in her face and the promise of a whole weekend before her, she felt buoyed up with hope. She had pressed one of her orange flowers in a book in her travel bag to be able to show Lucas Clairmont, for she knew flowers in this season would have cost him a fortune that he did not possess and she wanted him to know, at least, that she had appreciated the gesture.

'Lillian!' Her name was called and she turned to see who summoned her. Cassandra St Auburn walked towards her, her bright red hair aflame and the sweetness in her face all that Lillian remembered.

'You came! I thought perhaps that you would not.'

'Indeed, it is such a lovely spot I should be loathe to miss out. Lady St Auburn, this is Lord Wilcox-Rice. It was noted on my invitation that I could bring a partner.'

'Yes, of course.' Cassie shook the outstretched hand

and Lillian detected disquiet. 'But I thought your aunt was coming…'

'Here I am, my dear, a little late to alight, but the bones are not quite as they used to be.' Jean thanked the servant who had helped her and turned to the house. 'I was here when I was about your age with Leonard St Auburn.'

'My husband's grandfather. He is still here, though he spends much of his day now in the library.'

'A well-read man, if I remember rightly. Very interested in the world of plants.'

Cassandra laughed and Lillian liked the sound. A happy and uncomplicated girl! Sometimes she wished she could have been more like that.

'Most of the party are in the conservatory,' she continued on. 'Would you join us there after you refresh yourselves?'

'That would be lovely,' Lillian answered as they were ushered inside, the quickened beat of her heart steadying a little as they mounted the staircase.

Twenty minutes later they walked towards the group of guests standing around a table well stocked with food and drink.

Lucas Clairmont was nowhere in sight and part of her was annoyed that she could not have met him here informally. The Earl of St Auburn, Nathaniel, came over to join his wife. He had once rather liked her, Lillian recalled, when she had first come out, though it was such a long time ago she doubted he would remember it.

'Miss Davenport!' His smile was welcoming. 'And

Lord Wilcox-Rice.' Her Aunt Jean had elected not to come downstairs, but have a rest so that she would be refreshed for dinner. 'We are very pleased that you could both make the journey.'

He placed a strange emphasis on 'both' and Lillian saw a quick frown pass between the St Auburns, an unspoken warning from Cassandra, she thought were she to interpret it further. Did they already perceive her and John as a couple? She swallowed back worry.

'You have a large number of people here. Do you expect any more?' Her mind raced. If Lucas Clairmont did not come after sending her the invitation she would never forgive him!

'A few of the neighbours will come tonight for dinner and Mr Clairmont will bring Lady Shelby down from London.'

'Caroline Shelby?' John's voice had the same ring of masculine appreciation that she had heard in the tone of each man who had discussed the newest beauty on the London scene.

'She couldn't leave town any earlier so Nat asked his friend to wait and escort her.'

Lillian felt the muscles in her cheeks shake, so tight did she try to hold her smile. If Clairmont had invited her here to flirt in front of someone else... Lord, the whole weekend would be untenable and she wondered how she might return to London without causing conjecture.

No. Her resolve firmed—she would not turn tail and disappear. For five days now she had been walking on eggshells at every single social occasion just in case she should see him, her words rehearsed so as to deliver the nonchalant greeting she wanted.

She needed to thank him for the flowers and move on to the next part of her life, and if memory served her well she knew him to be off to America in merely a few weeks' time.

Luc waited as the girl gathered her shawl and minced to the carriage. Her chaperon, a woman in her mid-forties, followed behind her. Lord, would they ever be ready to go? He looked at his watch and determined that Lillian Davenport should have already arrived in Kent.

Would Nathaniel have told her of the reason for his lateness?

Caroline Shelby placed her hand in his as she gained the carriage steps and kept it there long after the need lapsed. Extracting his fingers, he put his hands firmly by his side, sitting on the seat opposite from the two women and looking out of the window.

'It should take an hour,' he said with as little emotion as he could muster.

Caroline giggled, the sound filling the carriage. 'They say the St Auburns have a beautiful house?'

'Indeed they do.'

'They say if you rode from one end of the estate to the other it may take all of a day.'

'It may.'

The echo of Virginia loomed large. To go from one end of his property to the other would take a week and he missed it with an ache that surprised him.

'I should love to see it on horseback. Do you ride?'

He nodded, hoping she did not see this affirmation as an invitation.

'Then we must find some horses and venture out,' she replied and his heart sank at the sentence.

'I have some business with the Earl—' he began but she interrupted him.

'But you could find an hour or so for a lady who has asked you?' Her hand closed over his and the chaperon looked away.

'Certainly.' Luc resolved to make a large party of this sojourn even as he removed his fingers yet again from hers.

Forty-eight long minutes later the St Auburns' country seat came into view and the woman who sat next to Lady Shelby finally seemed to deem it time to haul the antics of her young charge in.

'Your hat is a little crooked, dear,' she said, deft fingers straightening the bonnet that had come askew when she had fallen forwards against him on one of the more rutted sections of the road. 'And you really ought to replace your gloves.'

The sight of the house as they swept on to the circular drive was welcome and it seemed as if many of the houseguests still languished in the glassed-in conservatory, enjoying the last rays of the sun. He easily picked out Lillian, her pale hair entwined today into one single bunch, simple and elegant and the white gown complimenting her figure. She had not seen him, but was talking to Cassandra and next to her stood…John Wilcox-Rice.

'Damn.' He swore beneath his breath, glad for the

chance to vacate the carriage and escape the company of the irritating Lady Shelby and her dour chaperon.

Nathaniel met him first. 'Wilcox-Rice is here.' A warning flinted strong.

'I saw him.'

'Should I stand between you?'

'To keep the peace, you mean?'

'He is rumoured to have offered for her hand. If you mean to pursue that gleam I can see in your eyes…'

'Have patience, Nat. Any protection that you feel the need to give me will be relinquished in a few weeks.'

'You think that you'll be on that boat?' A strange smile filled the eyes of his friend.

'Of course I will be. My passage is booked and paid for. There is nothing to hold me here.'

'Or no one?'

Luc laughed suddenly, seeing where it was Nathaniel was going with this line of question. 'I tried marriage once.' His words were bleak and he hated the tightness in them.

'Elizabeth was a woman who would drive anyone to the bottle. God knows why you still wear her damn ring.'

Luc felt a singular shot of fury consume him. 'I wear it because it reminds me.'

'Reminds you of what?'

'Never to make the same mistake twice.' He grabbed a drink of fruit punch from the table as he moved away.

Lillian turned as Lucas Clairmont downed a large glass of punch, the lot hardly touching his throat before he helped himself to another.

He looked angry and she could not quite reconcile this man with the one who had sent her flowers and kept silent about a scandal that could easily ruin her. The bruising around his eye was largely gone and the velvet of his dangerous glance made her wary and uncertain. Caroline Shelby seemed bent on following him and Lillian could well see why she had been often named as the most beautiful girl of her Season. Wilcox-Rice beside her laid his hand beneath Lillian's elbow in a singular message of claim and she saw Clairmont take in the movement.

Caught between convention and other people's expectations, she could do nothing save for smile, her practised speech of thanks buried under the weight of a careful control.

'Miss Davenport.' When she gave him her hand he held it briefly. The warmth of his skin made her start with the recognition of his touch.

'Mr Clairmont. It is nice to see you once again.'

He dropped contact almost immediately.

'You two know each other?' Cassandra was astonished.

'A little.' Her words.

'Not well.' His.

Cassie's giggles drew the attention of Caroline Shelby as she gained their small circle.

'What a lovely party! I knew I should have left London earlier. If it had not been for you, Mr Clairmont, I should not even be here by now. I hope that I have not missed too much, for you all seem very festive.'

'I am certain you are quite in time, Lady Shelby,' Lillian returned.

'Miss Davenport. How wonderful that you should be

here. I have long admired your sense of style and bearing and your dress—' she gestured to the white moiré silk '—why, it is just so beautiful.'

'Thank you.'

'My friend Eloise says you have your clothes made in England, but I think that cannot be true as the cut and cloth is just too wonderful and I said to my mother the other day that we should ask you about your seamstress and use her ourselves because…'

Was she nervous, Lillian thought, switching out of the constant barrage of never-ending chatter, or just frivolous? She made the mistake of glancing at Lucas Clairmont and almost laughed at the comical disbelief on his face. Lord, and he had had a whole hour of it coming down from London. No wonder he had almost leapt from the coach as soon as it had stopped.

'Do you enjoy flowers, Miss Davenport?' Caroline's shrill and final question pierced her ruminations.

'I do indeed.'

'Is not the garden here just beautiful? All in shades of white, too. I suppose with your penchant for the paler hues you would prefer your flowers in the same sort of palette?'

Lillian smiled. Now here was an opening she could take, and easily. 'Lately I find that I have a growing preference for orange.'

She caught the expression of puzzlement on Lucas Clairmont's face, but with John at her side could make no further comment.

'Orange?' The girl opposite almost shouted the word. 'Oh, no, Miss Davenport, surely you jest with me?'

When Cassandra St Auburn suggested that the party now retire to dress for dinner Lillian could do nothing but lift her skirts and follow, noticing with chagrin that Lucas Clairmont did not join them.

Chapter Eight

Luc took a sixteen-hand gelding from the stables of St Auburn and rode for Maygate, a village a good ten miles away. He was tired and using the last light of dusk and the first slice of moon to guide him he journeyed west.

Dinner would still be a few hours away and he felt the need to stretch his body and feel the wind on his face and freedom.

Lord, how the English enjoyed their long and complicated afternoon teas, something which in Virginia would have been thought of as ludicrous.

Virginia and a green tract of land that reached from the James to the Potomac. His land! Hewed from the blood, sweat and tears of hard labour, the timber within his first hundred acres bringing the riches to buy the rest.

A piecemeal acquisition!

He ran his thumb across the scar on his thigh, feeling the ridges of flesh badly healed. An accident when the

Bank of Washington was about to foreclose on him and he had no other means of paying to get the wood out. He had dragged it alone along the James by horse, unseated as a log rose across another and his mount bolted, pushing him into the jagged end of newly hewn timber. The cut had festered badly, but still he had made it to Hopewell and the mill that would buy the load, staving off the greed of the bank for a few more months.

Hard days. Lonely days.

Not as lonely as when Elizabeth had come, though, with her needs and wants and sadness.

No, he would not think of any of that, not here, not in the mellow countryside of Kent where the boundaries of safety were a comfortable illusion.

'Lately I find I have a growing preference for orange.' The words drifted to him from nowhere, warming him with possibility. Was it the flowers he had given her she spoke of? He shook his head. Better for Lillian Davenport to marry Wilcox-Rice than him and have the promise of an English heritage that was easy and prudent.

He stopped in a position overlooking a stream, the shadows of night long as he ran his fingers through his hair. Such dreams were no longer for him and he had been foolish to even think they could be. He should depart again tonight for London, leaving Lilly with her enticing full lips and woman's body to his imagination. But he could not. Already he found himself turning his horse for home.

Lillian felt like a young girl again, this dress not quite fitting and that one not quite right. She was glad for the help of her lady's maid and glad too that her aunt Jean was still in bed, her headache having turned into a cold.

When she finally settled on a gown she liked she walked to the window and looked out. The last of the daylight was lost, the moon rising quickly in the eastern sky and the gardens of St Auburn wreathed in shadow. She was about to turn away when a lone rider caught her eye, his gait on the horse fluid. No Sunday rider this, the beat of the hooves fast and furious.

Lucas Clairmont. She knew it was him, the raw power of his thighs wrapped about the steed in easy control and the reins caught only lightly as the animal held its head and thundered on to the gravelled circle of the driveway.

Caught in the moonlight, hair streaming almost to his shoulders and without a jacket, he looked to her like the living embodiment of some ancient Grecian God. What would it be like to lie with such a man, to feel him near her, close?

Shocked, she turned away. Ladies did not ponder such fantasies and she had been warned many times of the man that he was. Yet surely a light flirtation was a harmless thing and, perhaps, if she were generous, she could place her clandestinely bought kiss into that category. But she should take it no further. To cross the line from coquetry into blowsy abandonment would be to throw away everything that she had worked hard for all her life. Stepping to the mirror, she looked at herself honestly, observed eyes full of anticipation and the smile that seemed to crouch there, waiting.

For him!

Adjusting her chemise so that a little more flesh than usual was showing, she smiled, still proper indeed, but bordering on something that was not. This wickedness that had leaked into her refined formality was freeing somehow, a part of her personality that had until lately lain dormant and unrealised.

'Oh God, please help me.' Spoken into the silence of her room, she wondered just exactly what it was that she was asking. For absolution of sin or for the strength to see her virtue in the way she had always tried to view it? Shaking her head, she sought for the words to cancel such a selfish prayer and found that she couldn't. There was some impunity received, after all, in asking for celestial help and a sense of providence. Tonight she would need both.

Proceeding in to dinner on the arm of the Earl of St Auburn, Lillian was surprised when Clairmont found his seat next to hers. Status and rank almost always determined seating after the formal promenade and she was astonished to see John consigned to a place at the other end of the table and looking most displeased. Cassandra St Auburn raised her glass and Lillian wondered at the definitive twinkle in the woman's glance. Had she planned this? Was there some communal strategy behind the reason for her invitation? Well, she thought, the usual nerve-racking worry of seating seemed to have been done away with completely and the lack of any remorse was, if anything, refreshing.

At her own dinner parties the seating arrangements were what she always hated the most in her fear of offending some personage of higher status than the next one.

Determining to think no more of it, she took a quick peek at the American. His hair was slicked back tonight, still wet from a late bath she supposed after the exercise that he had taken.

'I saw you return from your ride.' She spoke because she found the growing silence between them unnerving.

'After the carriage trip I needed to blow away the cobwebs.' A loud trill from Caroline Shelby two places away punctuated his words. 'Need I say more?' He smiled as she looked shocked. 'It must be difficult to always be so virtuous, Miss Davenport.'

'I am hardly that, Mr Clairmont.' The kiss they had shared quivered between them, an unspoken shout. 'You of all people should know it.'

'Your small experiment to…determine emotion can hardly be consigned to the "fallen woman" basket. Nay, put it down instead to any adult's healthy pursuit of knowledge.'

He was more honourable in his dismissal of her lapse than he needed to be and a great wave of relief covered her. With shaking hands she took small sips of her wine and then laced her fingers tightly together.

'I thank you for such a congenial summary, but my actions the other day were much less than what I usually expect from myself.'

'As a dubious consolation I can tell you that the wisdom of age dims such exacting standards. When you are as old as I am you will realise the freedom of doing just as one wills.'

'Like fighting with my cousin at the Lenningtons'?'

'Or sending a beautiful woman flowers.'

She was silent, the last rejoinder putting a halt to her fault-finding. *Beautiful.* He thought her that?

'How old are you, Mr Clairmont?' She hated herself for asking the question in the face of everything that had passed between them.

'Thirty-three and judicious beyond my years, Miss Davenport.'

'Some here might call you a gambler?'

'Which I am.'

'And a cheat?'

'Which I am not.'

'There are even rumours circulating that hint at the possibility that you have killed people.'

'More than one?' His eyebrows rose in a parody of an actor on the stage, though when she pulled back he laughed. ' "*A man can smile and smile and be a villain,*" ' he quoted, a new wickedness supplanting the guile.

'You are a puzzle, Mr Clairmont. Just when I think to understand your character you surprise me.'

'With my knowledge of Shakespeare?'

She shook her head. 'Nay, with your intuition on the very nature of mystery!'

'I've had years of practice.'

'And years of debauchery?'

Again he laughed, though this time the sound was less feigned. 'Mirrors and smoke are not solely the domain of the stage, Lilly.'

'Miss Davenport,' she corrected him. 'So are you telling me that what I see is not who you are?'

He tilted his drink up to the light. 'Does not everyone have a hidden side?'

The chatter around her seemed to melt into nothingness and it was as if they were alone, just her and just him, the recognition of want making her feel almost dizzy. Clutching at her seat, she turned away, the room spinning strangely and her heartbeat much too fast.

She was pleased when a delicate pheasant soup was placed before them as it gave her a chance to pretend concentration on something other than Luc Clairmont, and the turbot with lobster and Dutch sauces that followed were delicious.

Lady Hammond, a strong-looking older woman sitting opposite, regaled them on the merits of the hunting in the shire of Somerset as the entrée and removes were served, and by the time the third course of snipes, golden plovers and wild duck came out the topic seemed to have moved on to the wealth and business advantages available in the colonies.

'How do you see it, Mr Clairmont?' one of the older guests asked him. 'How do you see the opportunities in the area around Baltimore and Chesapeake Bay?'

'Men with a little money and fewer morals can do very well there. My uncle's land, for example, was swindled for a pittance and sold for a fortune.'

'By fellow Americans?'

'Nay, by an Englishman. The new industries are profitable and competition is rife.'

The sentence bought a flurry of interest from those around the table and John Wilcox-Rice was quick to add in his penny's-worth. 'It seems that the fibre of our society is threatened by a new generation of youth without morals.'

The Earl of Marling seconded him. 'Integrity and honour come from breeding, and the great families are being whittled away by men who have money, but nothing else.'

Looking down at Luc Clairmont's hand between them, Lillian noticed his knuckles were almost white where he gripped the seat of his chair. Not as nonchalant of it all as his face might show.

Wondering at his manner she was distracted only when a crashing sound made her turn! Lord Paget was drunk and his wife was trying to settle him down again in his seat, the shards from a broken glass spilling from the goblet to the tablecloth and dribbling straight into the lap of John Wilcox-Rice.

Pushing his seat back, John tried to wipe away the damage and Paget in his stupor also reached over to help him, his fingers touching parts that Wilcox-Rice was more than obviously embarrassed by. The tussle that ensued knocked the first man into a second and the tablecloth was partly dragged away from the table, bringing food and wine crashing all around them.

Luc Clairmont was on his feet now as Paget went for Wilcox-Rice.

'Enough,' he said simply, pulling the offender back and blocking an ill-timed punch. 'You are drunk. If you leave with your wife now there will be little damage come morning.'

Paget's wife looked furious, both at her husband's

poor behaviour and at Luc Clairmont's interference, but it was Paget who retaliated.

'Perhaps you should be getting your own house into order, Clairmont, before casting aspersions on to ours. You were, after all, expelled from Eton and many would say that you still haven't learned your lesson.'

'Would they now?' His drawl was cold and measured, the gold of his eyes tonight brittle.

'Leave him, my dear, for he is not worth it. If St Auburn wishes to make himself a laughing-stock by insisting the American is a gentleman, then let him.' Lady Paget seemed to be supporting the stupidity of her husband, no thanks being given for the assistance she had received from the man she now railed against.

Anger seized Lillian.

'I would say, Lady Paget, that your manners are far less exacting than the one you would pillory. From where I sit it seems that Mr Clairmont was only trying to make certain that Lord Paget's flagrant lack of etiquette did not harm any of the other ladies present. I for one am very glad that he intervened, as your husband's behaviour was both frightening and unnecessary.'

With a haughty stare she looked about the table, glad when the nods of the others present seemed to support her assessment. Sometimes her position as the queen of manners was an easy crown to wear and a persuasive one. She felt the anger swaying back to the Pagets and away from Luc Clairmont as the wife picked up the heaviness of her skirts and followed her husband, an angry discourse between them distinctly heard.

Lillian did not look around at Lucas Clairmont or

question his silence. Nay, she was a woman who knew that if you left people to think too much about a problem then you invariably had a larger one. Consequently she swallowed back ire and began on a topic that she knew would surely interest all the ladies present.

Luc sat next to her and hated the anger that the Pagets' stupid comments had engendered in him. England was the only place in the world, he thought, where the deeds of the past were never forgotten nor forgiven, and where misdemeanours could crawl back into the conversation almost twenty years on.

For now, though, Lilly was chattering on forever about dresses she had seen in Paris in the summer, and if he had not been so furious he might have admired her attention in remembering the detail of such an unimportant thing.

Not to the women present, however! Each one of them was drinking in her every word and as the servants scooped away shards of china and crystal, replacing the broken with the whole, it was as if there had never been a contretemps. When the dessert of preserved cherries, figs and ginger ice-cream arrived, he noticed that everyone took a generous portion.

Warmth began to spread through him. Lillian Davenport had stood up for him in front of them all, had come to his aid like an avenging angel, her good sense and fine bearing easily persuading everyone of the poor judgement the Pagets had shown.

Indeed, she was lethal, a pale and proper thunderbolt with just the right amount of ire and refinement.

No one could criticise her or slate her decorum and

it was with this thought that her offered kiss was even the more remarkable. Lord, did she not realise how easily she could fall, how the inherent nature of man would make any mishap or misconduct accountable in one so loftily placed?

He worried for her, for her goodness and her vulnerability and for the sheer effort that it must take to stay at the very top.

This weekend had been his doing, his own need to see her alone and overriding every other consideration for her welfare. And she had repaid this selfishness with dignity and assurance.

Respect vied with lust and won out. He would do nothing else to bring her reputation into disrepute. That much he promised himself.

He had not come near her since the Pagets had left, the tea taken in the front salon a sedate and formal sort of an affair, with Lucas Clairmont placing himself on the sofa the furthest away from where she sat.

Indeed, after her outburst she thought he might have been a little thankful, but he made no effort at all to converse or even look at her, giving his attention instead to Caroline Shelby and her simpering friend.

Nathaniel St Auburn at her side turned to her to speak. 'I see you had much to talk about with Mr Clairmont earlier on, Miss Davenport?' St Auburn's question was asked in a tone indicating manners rather than inquisitiveness. 'He was an old school friend of mine at Eton,' he enlarged when he saw her surprise. Lillian pondered the thought.

'I didn't realise that he once lived in England.' The cameo of a younger Lucas Clairmont intriguing her. 'He seems too…American?'

Nathaniel chuckled, but there was something in the sound that made her think. She pressed on.

'Have you ever visited him in Virginia?'

'I have.'

'And you enjoyed it?'

'I did!'

Lillian grated her teeth, wishing that his answers might be enlarged so as to give her an insight into the personality of the man sitting across the room from her.

'Mr Clairmont says his home is near a river. The James, I think he said. Does he have family there?' She hoped that the interest she could hear in her words was not so obvious to him.

'His wife was from those parts, but she died in a carriage accident. A nasty thing that, because Luc blamed himself, as any gentleman of sensitivity might.'

Relief bloomed at Luc Clairmont's innocence in his wife's demise. After all the darker conjectures in society, Lillian was pleased to find out that the cause of the woman's death had been an accident, though she had a strange feeling that St Auburn's words were carefully chosen. In warning or in explanation? She could not tell which.

'So you think him a sensitive man?'

'Indeed I do, but I can see by your frown that you may not?'

'I have heard things…'

He did not let her finish. 'Give him a chance,' he said

softly and she almost thought that she hadn't heard it before he turned away.

Give him a chance! Of what? She felt again the warmth of Lucas Clairmont's arm against hers where they had not quite touched at the dinner table. If she had moved closer she might have felt him truly, but she had not been brave enough to try. Not there, not then, not with such hooded enquiry seen in so many eyes.

Lord, she seldom came to these country weekend parties and knew now again why she did not. She was stuck here at least till the morrow, any means of escape dubious with her aunt in tow.

John next to her interrupted, making his displeasure known. 'Surely you can see, Lillian, just how the sort of outburst you gave at dinner is damaging? Far wiser indeed to let these small spats run their course and stay well out of it.'

'Even if I should perceive the criticism unfair?' she returned. His social mannerisms were becoming more and more annoying tonight with every new piece of advice that he offered her.

'You are a lady of breeding and cultivation. It is not seemly to be defending a man who has neither.'

'Paget was hardly in order.'

'He was not expelled from Eton for stealing either.'

'Stealing?' The word caught her short.

'Clairmont the youth took a watch from the head-master's study and hid it in his blankets. When it was found he admitted the theft and was sent down.'

Lillian felt her hands grip her side. Why was nothing ever easy as far as Lucas Clairmont was concerned?

Why could she not find out something noble and virtuous about him instead of being plagued with a never-ending lack of moral fibre?

And why would a small boy steal a watch anyway? For money? To know the time? She could fathom neither the reason nor the risk. Why indeed had he not hidden it in a place no one would ever think to look? She took in a breath. No. She must not excuse him and take his side. Not for theft!

She was pleased when the older guests began to take their leave and was able to gladly follow, John accompanying her upstairs to her room.

'It has been a pleasure to be in your company today, Lillian,' he said as she opened her door, and she had the distinct impression that he was angling to kiss her again.

Consequently she sneezed three times, holding her handkerchief across her mouth and sniffing.

'My goodness, perhaps I have caught Aunt Jean's cold?'

'Will I call the housekeeper and ask her for some medicine?' The amorous look in his eyes was completely overtaken by concern.

'No, please do not bother. If I just go to sleep early…' She stopped and sneezed again and he moved back.

'Well, I suppose this is goodnight?' The words were said awkwardly and with disappointment.

'Thank you for walking me up.'

'It was my pleasure.'

She stepped inside and closed the door, standing still on the other side and replacing her handkerchief in her pocket. One night down and one more to go! Tomorrow she would make certain that she came up with the women in order to ensure no repeat performance of John's eagerness in seeing her alone.

Chapter Nine

A riding expedition seemed to be the entertainment for the next afternoon and as a keen horsewoman Lillian was looking forward to the freedom of racing across the Kentish countryside, though the eastern sky was draped in black billowing cloud.

Lucas Clairmont was again distant; he had tipped his hat as he had passed her, making his way to his horse, but he neither stopped in conversation nor offered to help her mount. John on the other hand was all attentive vigilance and her heart sank. Lucas Clairmont was due to return to America at the end of December, and would not return for many a long, long year, if ever. She was running out of time, the month of December almost upon them, and her father's demands of a Christmas engagement beginning to look more and more worrying.

Pulling her cloak around her neck to make the fur collar sit up, she ordered the horse on. A sorrel mare, it was neither fancy nor plain and its disposition as far as she could tell was pleasant. A horse much like the man who rode beside her, seeing to her every whim.

Caroline Shelby's mount trotted between St Auburn and Luc, her laughter returning on the eddy of wind to the rear of the pack. Three other couples completed the group, the Pagets conspicuous by their absence; Lillian presumed them to have packed their things and left. She sighed, hoping her father would not meet the odious man at his club and hear the story of her defence of Mr Clairmont as only he would probably see it. She seldom made enemies of people and the fact that she had worried her.

'Lady St Auburn has not joined us this morning.'

John's tone was puzzled.

'Perhaps she will later,' Lillian ventured, though she, too, had been surprised by Cassandra's absence. In fact, if she thought about it, she was also surprised by the closeness of the relationship between the St Auburns and Luc Clairmont. Nathaniel had said that he had been to see him in Virginia. Had Cassandra gone as well? Tonight she would make certain that she asked Cassie of the details and ask her also as to the size of any land Lucas Clairmont owned.

If only he were…what? she ventured. Rich? Well liked? Connected to the right people? Her musings took on a shallowness that she would have thought abhorrent in others. Yet she could not pursue a man whose very presence aroused such strong condemnation in those about him.

The strictures and codes that applied to everyday social life were after all there for a reason and the protection that they afforded was comforting. Even John's own layer of conventionality heartened her, for at least she could control him.

Luc Clairmont would be raw and ungovernable. The words made her wonder. He would not be repelled by a few false sneezes as John had been last night or distracted along any lines that she might favour. He would not be cajoled or dominated or managed. She remembered his kisses and her own unrestrained reaction to them and breathed in hard.

No. No. No.

Safety lay in correct behaviour, just as ruin lurked in the narrow margins of error and she would do very well to remember it. Sighing loudly, she tipped her head to the sky and decided that his entrancement with the Shelby heiress was probably for the best, though another feeling lingering beneath propriety wanted to scratch the woman's eyes out. Oh, she was beautiful, there was no doubt about that. But she was also more than forward, a girl who would eye up her quarry and go for it, and here her quarry was definitely Lucas Clairmont.

The clap of thunder came as they wound their way into a meadow almost at the edge of the St Auburn land, and everybody reined in their horses. Everyone, that is, except for Caroline Shelby, whose mount bolted towards a copse some few hundred yards away. Her screams this time were truly alarming, the timbre of them sending Lillian's own heels against the flank of her steed in pursuit.

Luc Clairmont, however, was in front of her already,

his stallion galloping down upon the smaller mare and catching up with each long stride.

'Keep your head down,' he called to the terrified girl, 'and hold on.'

Caroline Shelby, however, seemed frozen solid, her gait unsteady and swaying. Another few yards and she would be off and if the stirrup wrapped about her boot was not freed she would also be dragged.

'Get your boots out of the stirrups,' Luc was now yelling. 'Or you will be unseated and caught.'

'I ca…aaa…aan't.' At least some advice seemed to be getting through even though she chose to ignore it, lying across her horse in a position that suggested pure and frozen terror.

Luc was at her side, leaning down wide from his own horse in a way that made Lillian's heart flutter. Goodness, if he were to fall in this position he would be under the hooves of both mounts and the jagged up-standing stones that scattered the field were not helping his cause either.

She shouted to him to be careful, sheer muscle and strength now keeping him in his seat, his centre of gravity so tilted as he tried unsuccessfully to rein in Lady Shelby's horse.

Freeing his feet from his stirrups as the edge of the copse bore down upon them, in a daring leap of faith he jumped from his horse to the other and grabbed on the reins, the bridle pulling at the horse's mouth and bringing its head back in a jerk.

The leafy green branches of the first oaks swiped him as he stopped, Caroline Shelby's crying now at a fever pitch as she clung to him, arms entwined about his neck as though she would never let him go.

Lillian drew her own horse up a second or so later and slid off.

'Are you hurt, Lady Shelby?' she asked anxiously, and caught the golden glance of Luc Clairmont.

'Not as badly as I am,' he drawled and extricated himself from the woman's grasp, jumping down from the horse. Touching a bloodied cheek he smiled, but after the fear of the last few moments any humour was lost on Lillian. She almost lifted her riding crop and hit him.

'Hurt? You could have been killed!' She made no attempt at all to curb her shout. 'You could have fallen and broken your head open on the stones or been trampled by the hooves of these frightened horses.'

Caroline Shelby's cornflower-blue eyes were now upon her, her terrified shrieks silenced. Gracious, Lillian thought, I have become exactly like her with such an outpouring of words. She clamped her mouth shut and turned away, bringing her whip down against a tree branch, liking the way the brown leaves fell at the action.

She was shaking, she felt it first in her hands and then in her stomach and as she took another step in the direction of her horse, a light-headed strangeness suddenly overcame her, a dry-mouthed fear that was overwhelming. Then the ground was swallowed by blackness and she could not stop her fall.

Luc caught her as she staggered the last few paces, her soft smallness easy to lift, her pale hair undone from its tight chignon as her hat fell to the ground. Her hair tumbled silver across his chest as he placed her gently on the grass.

'Lilly. Lilly.' He tapped her cheek and was rewarded by her eyes opening, shadow-bruised in uncertainty as she tried to sit up.

'Stay still. You fainted.'

'I…never…faint,' she returned, though a frown deepened as she realised that indeed she just had. 'It was your foolishness that made me…'

'I'm not hurt.'

Her thumb reached up to touch the blood on his cheek. He turned into the contact.

'From the branches,' he qualified, 'and just a scratch.'

Sweat marked her upper lip now and made her skin clammy. God, he could see Wilcox-Rice bearing down and he did not look happy. Behind him came the Hammonds. Nat was last and Luc could have sworn he had a smile on his face.

'I wanted to tell you that I felt something, too.' Her words were softly whispered, just before John claimed her and Lady Hammond bent to his side.

The kiss. She spoke of that? He knew she did. The words on the card he had sent said the same thing. Caroline Shelby stood behind him now, looking at them strangely, gratitude mixed with shock. Had she heard? Would she say? He made much of picking his hat up and wiping it against his riding breeches.

'It seems the world is full of damsels in distress today,' he quipped and stepped away, hating to leave Lilly behind him with a fear of everything in her ashen face and pale eyes.

* * *

Everybody fussed over her, made her comfortable, tucked in her blankets and fluffed her pillows. Aunt Jean, Lady Hammond and Caroline Shelby. Even Cassandra St Auburn with her red hair floating about her face, and looking the picture of glowing good health. Why had she not joined her guests and could she get her alone for five minutes to ask the questions that she wanted to?

Lillian was glad in a way for this bed, glad to be sequestered in a room far away from the chance of meeting Lucas Clairmont again after her last whispered and most unwise remark.

'I wanted to tell you that I felt something, too.'

What had she been thinking? She shut her eyes against the horror of it all and Aunt Jean's voice was worried as she shook her arm.

'Are you feeling poorly again, my dear? Should I send for your father?' Her query was accompanied by a hacking cough that made Lillian draw the sheet further over her face for fear of catching it.

'No, I am perfectly all right, Aunt.' *And perfectly stupid,* she added beneath her breath.

Could she just stay hidden, pleading some illness that was inexplicable? But how then could she journey home? Gracious, if she had been in London this would have been a whole lot easier, but she was here at a country house an hour's drive away and in close proximity to a man to whom her reaction gave her a lot to be concerned over.

She could not trust herself, she decided, doom spreading at the conclusion.

She was now a feckless and insubstantial woman

who did not trust her own mind and whose opinion was forever yo-yoing between this idea and that one.

To love him!

To love him not!

A man can smile and smile and be a villain!

Lucas had said so as he had spoken of his own shadows and mirrors and alluded that she might have her secrets too. Well, she did, and it was a secret that she could never tell anybody.

She…loved…him.

And she had done from the very first second of laying her eyes upon him outside the retiring room at the Lenningtons' ball. Loved a man with a smile in his eyes and a voice that held the promise of every single thing that she was not.

Brave. Free. Wild. Untethered.

And today with the chance of death dogging his bravery she had recognised it, her very heart pierced with the impossibility.

'Oh, Lord God, help me, please…'

The prayer circled in her head, another petition to smite from her soul the horrible recognition of what was there.

Cassie St Auburn now sat on a chair near her bed, all the other women gone for the moment, and yet in her newly found revelation she did not dare to ask anything about Lucas Clairmont. What if he was a villain? What if he truly did inhabit the underworld of crime and gambling? What if she as a friend who knew him well warned her off?

'I am glad to see you better, Cassandra,' she began, at least filling the silence with something.

'Oh, I am only ever sick at mid-day. After that I am always much recovered.'

Lillian could not quite get the gist of her illness.

'I am pregnant,' Cassandra St Auburn laughed. 'Already halfway along.'

A great surge of envy overcame puzzlement. Cassie had a husband who loved her and was now awaiting her first child. With her smiles and happiness she had a life that Lillian suddenly felt was very far from her own. A solitary quiet life, her father's daughter, and burdened with a stalwart code of behaviour that was beginning to look faintly ludicrous and infinitely lonely.

'Lord Wilcox-Rice has been asking after you almost hourly,' Cassie continued, 'though I have made it clear to him that you need your rest.'

'Thank you.'

'Nat also had the doctor look at Mr Clairmont's injuries, but apart from a torn nail and a cut that has needed to be stitched across his cheek he is in fine form. He also asked after your health.'

'He did?' She tried to keep the interest from her question, but knew that she had not succeeded.

'Indeed. He felt somehow responsible for your faint.'

Lillian nodded and looked away. 'I thought that he might have been killed.'

'Nathaniel says that Lucas is a man who can easily look after himself.'

'I do not doubt it.'

'The wound on his cheek makes him look even more unruly than he normally does.'

'But it is not deemed dangerous to his health?'

Lillian hated the tremor of worry in her words and hoped Cassie would not detect it.

'I doubt the doctor could have made Lucas stay in bed to rest even had the injury been worse.'

'I believe Mr Clairmont will be returning to America at the end of December? Has he already arranged passage?' Goodness, and she had promised herself that she would find out nothing, but Cassandra stood and looked at the time on a clock by the bedside table.

'I must not wear you out as the doctor asked for quiet and I think it might be wise for you to sleep.'

When she was gone Lillian wondered about her quick exit. Her hostess had not wished to answer any questions about Lucas Clairmont, that much she could glean. Why ever not? Were the St Auburns in on some sort of ruse? The headache she had been pretending for the past hour suddenly became real and she closed her eyes against the growing pain.

Caroline Shelby waylaid Luc in the drawing room after dinner and he wished he had left the salon when the other men had. She looked rather excited, her colour high and her eyes bright.

'I would like to thank you again for your help, Mr Clairmont.'

As she had already thanked him numerous times he held his counsel and waited.

'I would also like to ask you a question.' She looked around to make certain that there was no one behind her, eavesdropping. When she saw the coast was clear she continued, albeit a little more softly. 'I would like to ask you of the relationship between you and Lillian Davenport?'

'Miss Davenport?' A hammer swung against the beat of his heart. She had heard Lilly's words and everything was dangerous. Fury leaked into caution and into that came the obvious need for sense.

'I stopped her falling when she fainted. Something I would have done for any woman.'

'Any woman?' Lady Shelby looked relieved. 'So there are no special feelings between you?'

'There are not. I barely know her.'

'Then would I be remiss to ask you if you might accompany me home on the morrow? I need to be back in London and would appreciate an escort.'

'Of course,' Luc answered. 'I would be delighted.'

When she had left he poured himself a large cold drink of water.

Nat found him forty minutes later sitting watching the night through the opened curtains.

'You are not in bed?'

'I am leaving with Caroline Shelby first thing in the morning.'

'A change of plans, then?'

'The woman came right out and implied I had feelings for Lilly Davenport.'

'Lilly?'

'And I haven't.'

'Of course not.'

'I would ruin her.'

'Lord, Luc. Sometimes I think that you are too hard on yourself and Virginia is far from here.'

'It is my home, the only one I have known.'

'Only because you refused to ever come back.'

'No.' Anger was infused in the word. Real anger. 'You do not understand…'

'And God only knows how I wish I could, but you will not let me in! There is something you are not telling me, and if there is one person in the world who owes you a favour you are looking right at him. After Eton…'

'None of it was your fault, Nat.'

'It was me who stole the watch, remember, and you who took the blame.' This confession was said with such a sense of doom that Luc began to laugh.

'Lord, Nathaniel, it was your damn watch in the first place and the master had no right in taking it.'

'Still, it was not one of my finest moments and I always regretted such a lapse in courage.'

'You just wanted your property back and I was desperate to be gone. Each of us gained what we hoped for. You know that.'

'If you had stayed in England, I could have helped you.'

'Getting expelled from Eton saved me, because with my mother and father out of the country, I had a chance to escape them and become my own man.'

'You were fourteen.'

'Going on twenty.' Luc took another sip of the water in his glass. 'And you and Hawk were the only damn friends that I ever had there.'

'Not much of a friend, I fear. Look at Paget bringing up the past like it was yesterday.'

'He is a man who still has much of the boy in him.'

'And there is the trouble of it all, Luc. People here are long on memory and short on forgiveness and without a family name to shelter behind you are open game. If we came back to town and you moved in with us…'

'I think it wiser to keep a distance, Nat.'

'Because of your intelligence work? You said it was over and finished. You said that you no longer worked for the army in any capacity.'

'I don't, but there are remnants of other things that don't so easily fade.'

The moon suddenly came out from behind the clouds and through the open curtains the landscape around this tiny corner of Kent was bathed in light. Touching the newly stitched scar on his cheek, Luc stood and downed the last of his drink. 'You're a family man now, Nat, with the promise of a child come the summer. Concentrate on those things, aye.'

On the silver lawn an owl swooped, its talons catching a field mouse in full flight, taking it up into the sky, a small and struggling prey that had been in the wrong place at the wrong time.

Like himself as a youngster, Luc thought, and unlatched the ties so that the curtains fell across the scene in a single heavy tumble of burgundy velvet.

Chapter Ten

'There is some evil afoot, Lillian,' her father said quietly as she lifted the first of the Christmas garlands into place around the hearth in the blue salon. 'Lord Paget has been found dead at his house this morning.'

Lillian fastened the bough of pine before turning, trying to give herself some sense of time.

'But he was with us at the weekend at the St Auburns.'

'Which brings me to the very reason that I mention it. Some are saying that his death is suspicious for there was an argument, it seems, between him and Clairmont. The American has been taken in for questioning.'

'But Mr Clairmont did not cause the argument, Father, he tried to stop it.'

'Oh, well, no doubt the constabulary will get to the bottom of what happened and it's hardly our problem. From all accounts the man is a renegade and why he continues to frequent the soirées of the *ton* eludes me.

I for one would not give him the time of day.' Standing beside her, he put his hand up to the greenery. 'That looks lovely—will you place one on the other side too?'

Lillian nodded, though the Christmas spirit had quite gone out of her as she thought back to the weekend.

Luc Clairmont had already left when she had finally risen on the Sunday morning, accompanying Lady Caroline Shelby back to London! He had not stayed to find out more about her hastily whispered promise of feeling 'something' and had not tried to contact her since.

Could he have murdered the man? For an insult? Her whole world was turning upside down and she had no way of stopping it doing so.

The pile of decorations she had had the maid bring down from the attic lay before her, a job she usually enjoyed, but now... She looked over at the tin soldiers and varnished collages, the paper cornucopias all waiting to be filled and the hand-dipped candles that she had so lovingly fashioned last year. A pile of gay Christmas cards lay further afield and the dolls she used every Yuletide in the nativity scene beneath the tree were neatly packed in another box. All waiting!

When a maid came to say that there was a caller and gave her the card of Caroline Shelby, she was almost relieved to be able to put off the effort of it all.

'Please show her up,' she instructed the girl and Lady Shelby appeared less than a scant moment later.

'Miss Davenport! I am so sorry to intrude, but I have come on a matter of a most delicate sort.'

Gesturing for the newcomer to sit, Lillian took the chair opposite and waited for her to begin. 'It's just I do not know what to do and you are so sensible and seem to know just exactly what next step to take about everything.'

Lillian smiled through surprise and felt a lot older than the young and emotional girl opposite.

'The thing is that I have found myself becoming increasingly attracted to Mr Lucas Clairmont from Virginia and I came because I heard you talking to him when you were recovering after your faint.'

'I beg your pardon?' Of everything Caroline Shelby might have said this was the most unforeseen, and she hoped her own rush of emotion was not staining her face.

'At the St Auburns'. I heard you say that you felt something for him.'

Lillian made herself smile, the danger in the girl's announcement very alarming. 'Perhaps you have made an error, Lady Shelby, for I am about to be engaged to Lord Wilcox-Rice.'

The woman looked uncertain. 'I had not heard that.'

'Probably because you were too busy fabricating untruths,' she returned. 'John and I have been promised to each other for the past three weeks and my father has given us his blessing.'

Caroline Shelby stood, placing her bag across the crook of her arm. 'Oh, well then, I shall say no more about any of it and ask most sincerely for your pardon of my conduct. I would also ask you, in the light of all that has been revealed, to keep the words spoken between us private. I should not wish any others to know.'

'Of course not.'

She rang the bell and the maid came immediately.

'I bid you good afternoon, Lady Shelby.' Lillian could hear the coldness in her words.

'Good afternoon, Miss Davenport.'

Once the woman had gone she sat down heavily on the couch. Gracious, could this day become any worse? She did not think that it possibly could although she was mistaken.

Half an hour later John Wilcox-Rice arrived beaming.

'I have just seen Lady Shelby and she led me to believe that you had had second thoughts about our engagement.'

Lillian looked at him honestly for the first time in weeks. He was an ordinary man, some might even say a boring man, but he was not a murderer or a liar. Today his eyes were bright with hope and in his hands he held a copy of a book she had mentioned she would like to read whilst staying at the St Auburns'. She added 'a thoughtful man' to her list.

'Perhaps we should speak to Father.'

Ernest Davenport broke open his very best bottle of champagne and poured four glasses, her aunt Jean being summoned from her rooms to partake in the joyous news.

'I cannot tell you how delighted I am with this announcement, Lillian. John here will make you a fine husband and your property will be well managed.'

Her aunt Jean, not wishing to be outdone in gladness, clapped her hands. 'When did you think to have the wedding, Lillian?'

'We can decide on a date after Christmas, Aunt,' she replied, the whole rigmarole of organising the occasion something she did not really wish to consider right now.

'And a dress, we must find the most beautiful gown, my dear. Perhaps a trip to Paris to find it might be in order, Ernest?'

Her father laughed, a sound Lillian had not heard in many months and her anxiety settled. 'That seems like a very good idea to me, Jean.'

John had come to stand near her, and he took her fingers in his own.

'You have made me the happiest of fellows, my dear Lillian, the very happiest.'

My dear? Goodness, he sounded exactly like her father. What would she call him? No name at all came to mind as she went over to the drinks table and helped herself to another generous glass of champagne, turning only when Eleanor was shown in by the maid, a look of surprise on her face.

'I have just been given the news,' she said, 'and so I have come immediately. Mama and Papa are returning from the country tonight so the timing could not have been better.'

With a smile she enveloped Lillian in her arms. 'And you, sister-in-law—' the words rolled off her tongue in an impish way '—I didn't have an idea that you two were so close and you let me know nothing! Was it the sprig of mistletoe that settled it? When shall the ceremony take place? Do you already have your bridesmaids?'

Everyone laughed at the run of questions, except

Lillian, who suddenly and dreadfully saw exactly what she had done. Not just she now and John, but her family and Eleanor and a group of people whom she did not wish in any way to hurt.

Taking a breath, she firmly told herself to stop this introspection and, finishing the champagne, bent to the task of answering the many questions Ellie was pounding her with.

A sensible and prudent husband...

The five words were like a mantra in the aching centre of her heart.

They had finally gone. All of them. Her father to his club and her aunt to a bridge party at an old friend's house. Eleanor and John had returned home to see if their parents had arrived from the country.

Four days ago she had fancied herself in love with one man and today she was as good as married to another. The very notion of it made her giggle. Was this what they termed a hysterical reaction? she wondered when she found it very hard to stop. Tears followed, copious and noisy and she was glad for the sturdy lock on the door and the lateness of the hour.

Carefully she stood and walked to the book on the shelf in which she had pressed one orange bloom. The flower was almost like paper now, a dried-up version of what it once had been. Like her? She shook her head. All of this was not her fault, for goodness' sake! She had made a choice based on facts, a choice that any woman of sound mind might have also made.

The Davenport property was a legacy, after all, one

that needed to be minded by each generation for the next one. The man she would marry had to be above question, reputable and unflinchingly honest. He could not be someone who was considered a suspect in a murder case. Besides, Luc Clairmont had neither called on her in town since she had made her ridiculous confession nor tried in any way to show he reciprocated her feelings.

Her fingers tightened on the flower. She was no longer young and the proposals of marriage, once numerous, had trickled away over the past year or two.

Caroline Shelby's exuberant youth was the embodiment of a new wave of girls, a group who had begun to make their own rules in the way they lived their lives.

Poor Lillian.

The conversation from the retiring room over three weeks' ago returned in force.

Everything had changed in the time between then and now! A tear traced its way down her cheek, and she swiped it away. No, she would not cry. She had made the right and only choice, and if John Wilcox-Rice's kisses did not set her heart to beating in the same way as Luc Clairmont's did, then more fool she. Marriage was about much more than just lust, it was about respect and honour and regard and surely as the years went by these things would gain in ascendancy.

Feeling better, she placed the flower back in the book and tucked it on to the shelf. A small memento, she thought, of a time when she had almost made a silly mistake. She wondered why her hands felt so empty when the orange bloom was no longer in them.

* * *

His father's face was above him red with anger, the strap in his hands biting into thin bare legs. Further off his mother sat, head bent over her tapestry and not looking up.

Screaming when silence was no longer possible, William Clairmont's beating finally ceased, though the agony of his parents' betrayal was more cutting than any slice of leather.

'Another lesson learnt, my boy,' his father said, trailing his fingers softly down the side of his son's face. 'We will say no more of this, no more of any of it. Understood?'

Luc woke up sweating, trying to fight his way out of the blankets, cursing both the darkness and the ghost of his father. If he had been here now, even in a celestial form, he would have made a fist and beaten him out of hiding, the love that most normal fathers felt for their children completely missing in his.

As fury dimmed, the room took shape and the sounds of the early morning formed, shadows passing into the promise of daylight. He hadn't had this particular dream for years and he wondered what had brought it on. Nat's mention, he supposed, of the Eton fiasco, and the events that had followed.

The knock on the door made him freeze.

'Everything in order, Luc?' Stephen Hawkhurst's head came around the portal, the fact that he was still in his evening clothes at this time of the morning raising Luc's eyebrows.

'You've been out all night?' The smell of fine perfume wafted in with him.

'You refused to join me, remember? Nat had an

excuse in the warm arms of his wife, but you?' He came in to the small room and lay across the bottom of the bed, looking up. 'Elizabeth has been dead for months and if you don't let the guilt go soon you never will.'

'Nathaniel's already given me the same lecture, thanks, Hawk.' Luc didn't like the coldness he could hear in his own words.

'And as you have not listened to either of us I have another solution. Leave this place and move in with me and I'll throw the grandest ball of the Season and make certain that anyone who is anyone is there. Properly done it could bury the whispers of your past for ever, and as the guest of honour with Nat and me beside you, who would dare to question?' A smile began to form on Stephen's face. 'You're a friend of Miss Davenport's. If we can get her and her fiancé to come, then all the others will follow.'

'She is engaged to Wilcox-Rice!' Luc tried to keep his alarm hidden.

'I heard it said this evening and on good authority that the wedding will be after Christmas…'

'The devil take it!' Luc's curse stopped Hawkhurst in his tracks.

'What did I miss?'

'Nothing, Hawk,' Luc replied, 'you missed nothing at all, and I should have damned well known better.'

A whoop of delight made his heart sink. 'You are enamoured by Miss Davenport? The saint and the sinner, the faultless and the blemished, the guilty and the guiltless. Lord, I could go on all night.' Hawk was in his element now, fingers drumming against the surface of the blankets as he mulled over his options. Luc sat up against the headboard and wished to hell that he had said nothing.

'I suppose you could always hope that Wilcox-Rice will bore her to death?'

'I could.' From past experience Luc knew it was better to humour him.

'But with the wedding planned for early next year that probably won't give you enough time.'

'That soon?'

'Apparently. Davenport is her cousin, you know that, don't you, so when you wrap your arm around his neck next time, best to do it out of sight of your lady.'

'She isn't my lady.'

'An attitude like that won't effect any change.'

'Enough, Stephen. It's early and I am tired.'

His friend frowned. 'Nat and I were the closest to brothers you ever had, Luc, so if you want to talk about anything…'

'I don't.'

'But you would not be adverse to the ball?'

'You were always the problem solver.'

'Oh, and another thing. When I was out tonight I heard from a source that the police have determined Paget's death as suicide and we both know what that means.'

'I won't be had up for his murder!'

'If you stopped harassing Davenport and quit the gambling tables, you wouldn't be a suspect and, to my mind, Daniel Davenport isn't worth the trouble no matter what he has done to make you believe otherwise.'

'My wife might have disagreed.'

'Elizabeth knew him?' Surprise coated the query.

'If the letter Davenport sent her was any indication of the feelings between them, she knew him very well.'

'Hell.' Luc liked the shock in Hawk's word, for he had begun to question his own reactions to all that he was doing.

'If you kill him, you'll hang. Better to do away with him on some dark night far from London'

'Shift the blame, you mean?' He laughed as Hawk nodded and felt the best he had done in months.

'On reflection I don't think it was all her fault. Towards the end I liked her as little as she did me.' Honesty was a double-edged sword and Luc wished he could have had Hawk's black-and-white view of the picture.

'When did you become so equitable?'

Unexpectedly Lillian's face came to Luc's mind. She had tempered his anger and loneliness and despair and replaced his feeling of dislocation with a trust and belief in goodness that was…staggering and warming all at the same time.

'It's age, I think.' He smiled as he said it and knew that his words were a complete lie. As the first birdsong lilted into the new morning Stephen stretched and yawned.

'I have to go to sleep. Goodnight, Luc.'

'Goodnight, Hawk.'

When his oldest friend simply curled up at the bottom of his bed and was soon snoring, Lucas smiled. There were definitely advantages to being back in England and Stephen was one of them.

* * *

The following morning he left Stephen still asleep in his lodgings and walked along the Thames, the winter whipping the river into grey waves that swelled up the embankment and threatened to engulf the pathway. He didn't want to go to a club or a tavern or even to the Lindsay town house where he always felt welcome. No, today he simply walked, on past the Chelsea Hospital and down the route that the body of Wellington must had been taken during his state funeral last November. A million people had lined the streets then, it was said, and they would again at the next funeral, the next celebration, the next public function that caught the fancy of a nation.

Life went on despite a wife who had betrayed him and an uncle who had died well before his time.

Stuart Clairmont!

Even now the name was hard to say and he ground his teeth together to try to stop the sorrow that welled up over the thought. A man who had been the father his own never was. A man who had loved and nurtured a lost child newly come from England and given him back the sense of purpose and strength that had been leached away from him under the punitive regime of a father who thought punishment to be the making of character.

He still bore the scars of such bestial brutality and still hated William Clairmont with all the passion of a young boy who had never stood a chance.

Where was Lilly? he wondered, the news of her engagement angering him again. She would marry a man who was patently wrong for her, a man who neither kissed her with any skill nor fought with a scrap of dexterity. He remembered the feeble slap Wilcox-Rice had given Paget before he had intervened, the breathless sheen on his face from the effort of doing even that, pointing to a spouse who would not protect a wife from anyone.

The flaws in his argument pressed in. John Wilcox-Rice was a man who would not have enemies, his life lived in the narrow confines of an untarnished society. Why should he need to be adept at the darker arts of survival, the things that kept a man apart and guarded? As he was!

The number of differences between Lillian and him spiralled upwards as he ran for the omnibus, and as the conductor inside issued him a ticket for the cramped and smelly space he was certain that the permitted twenty-two passengers was almost twice that number.

Chapter Eleven

No one was speaking to Lucas Clairmont, Lillian saw as she walked into the Billinghurst soirée that evening and found it was divided into two distinct camps.

Oh, granted, the Earl of St Auburn and Lord Hawkhurst leaned against the columns on his side of the room, the smiles on their faces looking remarkably genuine, but nobody else went near him.

It was the death of Lord Paget, she supposed, and the fact that much was said about the card games Lucas Clairmont was involved with. Gossip that did not quite accuse him of cheating, but not falling much short either.

'Mr Clairmont does seem to inspire strong feelings in people, doesn't he?'

Lillian looked around quickly, trying to determine if her friend was including herself in that category.

Lucas Clairmont looked vividly handsome on the other side of the room, dressed in a formal black evening suit that he looked less than comfortable in.

'If he is here and not languishing in a London gaol, my guess would be the police thought him to have no knowledge of Lord Paget's death.'

Anne Weatherby at her side laughed at the summation. 'You are becoming quite the defender of the man, Lillian. I heard it was your testimony at the St Auburns that had the Pagets fleeing in the first place.'

'And for that I now feel guilty.'

'Well, your husband-to-be seems to have no such thoughts. He looks positively radiant this evening.'

John crossed the room towards them, Eleanor on his arm, and indeed he did look very pleased with himself.

'I have it on good authority that Golden Boy is set to run a cracking first at Epsom this year and as he is a steed I have a financial stake in the news is more than pleasing. Is your father here, Lillian? I must go and impart the news to him.'

Eleanor watched as her brother chased off again across the room and entwined her arm through Lillian's.

'I do believe that John loves your father almost as much as he loves you. He is always telling me that Ernest Davenport says this and Ernest Davenport says that. My own papa must be getting increasingly tired of having the endless comparisons, I fear, though in all honesty John hasn't seen eye to eye with him for a very long time. The inherent competition, I suspect, between generations so closely bound. I often wonder if a spell in India or in the army might have finished my brother off well? Pity, perhaps, that that avenue is no longer available.'

Lillian tried to imagine John in the wilds of the Far

East and found that she just could not. He was a man who seemed more suited to the ease of the drawing room.

Lucas Clairmont on the other hand never looked comfortable confined in the small spaces of London society. Oh, granted, he had a sort of languid unconcern written across him here as he conversed with his friends, but he never relaxed, a sense of animated vitality not quite extinguished. He also always stood with his back against the wall, a trait that gave the impression of constant guardedness. The guise of a soldier, perhaps, or something darker. She had read the stories of Colquhoun Grant and there was something in the character of Wellington's head of intelligence that was familiar in the personality of the man who stood opposite her.

As if he sensed her looking at him, his eyes turned to meet her own, dark gold glinting with humour. Quickly she looked away and made much of adjusting the pin on her bodice. When she glanced back, he no longer watched her and she squashed the ridiculous feeling of disappointment.

Turning the ring John had given her on her betrothal finger, she tried to take courage from it as she listened to the conversation between Anne and Eleanor.

'I hear that congratulations are in order,' he said in a quiet tone as they met an hour later by one of the pillars in a largely deserted supper room. 'Your groom-to-be must have made great strides in the art of kissing a woman.'

'Indeed, Mr Clairmont,' Lillian replied, 'and although

you may not credit it, there are, in truth, other things that are of much more importance.'

'There are?' His surprise made it difficult to maintain her sense of decorum.

'A man's reputation for one,' she bit back, 'is considered by a careful bride to be essential.'

'And are you a careful bride, Lilly?'

'Lillian,' she echoed, ignoring the true intent of his question. 'And careful in the way of being certain that John has at least never been a suspect in murder.'

'Because he plays everything as safely as you do?'

She turned, but he caught at her arm, not gently either, the hard bite of his fingers making her flinch. 'Perhaps you might wait till the findings of the police are made public before naming me guilty.'

'Why?' she retaliated. 'If you keep the company of gamblers and card sharps and are often covered in the bruises and markings of a man who goes from one squabble to the next, why indeed should I give you any leeway?'

'Because I hope you know by now, Lilly, that I am not quite as black as you would paint me.' His accent was soft but distinct, the cadence of the new lands on his tongue.

'Do I, Lucas? Do I know that?'

It was the first time she had called him by his Christian name and the warm glow in his eyes alarmed her. There was something else there too. A vulnerability that she had not seen before, an unprotected and exposed need that tugged at her because it was so unexpected.

'Marrying one man because of the faults of another is not the wisest of choices.'

'So what is it then you would suggest?'

He laughed, the sound filling the empty space around them. 'Come away with me instead.'

The room whirled, a yearning ache in her body that she was completely astonished by. If only he meant it. If only the laughter that the invitation had been accompanied with did not sound quite so offhand. So casual!

'And spend the rest of my life wondering when a noose would be placed about your neck?'

'I had nothing to do with the death of Paget, if that is what you are implying.'

'You were asked to leave Eton.'

'I was a boy…'

'Who stole a watch?'

Again he began to laugh. 'Such a crime…' But she allowed his amusement no further rein.

'I am the only heir to Fairley Manor, Mr Clairmont, and in England we protect our assets by marrying wisely.'

He tipped his head and in the light of the room Lillian saw the beginnings of a reddened scar that snaked from his right ear into the collar of his shirt.

'A long-ago accident,' he qualified as he saw her uncertainty.

But she was transfixed. This was no simple wound that would take a day or two to mend. She imagined both the pain and the tenacity needed to recover from such an injury and in her conjecture also saw the wide and yawning gap that lay between them. Who had tended him in his hours of need, wiped his brow and brought him water? She had heard it said he had left for America as a boy, but there had been no mention of any family.

'Did your parents go with you to the Americas?'

He looked puzzled at her change of topic. 'My parents?'

'The Earl of St Auburn implied that you were barely above fourteen when you left Eton and that you sailed from England very soon afterwards.'

'I had an uncle there already.'

'So you took passage alone?'

'Worked my way there actually as a deckhand on the *Joanna*. Forty days was all it took between London and New York—the seas and winds were kind.'

Marvelling at his description, she imagined a child making his way across the world to a different shore, the mantle of being labelled a thief on his shoulders and alone. Why had his parents not gone with him? She sensed he wanted no more questions as he stood there, the candles above setting his hair to a shade of lighter brown amongst the ebony, curling long against his nape.

'Wilcox-Rice will never make you happy.' The words seemed dragged from him.

'Whereas you will?'

He smiled at that. 'There are things more important than a certain cut of cloth or which fork one uses at a banquet table, Miss Davonport.'

'You think that is what defines me?'

'Partly.'

She hated the truth in his words and the answering

echo of it in her own mind. 'The sum of my pieces must be awfully galling to you then, Mr Clairmont, just as the sum of your own is as equally trying to me. I think a passably good kiss in a man who seems to eschew every other moral principle would not sustain a relationship for even as long as a month.'

'Do you now?' Ground out. Barely civil.

Lillian stood her ground. 'Indeed, for it has come to my ears that the whisper of friendship and respect is a most underrated thing in any marriage.'

'Which unfulfilled brides have told you that nonsense?'

Shock held her rigid. 'Perhaps it was naïve of me to expect that you might consider such a sentiment with an open mind.'

'An open mind?' He laughed. 'When your own has just condemned me as a murderer.'

'Paget was a man you seemed to have much reason to hate.'

'I concede. Put like that my case seems hopeless and if a thought is as lethal as a bullet…'

When she allowed a smile to blossom he took the small chance of it quickly.

'Stay the night with me, Lillian. See what it is you will miss if you marry John Wilcox-Rice.'

The shock of his question was only overrun by the stinging want in her body. 'I could start with ruination—'

He broke into her banter. 'I would never hurt you, at least believe that.'

She saw the way he looked about to make certain no person lay in earshot, saw the way too he kept his hands jammed in his jacket pockets and his face carefully bland. They could for all intents and purposes be discussing the weather should a bystander take the time to watch them.

'If by some misguided logic I should chance to consider such a risky venture, where would you imagine this tryst to take place? I should not wish to shed my inhibitions in a dosshouse, after all.'

'Someone has told you my address?'

The dimple in his cheek was deep and she tried not to let the beauty of his face daunt her.

'Come away with me, then. I have a house in Bedfordshire.'

'I could not possibly…'

'You could buy a kiss when you barely knew me. Take that one step further.'

John Wilcox-Rice's voice sounded behind her. 'Lillian, I have been looking for you.' His words were wary and distrustful.

'Mr Clairmont has just extended an invitation to us to call in at his house in the country.' She watched as amber flared, catching her glance in a hooded warning.

'I doubt we shall be in the district, Clairmont, and I thought I had heard it said that you were taking passage home very soon.'

'Unless the police have need to keep me in London.'

John stuttered at such nonchalance. A challenge. A provocation. A carefully worded gauntlet thrown into the ring between adversaries and John with no notion at all as to what he fought for.

Her!

The beat of Lillian's heart thickened in the dawning realisation that she was the prize, a situation that she had not had the experience of since her first year of coming out, and the band of white gold and diamonds on the third finger of her left hand felt tight, a small message of control and limit that constricted everything.

Oh, for the chance of another kiss? No, there wasn't the possibility for any of it, especially here with her father and aunt close and a fiancé who allowed her not a moment's respite. If only she might lay her fingers in those of the American opposite and simply walk, now, away from it all.

Like her mother had!

She shook her head and the moment of madness passed, evaporated into expectation and duty. Lillian or Lilly. The white and careful promise of obligation and discretion counterbalanced against the wilder orange flair of excitement and thrill.

The very same choices Rebecca had mismanaged all those years before and look where it had taken her: a deathbed racked with self-reproach and contrition.

She inclined her head as she allowed John Wilcox-Rice to take her arm and lead her out into the ballroom proper, the music of Strauss settling her fears as it swirled and eddied about them. Many in the pressing crowd smiled at them, the illusion of a wondrous young love, not such a difficult one to pass off after all.

John leaned in as they performed the waltz, the ardour that had been apparent at the St Auburns' the night he had escorted her to her room as obvious here.

She felt his fingers splayed out across her back.

'This is the dance of lovers, Lillian. Appropriate, don't you think?'

It took all of her composure not to break his hold and pull away.

'If you could give some consideration about naming a date for our nuptials, and preferably one in the not-too-distant future, you would make me the happiest of men.'

Lillian faltered. 'With all the Christmas preparations I have been busy.'

'What of February, then?'

'I had thought of the summer,' she returned and his face fell.

'No, that is too long.' The forceful tone in his voice surprised her. 'It needs to be earlier.'

Nodding, she retreated into silence. Earlier? The very word was like a death knell in her heart.

'If you don't approach her soon the night will be gone, Luc.' Hawkhurst's voice was insistent. Already the clock was nearing the hour of two.

'I think I made myself more than clear to Miss Davenport an hour or so back, Hawk.'

'And she wanted none of you?'

'Exactly.'

'Well, that's a first. So you're going to give up just like that?'

'I am. She intimated that she thought I had some hand in the death of Paget.'

'You are here for a month and life becomes interesting again. To my mind, however, Lillian Davenport seems downright miserable and the stuffed shirt of a fiancé looks as though he is hanging on to her arm for dear life. Even her father looks bored with his conversation and that's saying something.' He stopped, and Luc didn't like the way he smiled. 'Her aunt on the other hand is eyeing you up with a singular interest.'

'She probably wants to chastise me on behalf of her son.'

'No, the glance is one more of a measured curiosity.'

'Then perhaps she was a particular friend of Albert Paget and is trying to work out how I did away with him.'

'Well, no doubt we will discover the truth in a moment. She seems to be heading this way.'

'Alone?'

'Very.'

'Mr Clairmont.' Jean Taylor-Reid's voice carried across the room around them and, ignoring Hawkhurst altogether, she went straight to the heart of what was worrying her. 'I think my niece seems to have taken up your cause as a man who needs improvement and so I have come to warn you. There are many here who say that the misdemeanours of your youth would make it difficult for you to fashion a future here in London.'

'Is that what they say, Lady Taylor-Reid?' He looked around pointedly. 'England has long since ceased to frighten me with its obsession with the importance of family name and fortune.'

'Then you are inviting problems for yourself.'

'I beg your pardon?'

Ignoring his perplexity, she carried on. 'The protection offered by a family name is irrefutable and the name of Davenport is one I should wish to keep untainted. If my son Daniel has done anything to offend you...' She swallowed back tears and stopped, and Luc, who could not for the life of him work out where she was going with this, remained silent.

'I would plead with you to ignore him. He may not be the easiest person to like, but if he should die...' Her voice petered out, but, taking a breath, she continued more strongly. 'I would, of course, offer you something in return. There are whispers, you see, that you are more involved in the Paget death than you let on. Perhaps this might be a wise time to simply return to America—slip out on the next tide, so to speak. There is a ship leaving for Boston in the morning that has a berth which is paid for.' She pressed a paper into his hands. 'You will find all the details here, Mr Clairmont, and the captain is amenable to asking no questions.'

'Leaving both your son and niece safe from my person?'

'I think we understand each other entirely.'

She did not wait to see if he agreed, but moved away, back to the side of Lillian's father who watched with open anger. A small greying woman with a slight stoop and the iron will of a doyenne who would do anything to protect the reputation of her family.

'Perhaps Davenport learned the art of getting his own way in everything from the unlikely breast of his mother.'

Luc laughed at Stephen's reflection, though Lilly pointedly looked away from him, the tip-tilt of her nose outlined against the wall behind.

Beautiful. And careful. A woman whose life was lived and measured by the right thing to do. He should take note of Jean Taylor-Reid's warning, should leave Lillian Davenport to the faultless standards of an exacting *ton* and to a fiancé who would for ever be circumspect and judicious. But he could not, not when she had whispered her feelings to him after she had fainted and her guard was down, not when she had admitted that her favourite colour was orange when it was so plainly not.

He finished his glass of lemonade and placed the container on a low-lying table beside him. If he did not act tonight, tomorrow might be too late, the aunt's proclivity to interference worrying and his own problems with Davenport throwing him into a no-man's land of wait and see.

He had never let anyone close, his wife's death a part of that equation in a way he had not understood before. Lillian was drawing something out of him that he thought was gone, shrivelled up in the miserable years of both his youth and his marriage. But it had not. Tonight as he watched her across the room in her white dress and with the candlelight in her hair, the hard centre of his heart had begun to thaw, begun to hope, begun again to feel the possibility of a life that was…whole.

Swearing to himself, he turned away from Hawk and strode out on to a balcony near the top of the room.

The strains of Mozart rent the air, soft, civilised, a thread of memory from an England that had never quite left him. A great well of yearning made him swallow. Yearning for a home. Yearning for Lilly and her goodness, and sense and trust and honesty.

In the window of a salon downstairs he could see a Christmas tree glowing, the candles on its bough promising all that was right and good with the world. Elizabeth had never fussed with such traditions, preferring instead an endless round of visiting. A woman who found solace in the busy whirl of society.

He ran his hand through his hair. If he was honest he had married her for her looks, a shallow reason that he had had much cause to regret within the first year of their life together. But he had been nearly twenty-seven and the land he had spent breaking in with Stuart had taken much of his time since first arriving in America. When she had come after him with her flashing eyes and chestnut curls he had been entranced.

He had never loved her! The thought made him swear because even in his darkest hours he had not admitted it to himself. Why now, though? Why here? He knew the answer even as he phrased the question. Because in the room beside this one a woman whom he felt more respect for than any other he had met in his life laughed and danced and chatted.

'I think my niece seems to have taken up your cause as a man who needs improvement and so I have come to warn you.'

The old woman's voice rang true in his conscience as he opened the door and searched the space inside, and as luck might have it Lilly separated herself from her family group and retired to a small alcove at one end of the room. Had she seen him coming? Lucas did not know. All he knew was that he was beside her in the quiet dimmed space and that her warmth beat at his coldness, living flame in her pale blue eyes. He could no longer be circumspect.

'Your aunt has just warned me away from you. She thinks I may be a corrupting influence.'

'And are you, Lucas? Are you that?'

He shook his head, her very question biting at certainty. He wanted to say more, but found himself stymied; after all, there had been much he had done in his life that she would not like. As if she could read his mind she faced him directly.

'I do not understand what this thing is between us, but how I wish that it would just stop.' She laid her hand across her chest as if her heartbeat was worrying her, and the sensation building inside him wound tighter, dangerously complete. There was no room left for compromise or bargain.

'I want you.' Sense and logic deserted him as his thumb traced a line down the side of her arm, the silver of her hair falling like mist across the blackness of his clothes.

Fragile. Easily ruined.

Even that thought did not have him pulling away, not tonight with this small chance of possibility all that was left to him. Now. Here. Only this minute lost in the luck of a provident encounter and a hundred-and-one reasons why he should just let her go. Her fingers joined his thumb and he chided himself, the thin daintiness of white silk sleeves falling over his fist like a shroud. Hidden.

'Lord.' He pulled back as he closed his eyes and swore, a softer feeling tugging at lust and settling wildness.

'Lilly.' Her name. Just that. He could not even

whisper what it was he desired because even the saying of it would take away the beauty of imagination and, if memory was all he was to be left with, he would not spoil even a second of it by a careless entreaty.

He had both power and restraint. The disparity suited him, she thought, as the heat inside her crumbled any true resistance and the incomprehensible fragment of time between separation and togetherness ended. Like a dream, close as breath. Melding simply by touch into one being. She heard the echo of his heartbeat, fast and strong, felt the tremble of his fingers as they trailed down silk and met flesh beneath the lace at her elbows. Her own breath shallowed, roughly taken, the very start of something she could no longer fight, no words to deny him. Anything. She had had enough of denial and of pretending that everything she felt for him was a ruse.

Tears welled as she swallowed. 'If you kiss me here, I shall be ruined.'

There was no choice left though, for already her body leaned across, breasts grazing his shirt beneath an opened jacket, nipples hardened with pure and simple desire. He was her only point of connection in the room, her north to his south, balanced and equal. Even facing havoc she wanted him, wanted him to touch her, to kiss her as he had before and show her what it was that could exist between a man and a woman when everything was exactly as it should be.

Before it was all too late. She did not dare to fight it any longer for fear of a loss that would be more than she could bear! A single tear dropped on to her cheek and she felt its passage like a hot iron, wrenching right from wrong, and changing before to after. No will of her own left. Just what would be between them, here in this room, fifteen feet from her father and fiancé and from three hundred prying eyes.

'Ah, Lilly, if only this were the way of it.' His voice was sad with a hint of resignation in the message as he lifted her hand and kissed the back of it. She felt his tongue lave between the base of her fingers, warm and wet with promise. When he moved back she tried to hold him, tried to catch on to what she knew was lost already. But he did not stay, did not turn as he left the alcove, light swallowing up both shadow and boldness.

Gone.

Alone she trembled, her fists clenched before her, the words of a childhood prayer murmured in a bid for composure, and her nails biting into the heated flesh of her palms.

Life is like a river and it takes you where you are meant to be.

Here. Without him!

She looked out into the night, a myriad of stars above shifting bands of lower cloud. The weather had changed just as she had. She could feel it in her blood and in the rising welling joy that recognised honour.

Lucas Clairmont's honour just to leave her, safe. Taking a deep breath for confidence, she turned and almost bumped into the Parker sisters, cold horror on their faces. The beat of her heart rose so markedly that she felt her throat catch in fear. Coughing, she tried to find speech. Had they seen? Could they know?

'It is a lovely evening.' Even to her ears the words sounded forced, the tremble in them pointing at all that she tried so hard to hide.

But they did not answer back, did not smile or speak. No, they stood there watching her for a good few minutes until the youngest girl burst into copious tears and she knew that the game was up.

A woman she presumed to be a relative hurried quickly to their side and then another woman and another, watching and pitying.

'Miss Davenport let Mr Clairmont kiss her hand and she was standing close. Too close. She is after all betrothed to Lord Wilcox-Rice and I am certain that he would not like this.'

'Hush, Miriam, hush.' Another woman now came to their side, and the voice of reason and restraint might have swayed resolve had the older sister not also begun to sniff.

The whispers of interest began quietly at first, spreading across the ballroom floor like the ripples in a still summer pond after a large stone was thrown in carelessly. Wider and wider the curiosity spread, the fascination of intrigue shifting the weight of anger away from sympathy.

Her father's face was pale as he came towards her and there was a violent distaste on John's as he did not. Lillian saw her Aunt Jean frown in worry and heard the music of the orchestra wind into nothingness.

The sounds of ruin were not loud!

The colours of ruin were not lurid!

They were bleached and faded and gentle like the touch of her father's arm against her own, his fingers over hers, protective and safe.

'Come, Lillian,' he said softly, 'I shall take you home.'

Chapter Twelve

Luc left the Billinghurst town house and walked through the night, deep in his own thoughts as to what he should now do.

Lord, what might have happened had he stayed? He would have kissed her probably, kissed her well and good, and be damned with the whole effort of crying off.

'God help me.' The strain of it all made him breathe out heavily as he turned into a darkened alley affording a quick way back to his rooms.

Would Lillian have slapped his face and demanded an apology?

He could not risk it. Not yet. Not before she had had a chance to know his character and make her own choice as to whether she might want something more.

He swore again. He had always been a man who had carefully planned his life and made certain that the framework of his next moves were in place before he ventured on.

But here…he did not know what had just happened. How had he lost control so badly that he would risk her reputation on a whim?

In retrospect the full stupidity and consequences of his actions were blatantly obvious.

Lillian had not looked happy. She had not caught at his hand to hold him back, glancing instead towards the others in the room, towards her fiancé and her father, as her eyes had filled with tears.

How could he have got the whole thing so very, very wrong? Why the hell had he risked it all, anyway? Anger began to build. He was a colonial stranger with little to recommend him and a woman who sat at the very pinnacle of a society making much of material possessions would hardly welcome his advances in such a very public place.

'If you kiss me here, I shall be ruined.' Had she not said that to him as she had drawn back? Ruined by his reputation, ruined by his lack of place here, ruined by the fact that he had never truly fitted in anywhere save the wilds of Virginia with its hard honest labour and its miles of empty space.

Lord, he had lost one wife to the arms of another man because he had never understood just exactly what it meant to be married. Commitment. To stay in one place. Time. To nurture a relationship and sustain it even in the hours when nothing was easy. The example of his own parents' marriage was hardly one to follow and his uncle had never taken a wife at all.

He had never understood the truth of what it was that made people stay together through thick and thin, through the good times and the bad. Indeed, incomprehension was still the overriding emotion that remained from the five years of his marriage.

A noise made him turn and three men dressed in black stood behind him. His arm shot out to connect with the face of the first one, but it was too late. A heavy wooden baton hit him on the temple and he crumpled, any strength in his body leached into weakness.

As he fell he noticed a carriage waiting at the end of the alley, and he knew it to be the Davenport conveyance. For a second he was heartened that perhaps they were here to save him, but his hopes were dashed as a heavy canvas sack was placed over his head.

'The woman said to take him to the docks and that a man would meet us there.'

The woman?

She?

Lillian?

As the dizzy spinning unreality thickened he welcomed the dark whirl of nothingness, for it took away the bursting pain in his head.

Lucas Clairmont did not come as Lillian thought that he would. He did not come the first morning or the second and now it was all of five days past and every effort her father had made to find him had been fruitless. A man who had walked from the ballroom and out into the world, leaving all that was broken behind him.

He was not in his rooms in London and neither Lord Hawkhurst nor the St Auburns had any idea as to where he had gone. She knew because her father had spent the hour before dinner in her room explaining every ineffective endeavour he had made in locating the American.

'It is my fault all this has happened,' he said solemnly, running his fingers through what little was left of his hair. 'I pushed you into something untenable and your mind has lost its way.'

This melodramatic outburst was the first thing that had made Lillian smile since they had left the Billinghurst ball.

'I think it is more likely my reputation that is lost, Father.'

Ernest Davenport stood, the weight of the world so plainly on his shoulders and the heavy lines on his face etched in worry.

'I don't think Wilcox-Rice will forgive you. Even his sister is making her views about your transience well known.'

'I did not wish to hurt them.'

'But you did.'

No careful denial to make her feel better. She imagined the Wilcox-Rice family's perception of her with a grimace.

'And the worst of it is that you did it all for nothing. I do not now know, daughter, that you will ever be married. I do not think that avenue of action is open to you after this.'

'But you will support me…' Fear snaked into the empty sound of her voice.

'Jean says that I should not. She says that you are

very like your mother and that your lustful nature has been revealed.'

'No. That's not true, Father.'

'Everyone is speaking of us. Everyone is remembering Rebecca in a way that I had thought forgotten. We are now universally pitied, daughter. A family cursed in relationships and fallen from a lofty height.'

'All for a kiss on the back of my hand?'

'Ah, much more than that, I think. At least here in this room between us I would appreciate it if you did not lie.'

She remained silent and he inclined his head in thanks, honesty a slight panacea against all that had been lost.

'I think a sojourn in the north might be in order.'

'To Fairley Manor?' The same place as her mother had been banished to.

Her father's face crumpled and he drew his hands up to cover the grief that he did not wish her to see, and in that one gesture Lillian realised indeed the awful extent of her ruination and the folly of it.

'If you could find Lucas Clairmont, I am certain—'

Ernest dropped his hands and let irritation fly. 'Certain of what? Certain that he will marry you? Certain that this will be forgotten? Certain that society will forgive the lapse in judgement of someone whom they looked up to as an example of how a young woman should behave? You do not understand, do you? If it had been some other less-admired daughter, then perhaps this might have blown over, might have dissipated into the forgotten. But for all your adult life you have been lauded for manners and comportment. Lillian Davenport says this! Lillian Davenport does that! Such a stance has made you enemies in those who have not been so admired and they are talking now, Daughter, and talking loudly.'

She stayed silent.

'Nay, we will pack up the townhouse and retire to Fairley. At least there we can regroup. Jean, Patrick and Daniel will of course accompany us with the Christmas season almost here.'

Lillian's heart sank anew.

'And then we will see what the lay of the land is and make our new plans. Perhaps we could have a trip somewhere.'

So he would not abandon her after all. She laid her fingers across his.

'Thank you, Father.'

He drew her hand up to his mouth and kissed the back of it, a gesture she had not seen him perform since before her mother had left and the small loyalty of it pierced her heart.

When he was gone she pulled out a drawer in her writing desk and found a sheet of paper. She could not just leave such a silence between her and John and Eleanor Wilcox-Rice. With a shaking hand she began to apologise for all the hurt that she had caused them; when she had finished she placed the elegant gold-and-diamond ring in its box next to the note, pushing back relief. She would have it delivered in the morning. At least in the vortex of all that was wrong she was free of this one pretence.

Lucas Clairmont was gone. Back to America,

perhaps, on a ship now heading for home? He had not contacted her, had not in any way tried to make right the situation between them.

Ruined for nothing!

The mantra tripped around and around in her head, a solemn and constant reminder of how narrow the confines of propriety were, and how completely one was punished should no heed be taken of convention.

Lord, she could barely believe that this was now the situation she would be in...for ever? Even the maid bustling into the room failed to meet her eyes, stiff criticism apparent in each movement.

Lunch that afternoon was a silent drawn-out affair, each person skirting around the disaster with particular carefulness.

Her youngest cousin Patrick was unexpectedly the one who remained the kindest, setting out all his *faux pas* across the years with an unrivalled honesty.

'It is an unfair world, Lillian, when women are disadvantaged for the actions of a cad. If Luc Clairmont should walk through this door right now, I would bash his head in.'

'Please, Patrick.' Jean's protests fell on deaf ears.

'And then I would demand retribution, though God knows in what form that might take, given his light purse—'

'I think your mother would prefer to hear no more.' Her father's voice was authoritative and Patrick stopped, the loud tick of the clock in the corner the one sound in the room.

'The Countess of Horsham's good opinion that no American is to be trusted has come to pass,' her aunt continued after a few moments. She lifted her kerchief and wiped at her watering eyes. 'And now we shall have no trip to Paris. For the wedding gown,' she qualified, noticing the puzzlement of the others.

'I should think that the lack of a shopping excursion is the least of our worries,' Ernest said, waiting as the servant behind reached over to remove his empty plate. 'But if we are to have any hope of weathering this disaster, we also need to put what is past behind us and move on.'

'How?' Jean returned quickly. 'How is it that we should do that?'

'By the simple process of never mentioning Lucas Clairmont's name again.'

Her aunt was quick to agree and Patrick followed suit. 'And you, Lillian?' her father said as he saw her muteness. 'How do you feel about the matter?'

'I should like to forget it, too,' she answered knowing that in a million years she would never do so, his pointed lack of contact a decided rejection of everything she had hoped for.

But as the days had mounted and the condemnation had blossomed, even amongst those who had no reason to be unkind, anger had crawled out from underneath hurt.

Why had he followed her into the dim privacy of the alcove if all he meant to do was leave her? Surely his actions had not been that mercenary?

Lilly. The way he had said her name, threaded with the emotion of a man whose control was gone, and whose touch had burnt the fetters off years of restraint, leaving her vulnerable. Exposed.

Her father's voice interrupted her reveries.

'We will leave for Fairley in the morning and shut the house here until the end of January. Some of the servants will stay to complete the process before they come on to us. If we are lucky this…incident may not have filtered out to the country and perhaps we may even entertain on a smaller scale. I hope, Patrick, that you in particular will not find the sojourn too quiet.'

Lillian gritted her teeth, though she was hardly in a position to remind her father of her own need for some company. The winter stretched out in an interminable distance: Christmas, New Year, Twelfth Night and Epiphany. All celebrations that she would no longer be a part of, her newly purchased gowns hanging in the wardrobe for no reason.

As the terrible reality of her situation hit her anew she pushed back her plate and asked to be excused. The eyes of her family slid away from her agitation, another sign of all that she had cost them in her error, for the invitations that had once strewn the trays were now dried up, and the few that pertained to a time in the future cancelled by yet another missive.

Her entire family had become *personae non gratae* and she had not stepped a foot outside the house in all of five days. Even the windows overlooking the park had been out of bounds—she often saw curious folk looking up and pointing.

Poor Lillian Davenport. Ruined.

Suddenly she could not care. She could not hide for

ever. She was twenty-five, after all, and hardly a woman who had been caught in flagrant *déshabillé*.

Pulling on her heavy winter coat, her hat and her gloves, she called for the maid and the carriage to be ready to leave.

'I am not certain that the master—' The girl stopped when she noticed her expression. 'Right away, miss.'

Within the hour she was at her modiste trying on a dress she had ordered many weeks ago and Madame Berenger, the dressmaker, was polite enough not to ask anything personal, preferring instead to dwell on the fit and the form of the gown.

'It is beautiful on you, Miss Davenport. I like the back particularly with the low swathe across the bodice.'

Turning to the mirror, Lillian pretended more interest in the dress than she felt because a group of women she recognised had entered the shop.

An awkward silence ensued and then a whispering.

'It is her.'

'Has she seen us?'

Lillian tried not to react, though the hands of the modiste had stopped pinning the hem as though waiting for what might occur next.

'Perhaps now is not a good time to be here.' Christine Greenley spoke loudly, but the young assistant who had rushed to attend to the new arrivals assured her that there were seamstresses ready to help them.

'That may very well be the case, but will Miss Davenport be here long?' Lady Susan Fraser was not so polite. 'I should not wish to have to speak to her.'

No more pretence as silence reigned, the sound of a pin falling on to the wooden floor louder than it had any need to be.

Lillian thanked the woman kneeling before her and picked up the skirt of her gown so that she would not harm the fragile needlework. 'Please do not leave on my account, Lady Fraser, for I have finished.' The walking distance seemed a long one to the welcomed privacy of the curtains in the fitting room, her ingrained manners even giving her the wherewithal to smile.

Behind the velvet curtains her hands shook so much that she could barely remove the garment; when she looked at herself in the mirror it was like seeing a stranger, eyes large from the weight she had lost in the past week and dark shadows on her cheeks. Taking three deep breaths, she prayed for strength, her maid's shy call on the other side of the curtain heartening her further.

'Can I help with the stays, Miss Davenport?' she queried, her face full of worry when Lillian bade her enter and her fingers were gentle as she pulled the boned corset into position and did up the laces.

When they came from the room the group was still there however, the oldest lady stepping into her path as she tried to leave.

'I am sorry for your plight, Miss Davenport.'

Her plight. Just what was she to say to that?

'Thank you.' Her words were a ludicrous parody of good manners. Ever the gracious lady even in ruin!

'But at twenty-five you really ought to have known better.'

'Indeed I should have.' Another inanity.

'If I could offer you some advice, I would say to go to Wilcox-Rice cap in hand and beg his forgiveness! With a little luck and lots of genuine apology, perhaps this situation could be remedied to the benefit of all those involved.'

'Perhaps it may.'

Perhaps you should mind your own business. Perhaps you should know that your son has propositioned me many a time in a rude and improper manner.

Layers.

Of truth. One on top of the other and all depending on the one beneath it.

And Luc Clairmont. What was his truth? she wondered, as she walked out on to the pavement, carefully avoiding meeting the eyes of anyone else before entering the waiting carriage and glad to be simply going home.

Lucas awoke to the sound of water, the deepness of ocean waves, the hollow echo of sea against timber and wind behind canvas sails. He was in the hull of a ship! Trying to swallow, he found he could not, his mouth so dried out that it made movement impossible.

An older man sat on the table opposite watching him.

'Ye are thirsty no doubt?'

Luc was relieved when the fellow stood and gave him a drink. Brackish water with a slight taste of something on the edge of it! When he lifted his hands to try to keep on drinking, he was pleased that his captors had not thought to bind him. The rattle of chains, however, dimmed that thought as he saw heavy manacles locked on his ankles.

'Where are we?' His voice was rough, but at least now he could speak.

'My orders were ye are not to be told anything.'

Luc attempted to glean from his fob watch some idea of the time, but the silver sphere was gone. Gone, like his boots and his jacket and cravat. Glancing across at a porthole at the far end of the cabin, he knew it to be still dark.

A few hours since they had taken him? Or a whole day? He had no way of determining any of it. His head ached like the devil.

'You hail from Scotland?' He tried to make the question as neutral as he possibly could, tried to get the man talking, for in silence he knew he would learn nothing at all.

'Edinburgh, and before that Inverness.'

'I'd always meant to go north, but never did. Many say it to be a very beautiful land.'

'Aye, that it is. After all this—' he gestured around him '—I mean to go back, to live, ye understand.'

'If you help me off this ship, I could give you enough money to buy your own land.'

The other frowned. 'Ye are rich, then?'

'Very.'

The Scotsman eyed him carefully as if weighing up his options, the pulse in his throat quickening with each and every passing second. The sly look of uncertainty was encouraging.

'Are you a good judge of men?' Luc's question was softly asked.

'I like to think I am that, aye.'

'Then if I told you I am an innocent man who has done nothing wrong at all, would you believe me?'

The answer was measured.

'Any murderer could plead innocence should his life depend on it, but I've yet to see a man brought to this ship in the middle of the night who has not walked on the shady side of the law.'

Luc smiled. 'I would not expect you to do anything more than to look away for five minutes after unlocking these chains.' He gestured to the manacles at his ankles.

'I'd be a dead man if I did that.'

'Throw them overboard after me, then, and say that I jumped in.'

'Only a fool would attempt to swim while bound.'

'A fool or a desperate man?'

Silence filled the small cabin.

'When?' One small word imbued with so much promise!

Luc answered with a question of his own. 'Where are we headed?'

'Down to Lisbon.'

'Through the Bay of Biscay?'

'We have already sailed through those waters and have now turned south.'

'The warmer currents, then, off the coast of Portugal? If I jumped, I'd have a chance.'

'And my money?' The thread of greed was welcomed.

'Will be left at the Bank of England in Threadneedle Street, London, under my name.'

'Which is?'

'Clairmont. Lucas Clairmont. You could claim it when you are next back in England and then leave the ship for your hometown.'

'If ye die during this mad escape, I cannae see much in it for me.'

'Go to Lord Stephen Hawkhurst and tell him the story.' Luc pulled his wife's ring from his finger and placed it on the ground in front of him, the gold solid and weighty in the slanting shaft of light from the porthole. 'I swear on the grave of my grandmother that he will pay you five hundred pounds for your trouble, no matter what happens to me.'

When a cascade of expletives followed Luc knew that he had him. Still, there was more that he might be able to learn.

'Who brought me on to this ship?'

'Three fellows who paid the captain for your passage. There was some talk of a woman who wanted ye gone from England if memory serves me well.'

Closing his eyes against the stare of the other, he tried to focus and re-gather his strength whilst thanking the James River for its lessons in swimming from one wide edge of it to the other.

Not Davenport money, he hoped. Not Lillian regretting her intimacy in the alcove at the Billinghurst ball, a dangerous stranger who would be menacing to her? A few pounds and an easy handover! No, for the very life of him he could not see Lillian ever performing an illegal act no matter what duress she might be under. Her aunt Jean, then? Lord, that made a lot more sense. Perhaps he was on the same ship she had bought a passage on for him, though he knew the paper in his pocket to be gone.

Already the man had brought the key from the table and unlocked the manacles. The chains fell limply around his ankles as he stood, towering over his shorter captor.

'What usually happens to those you take on the ship under the cover of darkness?'

'At a rough guess I'd say Lisbon would be the last place they ever saw in this life.'

The choice was made. Luc stripped off his shirt and tied it about his waist. He wished he could have picked up the wooden chair near the table and dashed it to pieces, taking the largest piece as ballast. But he did not dare to, for fear the noise would attract others who would not be as willing to barter.

'How do I leave the ship?'

'If you follow me, I will show you, but be quiet mind.' Lifting the chains, the Scotsman muffled their sound in the folds of his jacket as Luc followed him out into the darkness.

Chapter Thirteen

The tapestry in Lillian's hands was almost finished, an intricate design of fish and fowl wrought in the tones of grey and cream. The belated completion of half-finished projects such as this had been one of the positive things to come out of her enforced isolation and other embroideries still to be done lay in the basket at her feet.

Two weeks now since she had had any word from Lucas Clairmont. Fourteen days since her life had been changed completely by a man who had never wanted anything more than a dalliance. She hated him for it, and hated too the sheer and utter waste of effort it took to loathe him, a depression of spirit all that was left of wonder. From love to hate in fourteen days, tripped in an instant into a ruin she could barely comprehend.

Tears pooled behind her eyes and she willed them away, the picture before her blurring in sadness, though a commotion at the front door made her stand, voices shouting and the raised anger of her father and cousin. Another voice too, lower, familiar, the sound of a tussle and running feet.

'Lucas?' His name was snatched from her lips in a whisper as she ran, through the blue drawing room and into the hall, threads of grey and cream trailing in her wake.

Blood was everywhere, across Luc Clairmont's nose and eyes swelling shut under the fist of her cousin and his friend and he was not fighting back, the crack of his head as he fell on the marble leaving him dazed upon the floor.

'What is happening?' Her voice. Loud in the ensuing silence.

'He deserved it.' Patrick's explanation, the grazes on his fists bleeding anew even as he wiped them against the white linen of his shirt.

Did he? Does he? The question flared in her eyes as she stood between her father and her cousin, the opened door of the house letting in the stares of those servants who worked the gardens and also the wet of the driving western rains. She did not come forwards. She could not, two weeks of anger and hurt unresolved even in his re-appearance and a stiffening distance widening between them.

When he coughed and his amber eyes hardened before sliding away from her own, she knew that she had lost the chance of atonement, the feelings that had been between them withered into the unknown, two strangers brought to this place by circumstances that now seemed almost unbelievable.

She did not understand him, had never known who

he was or what he wanted, an outlander who had strode into her life with the one sole purpose of disrupting it. And still was!

Her father's distress added to her own and with a sob she turned away, the silence left behind her telling. Lucas Clairmont did not call her back or try to stop her, the sound of her running feet against marble the only noise audible save for the frantic beating of her heart.

An hour later her father knocked on the door. He had changed his clothes, she saw, his shirt removed for a clean fresh one and his jacket and cravat in place.

Very formal for a country evening and no guests expected. Her mind began to turn.

'Lucas Clairmont would like to speak to you.'

'I do not think—'

'He is in the blue drawing room and I have told him you will be down immediately.'

Her glance went to his, but she could learn nothing there. 'I can see no point in prolonging what we both know will be the outcome of any meeting, Father.'

'You need to hear him out, Daughter. I have told him that after you have seen him he must leave and he has given me his word that he will.'

Still another barb to her heart! One last meeting. One final goodbye. Her fingers threaded through the hair that had fallen from its place beneath the shell comb at her nape and she tucked the strands back.

'Very well. I will be down in five minutes.' Her father's relief at her decision was faintly irritating, but she would not change or tidy herself up further. She would not stand there to be dismissed with her heart on her sleeve, and the weight of a ruined reputation between them. This was his fault every bit as much as hers and she would be the first to let him know it.

He looked worse than he had done an hour ago, new wounds upon his left cheek and fresh blood encrusted around the nails of the hand that she could see.

'Lillian.'

A sign, for he had seldom before called her that. There was flat anger in his glance.

'Your father has told me of the circumstances that have brought you and your family here and I would like to say that I am sorry—'

She could not let him finish. 'There is absolutely nothing to be sorry about, sir. We erred and we will pay. Society's rules are most explicit in that regard and any apology you might now wish to ply me with is by far and away too late.' The brisk distance in her voice pleased her, made her stronger.

'The price perhaps for you personally is rather steep and in that regard I would like to offer—'

'Oh, please—if it is something more permanent that you now feel compelled to tender, know that I should never accept it.'

He frowned, but remained silent, his hands now firmly jammed in a jacket borrowed from her father. She recognised the cut of cloth and colour. Too small on him, the seams straining at the stitching on his side. His lack of argument fortified her.

'We barely know each other and what little we are

cognisant of has resulted in disaster. My reputation is as ruined as your face! A truce of sorts! Surely now we should own up to what was never meant to be.'

'You would give up that easily?' His voice broke any polite restraint that she thought to hold on to.

'Give up what, sir? You are a mystery to me. A man who flirts with the affairs of the heart with no true understanding of what it all means. I trusted you, Mr Clairmont. I thought that you may have cherished what I had so senselessly offered, but you did not and then I understood. You are a gambler, a stranger, a liar and a cheat. It could never have worked between us, never, for I, unlike you, feel a certain responsibility to the titles I have inherited and to the rules and regulations that govern this land.'

'So in effect what you are saying is that I am not rich enough for you, Miss Davenport, not as well born as you have come to expect, and that that does matter?' The swollen flesh around his lips made the words slurred, a small vulnerability that she did not wish to notice.

'I am saying that you should go. That we should place this…madness into the slot to which it belongs.'

'Untenable?'

'Exactly.' Lillian's fervour broke as he looked up at her and the word wobbled into a silence caught between then and now.

Then there was a chance and now there was not.

'And you would have no wish to know why I was away from London for these past weeks?'

'I would not. It is beyond the time for excuses and

explanations and nothing you could say would make me believe that you did not realise that I was so badly compromised when you left the Billinghurst ball.'

'Nothing?' The word was phrased in a way she could not quite understand. 'I see.'

'I am glad that you do.' She shook her head, and tried to push back a rising grief. This was it. He would leave, hating her. Biting her top lip, she whirled around and made for the door, ignoring his plea to stop as she flew up the stairs and away.

Ernest Davenport read the documents laid out on his desk, the lawyer David Kennedy watching him from across the library with interest.

'So you are telling me that the man, far from being a pauper, has a series of large estates in Virginia and enough money to buy me out five times over?'

'Even that may be a conservative estimate.'

'You are also saying that this proposal of marriage comes with the distinct proviso of allowing none of this information to be leaked to my daughter should I choose to accept it.'

'Well, not you personally, you understand. This is not the dark ages where a recalcitrant daughter is dragged screaming to the altar, after all. But I put it to you that your daughter's reputation had been…sullied and that this is the quickest and most beneficial way of making certain she is once again accepted back into society. I would also say that my client is most anxious that the lady not marry him just for his money, which accounts for the secrecy.'

'Why would he do this? Why would Lucas Clairmont want a betrothal to a woman who has much reason to hate him?'

'The motives of clients are something in my fifteen years at the bar I have never yet truly understood, sir. I am but the messenger, the simple emissary of news and deeds.'

'You are also held by a retainer, I should imagine?'

'That is correct, but I never accept a client without express knowledge of the honour of his character.'

'So you are saying he is not a charlatan?'

'I am, sir. I would also say that, as a father myself, I should be very cautious about turning down such a fortune.'

'Indeed.'

'My client also has a desire to have this union quickly completed.'

'How quickly?'

'It is my client's hope that Miss Davenport would be his bride by the beginning of next week. To that effect he has procured a special licence enabling the marriage to take place anywhere and at any time.'

Ernest lifted his pen, the nib carefully inked as he bent to it.

'Tell him that she agrees. Tell him that the wedding shall take place in the chapel here at Fairley Manor and tell him that if he hurts her again I will seek him out and kill him.'

'I shall relate each word to him, sir.' A small sense of the absurd was just audible.

'You do just that, Mr Kennedy.'

* * *

'You did wha-aa-at?'

'I accepted Mr Clairmont's proposal of marriage on your behalf, Lillian, because I think as a parent it is the only wise and proper thing to do.'

'Proper? Wise? He is a pauper and a liar, let alone a gambler. Are you telling me that you are happy to place the very future of Fairley into the hands of a man who will in all likelihood bleed it to death?'

'I am.'

'You are mad, Father. You cannot mean to do this, to tie our fortune to one who has proven to be so very untrustworthy.'

'I think, Lillian, that you besmirch his character too harshly. I think if you could find it in yourself to look upon this match as something that might indeed be of benefit to you both—'

'No!'

'The licence has been procured and the wedding is set for Monday.'

Monday for wealth
Tuesday for health
Wednesday the best day of all…

The ditty of days to marry turned in her head like some macabre promise.

'I do not believe this. Is he blackmailing you or threatening you in some way?' The horrible realisation made Lillian feel faint. This was not her father. This was not the careful and prudent man who would cut off his right arm rather than let the estate of Fairley Manor pass into the hands of an unsatisfactory groom.

'If he were, I should instruct you to turn him down.'

'And if I do just that, regardless?'

'Then we shall be for ever marooned here in Hertfordshire, neither a part of society or of village life because of your one unmindful mistake.'

Her mistake! The sacrifice of herself or of her family?

'If you force me into this travesty, Father, I will not forgive you for it and I will never understand it.'

'I beg to disagree, Daughter, for honestly in time I think that you will.'

She made no real effort with her wedding gown. In fact, at the very last moment she chose to wear a cream organza gown from her last Season because the new dress from Madame Berenger suggested an exertion that she felt far from making. In her hands, however, she held fragrant white winter daphne from the Fairley glasshouse because a small part of her could not quite abandon all form of good taste.

Lucas Clairmont stood at the top of the aisle watching her. She had not seen him since she had stormed away from him and the bruises were today a lurid green and yellow, his left eye still largely swollen. The way he held his right hand against his ribs also suggested substantial pain. His whole life seemed to tilt between contretemps, she thought, never settling into the easier peace of a comfortable and gentlemanly existence.

The tears that had not been far from her eyes all week banked yet again, the differences between them boding ill for any future they might be able to fashion.

The guests on her side of the chapel were packed into the pews with standing room only at the back. On his side, however, two couples sat. The St Auburns and Lord Stephen Hawkhurst, accompanied by a very old man.

Concentrating on the vase of flowers on a table behind the font, she noted them to be aged white carnations, some relative's clumsy touch evident in the overdone blooms and the fussy paper decorations around all the pews. She wanted to rip them away as she walked, but her dress was taking all of her attention, the wide skirt requiring a certain walk so that the material did not snag on the overhangs of the oak seats.

When the music stopped she stopped too, beside her husband-to-be, his clothes today surprisingly well tailored. Had Lord Hawkhurst leant him a frockcoat? she wondered, and then dismissed the whole thought. It did not matter what he wore or how he looked. It did not matter that today he had made an effort with his attire she had not seen him make before. Perhaps he felt with the windfall of her dowry he had to be more careful to fit in, though when she took a quick peep at him he hardly looked overawed by a congregation of people far and away above him in rank, position and finances.

Even with his cuts and bruises he looked…confident. A man in the very place that he wanted to be!

Would she ever understand him? Would he ever know just how much he had hurt her? Her father obviously had some idea, the worry on his face making him look old and tired.

The clergyman raised his Bible. 'We are here today to marry Lucas Morgan Clairmont and Lillian Jewell Davenport.'

Lillian Clairmont! As the service continued the words that the priest wanted from her were difficult to say.

'…to love and to cherish from this day forward until death do us part.'

Such an empty troth! She wondered why an omnipotent God did not smite the church with an earthquake or a shower of hail or at the very least inveigle his man to question the intent. But the clergyman droned on as if it had oft been his misfortune to marry a less-than-jubilant bride.

Nothing about this wedding was anything like she had imagined it would be; when Lucas Morgan Clairmont reached out for her hand and slid the ring on her finger, it seemed like just another extension of an awful day.

The wedding band was a lurid yellow gold and embossed with a heavily set ruby, a ring that worked on the premise that bigger was better and that comfort was barely to be considered. No cheap piece either, but one fashioned only with the wish to impress.

Had he stolen it? Had he won it in a game of cards? She tucked her hand away into the folds of her skirt and wished he had not given her such an obvious piece. In contrast, the band she had given him was of classic plain gold and engraved with their initials and a date.

When the priest intimated that the bride and groom

might now kiss, Lucas merely shook the suggestion away and turned for the door, leaving her to follow in his wake as she tried not to catch the eyes of all those present on her side of the church. The wedding dress bumped against her legs as she hurried to keep up.

Lord, when the hell would this be over? Luc thought, as he tried to maintain a peace of mind that he had not felt in all the days since being back in England.

He had hit the water with a shock of fear, ten miles off a coast he had no knowledge of and the black ink of ocean stretching for ever. It was only for Lillian that he had kept going, stroke after stroke through the currents and the endless waves, the sea in his eyes and nose and throat. Yet now? His wife looked as though she hated him and her aunt Jean Taylor-Reid behind gave the impression of a woman seeing a ghost back from the dead.

Luc breathed out, wishing he might confront Lillian's aunt with his accusations and knowing at this minute that he just could not.

Lord, what was it he was doing? He had made the mistake of marrying badly once before and the first thrall of exaltation he had felt when Lilly had agreed to marry him was now fading into apprehension.

He hated weddings, hated the empty promise of them and the forced joviality that was almost always accompanied by a large dollop of uncertainty.

At least at his last wedding the bride had worn a dress that let him get near her and the words she had given were edged in hope rather than anger. Yet look where that had got him!

Lillian had barely glanced at him and had snatched her hand from his as soon as the ring was placed on her finger, the special licence he had purchased suddenly looking like a reckless thing.

Better perhaps to have taken her professed dislike of his character at face value and departed for America, where his lands and houses waited and the living was easy.

Easy? He could not have said that even three months ago with the guilt of Elizabeth crippling him and a drinking problem he could do little about.

Lilly with her pale goodness seemed to have cured him, made what before was impossible, possible. A woman he respected and liked. No, he could not just walk away.

'You look pensive, Luc?'

Hawk offered him a glass of lemonade and he took it.

'I was thinking that my bride doesn't look particularly happy…'

'Nat said that Cassie was as miserable at their wedding.'

'She ran away from him the next day, remember?'

Stephen smiled. 'I had forgotten about that.'

A flash of cream to one side of the room had them both turning.

'It seems that Alfred has made himself known to your new spouse. How long do you think it will be before she realises my uncle is somewhat soft in the head?'

'About now, I'd say,' Luc interjected. 'He seems to

be trying to extract my wedding ring from her finger. Perhaps you could persuade him not to, Hawk.'

But before either man had moved Lillian had solved the problem completely. With little fuss she removed the band and handed it to him, watching as he held it up to the window for a better look at the jewel in the light.

'Well,' said Hawk, 'that's a first. Usually they run screaming from him.'

'She didn't wait to collect the ring back either,' Luc added as he watched her move on. 'Do you think she has any notion as to how much it is worth?'

'She is a lady of taste, Lucas. Of course she knows it and right down to the last copper farthing, if I had my guess.'

'Then why would she just leave it with him?'

'Your grandmother was never one known for her artistic eye.'

'She was given the piece by the Duke of Gloucester's mistress.'

'And it shows!'

Seen like that, Lucas felt the first twinge of uncertainty. 'I'll buy her another one, then.'

'I think the ring's the least of your worries, Luc. Your bride looks miserable.'

'She thinks I deserted her intentionally.'

'You didn't tell her about the kidnapping? Why the hell wouldn't you tell her that?'

When he remained quiet, Stephen swore.

'God. You think she had something to do with it…'

'No.' The word was said loudly and had people turning. He remembered back to the lies Elizabeth had told. Little lies at first and then bigger ones as he had struggled to understand her anger and her moods. From Lillian he could not weather lies.

When Nathaniel broke into the conversation by slapping him on the back and indicating that the speeches were just about to start, he was relieved. Tempering worry, he walked to the head of the room to stand next to Lily.

Her newly acquired husband had been conversing happily with his friends whilst she was struggling to keep a thinly held composure. The absurdity of their marriage just kept on escalating. He was enjoying himself whilst she was so plainly not, her ugly dress hampering all sense of confidence and the horrible wedding ring lost into the hands of an ancient simpleton.

Stephen Hawkhurst's uncle it was said when she had asked his identity, a man who had been a little simple for years. Her hand crept to a growing headache about her temple as the speeches she had been dreading were called for. What would Lucas Clairmont say? Or her father?

Was this the part when the whole affair erupted into the fiasco it truly was? Surreptitiously she looked around to see where her cousin Daniel stood and was glad to find him missing. At least that was one less thing to worry about! Patrick, however, seemed bent on shadowing her every move, whether from a stance of protection or a desire to flex his muscles again, she could not be sure. Outside the rain beat against the roof.

Happy be the bride the sun shines on...

Today all she could think of were rhymes that scoffed at any inherent hope she might try to muster.

Her father began the toasts, raising up his glass and waiting for silence. 'To the bride and groom,' he said eventually when the room was quiet, his eyes settling on her. 'May they enjoy a long and joyous life together!'

'And fruitful,' someone called out, a rumble of amusement rippling around the room.

Not from her, though! The crass reminder of what this night could bring was suddenly and terribly in Lillian's mind. Would Lucas Clairmont expect fruitful, knowing what he did? Could he in all conscience demand what it was she had offered less than an hour ago before a man of God, knowing her feelings about this charade?

To love and to cherish...

Such tiny words for all that they implied.

Goodness, she thought, fixedly staring at the floor as the lump of terror in her throat congealed...if he thought that I might... She chanced a quick glance at her husband and the brittle smile that he gave back did nothing to reassure her. No, the opposite, in fact, because in the amber light she caught a glimpse of the lust that *fruitful* engendered, a very masculine understanding of all that a wedding night meant.

She shivered again and unexpectedly Lucas Clairmont moved closer, the light wool in his blue frockcoat resting against the thin layers of silk and organza across her arm. As a measure of comfort? She hoped that he had meant it such, but was doubtful. Anne Weatherby and Cassandra St Auburn standing together across the room both smiled at her, a tinge of anxiety in their looks, and Lillian wished Eleanor Wilcox-Rice might have come, too, but of course in the circumstances she could not, the stiff letter she had had in answer to her own note implying the desire for no further correspondence. She smoothed down the growing crinkles in her dress as attention swung back to her husband, alarm setting her heart to racing at a pace she felt worried about as she saw that it was now his turn to reply.

'Please, Lord, let him speak with authority and honour.' The whisper of prayer hung in the empty corners of her pride.

Lucas paused for a moment as though thinking of what it was he wished to impart; when he did begin speaking, he sounded neither breathless nor nervous.

'Ernest Davenport has given me the pleasure of taking his only daughter's hand in marriage and I would like to thank him for his generosity.' Lillian wondered why her father looked away, a rising blush evident upon his cheeks. Had she missed something important? 'I have known Lillian…' He halted, as though he would have perhaps preferred to use Lilly, but had decided against it. 'I have known Lillian for only a short while, but in that time have come to realise that she has all the attributes of an admirable wife. So it is with great pride that I stand before you all as her groom today and thank you for your presence here.'

Nothing of love or respect or even friendship! Lillian worried her bottom lip as he continued. 'Please raise your glasses and drink to my wife.'

When her name echoed around the room she inclined her head in thanks, her eyes widening as Stephen Hawkhurst's uncle stood from the chair in which he sat.

'Your ring's been blessed, did you know?' he began. 'The fairies came before and sanctified your union. It is not often that this happens, in fact, I have not seen the little folk in years, not since my brother's wedding in the March of 1816 when they came…'

Lord Hawkhurst had reached his uncle by now and taken him by the arm, meaning to lead him away. Lillian noticed that he did so gently but the old man wasn't finished.

'Yours will be a happy and long marriage, I am certain of it…' But now his voice was distant, the mere echo of it lying in the silence of the room. Lucas, however, did not seem content to leave it at that as the first awkward titters of embarrassment and fluster began to flow.

'Lord Alfred Hawkhurst was a soldier who took a bullet in the head for his country in the second Peninsular campaign under Wellington. In doing so he saved twenty of his regiment from certain death and as a hero deserves at least compassion.'

The snickering stopped.

An old hero in the guise of a fool! Her wedding in the guise of a celebration! Her husband in the guise of a man who held honour above the easier pathway of saying nothing!

For the first time in weeks she liked Lucas Morgan Clairmont again and was heartened by it.

Chapter Fourteen

It was almost four o'clock and Lucas knew that the time had come to take his bride and go home to Woodruff Abbey, an hour and a half away on the Northern Road.

He had toyed with the idea of paying for a room at the Elk and Boar Inn, a point that broke the journey halfway, but with the indifference marking Lillian's face had decided that being cramped together in a small space might not be the wisest thing to do.

Indeed, he even wondered about the carriage ride and wished that Hawk and his uncle had made plans to stay at Woodruff until the morrow. Such a desperate thought made him smile and as he did so he caught his wife looking at him.

'If you are ready to leave, I thought we might go?'

'Go where?' Her astonishment gave him the impression that she had expected to stay at Fairley Manor.

'My home is in Bedfordshire. A place called Woodruff Abbey.'

'And it is yours?'

He could not help but hear the catch of surprise in her voice. 'I only recently came into the inheritance.'

The interest that crossed into her eyes was tempered by disbelief, the whole charade of whom and of what he was here in England mirrored in pale blue uncertainty.

He hoped that Lillian would not hate the Abbey, would not demand the perfection of Fairley, would not turn up her nose at the shabby beauty of a house that was coming to mean a lot to him.

Lord, let her like it!

The emptiness of his last few years made him swallow and he knew that he could not survive should this marriage prove as disastrous as his first.

Ernest Davenport, seeing their intent to leave, came up to speak, his eyes watering a little as he held the hand of his daughter.

'I shall journey to see you for Christmas, Lillian.'

Lucas noticed how his wife's fingers curled about that of her parent as if she was desperate not to let him go. 'If you would wish to come sooner…' she began, but Davenport stopped her.

'Nay, the first weeks in a new marriage are for you and your groom alone. But I would just speak to your husband privately, for a moment?'

Lillian made a show of bidding her remaining family goodbye as Luc walked to the window with her father.

'This unconventionality of telling my daughter little about the state of your finances will be obeyed by me only until I see you again in a fortnight. Do you understand?'

Lucas nodded. Davenport had kept his word thus far and he was thankful for it, but with Christmas less than two weeks away he knew that he was running out of time.

'And if I hear that there has been anything untoward happening...'

'I would never hurt your daughter.'

'Your lawyer gave you my message, then?'

'He did, sir.' Lucas remembered David Kennedy's less-than-flattering summation of Ernest Davenport's parting words.

'I notice that she is not wearing her wedding ring?'

'No, it is here in my pocket.' He had retrieved the band from Hawk's uncle once the old man had lost interest in it.

'It does not look like a piece that my daughter would be fond of. If I might offer you some advice, having it reset completely may be the wiser option.'

Lilly's father and Hawk felt the same way?

Luc felt a strange sense of kinship with the man opposite. He was, after all, a father just trying to do his best by his daughter.

'I shall certainly think about it, sir.'

Lillian shifted in her seat when the carriage began to slow almost two hours later, pulling off the road and slipping through intricate wrought-iron gates. It had been a silent trip to Woodruff Abbey as two of her maids had shared the space with them, the lack of privacy allowing nothing personal at all to be said and slanting rain the only constant noise of the journey. When they rounded the last corner, she saw that the house before them was like something from another century.

'It needs a lot of work,' Luc declared as he leaned across to look at it and Lillian thought she detected a hint of apology in his voice.

In the growing darkness she could only just make out the newly weeded verges around the circular drive and the piles of pruned branches heaped to one end of a low-lying addition. Could this have been where her husband had been in the last weeks? Trying to make something of his windfall?

'The lines of the building are beautiful.' In all her hurt she found herself reassuring him and was rewarded with a smile as a footman drew down the steps, Lucas's hand coming to assist her after he had alighted.

Lillian was surprised by the bareness of the place as they walked in, though there was a certain beauty in the ancient rugs and the few pieces of furniture that were on display. An old dog roused itself from beneath a table and stretched, before coming to see just who the new arrivals were and three long-haired cats watched them from a small sofa placed by the stairway.

'This is Royce, the mongrel,' her husband said as he bent to pat the dog, its tongue licking the inside of his palm with a considerable force. For Lillian, who had never had much contact at all with animals inside a house, the plethora of pets was alarming. 'He is at least fifteen years old, although Hope believes him to be older still.'

'Hope?'

Lord, she thought, the tale she had heard of his

children ensconced in some house suddenly taking on a frightening reality.

'You will meet her and her sister tomorrow.'

Before she could answer an old man appeared, a similar-aged woman behind him pulling away the strings of a well-used apron as she too shuffled forwards.

'Mr Lucas,' she said, taking his arm with delight. 'You are back already?' Her glance took in them both. 'And with your lady wife, too?'

'Lillian Clairmont, meet Mr and Mrs Poole, my housekeeper and head butler.' The appellations seemed to please the older couple and she was astonished by the fact that her husband kept up such friendly terms with the serving staff that he would introduce them like equals. The Americans were odd in such ways, she surmised, giving the woman a polite but reserved smile.

'Well, I have your room ready, sir, and the eiderdown I embroidered myself over the winter months is just this week finished, so no doubt you will be warm and toasty.'

Your room? Warm and toasty? These words implied exactly what Lillian did not wish to hear at all, though the small squeeze her new husband gave her kept her mute.

'I am certain everything will be well prepared, but as we are tired would it be possible to send up a tray with some food?'

Goodness, in England these words were never used to serving staff—they implied a great deal of choice on behalf of the paid attendants. As a new landlord and employer, Lucas Clairmont had a lot to learn. The sneaking feeling that he could well be getting duped with his household expenses also came to mind, though the couple before her did not, in all truth, look like a dishonest sort, but merely rather strange and doddery.

The same headache that she had been cursed with all day suddenly began to pound and despite everything she was pleased to be led upstairs by her husband and into a bedroom on the second floor.

It was a chamber like no other she had ever been in, bright orange curtains at the windows and a red and purple eiderdown proudly slung across a bed that was little bigger than a single one.

On a table were bunches of wildflowers in the sort of glass jar that jam was usually found in and beside that lay a pile of drawings. Children's drawings depicting a family in front of a house, two small girls in pink dresses before a couple holding hands.

'Charity likes to draw,' her husband explained, picking up the sheath of papers and rifling through them. 'I think she has a lot of talent.'

He held up another picture of the same black-and-white dog downstairs, though this time Royce sat in a field of wildflowers, the sun above him vividly yellow. With no idea at all of the stages of refinement in a child's artistic ability, Lillian had to admit to herself that it seemed quite well done. Indeed, the artist had exactly copied the slobbery mouth and the matted coat, though the angel complete with halo perched before it was an unusual addition.

'Charity always draws her mother in these things,' Lucas explained when he saw her looking. Finding the first drawing, he alerted her to the same angel balanced on the only cloud in the sky.

'Her mother was your first wife?'

He shook his head and the whole picture became decidedly murkier. 'No, their mother was my wife's sister.'

Lillian sat down. Heavily. 'You dallied with your wife's sister?'

'Dallied?' His amber eyes ran across her face, perplexity lining gold with a darker bronze. 'I did not know her at all.'

'I thought—they say you are their father. How could you not have known her?' Lillian no longer cared how her voice sounded, perplexity apparent in every word.

A deep laugh was his only answer. The first time she had heard him laugh since…when? Since he had held her in the drawing room in London and shaken away her feebly offered kiss. The chamber swirled a little, dizzy anger vying with horror as she realised well and truly that she was now married to a man who appeared to have absolutely no moral fibre. And that she still wanted him!

'The children are my wards. I am not their father, but their guardian.'

'Oh.' It was all that she could say, the rising blush of her foolish deduction now upon her face as he crossed the room to fill a glass of water from a pitcher and drank it.

'Do you want one?' he asked as he finished and when she nodded he refilled the same glass and handed it to her.

Married people shared beds and houses and glasses of water, she ruminated, and the thought made her suddenly laugh. A strange strangled sound of neither mirth nor sadness. She imagined that if she could have seen the ex-

pression on her face she might look a little like the baffled
angel in Charity's drawings—a woman who found
herself in a position that she could not quite fathom.

Unexpectedly a tear dropped down her cheek and
Lucas moved forwards, his thumb tracing the path of
wetness with warmth.

'I know that this is all different for you and that the
house is not as you may have hoped it to be, but—'

She shook her head. 'It is not the house.'

'Me, then?'

She nodded. 'I do not really know you.' She refused
to look at him as she said it, and refused to just stop
there. 'And now this room with one bed between the
two of us…'

'Nay, it is yours. Tonight I shall sleep elsewhere.'

The relief of that sentence was all encompassing, and
she swallowed back more tears. She never cried, she
never blushed, she had never felt this groundless
shifting ambivalence that left her at such a loss, but
here, tonight, she did not even recognise herself, a quiv-
ering mannerless woman who had made little effort
with anyone or anything for the whole of her wedding
day and was now in a room that looked like something
out of a child's colourful fairytale.

And yet beneath everything she did not want her
pale and ordered old life back, and it was that thought
more than anything that kept her mute.

She looked as if she might crumple if he so much as
touched her, looked like a woman at the very end of her
tether and the fact that the water in the glass had stained

the front of her cream bodice and gone unnoticed added further credence to his summations.

His new wife was beautiful, her cheeks flushed as he had never seen them before and her skirt pushed up at such an angle that he could glimpse her shins, the stockings that covered shapely ankles implying that the rest of her legs would be just as inviting.

The direction of his thoughts worried him and to take his mind off such considerations he took the wedding ring from his pocket and laid it in his hand.

'I retrieved this from Lord Alfred.'

She remained silent.

'Though I have had advice that the setting may not be quite to your taste?'

A look of sheer embarrassment covered her face. 'No, it is perfectly all right.'

Manners again, he thought, and it was on the tip of his tongue to insist otherwise when she stood and put out her hand.

'I am sorry for the careless way I treated your ring.'

She did not say that she liked it, he noticed, as he took her left hand into his own, the fingers cold and her nails surprisingly bitten down almost to the quick.

At the very end of her forefinger was a deep crescent-shaped scar, the sort of mark a knife would make, but he said nothing for fear of spoiling the moment as he slipped the band back upon her finger.

A sign that things could be good or a shackle that held her to him despite every other difference?

'How old was your wife when she died?' The question unsettled him, but he made himself answer.

'Twenty-four. Her name was Elizabeth.'

'And you met her in Virginia?'

'She was the daughter of an army general who was stationed near Boston.'

'Nathaniel said that she was killed in an accident?'

The anger in him was quick, spilling out even as he tried to take back the words. 'No. I killed her by my own carelessness. It was a rain-filled night and the path too difficult for a carriage.'

'Did you mean for her to die?' Lilly's voice was measured, the matter-of-factness within it beguiling.

'No, of course I didn't.'

'Then in my opinion it was an accident.'

Light blue eyes watched him without pity. Just an accident. In her view. Perhaps she was correct? The hope of it snatched away his more usual all-encompassing guilt and he breathed out, loudly.

'Are you always so certain of things?' This was a side of her he had not seen before.

The answering puzzled light in her eyes reminded him so forcibly of the time that he had kissed her in London he had to jam his hands in his pockets just to stop himself from reaching out again.

Not now. Not yet. Not when she so plainly was frightened of him.

'Certain? I used to think I was such, but lately…' The shadows of the past week bruised her humour, and because of that he tried to explain even just a little of what lay unsaid between them.

'When I left London the night of the ball I had no notion that anyone had seen us, and I should like to explain just what happened next—' He stopped as she shook his words away.

'My ruination was as much my fault as it was yours. More, perhaps, for at least you had the foresight to stop it at a touch.'

'You wanted me to keep going?'

The very thought of it had the blood rushing to places that he knew would show and he turned. Lord, suddenly he wanted all the promise of a wedding night, all the whispers, soft words and touches, the burning pleasure of release and elation.

'I do not know…perhaps…?'

Given as a gift of honesty. The squeeze of relief in his heart made him giddy. Not at all like Elizabeth then, he thought, for she had seldom been truthful when it suited her not to be.

A knock at the door allowed the entry of two young maids who efficiently set out steaming dinners on trays at the table. A bottle of water was added to the fare just before they left.

'You do not drink wine?' she asked as they sat down to the supper.

'After the carriage accident I drank too much…'

'And then you met my cousin, whom you seem to dislike?'

Luc felt himself tense up. Lord, how was he to tell her anything, a woman who had been cocooned by a genteel and refined upbringing? He could see it in her skin, in the softness of her hands, in the worry of her eyes and in the shake of her voice. Tonight was her wedding night, damn it, and she could not wish to hear anything so sordid. Forcing a smile, he raised his glass to her. 'There is much in my life that has been more difficult than your own, and there are things that I have done that I am now sorry for.'

'Things?'

He laughed, more out of sheer unease than anything else, and hated the way her smile was dashed from her eyes.

'Things that I am not proud of now, but were at the time necessary.'

'To survive?'

He nodded. 'Survival here is a simpler process. Break the rules in England and you are banished. Break them in Virginia and you are left fighting for your life.'

'As you have been?' Her eyes deliberately ran across the scar on his neck. He saw the fear in them and his hand caught hers, his fingers running along the inside of her opened palm, stroking, asking.

For a chance, for a second chance, the softness of her skin against his just a small reminder of all that was different between them.

Lilly closed her eyes and felt. For this one moment in her wedding day she just felt what it was other brides might, the trail of his fingers evoking a thrall in her she had only ever known once before. With him.

Was this an answer?

An easy ending to everything that was different between them. A bride and groom thrown together not by love, but by ruin.

She knew nothing of his life or his beliefs, nothing

of his family or his country or the things that he knew as right and wrong. If they made love here and now it would be just that, bodies touching where minds could never follow, a shallow knowledge of desire that had nothing to do with the heart.

When she pulled away he let her go and stood with his hands by his side, watching, a man of honour and constraint, but one with enough questions in his eyes to make her understand what it was he asked.

If not now, then when?

The fire of his appetite was easy to interpret. Such a masculine simplicity! For a second the very sincerity of it made her pause, no pretence or artifice, no false posturing at something else either.

Not love, but need, his man's body bristling with something she did not understand yet, but knew enough to be wary about.

'If you could be patient.'

He nodded stiffly, the bronze in his eyes brittle. All of a sudden the sheer and utter amazement of sharing a meal at night and alone was scintillating. Exhilarating.

No longer single, but married.

The very idea of it seeped through her body in an unexpected warmth, as her memory of the one kiss he had given her began to tug at a power deep inside. It overwhelmed her, this newness of being here, and she could barely take breath as a hot flush of what he might do to her again surfaced. Too raw. Too quick after such a day. A single trail of sweat ran between her breasts and the cream dress was not thick enough to hide what she knew with horror was suddenly on show.

Her nipples stood proud against the silk, pressing and swollen. What was it that a husband did to a wife in a marriage bed beneath the sheets under the cover of darkness?

She did not know. Had never known. Until now. Until a knowledge that was as old as time itself began to wind itself through an aching anticipation, the thickening throb of her womanhood making her languid, heavy.

If he saw he did not say anything, a man who had spent the day balancing her unhappiness, her cousins' anger and her father's uncertainty like juggling balls as he tried to get through a wedding he could hardly want, either.

Her mind remembered Lord Hawkhurst's uncle's words. *A happy and long marriage?* She wished suddenly that she could be brave enough to ask right here and now of his movements across the last weeks and of his hopes for the future, but she did not want to in case the answers were nothing like the ones she needed to hear.

The longing in her body was replaced by a wooden fear of everything. Two strangers sharing a meal without any idea as to who each other was, their wedding clothes and rings only a ludicrous parody.

Just silence.

And then another sound.

'Mr Lucas. Mr Lucas.' A child's voice from afar and as the door was flung open a small dark-haired girl bolted into the room, stopping briefly as her eyes sensed Lillian's presence, but then regrouping.

'You are home again. Mrs Poole said that we should wait until the morrow, but—'

'We?' He looked around just as she did and there at the door stood a more timid child, hair so blonde it was almost silver and eyes a wide pale blue.

'Charity wanted me to wait, but she is so much slower I could not.'

The other child came forwards, a shy smile of gladness gathering on her lips.

'Charity and Hope, this is Lillian Clairmont.'

Hope smiled at her, but the other child looked away.

'We were married today at her country home of Fairley.'

'This is your ring?' Hope's finger traced the band of gold on the hand that held her.

'Indeed it is.'

'Look, Charity. Isn't it lovely?' the dark-haired girl exclaimed and the smaller child nodded.

'And the lady wore that…?' A thread of something akin to disappointment startled Lillian, although Lucas did not seem to notice any criticism.

'She did and she looked very beautiful.'

'I will wear lace and silk and a tiara when I get married and I will have flowers in my hair.'

The appearance of a harried-looking governess at the doorway curtailed the amusements.

'I am so very sorry, sir. The girls were told to stay in their room and I thought that they were there until I heard footsteps and followed the sound.'

'Please could you come and tuck us in? Please, Mr Lucas.'

He looked at the time. 'If you do not mind, Lillian, it is late and the girls…'

'Indeed,' she answered back, trying to keep her tone light. 'They would obviously like you to settle them and I am very tired.'

He seemed to hesitate at that, as though he might have wanted to say more, but then thought again.

'Then I shall bid you goodnight.'

'Goodnight,' Hope parroted, and they were all gone, just the bustling sound of them receding into silence.

Lillian stared at the closed door with a growing amazement. Goodness, she thought, and turned to lift the lurid purple eiderdown around her shoulders, the quilting on the back of it catching her eye with the very fineness of detail.

A movement to one side of the room made her start as a large grey-and-white cat padded towards her.

'Shoo,' she said, but the word did not seem to change the animal's direction one bit as it lurched itself up on the bed, the sound of purring distinct and deep. Tentatively her hand went out, running across the thick fur, a quiet delight enveloping her.

'I said shoo,' she repeated, allowing the cat on to her lap even as she said it, the warmth of its body comforting in the cold of the evening. Soft paws pushed into her thighs, kneading the layers of silk and organza. Almost tickling.

The whole day had been a skelter of emotion. Up and down. This way, that way. Touching and distance. No true direction in any of it. She closed her eyes and breathed in, the ugly ring on her finger winking up at her with its bright deep red.

* * *

Damn, damn, damn, Luc thought, after he had tucked in the two children and gone back to his own room. The wilting ache of his body was as out of place here as his desperate attempt at ignoring the hard outline of Lillian's breasts against silk.

Take it slowly, he thought. Give her the time she wants! *'If you could be patient.'*

But even now he wanted to go back, wanted the promise of what could be, wanted to see the beauty of what lay beneath her dress, her nipples puckered with yearning. But he could not.

Careful, he thought. Go carefully. The reason for his ordeal at sea still worried him and the truth was not as yet such an easy path to follow.

He had married Lilly to save her reputation and any other feelings that were as yet unresolved lingered in a place he had no wish to explore. Had she had any hand in his disappearance? Had Jean Taylor-Reid acted alone? Did the woman have any true idea of the danger she had placed him in? Perhaps she genuinely thought she had bought passage for him to the Americas, an easy way of dealing with a problem that was becoming more and more complex.

The whole puzzle of it made him swear and he was tempted to open the brandy standing on his desk. But he didn't.

He needed to trust Lilly and she needed to trust him.

If he took her virginity in the guise of a man who was not exactly as he promised he was, he knew she would never forgive him.

Damn, he said again as the knowledge of what he could have just missed out on settled in his stomach like a stone.

Taking a drink of Mrs Poole's freshly made lemonade, he settled down to read the final part of Dickens's Bleak House, the title appropriate for all that he was feeling tonight.

Chapter Fifteen

'This hillock affords the best view of the place,' Lucas said as they stopped atop a cliff. 'I think it must have once been a river-bed, for the water has cut through the sandstone etching out the land. See, there is still the remains of a smaller stream.'

Lillian looked at where he was pointing. 'You have a good knowledge of geography.'

He shook his head. 'Rivers are the same anywhere. They divide the country with their own particular brand of frivolity and men must simply follow their course.'

'Like the river near where you live? The James, was it not?'

'And you have a good memory,' he returned before spurring his horse on and gesturing her to follow.

They had spent the morning wandering the wide lands of Woodruff Abbey, his attempt, she suspected, at keeping her busy and having enough space between them to make things…simple. No touching, no deeper conjectures, just the land and the choice of moving on once conversation foundered.

And yet she was enjoying the tour, enjoying the cold winter sun on her face and the exploration of an estate that was magnificent in its diversity. The caves they now stopped beside were mossed with lichen and carvings, sticks wedged as sentinels protecting angular sandstone facings.

This time he dismounted and came over to help her down. Having no other recourse but to accept, she waited as his hands came around her waist, her body sliding down the length of his until her toes met the ground.

Moving away as soon as she was stable, the material in his riding jacket strained across the breadth of his shoulders. Today he was neither the Lucas Clairmont who had kissed her in London nor the dangerous man at Fairley with blood on his face and anger in his eyes. The Lucas Clairmont of yesterday had disappeared, too, with his confidence and certainty. This man was gentler, more considerate, with no hint of demanding more than she would give him. A patient, self-controlled husband who had spent his wedding night alone!

She suddenly missed the man who would tease her and reach out unbidden, his golden reckless glance today well guarded, as if he was trying to be on his best behaviour.

Lillian's heart began to beat faster. Was that what he was doing? Nurturing patience?

'If you could be patient.' She had asked that of him yesterday. Had he retreated into trying? Warmth began to spread into the cold anger that the wedding had imbued, flushing the possibility of something very different.

'Jack Poole says these carvings have been here since before any written history.' His voice was tight, the facts given with a stiff correctness.

'So they don't really know who did them?' Sitting on the nearest rock, she hitched up her skirts to keep them from trailing in the dust.

'He says Viking travellers, thanes from the early part of the eighth century. People who crossed this part of England to battle the Saxon warriors fiercely defending themselves in the last free land of Wessex.'

His voice petered off as his eyes met her own, the bare facts of history irrelevant now in the growing silence. For the first time since she had met him she felt that she was in charge, the knuckles in his fist pressed white on the hand she could see, his wedding band glinting in the sun.

'An old history, then.'

He only nodded. A man who had probably reached the end of his patience!

'In which part of England did you live as a boy?'

'In the north-east,' he said obliquely. Telling her nothing.

'You seldom answer questions about yourself. I have noticed it.'

At that he laughed, but the sound of it was hard. 'Ask me anything.'

She pondered for a moment. 'Why did you steal the watch at Eton?'

'Anything but that.'

'Very well, then! How did you meet Nathaniel St Auburn and Stephen Hawkhurst?'

'At school. We were in the same year when we were all sent there at eleven and I was there for a good while. Holidays were also generally spent at St Auburn or Hawthorne Castle, Hawk's family seat in Dorset.'

'And what of your home? Your parents?'

'My father and mother were rarely home and when they were I stayed as far away as I could get.'

Lillian glanced up, this answer nothing like the others, a ring of truth and anger so desperately heard within it. But he did not look at her as he gazed across the wide valley, a few wildflowers even at this time of the year, caught in the change of seasons and the onslaught of winter. Brittle and temporary! She knew just exactly how they felt.

'You were an only child?'

He nodded, but the honesty of a second ago was gone. Regretting his outburst probably, she thought, by the look of the muscle that rippled to one side of his cheek.

'And they did not follow you to America?'

'No.'

'Then who did you live with when you got there?'

'An uncle. My father's brother. A fine man by the name of Stuart Clairmont.' He shook his head as she went to speak again. 'Are you always this curious?'

'You are my husband. Spouses ought to be curious about each other.'

'Very well, then,' he returned. 'Tell me something about you that nobody else knows.'

He saw the way her lips tightened, her pale eyes searching his face for what? For the right to see if what she wanted to say would be taken in the spirit that she gave it? He knew that look, had seen it on his own face in the mirror as a child when his mother had warned him not to tell anyone about anything that went on inside their family.

'I once read the Bible backwards,' she began. 'It was after my mother left my father for a lover who killed her.' She looked up. 'Not physically, you understand. There are other ways for people to die.'

Other ways? Small ways and large. Hearts that broke bit by bit until there was nothing left of any of it. Confidences that squeezed the very life out of living!

'Her lover was a man like you…secretive, dark…' Her voice broke on the confession.

Lord. Just like him! And in so many more ways than she knew.

But she did not let it go. 'If my father hears that I have told you this…'

'He won't.' The hands at the side of her gown were balled into tight fists.

'You promise me?'

'On my very life,' he returned, an odd expression that Nat and Hawk and him had used as boys when trading secrets.

'I had not meant to say, it was only…' She stopped.

'Only that I had aired my skeletons in the cupboard and you felt obliged to do the same?

He was pleased when she smiled. 'Only that.'

Far away the shape of Woodruff Abbey stood against a dark line of trees, nestled in a wide and fertile valley. Figures played on the lawn and on the circular sweep of driveway.

'How long have you been the children's guardian?'

'Since I put Woodruff into trust for them and named myself a trustee.'

'The place is not yours?'

'It is mine to use, but theirs to keep.'

'An expensive gift from a man with little in the way of chattels.'

'Children need a safe home to grow up in.'

'A home like the one you never had. Whatever happened to your parents' house? You have not mentioned it at all.'

'It was sold when they left England. Travel is expensive and my father could never abide the responsibility of chattels.'

'He sounds a selfish man.'

When he didn't answer she tried another tack. 'The little girls seem very fond of you?'

This time when he laughed Lillian felt the warmth of it and she liked the sound, liked the easy way he tipped back his head, liked the creases that marked the skin around his eyes when he did so. Not a dandy or a fop. No, her husband was a man whom the outdoors had marked in muscle and in tone, the bronze in his eyes startling sometimes against the darkness of his skin. Like now, outlined against the wideness of sky, a man who could have been one of those wild Danish thanes wandering this part of the land all those centuries ago. That was it exactly. He did not really fit into England with its gentle rhythms and thin watery sun.

And he was hers. For a lifetime. This man whom she did not understand, but wanted to, this man whose body called to her own in a way no others ever had before him. She felt humbled by his confession of the Woodruff trust, humble enough to offer him money and condolences for his lack of property

'Fairley Manor is a large estate. You should want for nothing with my dowry.'

'I would never challenge your right to Fairley, Lilly. I swear it. If you wanted, I could have my lawyer draw up a document to say just that.'

Lillian was speechless at his sincerity. How often in her life had she been pursued by swains who measured the value of the Davenport lands before the worth of taking her as a bride? Yet here was a man with little who would give it all back?

'Fairley is your heritage and, just as Hope and Charity need a home, so do you.'

The understanding in his answer was exactly what she needed and the awareness between them heightened.

Touch me! she longed to ask. Reach out first and touch me, for she could not do it, not after the words she had given him of squandering and patience and anger.

But he only swiped away a winged insect that dived down and laughed as she jumped back.

'It likes the light in your hair. How long is it when you wear it down?'

'My hair?' She blushed beetroot red. 'Too long, probably. I should cut it, but—'

'No.' A frown crossed his forehead, emotion skewered by his need for caution.

In answer she simply undid the net that held her

chignon in place, enjoying the feel of curls unravelling down her back, the length reflected by the greed in his eyes.

'It was patience I asked for,' she whispered softly, 'not distance.'

'Ah, Lilly,' he replied in return, 'have caution with what you think a husband might take from such an offer.'

Still he did not move.

'Perhaps a little?' Her tongue licked around the sudden dryness of her lips.

'A little?' His voice was husky as he reached forwards and brought him to her, not gently either, but moulded along the full front of each other so that she felt the hard angles of his body and the heat of his breath.

'Is this a little?' he asked as his lips came down upon her own, opening her mouth and plundering, one hand sliding up from her waist to fist in her hair and the other cupping her chin as though daring her to pull away.

She didn't, the taste of him exactly how she had remembered it in countless dreams, an invitation for more, his tongue laving against hers, the rocking of his body restless and every breath shared.

Heady delight in the fold of an ancient mountain and the wind playing with her hair, the shards of need swelling want in her belly, in her breasts, in the place between her legs that no man had ever touched.

She could not feel where she ended and he began, could not in truth stop him from doing anything that he wanted, the brutal slam of lust as desperate in her as she could feel it was in him. Just pleasure, on the edge of delight, just the boneless floating relief of what it was to be a woman, and at twenty-five it had been a long time coming.

When he finally broke off the kiss she pressed in, but he held her still, his breathing ragged and his voice hoarse.

'The rain is near and a little is never enough.'

His heart beat in the same rhythm as hers, matching exactly as her hands bunched at the material in his jacket, trembling with what had just happened, no control and no regrets either, the core of her being alive with the rightness of it.

This had nothing to do with the expectation of others, for no external thing could touch a freeing blazing truth that held all the other more normal concerns at a distance.

What if she had not constrained him with 'a little', what if she had just let him do what it was he seemed so very good at, up here on the high mountain with no one around them for miles?

Always a limit, the boundaries of her life reflected even in her loving. The thought made her frown as she tied up her hair, feeling a little like a fairytale princess who had been let out of a story for just a moment.

Princess Lillian. How often had unkind children called her that as she had grown up? The girl with everything!

Except a mother, and the rigid morals of her father the touchstone to his affection.

She took in a deep breath and moved away, not meeting the gaze of her husband, though his smile she could not fail to miss even from the corner of her eyes.

'For a woman who has barely been kissed in her life you have made remarkable progress.'

Not a criticism, then. With her confidence bolstered she faced him. 'I have had a good teacher.'

'And one with a lot more to show you yet.'

His laughter caught on the wind and the cloak she wore billowed as if even her clothes sought closer contact, both the strength and mystery in him evident in the way he watched her, as if 'just a little' would never be enough.

Chapter Sixteen

Lucas was not at breakfast at all the next morning, a fact that Lillian found strange; by the middle of the afternoon she was beginning to wonder just exactly where he was, for he had left in the early evening of the previous day and had been more than a little distracted. She had been glad when he had come to tell her of his need to leave Woodruff for a few hours because the kiss of the afternoon lingered still, clouding every reasonable argument she thought of that might stop her going further.

Her daydreams were vivid and passion-filled. No constraint on imagination after what had happened yesterday. Now her mind followed other paths, unbridled and giddy paths that had no mind for limits and no time for a marriage convened in name only.

The dress she wore today seemed to mirror all her thoughts, the lace trimming it barely covering places that she had always kept well shielded. She had put it on in hope that Lucas would be back to see it, but by midday had given up on that hope and had begun instead to explore Woodruff Abbey.

After a good half an hour she found a room off a conservatory at one end of the house containing a library whose shelves gave the impression of having never being culled since the first literate member of the family had begun to call the Abbey home. Sitting in a chair, she was looking at a book with various lithographs of Bath when she became aware of a rustling behind her, the quick order of quiet that came after it telling her that it was the children that she had met two nights back.

Hope and Charity.

Whilst wondering what mother in her right mind would saddle her children with such names, a small white winter rose hit her on the arm. And then another one.

Playing the game, she rose and picked them up, cradling them in her hand.

'Why, it is flower snow…'

The whispering stopped to be replaced by silence.

'Fairies send this to earth to remind children of their manners.' She looked around, making an effort not to glance in the direction of an old table that she knew them to be behind.

A small giggle could be heard.

'But this does not sound like a fairy laugh…?' She moved forwards meaning to take the game further, but Hope's face poked out before she could.

'It is us,' she said simply, like a child who did not have a great knowledge of how to play at make-believe and pretend. 'We picked the flowers from the garden yesterday before the rain,' she qualified, looking out of the windows that graced the whole wall of this wide room. Drops distorted the glass, the heavy greyness outside making everything colder within.

Charity came out from behind her, both children dressed in identical matching aprons.

'You have been doing your lessons?'

Hope's face contorted. 'We did not have to do anything until a month ago when Mr Lucas said that we must and he found us a tutor.'

'Learning is a good thing,' Lillian countered, gesturing to the book she held. 'Reading can give you many hours of happiness.'

The children did not answer, but looked at her with uncertain faces. Trying to find some topic that might be of more interest, she happened on the season.

'Do you make decorations with your governess?'

Both little girls shook their heads. 'Mrs Wilson tells us that we are too old for Christmas now.'

'Too old for Christmas?' Suddenly she felt unreasonably angry towards a woman who would tell two motherless little girls such a fib. 'No one is too old for Christmas. It is a fact.'

Hope crept closer. 'Last year we brought a tree in from outside. Mrs Poole let us thread paper to decorate it and she cooked lovely things like plum pudding. But this year it is different. We just have to study because Mrs Wilson tells us we have missed out on so much knowledge.'

Charity nodded behind her, giving Lillian the impression of hearing every word her sister said. So she was not deaf!

Different for Lillian, too, the bare lack of seasonal joy all around this room suddenly rankling. 'If I was able to find some paper and paint and scissors and glue, would you be able to help me decorate this room?'

'Now?'

'As it is only just over a week until Christmas we have no more time to waste.'

Charity's little head bobbed up and down, the first time Lillian had seen her decide something before her sister and for a second she opened her mouth as if she might speak, but she didn't, and with her blonde-white hair and pale eyes she suddenly reminded her of someone.

Herself as a young child! Trying to please. Apprehensive. Motherless. She swallowed back sadness, the great wave of grief catching her sideways. She had not cried when her mother had left because her father had needed strength and fortitude, and she had not cried after Rebecca's death either because by then the ingrained habit of coping had taken hold.

Coping!

How good once she had been at that.

'We have some silver ribbon and tiny pinecones in boxes in our room, Lilly. Would that be useful, do you think?'

'Indeed it would be.' Lillian placed the book she had been browsing back on to its shelf and held out her arms to the girls. When two small warm hands crept into her own she had the sudden thought that she had never before touched a child or even been close to one. And when her own fingers curled into theirs she also realised just how much she had missed out on.

Luc returned just as dusk was falling on the land, the rain that had been present all day as a downpour becoming more like a shower, the drops of it caught in the last shards of light.

Woodruff stood in a rainbow, its lines etched against a leaden sky. Like a treasure, he thought to himself, at the end of a rainbow. Lilly and Charity and Hope.

He pushed the gun he held into the saddlebag and took his knife from where it was hidden in his sock, tucking it in beside the pistol. His sleeve he pulled down too, the deep cut on his forearm so obviously from a blade he wanted no one to see it.

Daniel Davenport had just sat down for a drink in a pub near Fairley when Lucas had surprised him, and the two other fellows drinking with him, who were familiar, their hands filled today with drink instead of the batons in London when they had waylaid him on the city streets.

Davenport had scampered quickly away and Luc swore at the memory of it before looking up. The day was dark though it was barely evening and Christmas was close. Perhaps it was the seasonal tidings, then, that explained his leniency with the others' lives, discharging the pair into the hands of the local constabulary before making his way back to Woodruff. Even six weeks ago he would have had no compunction in killing them, but the influence of Lilly upon everything seemed to have trickled even into his need for revenge.

'Damn,' he muttered as a branch whipped across

him, pain marking his face when it dug into his aching arm, where one of the pair had surprised him with a hidden knife. The lights of the house were bright and the sound of music came from within.

Christmas music, he determined as he got closer.

Sing choirs of angels
Sing in exaltation
Sing all ye citizens of Heaven above

The first pelt of a heavier rain made him grimace as he turned his horse for the stables and prepared to dismount.

They had worked all afternoon on the library, pulling an aged pianoforte from its covers to set it up near the tree Mr Poole had cut for them, which was now adorned haphazardly in red and green and gold and silver. Stars, hearts and twirling paper cut-outs bedecked each branch and plaited chains ran from an angel at the very top: an angel fashioned from an old doll of Hope's. A roaring fire burned now in the grate and chased the dark shadowed coldness from the room.

Festive and bright, the smell of sharp evergreen was in the air and the sound of crackling chestnuts on the hotplate above the flames.

Not a white or a pale shade on show. Lillian thought of her perfectly decorated rooms at Fairley, so different from this, the expensive trimmings laid in exactly the same pattern each and every year.

Yet here with the children's governess on the pianoforte, Mrs Poole singing her heart out beside her and the children in their night attire snuggled in, Lillian felt a certain peace of spirit that she had never known before. She had never sung the carols like this at the top of her voice with no care for tune or melody, had never eaten her supper on a tray with mismatched utensils and a flower across the top of the plate that looked as if it had been in a storm for weeks. But Charity had picked it from the garden between the showers and handed it to her shyly, so Lillian had given it pride of place, the lurid blood-red reminiscent of Lucas's taste in blooms. Hope traced the shape of her wedding ring as the song came to an end, one of the cats trying to lick the icing sugar from her fingers.

'I do not like your ring much, Lilly. When I get married I shall have a slender band with one single diamond.'

Lillian laughed, the truth of it so naïvely and honestly given, and at that moment Lucas stepped into the room.

She was laughing, the children beside her in a library that was completely changed. Things hung everywhere, Christmas things, all hand-fashioned, he surmised, and a tree stood where before had been only a chair.

His library. Gone. Replaced by a grotto of light and sound, hot chocolate drinks on the tables and a pianoforte that he had not known was there.

His arm ached and the faces of those he had tracked today danced macabrely before him.

Juxtaposition.

His life had always been full of it. But here tonight it was a creeping reminder of wrongness, a shout from the empty spaces he inhabited and people who made the world a place unsafe.

He tried to smile, tried to feel the warmth, tried to know all that it was he knew he missed, his sodden clothes making him shiver unexpectedly.

'Lucas.' Lilly's voice was soft and the children acknowledged him from her lap.

'I am wet. If you would give me a moment to change.'

He turned before anyone could say otherwise because shaking began to claim him, deep and strong, the blood loss from his arm, he suspected, combined with the extreme cold on a long ride home. 'I will be back soon…' he called the words over his shoulder and when the music began to play again he was pleased.

Glory to God
In the Highest
Oh, come let us adore him…

Something was not right, she could tell it in his laboured gait and in the sound of his words. A hidden sound that she knew well, her own voice having the same timbre in it for all those years.

'*No, I am all right, Father, I will be down soon.*'

If only her father had not believed her. If only he had come in to her room and held her warm against the demons and the regrets and the guilt of everything that had happened with her mother. But he had not and she had got better and better at hiding what she wanted others not to see. Like Lucas tonight!

Settling the children on the pillows and excusing herself, she walked up the stairs to the second floor.

The door to his room was shut, a room she had discovered today on their search for materials to use for the decorations and she could hear nothing inside.

Deciding against knocking, she turned the handle and stepped in.

He lay on his bed fully dressed, one hand across his face, the wetness of the night staining the counterpane dark and he shivered violently.

'I will be down soon, Lillian.' He did not remove his hand, did not try to rise or sit or converse further. The skin she could see around his lips was blue.

Fright coursed through her. 'You are ill?'

'No, I am c-cold. If you could just leave…'

One golden eye became visible through the slit of his fingers when she did not go. 'If you could hand me the b-blankets?' Tiredness ringed his eyes, a crippling desperate tiredness that did not just come from lack of sleep, his speech slurred into a stutter. She noticed how his left arm lay limp by his side, the deeper stain of blood showing at his wrist.

Blood! Hurrying over, she took his fingers into her own. Freezing.

'I will call a doctor.'

He shook his head and dry terror coated Lilly's mouth. Not a simple accident, then, if he thought to hide it! Carefully she rolled back the sleeve and the long thin jagged wound took away her breath.

'Who has done this?

Silence reigned and she had the impression that he

was holding in his breath until he could cope with the pain. 'It was my own fault,' he finally said and she knew she would hear no more.

'It looks deep.'

'Are you very good at s-stitching?'

'Tapestries. Embroideries. I can sew up the hem of a gown if I have to…' Suddenly she saw where this was going and her voice petered out.

The side of his lips curled up. 'I am certain then that th-this will give you no b-bother. But it will n-need to be cleaned first.'

'With what?' Lillian felt her teeth clench in worry. She had had no practice of this sort of thing ever. Oh, granted, she had dealt with headaches before and the occasional bruise, but a conserve of red roses and rotten apple in equal parts wrapped in thin cambric did not quite seem the answer here.

'Alcohol. The more proof the better, and boiling water. If you fetch Mrs Poole, she will know what to do.'

Lillian suddenly felt sick to her stomach. 'This has happened before?'

He turned away from her criticism, a man only just dealing with the agony of his arm and not up to telling any more of the truth. She jumped up in fright when his eyes turned back in his head and all that was left was the white in them. Quickly he shook himself and burning amber reappeared.

'If you die, Lucas Clairmont, two days after I have married you, I swear that I will strangle you myself.'

Her words were no longer careful, the shout in them surprising them both.

It made no sense, but she was beyond caring, beyond even the measuring of right and wrong. If he had killed someone today, then the reckoning of his soul would come to him later. Right now she just had to get him better.

With the room warmed by a blazing fire and his sodden shirt removed, Lucas's shivering finally stopped.

Mrs Poole brought steaming water and sharp scissors and all her movements gave the impression of a woman who had seen such things before.

'I was with Wellington's troops, my dear,' she explained when Lillian asked her. 'Marched with the drum, you see. It was how I met Mr Poole, for my first husband had been killed in Spain and widows did not stay that way for long.'

'And you saw injuries such as this one?'

'Many a time.'

'And they lived…' she whispered, 'those who had this sort of injury?'

'Of course they did. It's only if they took the fever after I would worry, though it is a pity he will not allow himself a good swig of brandy, for the ache would be a lot lessened.'

She handed a needle and thread to Lillian. 'Take little stitches and not too deep. Are you certain you would not like some brandy, my dear?'

Having already refused libation once, Lillian shook her head. She needed to be completely in control for the task in front of her and wished for the twentieth time that Mrs Poole's eyesight had been better.

Still, with the long explanation as to what the housekeeper could and could not see behind them, Lillian thought it only right that it should be her doing the repair work.

'I've had stitches before,' Lucas said to her as she readied herself for the task, trying to put it off for as long as she could. 'I don't usually weep.'

The tilt of his lips told her that he was attempting to take some of the tension from the moment, though the sweat on his upper lip gave a different story again. Not quite as indifferent as he would have her think! Her heart beat so violently she could visibly see the rise and fall of her bodice and it accelerated markedly again as she learnt that skin was a lot harder than cloth to push a needle through.

'I'm so sorry,' she whispered as he winced, the quick spring of red blood from the wound blotted by Mrs Poole as he looked away. Following his glance, she saw that the night outside was still heavy with rain and further afield the bright glow of lightning silhouetted the land.

'A storm is coming this way,' he said and Mrs Poole interjected.

'There is talk of snow, sir. Perhaps it will be a white Christmas after all.'

The weather was a benign topic as the needle sliced through flesh again and again, the stitches neat and tidy and his skin once jagged and open pulled together into a single light red line.

When it was done, Lillian put down her needle and stood, the magnitude of all that had happened washing over her in a flood of shock.

'Thank you.' In the soft light of flame his amber eyes were grateful, bleached in fatigue and something else, too.

Embarrassment.

When Mrs Poole bustled out of the room in search of a salve that was missing, Lillian also felt…shy. Wiping her hands against her skirt, the enormity of everything overcame her.

'If you are in trouble, perhaps I can help. My father has money and influence. If I talked to him and asked—'

'No, Lillian.' He winced as he shifted his position on the bed, the pale hue of his face alarming her.

His use of the fullness of her name surprised her as did the tone he used, as serious as she had ever heard him, his accent almost English.

'When I left you in the Billinghurst ballroom in London, I walked into a trap.'

'A trap?' She could not understand at all what he was telling her.

'Three men jumped me as I made my way home from the ball and the next thing I knew I was on a ship as a prisoner heading for Lisbon. I think Davenport money was used to make me…disappear.'

Lillian put her hand across her mouth to try to stop the horror that was building. 'I would never…'

'Not you.' His smile was gentle, relief showing over tenderness.

'My father?' The horror of his confession was just beginning to be felt. Lord, if it were her father…

'Not him either.'

'Daniel, then?'

'And his mother. A woman paid the money and the Davenport coach was waiting at the end of the alley.'

'Aunt Jean?' Horror tripped over her question. 'I cannot believe that my aunt would pay for something so… wrong.'

A flicker of a smile crossed his face, though there was something he was not telling her, something that marked his eyes with carefulness even as he stayed silent.

'When you did not come back, I thought perhaps you were in hiding, not wanting to be betrothed by force to me.'

He shook his head. 'I had my lawyer offer marriage as soon as I heard of…of how things were for you.' Lillian was glad he did not say ruined.

'And when my father accepted, I could never understand just how it was you persuaded him.'

A shutter fell across amber, the secrets between them there again after a few brief moments of honesty. The thought made her sad as she tidied the sheets on his bed.

'There are things we need to say to each other, Lilly, but not here like this. I need to at least be standing.' The corners of his lips pulled up.

'An explanation for your wounds, perhaps?' She gestured to his arm and unexpectedly he reached out, the strength in his fingers belying the pain.

'That, too,' he added and the brush of his thumb traced the lines of blueness on her wrist. A small caress! Quietly given as the distant storm rolled closer and a single bolt of lightning lit the room with yellow, thunder rattling the panes of glass in a celestial reminder of the paltriness of human construction and endeavour.

When his fingers tightened she did not pull away,

liking the warmth and closeness, watching the wind wild-tangled in the trees outside.

He was asleep before she realised it, his face in slumber so different from the watchful guardedness that cloaked him when awake. The scar on his neck was easily seen, his head tipped sideways so that the full length of it was visible, his opened collar making it even more shocking.

A small boy who had left parentless for the new lands across the sea. What had happened to him between then and now? she wondered. What possible excuse could he give for the scraps he was so constantly in?

'Please, God, don't let him be…bad,' she asked quietly of the omnipotent deity that she believed in, and then smiled at her own ridiculous description of Lucas's character.

Bad?

From whose point of view?

The world she lived in skewered slightly. Never before had she questioned anything. Rules. Regulations. Beliefs. All had been adhered to in the way of one who feared that even the slightest of detours might lead to chaos.

Well it had, here and now, but the feel of his fingers against hers and the sound of his breathing did not feel like anarchy.

No, it felt warm and real and right, the world held at bay by a promise far greater than fear.

'Love,' she said quietly into the darkness, the word winding around truth with its own particular freedom as Mrs Poole bustled back with a tray full of salves.

Chapter Seventeen

Lucas joined them for breakfast, the morning weather quieter than it had been in the night. Today, Lillian could almost feel the sun wanting to break through its binding mantle of cloud, though a thick blanket of twigs and leaves had been left on the part of the garden visible from the breakfast room.

Hope chattered beside her about the day and the night and the storm and the decorations that they had made yesterday. A never-ending array of topics and thoughts and so different from her sister, who sat in silence as she carefully spooned thick porridge to her lips.

'If your governess could spare you one day around lunchtime, I thought we could go and collect pine cones and berries for the Christmas fireplace. I used to do the same when I was a little girl.'

'At Fairley?' Luc asked.

She nodded. 'With my mother…' Amazement claimed

her. She could not remember the last time she had ever spoken of her mother in company, but as the questioning gazes of the two children fell upon her she fought to appear calm. 'She died when I was thirteen and I find it sad to think of her. Especially at Christmas.'

Unexpectedly Charity's warm hand crept into hers, the small honesty of it endearing. *You are not alone*, it said. *I'm here*.

Lillian looked at Luc, knowing that he had seen the gesture, and he tipped his head. This morning the whiteness of his shirt covered the generous bandage and his colour had returned to normal. A masculine virile man with more than just humour in his smile, for sensuality and appetite could be seen there, too. She knew by the responding lurch of her own body that it would not be long before pure desire ruled between them.

Looking away, she helped herself to scrambled egg and a piece of thick buttered toast. Scrambled like her thoughts, the rush of heat on her cheeks bringing her glance downwards so that her new husband might not see, might not know, might not understand that the resistance she had made such a show of was crumbling fast.

'I have something in my room for you, Lilly. When you have finished your breakfast and the girls have gone up to their lessons I would like to give it to you.'

His room was tidier than she had seen it last time, all the clothes put away and the myriad of papers and books stacked on his desk into two neat piles.

A well-read man, she determined, and tried to align that with one who gambled and fought. Often.

She noticed there were many books on boats and shipping and on a shelf behind him was a single ship on a plinth, its riggings intricate and complete.

'She's the *Rainbow*,' he said when he saw her looking, 'and one of the prettiest clippers ever built by Donald McKay. I saw her once in Massachusetts Bay before she made for the open sea with her long fine bow. She was designed to penetrate through the waves, you see, rather than ride over them.'

'You bought this model here?'

He nodded. 'In London. It will be shipped home to my uncle's house in Richmond after Christmas.'

'He likes ships as well?'

'Liked. He is dead.'

'Did your parents ever visit you in America?

'No, thank God.' When she frowned, he softened the criticism. 'My parents were more interested in each other than in me. My father was almost forty when I was born and heavy-handed with a boy whom they never understood. It was a relief when they left my upbringing to Stuart.'

'But you saw them again after you left England?'

He shook his head. 'They died a few years after I left, of the influenza. In Italy.'

She saw no sorrow in his eyes. Just fact and distance, the ties that more usually held a boy to his parents broken by misunderstanding.

'So you lived with your uncle.'

When he hesitated she knew that he had not. 'I lived on his land on the James and farmed it.'

'By yourself?'

'There were a few mishaps but I soon got the way of it and Stuart helped me.'

'Did one of the mishaps lead to the scarring on your neck?'

Before he could stop himself he pulled up his collar, the movement making Lillian place her hand upon his arm. 'It was not meant as a censure,' she said softly.

'I have other scars as well,' he returned and the air around them changed.

Other scars, other places. Where she could not see? Beneath his clothes and hidden. A singular vision of naked limbs entwined came to her, the thick burgundy cover on his bed loosely wrapped around them.

'I am not untarnished, Lillian,' he went on. 'Not like you,' he added, the husky American accent in his voice more pronounced than she had ever heard it. 'And I cannot help but notice that you rarely wear my ring.'

He brought her hand up between them, the nakedness of her finger making her frown.

'I took it off yesterday when I was painting with the girls…'

He leaned over and opened the drawer by his bed. 'I know. Mrs Poole found it and had it cleaned.' The large red ruby glinted at her, its familiar heaviness making it less…ugly, she thought, surprising herself. When he fitted it on to her finger she smiled.

In return he traced a line from her wrist to her elbow and then higher again when she did not pull away or turn.

'I want this marriage to be more than just a sham, more than separate beds. You mentioned patience and limitations, but I am thinking that I have run out of both.'

'I see.' Her answer was given with a smile.

'So if you thought to stop me, then I would say now is about the time…'

His fingers cupped the fullness of one breast through the layer of velvet, his burning glance holding her captive.

The feeling was exquisite. Thin want with need on the edge of it, and an answering spasm in her belly as the thrall of lust made her groan out aloud.

'Lucas?'

She whispered his name amongst the riding waves of hunger and heat, his leg pushing against the mound of her femininity.

'I would like to show you more than just a kiss under mistletoe, Lilly.'

His breath against her face was close. A locked door and as many hours as was needed.

She felt his fingers move across the cloth of her gown, bringing her to him. The length of their bodies fused into warmness, finding home, fitting perfectly.

When she tipped up her head he leant down, his mouth tasting hers, slanting across the small kiss she thought to offer and finding much, much more.

Heat. Hope. Thrall.

The pulse in her quickened, understanding what she knew only such a little of, yet wanting again what he had offered her once, the strength and core of his masculinity measured and fine.

And then hesitating.

'Why?' She shook her head, her breathing hoarse in the silence and the daylight bright. Not dark. Not hidden. No concealed and veiled mating.

'If we go any further, Lillian, I cannot promise to cease.'

'Cease?' Even the thought of it made her shake.

'It is not just a kiss I want this time.'

She felt her face flame, though his answering smile was tender.

'I would never mean to hurt you.'

'Hurt me?' Her eyes widened, reality coming between fantasy.

She heard him take in breath and hold it. His heart-beat quickened under the pads of her fingers at his wrist.

'When a man and a woman mate, the way of it is not always easy the first time.'

His words were whispered, the clock on his desk punctuating the passing seconds of silence. The caress of his breath on her cheeks made her turn towards him even as he began to speak again.

'Do you know anything of what happens?'

Lillian swallowed. 'A baby is made by the seed you place in my stomach.' Anne Weatherby had told her that once after a particularly large glass of wine.

'Well, not quite, sweetheart.'

Sweetheart? The word turned in her mind. Not a small endearment from a man who looked as he did.

Lucas's hands had now fallen lower, caressing her hips and her stomach and an ache of want made her press into him, unbidden. Asking for more even without the knowledge of what 'more' meant.

He began to move too, matching her rocking with his own. Give and take! The silent language of lovers through all the centuries of time. Faster and harder until her fingernails scraped down the skin of his arms, trying to understand what it was she asking for. Just this. Just them.

'Luc?' A question almost groaned. His fingers cupped her chin and he brought her face up so that his amber eyes burnt into hers as his other hand fell lower.

And lower as he lifted her skirt. The coolness of the winter air was strange against the heat of his fingers, and when he reached into what was hidden she tried to look away. He did not let her, holding his glance to her own as one finger gently found what it sought and eased in.

The rush of delight was elemental, uncomplicated and right. Opening her legs further, a thicker push followed, his fingers magic in what they engendered, a play of feeling and need and rapture.

The rising hardness against her stomach made her wonder. Was a man's need as great as hers, but nowhere near as well concealed? She smiled at the thought.

'Like a sheath, Lilly,' he said as he nuzzled her neck. 'I promise that you will fit me like a sheath.'

Snug? Close? Bound in skin?

Again he took her mouth, using his tongue in the same way he did his fingers, penetrating to find knowledge of her. Time seemed to stop as the day faded into only feeling, a nip of his teeth against the soft skin of her lips, his other hand pushing away the fabric covering her breasts and cupping the fullness before finding her nipple. And below his fingers bathed now in wetness.

The air between them quivered with all that he was doing to her, sweat building across the skin of her body as waves of need seemed to grow and grow and then recede again as he pulled away.

'No!' He laughed at her fervency, though his voice seemed hoarse and different.

'Not so fast. Not so fast.'

Peeling away her stockings, he settled her against the wall, her velvet gown a cushion against the cold and her skirt now riding high above the juncture of her legs. Naked. Bare. Waiting. Excitement built steadily, vying with impatience as he undid his trousers and slid them down. The billowing white of his cotton shirt contrasted against the brown of his skin, muscles firmed and well defined.

A beautiful man with golden eyes and night-black hair and enough experience to make all of this easy! Giddy delirium urged her on, her fingers coming to the abundance of his sex and feeling…him. Smooth, warm. Needing all of what was to happen next. No control. No limitations. Just all the hours before them and an aching yearning eagerness!

He brought her hand into his as he positioned himself at the juncture of her legs. Wetness flooded between them and she frowned.

'It is your body, sweetheart, saying that you want me.'

Now he lifted her slightly, gently piercing.

'Luc,' she cried as the first pains hit, his length buried within and straining.

He stopped instantly, his breath ragged and his eyes pleading.

'If you truly wish for me to cease…'

'No.' She whispered this time, for in the hurt she could detect some other want, a small question of flesh as he moved once and once again.

Bringing her legs around him, he tipped her hips and her weight upon his manhood changed from discomfort into another thing.

Some life-filled thing, her hands holding him in place as her mouth bit into the soft folds of his neck.

Not just her hurt, but his as well, the deep thrusts changing rhythm, harder and faster, careful wariness punctured by a building fervour as his hand covered her bottom. The crescendo of an ache made her throw her head back and just feel, the pulse of heat and light and loving. And sound. Her voice. Not restrained or polite or ladylike, but vivid and raw and loud.

Nothing hidden or covert! No shrouded thing as the pace of their breathing slowed and the world reformed again.

'This is what all married people feel…?' She had to ask.

'Only those who are lucky enough,' he returned and lifted her into his arms, the swell of her breasts displaced so that her nipples were easily on show.

When he laid her on his bed she sat there as he undid her gown and her stays, pulling the cloth from her nakedness, daylight revealing much more than just secrets.

'My God, you are so very beautiful,' he said slowly, unravelling her hair. 'Far more beautiful out of your clothes than in them and that's saying something.' The heavy drop of her tresses reached to the small of her back and the warmth was welcome.

Lucas wrapped his fingers in the gold paleness and brought it up to the light.

'So many different shades of pale, Lilly.' He had never seen hair her colour on anybody before, a changing kaleidoscope of corn and wheat and silver, her skin mirroring the delicate fineness. Carefully he shrugged off his shirt and stepped from his trousers, though when the bandage on his arm chaffed against his side he saw her wonder, all the other scars he had kept hidden beneath clothes visible as well today in the morning light.

Lillian's fingers traced the one on his thigh and then the smaller scar beneath his left rib. 'A bullet where I was not quick enough,' he said when he saw where it was she looked.

Her body glowed in unmarked glory, the long lines of her legs, the roundness of her bottom and the smooth beauty of her breasts. Only one finger held the slice of some accident. He found the hand and separated it from the others.

'I hurt it on a knife last year when I was quartering the first apple of summer.'

He laughed. Even her accidents were appealing. The ruby ring on her finger winked at him as he turned her hand.

'Do you still want this changed?'

She shook her head.

'I have grown used to it and it has grown used to me.'

'It was my grandmother's and the only possession I took with me from England. I wore it on a chain then around my neck so that it would not be stolen when I worked my passage. I never gave it to my first wife and now I know why. I was waiting for you.'

Her hand fisted tight and he leant to place a kiss on the back of her knuckles, laving the spaces between with his tongue, the trail of coldness making Lillian shiver.

Her husband. A man fashioned by hardship and loneliness and the absence of family that had shaped all of his life.

And now. What was he now? Just at this moment in this room with their skin against the daylight and the feel of each so known?

Lovers? Friends? Two halves of a whole made complete? The beginning of a life that glinted in the red stone on her finger, tantalisingly close.

'Love me, Lucas,' she whispered.

'I do,' he answered and his mouth came down to claim hers in reply.

He had left when she woke, the dent in the sheets where he had lain, cold and empty.

Her hand smoothed down the creases and she turned towards his side so that she lay watching the window, the smile that played at her lips pushing into the pillow with a shy incredulity.

'Goodness,' she whispered, remembering. She had always been so controlled, so restrained, so correct and careful and proper.

But not this morning!! The hours with Luc had cured her of ever being *proper* again, his hands in places she had not dreamed of, and showing her things she could never have imagined. Stretching, she felt elation rise. She was a wife in truth now, and one who knew the secrets of a marriage bed.

A tiny piece of misdoubt remained as she also

thought of the marks that crossed his body. No little accidents or paltry cuts. The scar on his leg ran from his groin to his knee and the one at his neck reached the blade of his shoulder. And that was discounting the long wound still beneath the bandage. She frowned. The man who had left England as a boy had had enemies; that much was certain. Still had enemies, she corrected.

Could she ask him about it? Would he tell her? Her father had seldom spoken to her mother of anything of importance. She knew because Rebecca had complained of it again and again to her friends when she thought Lillian was not listening.

Was this the way of marriage? She shook her head and played with her ring. In the light the stone shone red against the sheets, and in the newly cleaned yellow gold she saw markings. Slipping the bauble off, she brought it up to her eyes and read an inscription of three words held within the band.

Whither thou goest…

Lillian finished it off from memory in a whisper. '…I will go: and where thou lodgest I will lodge.'

She sat up, the declaration of devotion from the Book of Ruth making her heart thump. Did Lucas know these letters lay within the ring? Had he meant them for her? The band was an old one, fashioned, she imagined, some time in the last century, the worth of it considerable. Had it been only recently engraved or was it an ancient troth given between other lovers? His grandmother's, he had said, and the only worldly tie to a family lost to him. Slipping it back on, she clenched her hand inwards, the value of gold and precious stone as nothing compared to the worth of the words.

A shimmer of hope crossed her heart like a kiss beneath the magic of mistletoe or the first dusting of fine snow when the Christmas bells rang true.

New! Exciting! Full of promise!

Pushing back the sheets, she stood, donning a night-gown left on the oak chest at the foot of his bed, the material holding the smell of Lucas and the folds of fabric easily reaching to her feet. With care she pulled the bedding upwards so that the prying eyes of the maids she summoned would not see the chaos that such loving had wreaked and then she waited for a hot bath to be filled.

There were two men in the library with her husband when she went to find him a few hours later. Two men who looked nothing like refined country folk or city gentlemen.

Dangerous.

The word came out of nowhere and made her stop, fright replacing all that had been there a moment earlier, and Lucas's expression daunted her further.

'Lillian.' His tone was distant but polite as he moved in front of the visitors, shielding them from her gaze. 'I am busy now. If you could wait until later?'

'Indeed?' She could not keep the question from her response, though nothing showed on his face save guardedness.

Looking further on to the desk, she noticed a pile of paper bank notes of the larger denominations and beside them lay a gun. Not the elegant shape of a duelling pistol, either, but the serious contours of a lethal shooting tool. The small Christmas tree that Charity had made him as a present sat squarely beside it, its red and silver stars the reminder of a season of goodwill and peace.

Not here though!

Not in this room!

Not with men who looked like foreign sailors or thieves, their eyes falling away from her own even as she glanced at them. Her right hand crossed her left, feeling for her ring.

'I will await you in the blue salon,' she added frostily, accepting her husband's help with the door as she sailed through it, the wide sway of her gown breaking the growing silence with its own particular music.

Once outside she stopped and took stock. Lucas's arm was out of the sling Mrs Poole had fashioned for him, and the clothes he wore were riding ones. Could he have been out already?

Eight days until Christmas and her house was filling up with guns, blood money and ruffians of a foreign persuasion, not to mention the chilling anger that had dwelt in her husband's eyes before he had been able to hide it.

She took three deep breaths and heard the sound of a squeal from the stairs.

Rounding the corner, she saw Hope and Charity playing with a puppy who looked nothing like any other dog she had ever seen. And Hope was calling to it, as it leapt to try to take a ball.

Lillian walked forwards. 'Where did the puppy come from, poppet?'

'Mrs Poole brought it over early this morning and Mr Lucas said we could keep it because Royce is getting to be so old. Can we, Lilly?' This entreaty, given her husband's promise already made, was so unexpected that she could not help but nod. Charity's head was bobbing up and down, too, and Lillian thought for a second that the child might even speak, for she pursed her lips in the way of a 'please'.

This morning could not possibly become any stranger, she thought. A husband sequestered with men who looked like pirates and a puppy dog with baby fat showing through the ample folds of its pink-and-white skin.

But when Stephen Hawkhurst suddenly burst through the front door in full riding kit and without knocking, she revised her opinion.

It just had!

Chapter Eighteen

'I need to speak to Lucas!' he shouted, the anger in his words causing the children and the puppy to cower behind her.

Her glance took in the sword in his scabbard and the holster containing a gun.

'Why, what on earth could be wrong—?' she began.

'Lillian, I have been lodging at the inn in the village in case of trouble. Tell me where Luc is, for the others are right behind me and there are many of them.' The anguish in his tone was unmistakable though his words petered out as her husband strode into the room.

'What the hell is happening?'

Stephen's eyes widened with relief. 'They are here, Luc.'

'You've seen them?'

'From the hill beyond the village! A group of six men coming this way. They will be here within a few minutes.'

Crossing the salon in three strides, Luc pulled her and the children towards the stairwell, depositing the frantic puppy into Hope's arms.

'Go up to our bedroom, Lilly, and lock the door. There is a gun in the drawer. Do you know how to use a gun?'

She shook her head.

'Then pretend you do,' he answered back, not phased at all by her ignorance. 'If anyone comes into the room, point it at their chest and buy some time.'

'Time,' she parroted, the whole idea of what it was he wanted beginning to make her shake, but already he had turned away and the men she had seen in the library were priming their own weapons.

'Come on, girls,' she said in a tone that she prayed was reassuring. 'We have many more Christmas decorations to make.'

When she saw her husband smile at her, the warmth in her heart warred with the whole terrible possibility that she, Lillian Davenport, had married a murderous and unrepentant stranger whose very soul was in utter and mortal danger.

Lucas took a breath as he watched his wife leave, her ridiculous comment about making Christmas decorations wringing a kind of respectful disbelief in him, the power of a woman's ability to shield children from anything dangerous so intrinsic in feminine virtue.

Virtue!

When had virtue deserted his life? At fourteen, perhaps, when he had worked out a hard passage to America and learned things no youth should ever know.

At twenty when the land he was breaking in demanded the sweat of a man twice his size and when the bank had no time for an injury that had nearly killed him? Or when Elizabeth had died in the mad dash to the midwife in Hampton while in labour with Daniel Davenport's child?

Consulting his uncle's watch, he checked the time. Something prosaic about that, too, he thought as he did it, given that Stuart Clairmont had long since run out of the same commodity.

The stealth of vengeance stilled him and he flipped a coin.

'Heads I get the gateway.'

Stephen smiled. 'Tails, you have the front door.'

When the florin showed the face of Victoria, Luc pushed open the portal and ran for it. He breathed in when no gunshots were heard, relief overcoming everything as his fingers tightened on the stock of the gun.

The beat of his heart and the sound of his breathing in the damp closeness of the day were all he could hear, save the wind in the trees on the far side of the gardens as he made his way around the pathway. The orange rosehips of the winter roses hung from their brown branch. If he came out of this he would pick them on his return and take them up to his wife. And then he promised himself he would tell her exactly who he was.

Lillian set the little girls the task of making a list of Christmas games that they would dearly like to play. She had instructed Hope to write out the rules so that they knew exactly how each game went and for Charity to make an illustration of it.

'Will Mr Lucas be all right, Lilly?' Charity's voice? Perfectly formed words with a voice that was slightly husky.

Lilly dropped to her knees in front of the child, tears behind her amazement. 'You can speak, Charity?'

'Oh, she always could, to me.' Hope was dismissive of such a momentous occasion. 'But she loves you, too, and so she chose to speak. When our mother died she just stopped, but with you here just like our mama…'

Lilly's hand went out to the little girl's face, brushing her fingers against one pale soft cheek.

'Thank you, Charity. Will you speak to Mr Lucas, too?' A shy little nod confirmed that she would and Lillian took her into her arms. As a mother would cuddle a child. Her child. Her children. Lucas and her and Hope and Charity. When the little girl broke away after a moment and returned to her drawings, Lilly moved across to Lucas's desk, surreptitiously wiping away her tears of gladness.

His drawer was full of pens and pencils and to one side she recognised the red-wax stamp of the Davenport family on a letter.

Why would he have that? She did not dare to unfurl the seal in case she could not rejoin it, but she could see Daniel's writing on the outside. Placing the letter down, she dug deeper into the drawer and brought out a set of soldier's medals carelessly tangled and engraved with the name of Lieutenant Lucas Clairmont from the 5th Regiment of Infantry of the New York Militia. A date stood out. 1844. Counting backwards, she determined that would have made him all of twenty-four when he had received them.

To one side of his desk on a sheet of paper she saw her cousin Daniel's name scratched out beneath another. Elizabeth Clairmont, Lucas's first wife. Had they known each other in America? Could this be the reason for their feud and for the letter here with the Davenport seal?

Lord! She could barely understand any of it.

Had she made love to a man who would tell her nothing of the truth of his life, his whispers of something different more questionable now as she wondered if she was a part of the same charade? No. She would not think like that. She would not talk herself into the wronged woman until she had spoken with her husband and given him at least the chance to explain it all. When the shouts of anger from beneath the window drifted upwards she told Hope and Charity to stay down on the floor and peeked most carefully out from the very corner of the window.

To see a man take a shot at Lucas from the closest of distances!

'Damn it,' Luc swore as the bullet mercifully missed his head by the breadth of a farthing on its edge. 'You should have taken a body shot,' the soldier in him chided, though the man opposite was already re-cocking his pistol and he had no more time to lose.

His own bullet went true as the large man fell and a voice sounded out across the distance of the drive.

'If you don't come out now, I will shoot your friend.'

Daniel Davenport's voice, and then Stephen's!

'Don't do it, Luc. He will shoot me anyway—'

Hawk's voice was suddenly cut off. Not a shot, though. He had not heard that. The butt of a gun or the sharper bite of a sword? For Stephen's sake he prayed for the former.

Doubling back around the house, he had a good view of Davenport standing over Stephen and was pleased to see Lillian's cousin had absolutely no notion of him being there.

'Ten seconds or he dies. Nine…eight…seven….'

On the count of six Luc fired, the man to the left of Davenport falling without a fight.

'Damn,' he muttered, re-sighting his pistol and seeking the protection of the thick bough of a yew tree.

How many more men had Davenport brought and was Stephen still alive?

Looking around for anything he could use to his advantage, he found it in the heavy swathe of a hawthorn bush less than twenty yards away. If he could reach it, the plant would allow him an excellent cover to see around the whole side of the building.

Lillian saw Lucas meant to make a run for it, meant to leave his shelter and make for a spot further out and one that would allow him to see exactly where Lord Hawkhurst was. Goodness, if he should try she knew that he would never make it, the guns of those who held Hawkhurst firing before he would get there. If that happened they would be up the steps to the house next and she had very little wherewithal with which to protect the girls.

Could she open the window further and chance shouting out their positions? What if she threw something out to distract the men, to draw their fire this way whilst Lucas ran? The small solid wooden table next to her, for instance. She measured the width of the glass and, surmising it to fit, ordered Hope and Charity behind the sofa on the other side of the room.

Then she threw the piece of furniture with all her might, simply heaving it towards the middle of the glass and letting it go.

The shots came almost instantly, a wide round of them right at the window, pinging off its frame though one veered from the trajectory.

She felt it as a pinch, a tiny niggling ache that blossomed into a larger one, the red circle small at first and then spreading on the white of her dress. Breathing out, she sat down, her legs giving way to a dizzy swirling unbalance.

She heard the girl's screams through the numbing coldness and tried to take their hands, tried to reassure them, tried to tell them to stay down behind the sofa and out of harm's way.

But she couldn't because the dark and deepening blackness was leaching light from her world.

And then she knew nothing.

Luc was running, guns blazing past the hawthorn and around the corner, two men falling as he turned and another backing away.

Daniel Davenport. Today he looked nothing like the man from the drawing rooms of London and certainly nothing like the English lord who had held Elizabeth under his spell. No, today the fear in his eyes was all encompassing as the gun he cocked at Luc clicked empty.

His wife's lover.

Stuart's tormentor.

Retribution.

Pull the trigger and that would be the end of it. But he couldn't. Not in cold blood. Not with a man who looked him straight in the eyes.

'Kill him.' Stephen's words from the ground were said through pain and anger.

Lucas shook his head as Davenport spat at him, egging on a different and easier ending. But Luc merely smiled.

'Ruination to a man like this can be worse than death. When Society hears of your assault on my family home, you will never be welcomed in it again.'

The redness of Lillian's cousin's pallor faded to white, but Luc had more pressing matters to attend to. Giving the gun to Stephen and the gathering Woodruff servants he told them to lock Daniel up in the storeroom before he ran for the house and for Lilly, with every breath he took, praying she had not been hit by a stray bullet, though the girls' screams suggested otherwise.

'Lilly?' Her name called from a distance, a tunnel of blurred colour and a face close.

"Lilly.' He tried again and this time Lucas stood above her, dressed in the clothes he had been wearing when she…fell asleep? That wasn't right. It was night-time, and her curtains were shut, a lamp throwing the room into shadow.

'Thirsty.' She could barely croak out the word and when water was brought to her lips she tried to take big sips, but he drew it back.

'The doctor said just a little water and often.' Putting the glass on the table, he stepped back.

'Girls?'

'Are asleep after I promised them they could come to see you in the morning. Charity is chattering now even more than Hope. She sent you "a thousand kisses."'

'And Lord Hawkhurst?'

'Stephen is in the room next door with a bandaged head and two missing teeth.'

She nodded, the hugeness of all that had happened too great to contemplate right now. Lucas did not touch her, did not take her hand, did not sit on the empty chair beside the bed or fluff up her pillows. He looked angry, distracted and worried all at the same time.

Swallowing, the dryness in her mouth abated slightly from the liquid, but she did not even want to know what had happened to her until she could cope.

Closing her eyes, she slept.

He was still there the next time she awoke. He slumbered on a chair, one leg balanced on a leather stool with a picture of an elephant engraved into it. His hands were crossed over his midriff, his wedding band of gold easily seen, his chin shadowed by the stubble of a day's growth of beard.

As if he knew that she watched him, his eyes opened. Sleepily at first and then with great alarm.

'Lilly?' His word was loud, quick, the sound of desperate horror and then relief when she blinked. 'I thought you were…'

He did not finish the sentence, but she knew exactly what he meant.

'I'm that ill?'

'No.' He leant forward now, the bulk of his shape shading out the lamp behind him so that she could no longer really see his face.

'How long have I been asleep?'

He looked at his watch. 'Twelve hours.'

She wriggled her toes and her fingers and tried to lift her head.

'I was shot?

'The bullet passed through the flesh on your side. Another inch and…' He didn't finish.

'I found Daniel's name beneath that of your wife's…' She closed her eyes tight, the tears she wanted to hold back squeezing past and running down her cheeks into her hair. 'You risked everything for revenge?'

The look on his face was strained and tired, guilt marking gold eyes as plain as day. Turning away as he hesitated, she burrowed into her pillow, not wishing to hear anything else that he might say.

Hope and Charity came with Mrs Wilson in the late morning, the steaming porridge and freshly made bread they brought whetting an appetite that she had thought might never return again.

She could eat, she could smile, she could hold the girls' hands and pretend to them that all the violence and horror of yesterday was quite an adventure.

She did not ask where her husband was or where her cousin was. She did not dwell on what had happened to the bodies of those who had come to Woodruff with Daniel, or that when Lucas had aimed he had not meant to merely wound. He was a soldier trained for other things!

What else he was she did not know, did not want to know. He had lied and lied and lied and even for the time she had lain with him soft in the daylight with all the hours in the world to tell the truth, still he had not.

A dangerous man, a stranger, a husband who had risked his home for something that she didn't understand. She would not forgive him this. Ever.

She unclenched her fist as she saw Charity looking at her whitened knuckles and smiled.

She had to leave this place now, even with her side aching and the tiredness pulling her down.

'Would you both like to come with me today to see my house? My room has many toys that you might enjoy.'

The children's governess frowned deeply, but kept her counsel and for that at least Lilly was grateful.

The girls' quick smiles and nodding heads were much easier to deal with.

They reached Fairley Manor by lunchtime and her father was waiting for the coach with her aunt even as it came to a halt.

'Lillian.' He folded her in his arms and held her

there, his familiar strength and honesty a buffer against all that had transpired.

After a moment she pulled away and introduced the girls, pleased when her father asked one of the servants to take the children to the kitchens and give them a 'treat'.

In his library he closed the door and helped her to a seat. When Lillian caught her reflection in the mirror, she was astonished by her paleness and could see why her father looked as worried as he did.

Pride stopped her saying anything. Ridiculous pride, if the truth be known, given that the story must be all over the countryside by now, though her father did not seem to have heard the gossip. For that she was glad.

'Can we stay here, Father?' she ventured instead and the line of worry on his brow deepened.

'For tonight?' He seemed to be testing the waters.

'For for ever,' she returned and burst into copious tears.

She felt better after a brandy and a Christmas tart, the seasonal joy having its own way of dulling her problems.

'I should never have forced you into this marriage—there has been nothing but problems ever since. In my defence I might add that Lucas Clairmont charmed me.'

She smiled. Her first smile since lying in bed with her husband clad in nothing save air. She shook away the thought.

'Then we are alike in that,' she returned.

'Perhaps if we filed for divorce to the Doctor's Commons under the name of insanity, and then went to the House of Lords with a suit? Though then, of course, we would need an Act of Parliament to enable you to ever marry again.'

Lillian frowned. Goodness, to get into a marriage was so easy, but to get out of one…?

She could not think of it, not now. She needed to get stronger first and build up her courage.

Reaching over, she took her father's fingers in her own. Sorrow filled her, for him, for them and for a future so uncertain now.

'Are the children his?'

'No. He is their guardian. They are his wife's sister's girls.'

'Yet you brought them here? Does he know that you have?'

She shook her head. 'I did not speak to him about it, but they need a home without violence. They need to be loved and cherished and protected. I can do that.'

Her father smiled. 'I believe that you can, my daughter. Welcome home.'

Lillian watched the driveway religiously all that evening and all the next day, but Lucas did not come. Nor did Daniel. She wondered if she should say something of her cousin's part in the whole fiasco to her aunt and then decided against it, for what exactly could she say?

Your son is a murderer just like my husband.

Christmas was now four days off and the house was dressed in its joyous coat for the children's sake as Hope and Charity dashed from this tree to that one, oblivious to every adult nuance that passed above their heads, the delight of wrapping presents and setting out gingerbread men and marzipan candies a wonderful game. Twinkling lights now hung on fragrant boughs and garlands of fresh sprigged pine bedecked the mantel, the children's hand in everything.

And then finally Lucas came at dusk on the second evening.

She met him on the front steps, glad that her father had gone with his manager to look at some problem on the property, for at least she did not have to worry about his reactions.

Gesturing for her husband to accompany her upstairs, she took him to her bedroom, the intimacy of it affording her no problem with her state of mind.

'You lied about everything?'

He had the grace to look disconcerted. 'I did not tell you everything because I didn't want you involved—'

She stopped him, jumping in with such a shout the back of her throat hurt. 'Involved? When I am watching Lord Hawkhurst lying in a pool of blood whilst you shoot at my cousin like some wild-west gun-toting cowboy. And what of Hope and Charity? Two little girls exposed to fighting and shouting. I should not worry about that, I should not be involved?'

Pain crossed his face. 'Are the girls well?'

When Lillian nodded he looked so relieved that the anger she felt inside her was squashed down a little.

'I cannot even begin to understand a motive that would bring a man from America to England with the express purpose of killing another.'

'My wife had an affair with your cousin. I think that the child she carried was his.'

'Child?' The question spluttered to nothing on her lips.

Stopping, Lillian saw his heartbeat gather pace in the tender flesh at his neck.

'If he had been sorry I might have understood, could have forgiven. But he wasn't.'

He swiped his fingers through his hair.

'I was a soldier once.'

Lillian wondered as to his hesitancy in telling her of his involvement in a profession that was after all a noble one.

'I was seconded into intelligence work in my third year and I learned and did things that were not in any army rulebook. Once you know how to kill a man and do, you cross over a line. Whether or not it is for king and country you cross a line and you never come back from it. From that moment you are different…isolated, and the choices that are easy for every other person are not quite so for you.'

'You killed others in America?' The horror in his voice told her that he had.

'Not for fun or gain or glory. Not for that, you understand, but I have killed people. People who died because they believed in things that the military did not and sometimes they were good people…' He stopped again.

'Did you kill Daniel at Woodruff?'

'No.' She felt the relief at this denial until he continued, the world around her condensed into breath and heartbeat and pure raw fear!

'I wanted to, though. I came here to do just that, but found that I could not. When my uncle died, your cousin's name was the last thing on his lips. He had swindled him out of some land, you see, and made a fortune out of Stuart's infirmity. Paget had a hand in the bargain, too.'

'So when you mentioned the subject that night at the dinner table…'

'He knew that I knew.'

Vengeance. Retribution. Reprisal. The words shimmered in the air between them, harsh words actioned by a hardened man, used to blood and danger. A life for a life… She waited as he went on.

'The strangest thing about all of this is that it was not revenge in the end that saved me, Lillian. It was you.'

'Me?'

'I was married once to a woman who could not be happy, not with me, not with life, not with anything. The night she died her child was trying to be born…' The tremor in his voice was steadied by pure will-power. 'She would not stay at the house for she believed the midwife couldn't be trusted.'

'So you took her with you?'

'And overturned the carriage when she opened the door and threatened to jump out while shouting out the name of your cousin. I did not know exactly what that meant at the time, though now of course…' He shook his head. 'She died as I reached her.'

'My goodness! Were you hurt?'

'This scar…' His fingers traced the mark from his ear down to his collarbone. No slight injuries for him either, then, and a wife and child lost in betrayal.

'When I recovered and got back to the farm, I began to drink heavily. To forget.'

Water! She had never seen him touch anything stronger. The small pieces of a puzzle clicking into place. An explanation of what made a man complex. No easy choices. No one reason.

The truth. Not laundered. Not tampered with. Not piecemeal. There was beauty in a man who did not try to hide behind illusion.

The silence stretched, boundless, and it was Lucas who broke it first.

'When I saw you at the Lenningtons' you were… perfect. Perfect in a way that I was not, had never been.'

'Perfect?' She shook her head. 'No one can be that.'

'Can they not?' His eyes were softer now, not as glitter-sharp as they had been, the anger in them dimmed by honesty and relief. 'There is a cherub on the chapel ceiling at my home with eyes and hair just your colour. Beside it is a sinner who is being…saved, I would guess, saved as you have saved me!'

There was violence in his words, desperation in the way his fingers reached out to the bare flesh of her arm.

'I am not a bad man, Lilly, and I need you. Need you beside me to make sense of the world and to shape my own.'

He tipped her chin up so that her eyes met his, direct and hard, no denial in the movement, no gentle easy ask.

'I would never hurt you, Lillian. Never. I would only ever love you.'

The words were not soft either, tumbling from nothing into everything.

Love.

You.

Overwhelming need and fear mixed with waiting.

Only them in this fire-filled cold winter's evening, three nights before Christmas, bound in troth for ever, the silence of the house wrapped around them.

Waiting for just one movement.

Towards him.

She simply stepped into his arms, her tears wetting the front of his jacket, the buttons old and mismatched and the elbows patched with leather.

He was perfect for her, too.

They stood there for a long time, listening to the heartbeats between them and feeling the warmth, not daring to move towards the bed for fear her father would knock on the door and find them. No, not wanting anything to be ruined again by violence and hostility.

Finally her father came, the sound of his steps in the passage and then a knock on the door. He came through quietly, waiting as they parted though their hands were still joined.

'I have been told what has happened.' His glance caught Lillian's. 'You are all right?'

'Yes.'

His face creased into a smile. 'And he has given you his secrets.'

'Not quite,' Luc said and his fingers tightened around her own. 'I am a wealthy man, Lilly. My estates are numerous in Virginia, for timber is a lucrative trade.'

'Wealthier than my father?'

'I am afraid so.'

'Then the flowers did not break you?'

'I beg your pardon?'

'Your bunch of flowers! I thought at the time they must have cost you a small fortune so I saved one and dried it to show you.'

He shook his head. 'If you wanted a roomful, I could afford it.'

'But I don't,' she said solemnly and walked in to his waiting arms. 'All I want is you.'

The bells rang out from the village near Woodruff, tumbling Yuletide bells with joy on their edge, though they were muffled by the snow that had fallen all day, filling the windows with white and making ghosts of the trees in the garden.

They had eaten and danced and sang, and the sweet smells of cinnamon and spices hung in the air, the last of the visitors to Fairley finally gone and the big Bible in the front parlour closed from the many different readings. The whole day had been noisy and rushed and wonderful. None of the silent ease of Christmases past but all of a building excitement and joy, with the squeals of delight of Hope and Charity.

Goodness, she had changed completely in these few weeks, for she could not imagine again a pale and ordered Christmas, nor a home with as few guests as she had always cultivated.

Charity and Hope had made up games to play, Stephen had organised charades and Patrick had shadowed Lucas all day with questions of Virginia and its riches.

Her father had spent a quiet moment with her in the early afternoon, taking her aside to give her his present, the pearls that she knew had been her mother's.

'She was a person who made one wrong choice, Lillian. But before that she had made many right ones. You, for instance,' he said and kissed the tip of her nose.

It was the first time she had heard him talk of Rebecca since her death, and that gift was as important to her as the double strand of matched pearls that were strong in her memory.

'You told me once, Father, that I would thank you for this marriage and I do.'

'Lucas has let Daniel leave the country, so his stupidity shall not be the ruin of the Davenport name after all. I think even Jean understands the generosity of Lucas's gesture and has elected to go along with Daniel.'

She smiled at her father's relief, the burden of the family reputation one he had always taken so very diligently to heart.

'You look better than you have in a long while, Father.'

He smiled. 'I believe I am well because you are happy, my love.'

And much later when the moon hung high she smiled again as Lucas placed a kiss on her stomach where candlelight played across her skin.

'I want lots more children, Lilly. Sisters and brothers for Hope and Charity.'

The ruby caught in the light as she brushed the length of his hair from his face.

'I wanted to ask you about the inscription inside the ring.'

'I had it engraved in London for you.'

'But you did not know then that I would even marry you!'

'"*Whither thou goest, I will go.*" I knew that after our first kiss in your drawing room.'

'It was always just us then?'

'Just us,' he whispered back and, bringing a sprig of mistletoe from the cabinet beside the bed, held it above them, a wicked smile in his dancing amber eyes.

* * * * *

The Winter Queen

AMANDA McCABE

Amanda McCabe wrote her first romance at the age of sixteen — a vast epic, starring all her friends as the characters, written secretly during algebra class. She's never since used algebra, but her books have been nominated for many awards, including the RITA®, *Romantic Times* Reviewers' Choice Award, the Booksellers Best, the National Readers' Choice Award and the Holt Medallion. She lives in Oklahoma, with a menagerie of two cats, a pug and a bossy miniature poodle, and loves dance classes, collecting cheesy travel souvenirs and watching the Food Network — even though she doesn't cook. Visit her at http://ammanda mccabe.tripod.com and http://www.risky regencies.blogspot.com

Chapter One

❧❧❧

December, 1564

> …it is our deepest hope that, once at Court, you will
> see the great folly of your actions and rejoice at
> your happy escape from this poor match. The
> Queen has done our family a great honour by ac-
> cepting you as one of her maids of honour. You
> have a chance to redeem yourself and our family
> name through service to Her Grace. To discover
> what will truly make you happy. Do not fail her, or
> us.

Lady Rosamund Ramsay crumpled her father's letter
in her gloved hand, slumping back against the cushions
of the swaying litter. If only she could crush his words
out of her memory so easily! Crush the memory of all
that had happened since those sweet, warm days of
summer. Was it all just months ago? It felt like years,

vast years, where she had aged far beyond her nineteen years to become an old, old woman, unsure of herself and her desires.

Rosamund shivered as she tossed the crumpled letter into her embroidered bag, curling her booted feet tighter around the warmer that had long gone cold. The coals weren't even smoldering embers now. It made her think of Richard, and their professed feelings for each other. The kisses they had stolen in the shade of green, flowering hedges. He hadn't even tried to see her when her parents had separated them.

And now she was being sent away from Ramsay Castle, pushed out of her home and sent away to serve the Queen. No doubt her parents were sure she would be handily distracted there, in the midst of a noisy, crowded Court, like a fussing babe handed a glittering bauble. They thought that, with Queen Elizabeth's patronage and all the fine, new gowns they had sent with her, Rosamund would find another match. A better one, more suited to the Ramsay name and fortune. They seemed to think surely one handsome face was as good as another in a young lady's eye.

But little did they know *her*. They thought her a shy little mouse. But she could be a lion when she knew what she wanted. If only she knew what that was…

Rosamund parted the curtains of the litter, peering out at the passing landscape. Her parents' desperation to send her away was so great that they had launched her out into the world as soon as the Queen's letter had arrived, in the very midst of winter. The world beyond the narrow, frost-rutted roadway was one of bare, skeleton-like trees stretching bony branches towards a steel-gray sky. Thankfully, it was not snowing now, but drifts of white lay along the roadside in lumpy banks.

A sharp wind whistled through the bare trees, bitterly chilling. Rosamund's escorts—armed guards on horseback, and her maid Jane in the baggage cart—huddled silently in their cloaks. She had not heard a single word since they had stopped at an inn last night, and likely all would be silent until they at last made it to London.

London. It seemed an impossible goal. The palace at Whitehall, with its warm fireplaces, was surely just a dream, as the cozy inn had been. The only reality was this jolting, jarring road, the mud, the never-ending cold that bit through her fur-lined cloak and woollen gown as if they were tissue.

Rosamund felt the hollow sadness of loneliness as she stared out at the bleak day. She had lost her parents and home, lost Richard and the love she had thought they shared. She had no one, and was faced with making a new life for herself in a place she knew so little of. A place where she could not fail, for fear she would never be allowed home again.

She drew in a deep breath of the frosty air, feeling its bracing cold stiffen her shoulders and bear her up. She was a Ramsay, and Ramsays did *not* fail! They had survived the vicissitudes of five Tudor monarchs thus far, and had escaped unscathed from them all, with a title and fine estate to show for it. Surely she, Rosamund, could make her way through the Queen's Court without getting herself into more trouble?

Perhaps Richard would soon come to her rescue, prove his love to her. They just needed a plan to persuade her parents he was a worthy match.

Rosamund leaned slightly out of the litter, peering back at the cart rumbling along behind her. Jane sat perched among the trunks and cases, and she looked distinctly grey and queasy. It had been hours since they had left the inn, and Rosamund herself felt stiff and sore, even tucked up among the fur robes and cushions. Feeling suddenly wretched and selfish, she gestured to the captain of the guard that they should stop for a moment.

Jane hurried over to help her alight. 'Oh, my lady!' she gasped, fussing with Rosamund's white-wool cloak and gloves. 'You look frozen through. This is not a fit time for humans to be out and about, and no doubt about it!'

'It is quite all right, Jane,' Rosamund said soothingly. 'We will soon be in London, and surely no one can keep a warmer household or finer table than the Queen? Just think of it—roaring fires. Roasted meats, wine and sweets. Clean bedclothes and thick curtains.'

Jane sighed. 'If we only live to see it all, my lady. Winter is a terrible thing indeed. I don't remember ever seeing a colder one.'

Rosamund left the maid straightening the litter's cushions and headed into the thick growth of trees at the side of the road. She told Jane she needed to use the necessary, but in truth she really needed a moment alone, a moment of quiet, to stand on solid ground and be away from the constant sway of the hated litter.

She almost regretted venturing away from the road, as her boots sank into the slushy snow-drifts and slid across frozen puddles. The trees were bare and grey, but so closely grown she soon could not see her party at all. The branches seemed to close around her like the magical thicket of a fairy tale, a new and strange world where she was alone in truth. And there were no valiant knights to ride to her rescue.

Rosamund eased back her hood, shaking her silvery-blonde hair free of its knitted caul. It fell in a heavy mantle over her shoulders, blown by the cold wind. She turned her face up to the sky, to the swirling grey clouds. Soon enough, the crowds and clamour of London would shut out this blessed silence. She would surely not even be able to hear her own thoughts there, let alone the shriek of the wind, the rattle of the naked branches.

The laughter.

The *laughter*? Rosamund frowned, listening intently. Had she stepped into a story indeed, a tale of fairies and forest sprites? Aye, there it was again, the unmistakable sound of laughter and voices. Human voices too, not fairies or the whine of the winter wind. Still feeling under an enchanted spell, she followed the trail of that merry, enticing sound.

She emerged from the woods into a clearing, suddenly facing a scene from another world, another life. There was a frozen pond, a rough circle of shimmering, silver ice. On its banks crackled a bonfire, snapping red-gold flames that sent plumes of fragrant smoke into the sky and reached enticing tendrils of heat toward Rosamund's chilled cheeks.

There were people, four of them, gathered around the fire—two men and two ladies, clad in rich velvets and furs. They laughed and chattered in the glow of the fire, sipping goblets of wine and roasting skewers of meat in the flames. And out in the very centre of that frozen pond was another man, gliding in lazy, looping circles.

Rosamund stared in utter astonishment as he twirled in a graceful, powerful arc, his lean body, sheathed only in a black, velvet doublet and leather breeches, spinning faster and faster. He was a dark blur on that shining ice, swifter than any human eye could follow. As she watched, mesmerised, his spin slowed until he stood perfectly still, a winter god on the ice.

The day too grew still; the cold, blowing wind and scudding clouds held suspended around that one man.

'Anton!' one of the ladies called, clapping her gloved hands. 'That was astounding.'

The man on the ice gave an elaborate bow before launching himself into a backward spin, a lazy meander towards the shore.

'Aye, Anton *is* astounding,' the other man, the one by the fire, said. His voice was heavy with some Slavic accent. 'An astounding peacock who must show off his gaudy feathers for the ladies.'

The skater—Anton?—laughed as he reached the snowy banks. He sat down on a fallen log to unstrap his skates, an inky-dark lock of hair falling over his brow.

'I believe I detect a note of envy, Johan,' he said, his deep voice edged with the lilting music of that same strange, northern accent. He was not even out of breath after his great feats on the ice.

Johan snorted derisively. 'Envy of your monkeyish antics on skates? I should say not!'

'Oh, I am quite sure Anton is adroit at far more than *skating*,' one of the ladies cooed. She filled a goblet with wine and took it over to Anton, her fine velvet skirts swaying. She was tall and strikingly lovely, with dark-red hair against the white of the snow. 'Is that not so?'

'In Stockholm a gentleman never contradicts a lady, Lady Essex,' he said, rising from the log to take her proffered goblet, smiling at her over its gilded rim.

'What else do they do in Stockholm?' she asked, a flirtatious note in her voice.

Anton laughed, his head tipped back to drink deeply of the wine. As he turned towards her, Rosamund had a clear view of him and she had to admit he was handsome indeed. Not quite a peacock—he was too plainly dressed for that, and he wore no jewels but a single pearl-drop in one ear. And not the same as Richard, who had a blond, ruddy, muscular Englishness. But undeniably, exotically, handsome.

He was on the tall side, and whipcord lean, no doubt from all that spinning on the ice. His hair was black as a raven's wing, falling around his face and over the high collar of his doublet in unruly waves. He impatiently pushed it back, revealing high, sharply carved cheekbones and dark, sparkling eyes.

Eyes that widened as they spied her standing there, staring at him like some addled peasant girl. He handed the lady his empty goblet and moved towards Rosamund, graceful and intent as a cat. Rosamund longed to run, to spin around and flee back into the woods, yet her feet seemed nailed into place. She could not dash off, could not even look away from him.

'Well, well,' he said, a smile touching the corner of his sensual lips. 'Who do we have here?'

Rosamund, feeling utterly flustered and foolish, was finally able to turn around and flee, Anton's startled laughter chasing her all the way back to the safety of her litter.

Chapter Two

'Very nearly there now, Lady Rosamund,' the captain of the guard said. 'Aldgate is just ahead.'

Rosamund slowly roused herself from the stupor she had fallen in to, a hazy, dream-like state formed of the cold, the tiredness—and thoughts of the mysterious Anton, that other-worldly man of dark beauty and inhuman grace spinning on the ice. Had she really seen him? Or had he been a vision?

Whatever it was, *she* had behaved like an utter ninny, running away like a frightened little rabbit—and for what? For fear? Aye, perhaps fear of falling into some sort of enchanted winter spell. She had made a mistake with Richard—she would not do that again.

'You are a very silly girl indeed,' she muttered. 'Queen Elizabeth will surely send you home as quick as can be.'

She parted the litter curtains, peering out into the grey day. While she'd dreamed and fretted, they had left the countryside behind entirely and entered a whole new world, the crowded, bustling, noisy world of London. As her little entourage passed through the gate, they joined a vast river-flow of humanity, thick knots of people hurrying on their business. Carts, coaches, horses, mules and humans on foot rushed over the frosty cobblestones, their shouts, cries and clatters all a tangled cacophony to her ears.

Rosamund had not been to London since she was a child. Her parents preferred the country, and on the few occasions when her father had to be at Court he came alone. She was educated in the ways of Queen Elizabeth's cosmopolitan Court, of course, in fashion, dancing, conversation and music. But like her parents she preferred the quiet of the country, the long days to read and think.

But after the solitary lanes and groves, with only the bird songs for company, this was astounding. Rosamund stared in utter fascination.

Their progress was slow through the narrow streets, the faint grey light turned even dimmer by the tall, close-packed, half-timbered buildings. Peaked rooflines nearly touched high above the streets, while at walkway-level shop windows were open and counters spread with fine wares: ribbons and gloves, gold and silver jewellery, beautiful leather-bound books that enticed her more than anything; their colour and shine flashed through the gloom and then were gone as she moved ever forward.

And the smell! Rosamund pressed the fur-lined edge of her cloak to her nose, her eyes watering as she tried to take a deep breath. The cold air helped; the latrine ditch along the middle of the street was almost frozen over, a noxious stew of frost, ice and waste. But there was still a miasma of rotting vegetables, horse manure and waste buckets dumped from the upper windows, overlaid with the sweetness of roasted meats and sugared nuts, cider and chimney smoke.

The previous year had been a bad plague-year, but it seemed not to have affected the London population at all to judge by the great crowds. Everyone was pushing and shoving their way past, hurrying on their business, slipping on the cobbles and the churned-up, frozen mud. They seemed too busy, or too cold, to harass the poor souls locked in the stocks.

A few ragged beggars pressed towards Rosamund's litter, but her guards shoved them back.

'Stand away, varlet!' her captain growled. 'This is one of the Queen's own ladies.'

The Queen's own lady—gawking like a milkmaid. Rosamund slumped back against her cushions, suddenly reminded of why she was here—not to stare at people and shops, but to take up duties at Court. Whitehall grew closer with every breath.

She took a small looking-glass from her embroidered travel-bag. The sight that met her gaze caused nothing but dismay. Her hair, the fine, silver-blonde strands that never wanted to be tidy, struggled from her caul. She had hastily shoved up the strands after her excursion in the woods, and it showed.

Her cheeks were bright pink with cold, her blue eyes purple-rimmed with too many restless nights. She looked like a wild forest-spirit, not a fine lady!

'My parents' hopes that I will find a spectacular match at Court are certainly in vain,' she muttered, tidying her hair the best she could. She put on her feathered, velvet cap over the caul and smoothed her gloves over her wrists.

Having made herself as tidy as possible, she peeked outside again. They had left the thickest of the city crowds behind and reached the palace of Whitehall at last.

Most of the vast complex was hidden from view, tucked away behind walls and long, plain-fronted galleries. But Rosamund knew what lay beyond from her reading and her father's tales—large banquet-halls, palatial chambers, beautiful gardens of mazes, fountains and manicured flower-beds. All full of lushly dressed, staring, gossiping courtiers.

She drew in a deep breath, her stomach fluttering. She closed her eyes, trying to think of Richard, of anything but what awaited her behind those walls.

'My lady?' her guard said. 'We have arrived.'

She opened her eyes to find him waiting just outside the finally still litter, Jane just behind him. She nodded and held out her hand to let him assist her to alight.

For a moment, the ground seemed to rock beneath her boots; the flagstones were unsteady. The wind here was a bit colder at the foot of a staircase that led from the narrow lane in St James's Park up to the beginning of the long Privy Gallery. There were no crowds pressed close to warm the air, no close-packed buildings. Just the expanse of brick and stone, that looming staircase.

The stench too was much less, the smell of smoke and frost hanging behind her in the park. That had to be counted a blessing.

'Oh, my lady!' Jane fussed, brushing at Rosamund's cloak. 'You're all creased.'

'It does not signify, Jane,' Rosamund answered. 'We have been on a very long journey. No one expects us to be ready for a grand banquet.' She hoped. She really had no idea what to expect now that they were here. Ever since she'd glimpsed that man Anton spinning on the ice, she felt she had fallen into some new, strange life, one she did not understand at all.

She heard the hollow click of footsteps along flagstone, measured and unhurried, and she glanced up to find a lady coming down the stairs. It could not be a servant; her dark-green wool gown, set off by a small yellow frill at the neck and yellow silk peeking out from the slashed sleeves, was too fine. Grey-streaked brown hair was smoothed up under a green cap, and her pale, creased face was wary and watchful, that of someone long at Court.

As she herself should be, Rosamund thought—wary and watchful. She might be just a country mouse, but she knew very well there were many pitfalls waiting at Court.

'Lady Rosamund Ramsay?' the woman said. 'I am Blanche Parry, Her Grace's second gentlewoman of the Privy Chamber. Welcome to Whitehall.'

Rosamund noticed then the polished cache of keys at Mistress Parry's waist. She had heard tell that Blanche Parry was truly the *first* gentlewoman, as Kat Ashley—the official holder of the title—grew old and ill. Mistress Ashley and the Parrys had been with the Queen since she'd been a child; they knew all that went on at Court. It would certainly never do to get into their ill graces.

Rosamund curtsied, hoping her tired legs would not give out. 'How do you do, Mistress Parry? I am most honoured to be here.'

A wry little smile touched Blanche Parry's pale lips. 'And so you should be—though I fear you may think otherwise very soon. We will keep you very busy indeed, Lady Rosamund, with the Christmas festivities upon us. The Queen has ordered that there be every trimming for the holiday this year.'

'I very much enjoy Christmas, Mistress Parry,' Rosamund said. 'I look forward to serving Her Grace.'

'Very good. I have orders to take you to her right now.'

'Now?' Rosamund squeaked. She was to meet the Queen *now*, in all her travel-rumpled state? She glanced at Jane, who seemed just as dismayed. She had been planning for weeks which gown, which sleeves, which headdress Rosamund should wear to be presented to Queen Elizabeth.

Mistress Parry raised her eyebrows. 'As I said, Lady Rosamund, this is a very busy season of the year. Her Grace is most anxious that you should begin your duties right away.'

'Of—of course, Mistress Parry. Whatever Her Grace wishes.'

Mistress Parry nodded, and turned to climb the stairs again. 'If you will follow me, then? Your servants will be seen to.'

Rosamund gave Jane a reassuring nod before she hurried off after Mistress Parry. The gallery at this end was spare and silent, dark hangings on the walls muffling noise from both inside and out. A few people hurried past, but they were obviously intent on their own errands and paid her no mind.

They crossed over the road through the crenellated towers of the Holbein Gate, and were then in the palace proper. New, wide windows looked down onto the snow-dusted tiltyard. A shining blue-and-gold ceiling arched overhead, glowing warmly through the grey day, and a rich-woven carpet warmed the floor underfoot, muffling their steps.

Rosamund wasn't sure what she longed to look at first. The courtiers—clusters of people clad in bright satins and jewel-like velvets—stood near the window, talking in low, soft voices. Their words and laughter were like fine music, echoing off the panelled walls. They stared curiously at Rosamund as she passed, and she longed to stare in return.

But there were also myriad treasures on display. There were the usual tapestries and paintings, portraits of the Queen and her family, as well as glowing Dutch still-lifes of flowers and fruits. But there were also strange curiosities collected by so many monarchs over the years and displayed in cabinets. A wind-up clock of an Ethiop riding a rhinoceros; busts of Caesar and Attila the Hun; crystals and cameos. A needlework map of England, worked by one of the Queen's many step-mothers. A painting of the family of Henry VIII, set in this very same gallery.

But Rosamund had no time to examine any of it. Mistress Parry led her onward, down another corridor. This one was lined with closed doors, quiet and dark after the sparkle of the gallery.

'Some of the Queen's ladies sleep here,' Mistress Parry said. 'The dormitory of the maids of honour is just down there.'

Rosamund glanced towards where her own lodgings would be, just before she was led onto yet another corridor. She had no idea how she would ever find her way about without getting endlessly lost! This space too was full of life and noise, more finely clad courtiers, guards in the Queen's red-and-gold livery, servants carrying packages and trays.

'And these are the Queen's own apartments,' Mistress Parry said, nodding to various people as they passed. 'If Her Grace sends you to someone with a message during the day, you will probably find them here in the Privy Chamber.'

Rosamund swept her gaze over the crowd, the chattering hoard who played cards at tables along the tapestry-lined walls, or just chatted, seemingly careless and idle. But their glances were bright and sharp, missing nothing.

'How will I know who is who?' she murmured.

Mistress Parry laughed. 'Oh, believe me, Lady Rosamund—you will learn who is who soon enough.'

A man emerged from the next chamber, tall, lean and dark, clad in a brilliant peacock-blue satin doublet. He glanced at no one from his burning-black eyes, yet everyone quickly cleared a path for him as he stalked away.

'And that is the first one you must know,' Mistress Parry said. 'The Earl of Leicester, as he has been since the autumn.'

'Really?' Rosamund glanced over her shoulder, but the dark figure had already vanished. So, *that* was the infamous Robert Dudley! The most powerful man at Court. 'He did not seem very content.'

Mistress Parry sadly shook her head. 'He is a fine gentleman indeed, Lady Rosamund, but there is much to trouble him of late.'

'Truly?' Rosamund said. She would have thought he would be over the strange death of his wife by now. But then, there were always 'troubles' on the horizon for those as lofty and ambitious as Robert Dudley. 'Such as…?'

'You will hear soon enough, I am sure,' Mistress Parry said sternly. 'Come along.'

Rosamund followed her from the crowded Privy Chamber, through a smaller room filled with fine musical instruments and then into a chamber obviously meant for dining. Fine carved tables and cushioned x-backed chairs were pushed to the dark linen-fold panelled walls along with plate-laden buffets. Rosamund glimpsed an enticing book-filled room, but she was led away from there through the sacred and silent Presence Chamber, into the Queen's own bedchamber.

And her cold nerves, forgotten in the curiosities of treasures and Lord Leicester, returned in an icy rush. She clutched tightly to the edge of her fur-lined cloak, praying she would not faint or be sick.

The bedchamber was not large, and it was rather dim, as there was only one window, with heavy red-velvet draperies drawn back from the mullioned glass. A fire blazed in the stone grate, crackling warmly and casting a red-orange glow over the space.

The bed dominated the chamber. It was a carved edifice of different woods set in complex inlaid patterns sat up on a dais, piled high with velvet-and-satin quilts and bolsters. The black velvet and cloth-of-gold hangings were looped back and bound with thick gold cords. A dressing table set near the window sparkled with fine Venetian glass bottles and pots, a locked lacquered-cabinet behind it.

There were only a few chairs and cushions scattered about, occupied by ladies in black, white, gold and green gowns. They all read or sewed quietly, but they looked up eagerly at Rosamund's appearance.

And beside the window, writing at a small desk, was a lady who could only be Queen Elizabeth herself. Now in her thirty-first year, the sixth year of her reign, she was unmistakable. Her red-gold hair, curled and pinned under a small red-velvet and pearl cap, gleamed like a sunset in the gloomy light. She looked much like her portraits, all pale skin and pointed chin, her mouth a small rosebud drawn down at the corners as she wrote. But paintings, cold and distant, could never capture the aura of sheer energy that hung all around her, like a bright, burning cloak. They could not depict the all-seeing light of her dark eyes.

The same dark eyes that smiled down from the portrait of Anne Boleyn, which hung just to the right of the bed.

Queen Elizabeth glanced up, her quill growing still in her hand. 'This must be Lady Rosamund,' she said, her voice soft and deep, unmistakably authoritative. 'We have been expecting you.'

'Your Grace,' Rosamund said, curtsying deeply. Much to her relief, both her words and her salute were smooth and even, despite her suddenly dry throat. 'My parents send their most reverent greetings. We are all most honoured to serve you.'

Elizabeth nodded, rising slowly from her desk. She wore a gown and loose robe of crimson and gold, the fur-trimmed neck gathered close and pinned against the cold day with a pearl brooch She came to hold out her beringed hand, and Rosamund saw that her long, white fingers bore ink stains.

Rosamund quickly kissed the offered hand, and was drawn to her feet. Much to her shock, Elizabeth held onto her arm, drawing her close. She smelled of clean lavender soap, of the flowery pomander at her waist and sugary suckets; Rosamund was suddenly even more deeply aware of her own travel-stained state.

'We are very glad you have come to our Court, Lady Rosamund,' the Queen said, studying her closely. 'We have recently, sadly, lost some of our ladies, and the Christmas season is upon us. We hope you have come eager to help us celebrate.'

Celebrating had been the last thing on Rosamund's mind of late. But now, faced with the Queen's steady gaze, she surely would have agreed to anything.

'Of course, Your Grace,' she said. 'I always enjoy the Christmas festivities at Ramsay Castle.'

'I am glad to hear it,' the Queen said. 'My dear Kat Ashley is not in good health, and she seems to live more and more in old memories of late. I want to remind her of the joyful holidays of her youth.'

'I hope to be of some service, Your Grace.'

'I am sure you shall.' The Queen finally released Rosamund's arm, returning to her desk. 'Tell me, Lady Rosamund, do you wish to marry? You are very pretty indeed, and young. Have you come to my Court to seek a handsome husband?'

Rosamund heard a quick, sharp intake of breath from one of the ladies, and the room suddenly seemed to go suddenly still and tense. She thought of Richard, of his handsome blue eyes, his futile promises. 'Nay, Your Grace,' she answered truthfully. 'I have not come here to seek a husband.'

'I am most gladdened to hear it,' Queen Elizabeth said, folding her graceful hands atop her papers. 'The married state has its uses, but I do not like to lose my ladies to its clutches. I must have their utmost loyalty and honesty, or there will be consequences—as my wilful cousin Katherine learned.'

Rosamund swallowed hard, remembering the gossip about Katherine Grey, which had even reached Ramsay Castle—married in secret to Lord Hertford, sent to the Tower to bear his child. Rosamund certainly did not want to end up like her!

'I wish only to serve Your Grace,' Rosamund said.

'And so you shall, starting this evening,' the Queen said. 'We are having a feast in honour of the Swedish delegation, and you shall be in our train.'

A feast? Already? Rosamund curtsied again. 'Of course, Your Grace.'

Elizabeth at last released Rosamund from the force of her dark gaze, turning back to her writing. 'Then you must rest until then. Mistress Percy, one of the other maids of honour, will show you to your quarters.'

A lady broke away from the group by the fireplace, a small, pretty, pert-looking brunette in white silk and a black-velvet sleeveless robe.

Rosamund curtsied one last time to the Queen and said, 'Thank you, Your Grace, for your great kindness.'

Elizabeth waved her away, and she followed the other girl back into the Presence Chamber.

'I am Anne Percy,' she said, linking arms with Rosamund as if they had known each other for months rather than minutes.

Rosamund had no sisters, nor even any close female friends; Ramsay Castle was too isolated for such things. She wasn't sure what to make of Mistress Percy's easy-going manner or her open smile, but it *was* nice to feel she was not quite alone at Court.

'And I am Rosamund Ramsay,' she answered, not certain what else to say.

Anne laughed, steering Rosamund around a group of young men who hovered near the doorway. One of them smiled and winked at Anne, but she pointedly turned her head away from him.

'I know,' Anne said as they emerged from the Queen's apartments into the corridor again. 'We have been talking of nothing but you for days!'

'Talking of *me*?' Rosamund said in astonishment. 'But I have never been to Court before. And, even if I had, I would look terribly dull next to all the exciting things that happen here.'

Anne gave an unladylike snort. 'Exciting? Oh, Lady

Rosamund, surely you jest? Our days are long indeed, and always much of a sameness. We have been talking of you because we have not seen a new face among the ladies in months and months. We have been counting on you to bring us fresh tales of gossip!'

'Gossip?' Rosamund said, laughing. She thought of the long, sweet days at Ramsay Castle, hours whiled away in sewing, reading, playing the lute—devising foolish ways to meet Richard. 'I fear I have very little of that. No matter what you say, I would vow life in the country is far duller than here at Court. At least you do see people every day, even if they are always the same people.'

'True enough. At my brother's estate, I sometimes had to talk to the sheep just to hear my own voice!' Anne giggled, an infectiously merry sound that made Rosamund want to giggle too.

'Since I know so little of Court doings, *you* must tell me all *I* need to know,' Rosamund said. 'Maybe then the tales will seem fresh again.'

'Ah, now that I can do,' Anne said. 'A maid of honour's duties are few enough, as you will find. We walk with the Queen in the gardens, we go with her to church and stand in her train as she greets foreign envoys. We sew and read with her—and try to duck when she is in a fearsome mood and throws a shoe at us.'

'Nay?' Rosamund gasped.

Anne nodded solemnly. 'Ask Mary Howard where she got that dent in her forehead—and *she* is even the daughter of the Queen's great-uncle! But that is only on very bad days. Most of the time she just ignores us.'

'Then if our duties are so few what do we do with our time?'

'We watch, of course. And learn.' Anne paused in the curve of a bow window along the gallery. Below them was an elegant expanse of garden; neat, gravel walkways wound between square beds outlined in low box-hedges. The fountains were still, frozen over in the winter weather, the flowers and greenery slumbering under a light mantel of silvery frost and snow.

But there was no lack of colour and life. Yet more people flowed along the walkways, twining like a colorful snake in pairs and groups, their velvets and furs taking the place of the flowers.

Rosamund recognised Leicester's peacock-blue doublet, his black hair shining in the grey light. He stood among a cluster of other men, all more sombrely clad than he, and even from that distance Rosamund could still sense the anger etched on his handsome, swarthy face.

'We have no fewer than three important delegations with us for this Christmas season,' Anne said. 'And they all loathe each other. It provides us with much amusement, watching them vie for Her Grace's attention.' She lowered her voice to a confiding whisper. 'They will probably try to persuade you to plead their cause to the Queen.'

'Do you mean *bribes*?' Rosamund whispered back.

'Oh, aye.' Anne held out her wrist to display a fine pearl bracelet. 'But be very careful which faction you choose to have your dealings with, Lady Rosamund.'

'And what are my choices?'

'Well, over there you see the Austrians.' Anne

gestured towards one end of the garden, where a cluster of men clad in plain black and gray hovered like a murder of crows. 'They are here to present the case for their candidate for the Queen's hand—Archduke Charles. Truly, they are like the new Spanish, since King Philip has given up at last and married his French princess. No one takes them seriously, except themselves. And *they* are very serious indeed.'

'How very dreary,' Rosamund said. 'Who else?'

'Over there we have the Scots,' Anne said, turning to another group. They did not wear primitive plaids, as Rosamund would have half-hoped, but very fashionable silks in tones of jewel-bright purple, green and gold. But then, they did serve a very fashionable queen indeed. Perhaps Queen Mary made them wear French styles.

'That is their leader, Sir James Melville, and his assistant, Secretary Maitland. And Maitland's cousin, Master Macintosh,' Anne continued. 'They are the tall ones there, with the red hair. They certainly seem more lighthearted than the Austrians. They dance and play cards every night, and Her Grace seems fond of them. But I would not be too open and honest around them.'

'Why is that? Why are they here? Surely they can have no marriages to propose?'

'On the contrary. The Queen of Scots is *most* concerned with her own marriage prospects.'

Rosamund stared down at the Scotsmen in the garden. 'She seeks an English match? After being married to the King of France?'

'Perhaps. But not the one Queen Elizabeth would have her make.'

'What do you mean?'

Anne leaned closer, her voice such a soft whisper Rosamund could hardly make it out. 'Queen Elizabeth desires Queen Mary to take Robert Dudley as her consort. They say that is why she made him an earl last autumn.'

'Nay!' Rosamund gasped. 'But I thought the Queen herself…?'

Anne nodded. 'So do we all. It is passing strange. I'm sure Melville thinks so as well, which is why he bides his time here rather than hurrying back to Queen Mary to press such an offer.'

'So, that is why the Earl stalks about like a thunder-cloud?'

'Indeed.'

'But then who is the third delegation? How do they fit into these schemes?'

Anne laughed delightedly; every hint of the serious-ness she'd showed when discussing the Austrians and the Scots vanished. 'Now, they are a very different matter, the Swedes.'

'The Swedes?'

'They are here to present again the suit of their own master, King Eric,' Anne said. 'It seems he is in great need of a powerful wife's assistance, with war looming with both Denmark and Russia, and possibly France, and his own brother scheming against him.'

'He doesn't sound like a very attractive marital prospect,' Rosamund said doubtfully.

'Oh, not at all! That is why he was already rejected a few years ago. I'm sure Her Grace has no intention of accepting him—or not much.'

'Then why does she keep his delegation here?'

'Why, see for yourself!' Anne pointed as a new group entered the garden through one of the stone archways. They were a handsome gathering indeed, tall and golden, well-muscled in their fine doublets and fur-lined short cloaks, laughing and as powerful as Norse gods entering Valhalla.

And, right in their midst, was the most handsome and intriguing of all—the mysterious Anton, he of the amazing feats on the ice.

He carried his skates slung over his shoulder, shining silver against the black velvet and leather of his doublet. A flat, black velvet cap covered his inky-dark hair, but his radiant smile gleamed in the grey day.

The striking red-haired lady from the pond held onto his arm, staring up at him with a rapt expression on her sharp-featured face, as if her very breath depended on his next word.

Rosamund feared she knew very well how that woman felt. Her own breath was tight in her throat, and her face felt warm despite the chill of the window glass.

Think of Richard, she urged herself, closing her eyes tightly. Yet even as she tried to remember Richard's summer kisses, the way his arms had felt around her as he pulled her close, all she could see was a man spinning across the winter ice.

'That is why the Queen keeps them here,' Anne said. 'They have proved a great ornament to the Court—almost worth the trouble.'

Rosamund opened her eyes. Anton was still there, whispering in the lady's ear as she covered her mouth with her gloved hand, no doubt hiding a peal of flirtatious laughter.

'Trouble?' she murmured. Oh, aye; she could see where he would be a great deal of trouble, especially to a Court full of bored ladies.

'The Swedes and the Austrians detest each other,' Anne said cheerfully. 'The Queen has had to strictly forbid duels. And I am sure the Scots are involved somehow, though I have not yet devised how.'

'Oh.' Rosamund nodded, rather confused. She certainly did have a great deal to learn about Court life! Translating Greek manuscripts was simple compared to the complexities of alliances.

'That dark one there—Anton Gustavson, his name is,' Anne said, gesturing to the handsome Anton. 'He is only half-Swedish, they say. His mother was English. He has come to England not only on behalf of King Eric but on his own errand. His grandfather has left him an estate in Suffolk, a most profitable manor, and he wants to claim it. But he is in dispute with a cousin over the property.'

Rosamund watched as Anton laughed with the lady, the two of them strolling the walkways as if they hadn't a care in the world. 'I can scarce imagine a man like that in dispute with anyone. Surely he could charm the very birds of the trees into his hand?'

Anne gave her a sharp glance. 'You have met Master Gustavson, then?'

Rosamund shook her head. 'That is merely what I observe from watching him now.'

'Oh, you must be wary of such observations! Here

at Court, appearances are always deceiving. One never shows one's true nature; it is the only way to survive.'

'Indeed? And must I be wary of you, too, Mistress Percy?'

'Of course,' Anne said happily. 'My family, you see, is an old and wealthy one, but also stubbornly Catholic. I am here only on sufferance, because my aunt is friends with the Queen. But I will tell you this, Lady Rosamund—I am always an honest source of delicious gossip for my friends.'

Rosamund laughed. 'Tell me this, then, Mistress Honesty—who is that lady with Master Gustavson? Does he seek an English wife to go along with that new estate?'

Anne peered out of the window again. 'If he does, he has made a great mistake with that one. That is Lettice Devereaux, Countess of Essex—the Queen's cousin. Her husband the earl is away fighting the wild Irish, but it does not stop her making merry at Court.' She tugged at Rosamund's arm, drawing her away from the window and its enticing view. 'Come, let me show you our chamber. I will have much more gossip to share before the feast tonight.'

The feast in honour of those same quarrelling delegations, Rosamund remembered as she followed Anne along the corridor. It certainly should be a most interesting evening.

Perhaps if she wrote to Richard about it he would write to her in return? If he ever received the letter, that was. He was a country gentleman, not much interested in labyrinthine Court affairs, but he did enjoy a fine jest.

It was one of the things she had liked about him. That was if she still wanted to hear from him, which she was not at all sure of.

Anne led Rosamund back to one of the quieter, narrower halls. It was dark here, as there were no windows, and the torches in their sconces were not yet lit. The painted cloths that hung along the walls swayed as they passed. Rosamund thought surely the intrigues of Court were already affecting her, for she imagined all the schemes that could be whispered of in such a spot.

'That is the Privy Council Chamber,' Anne whispered, indicating a half-open door. The room was empty, but Rosamund glimpsed a long table lined with straight-backed chairs. 'We maids *never* go in there.'

'Don't you ever wonder what happens there?' Rosamund whispered in return. 'What is said?'

'Of course! But Her Grace does not ask our opinion on matters of state. Though she does ask us for news of Court doings, which is much the same thing.'

She tugged on Rosamund's arm again, leading her into what could only be the chamber of the maids of honour. A long, narrow, rectangular space, it was lined with three beds on each side. They were certainly not as large and grand as the Queen's own sleeping space. The beds were made of dark, uncarved wood, but they were spread with warm, green velvet-and-wool quilts and hung with heavy, gold-embroidered green curtains. A large clothes chest and a washstand stood by each bed, and the rest of the room was filled with dressing tables and looking glasses.

It was a peaceful enough space now, but Rosamund could imagine the cacophony when six ladies were in residence.

Her maid Jane was at one of the beds on the far end, unpacking Rosamund's trunks; she clucked and fussed over the creased garments. The satins, velvets, brocades and furs her parents had provided were all piled up in a gleaming heap.

'Oh, wonderful!' Anne exclaimed. 'You are in the bed beside mine. We can whisper at night. It has been so quiet since Eleanor Mortimer left.'

'What happened to her?' Rosamund asked, picking up a sable muff that had fallen from the pile of finery.

'The usual thing, I fear. She became pregnant and had to leave Court in disgrace. She is quite fortunate she didn't end up in the Tower, like poor Katherine Grey!' Anne perched on the edge of her own bed, swinging her feet in their satin shoes. 'Did you mean it when you told the Queen you were not here to find a husband?'

'Of a certes,' Rosamund said, thinking again of Richard. Of the letters from him she had never received. One man to worry about at a time was enough.

'That is very good. You must keep saying that—and meaning it. Marriage without the Queen's permission brings such great trouble. Oh, Rosamund! You should wear that petticoat tonight, it is vastly pretty…'

Chapter Three

'She wants you, Anton,' Johan Ulfson said. He was laughing, yet his tone was tinged with unmistakable envy.

Anton watched Lady Essex stroll slowly away along the garden pathway, her dark-red hair a beacon in the winter day. She peeked back over her shoulder, then swept off with her friends, their laughter drifting back on the cold wind.

He had to laugh, too. The young countess was alluring indeed, with her sparkling eyes, teasing smiles and her claims of vast loneliness with her husband away in Ireland. He could even enjoy the flirtation, the distraction from the hard tasks he carried here at the English Queen's Court. But he saw it—and Lettice Deveraux—for what they were.

And now he could hardly see the countess's red hair and lush figure. A vision of silver and ivory, of wide blue eyes, kept overtaking his thoughts. Who was she, that beautiful winter-fairy? Why had she run away so fast, vanishing into the mist and snow before he could talk to her?

How could he ever find her again?

'You are blind when it comes to a pretty face,' he told Johan, but he could just as well be talking of himself. 'The countess has other game in her sights. I am merely a pawn for her.'

He inclined his head towards Lord Leicester, who stood across the garden amid a cluster of his supporters. Everyone at this Court seemed entirely unable to move singly; they had to rove about in packs, like the white wolves of Sweden.

Lady Essex might have her sights firmly on *him*, but Leicester had his on a far greater prize. It would be amusing to see which of them prevailed.

If Anton would be here to see the end-game at all. He might be settling into his own English estate, the birthright that should have been his mother's. Or he might be back in Stockholm, walking the perilous tightrope at the court of an increasingly erratic king and his rebellious, ambitious brother. Either way, he had to fulfill his mission now or face unpleasant consequences.

Lady Essex was a distraction, aye, but one he could easily manage. When she was away, he thought not of her. That winter-fairy, though…

Perhaps it was a good thing he did not know who she was, or where to find her. He sensed that she would be one distraction not so easily put away.

'Pawn or no, Anton, you should take what she offers,' Johan said. 'Our days are dull enough here without such amusements as we can find.'

'*Ja,*' Nils Vernerson added, his own stare sweeping over the occupants of the frost-fringed gardens. 'The Queen will never accept King Eric. She merely plays with us for her amusement.'

'Is it better to be the plaything of a queen?' Anton said, laughing. 'Or a countess? If our fate this Christmas is only to provide entertainment for the ladies.'

'I can think of worse fates,' Johan muttered. 'Such as being sent to fight the Russians.'

'Better to fight wars of words with Queen Elizabeth,' said Nils, 'than battle Tsar Ivan and his barbaric hoards on the frozen steppes. I hope we are never recalled to Stockholm.'

'Better we do our duty to Sweden here, among the bored and lonely ladies of the Queen's train,' Anton said. 'They should help make our Christmas merry indeed.'

'If you ever solve your puzzle,' Johan said.

'And which puzzle is that?' said Anton. 'We live with so many of late.'

'*You* certainly do. But you have not yet said—do you prefer to serve the needs of the countess, or the Queen?'

'Or another of your endless parade of admirers,' Nils said as Mary Howard and two of her friends strolled past, giggling. Mary glanced at Anton, then looked quickly away, blushing.

'They are all enamoured after your great bouts of showing off on the ice,' Nils said, sounding disgruntled indeed.

'And now that the Thames is near frozen over he will have even more such opportunities,' Johan added.

'You can be sure all the ladies will find excuses to be in the Queen's Riverside Gallery just to watch,' Nils said. 'To blow kisses and toss flowers from the windows.'

Anton laughed, turning away from their teasing. He relished those stolen moments on the ice, speeding along with no thought except of the cold, the movement, the rare, wondrous rush of freedom. Could he help it if others too wanted to share in that freedom, in that feeling of flying above the cold, hard earth and all its complex cares?

'They merely want to learn how to skate,' he said.

'Skate, is it?' Nils answered. 'I have never heard it called *that*.'

Anton shook his head, twirling his skates over his shoulder as he strolled towards the palace. 'You should turn your attention to the feast tonight,' he called back. 'Her Grace deplores lateness.'

'So you have decided to be the *Queen's* amusement, then?' Nils said as he and Johan hurried to catch up.

Anton laughed. 'I haven't Lord Leicester's fortitude in such matters, I fear. I could not amuse her for long. Nor could I ever have Melville's and Maitland's devotion. To serve two queens, Scots and English, would be exhausting indeed. But we were sent here to perform a diplomatic task, *van*. If by making merry in Her Grace's Great Hall we may accomplish that, we must do it.'

He grinned at them, relishing the looks of bafflement on their faces. So much the better if he could always keep everyone guessing as to his true meaning, his true motives. 'Even if it is a great sacrifice indeed to drink the Queen's wine and talk with her pretty ladies.'

He turned from them, running up a flight of stone stairs towards the gallery. Usually crowded with the curious, the bored, and those hurrying on very important errands, at this hour the vast space was near empty. Everyone was tucked away in their own corners, carefully choosing their garments for the evening ahead.

Plotting their next move in the never-ending game of Court life.

He needed to do the same. He had heard that his cousin had recently arrived at Whitehall to plot the next countermove in the game of Briony Manor. Anton had not yet met with his opponent, but Briony was a ripe plum, indeed. Neither of them was prepared to let it go without a fight, no matter what their grandfather's will commanded.

But Anton could be a fierce opponent, too. Briony meant much more than a mere house, a mere parcel of land. He was ready to do battle for it—even if the battle was on a tiltyard of charm, flirtation and deception.

He turned towards the apartments given to the Swedish delegation, hidden amid the vast warrens of Whitehall's corridors. As he did, his attention was caught by a soft flurry of laughter. It was quiet, muffled, but bright as a golden ribbon, woven through the grey day and heavy thoughts.

'Shh!' he heard a lady whisper. 'It's this way, but we have to hurry.'

'Oh, Anne! I'm not sure…'

Curious, Anton peered around the corner to see two female figures clad in the silver and white of maids of honour tiptoe along a narrow, windowless passage. One was Anne Percy, a pretty, pert brunette who had caught Johan's devoted attention.

And the lady with her was his winter-fairy; her silvery-blonde hair shimmered in the shadows. For an instant he could hardly believe it. He had almost come to think her a dream, a woodland creature of snow and ice who did not really exist.

Yet there she was, giggling as she crept through the palace. She glanced back over her shoulder as Anton slid back into the concealment of the shadows, and he saw that it unmistakably *was* her. She had that fairy's pale, heart-shaped face with bright-blue eyes that fairly glowed.

For an instant, her shoulders stiffened and she went very still. Anton feared she'd spotted him, but then Anne Percy tugged on her arm and the two of them vanished around a corner.

He stared at the spot where she had been for a long moment. The air there seemed to shimmer, as if a star had danced down for only an instant then had shot away. Who was she?

His fanciful thoughts were interrupted by the clatter of Johan and Nils catching up with him at last.

'What are you staring at?' Nils asked.

Anton shook his head hard, trying to clear it of fairy dreams, of useless distractions. 'I thought I heard something,' he said.

''Twas probably one of your admirers lying in wait for you,' Johan laughed.

Anton smiled ruefully. If only that was so. But he was certain, from the way she had run away from him by the pond, that would never be. And that was a fortunate thing indeed. There was no room in his life for enchanting winter-fairies and their spells.

He found himself loath to ruin her happy sparkle with his dark, icy touch and uncertain future.

Chapter Four

The Queen's feast was not held in her Great Hall, which was being cleaned and readied for the start of the Christmas festivities, but in a smaller chamber near her own apartments. Yet it felt no less grand. Shimmering tapestries, scenes of summer hunts and picnics, warmed the dark-panelled walls, and a fire blazed away in the grate. Its red-orange glow cast heat and flickering light over the low, gilt-laced ceiling and over the fine plates and goblets that lined the white damask-draped tables.

Two lutenists played a lively tune as Rosamund took her place on one of the cushioned benches below the Queen's, and liveried servants carried in the heavily laden platters and poured out ale and spiced wine.

Rosamund thought she must still be tired from the journey, from trying to absorb these new surroundings, for the scene seemed to be one vast, colourful whirl, like looking at the world through a shard of stained glass where everything was distorted. Laughter was loud; the clink of knives on silver was like thunder. The scent of wine, roasted meats, wood smoke and flowery perfumes was sharper.

She sat with the other maids in a group rather than scattered among the guests, all of them like a flock of winter wrens in their white-and-silver gowns. That was a relief to her, not having to converse yet with the sharp-eyed courtiers. Instead, she merely sipped at her wine and listened to Anne quarrel with Mary Howard.

Queen Elizabeth sat above the crowd on her dais, with the Austrian ambassador, Adam von Zwetkovich, to one side and the head of the Swedish delegation to the other. Luckily, he was not the dark, skating man of the handsome smile, but a shorter, stockier blond man, who spent most of his time glaring at the Austrians. On his other side was the Scottish Sir James Melville.

But, if the dark Swede was not there, where was he? Rosamund sat with her back to the other table set in the U-formation, and she had to strongly resist the urge to glance behind her.

'Rosamund, you must try some of this,' Anne said, sliding a bit of spiced pork pie onto Rosamund's plate. 'It is quite delicious, and you have had nothing to eat since you arrived.'

''Tis not at all fashionable to be so slight,' Mary Howard sniffed, derisively eyeing Rosamund's narrow shoulders in her silver-satin sleeves. 'Perhaps they care not for fashion in the country, but here, Lady Rosamund, you will find it of utmost importance.'

'It is better than not being able to fit into one's

bodice,' Anne retorted. 'Or mayhap such over-tight lacing is meant to catch Lord Fulkes's eye?'

'Even though he is betrothed to Lady Ponsonby,' said Catherine Knyvett, another of the maids.

Mary Howard tossed her head. 'I care not a fig for Lord Fulkes, *or* his betrothed. I merely wished to give Lady Rosamund some friendly advice as she is so newly arrived at Court.'

'I hardly think she needs *your* advice,' Anne said. 'Most of the men in this room cannot keep their eyes off her already.'

'Anne, that is not true,' Rosamund murmured. She suddenly wished she could run and hide under her bed-clothes, away from all the quarrels.

'Rosamund, you are too modest,' Anne said. 'Look over there, you will see.'

Anne tugged on Rosamund's arm, forcing her to turn to face the rest of the chamber. She did not see what Anne meant; everyone appeared to be watching the Queen, gauging her mood, matching their laughter to hers. She was the star they all revolved around, and she looked it tonight in a shining gown of gold brocade and black velvet, her pale-red hair bound with a gold corona head-dress.

But one person did not watch the Queen. Instead he stared at her, Rosamund, with steady, dark intensity: Anton Gustavson. Aye, it was truly him.

He had been really beautiful in the cold, clear light of day, laughing as he'd flown so swiftly over the perilous ice, other-worldly in that aura of effortless happiness.

Here in the Queen's fine palace, lit by firelight and

torches, he was no less handsome. His hair, so dark it was nearly black, was brushed back from his brow in a glossy cap and shone like a raven's wing. The flames flickered in shadows and light over the sharp, chiselled angles of his face, the high cheekbones and strong jaw.

But he no longer laughed. He was solemn as he watched her, the corners of his sensual lips turned down ever so slightly. He wore a doublet of dark-purple velvet inset with black satin that only emphasised that solemnity.

Rosamund's bodice suddenly felt as tight as Mary Howard's, pressing in on her until she could hardly take a breath. Something disquieting fluttered in her stomach. Her cheeks burned, as if she sat too close to the fire, yet she shivered.

What was wrong with her? What did he think when he looked at her so very seriously? Perhaps he remembered how ridiculous she had been, running away from him by the pond.

She forced herself to lift her chin, meeting his gaze steadily. Slowly those lips lifted in a smile, revealing a quick flash of surprisingly white teeth. It transformed the starkly elegant planes of his face, making him seem more the man of sunlight and ice.

Yet his dark-brown eyes, shielded by thick lashes longer than a man had a right to, were still unfathomable.

Rosamund found herself smiling back. She could no more keep herself from doing it than she could keep herself from breathing, his smile was so infectious. But she was also confused, flustered, and she turned away.

Servants cleared away the remains of the meat pies

and the stewed vegetables and laid out fish and beef dishes in sweetened sauces, pouring out more wine. Rosamund nibbled at a bit of fricasséed rabbit, wondering if Anton Gustavson still watched her. Wondering what he thought of her, what was hidden behind those midnight eyes.

'Oh, why do I even care?' she muttered, ripping up a bit of fine white manchet-bread.

'What is it you care about, Rosamund?' Anne asked. 'Did one of the gentlemen catch your eye?'

Rosamund shook her head. She could hardly tell Anne how handsome and intriguing she found Anton Gustavson. Anne was already an amusing companion, and she surely could offer some sage advice on the doings at Court, but Rosamund feared she would not refrain from teasing.

'I will tell you a secret, Anne,' she whispered. 'If you swear to keep it.'

'Oh, yes,' Anne breathed, wide-eyed. 'I am excellent at secret-keeping.'

'I have no interest in Court gentlemen,' Rosamund said, 'Because there is a gentleman at home I like.' Perhaps that would make Anne let her alone!

'A gentleman at home?' Anne squeaked.

'Shh!' Rosamund hissed. They could say no more as servants delivered yet more dishes.

'You must tell me more later,' Anne said.

Rosamund nodded. She didn't really want to talk about Richard, but surely better that than Master Gustavson. She poked her eating knife at a roasted pigeon in mint sauce. 'How is so much eaten every night?'

'Oh, this is naught!' Mary Howard said. 'Wait until the Christmas Eve banquet, Lady Rosamund. There will be dozens and dozens of dishes. And plum cake!'

'We never can eat all of it,' Anne said. 'Not even Mary!'

Mary ignored her. 'The dishes that are not used are given to the poor.'

As the talk among the maids turned to Court gossip—such as who stole unbroken meats from tables which they were not entitled to—sweet wafers stamped with falcons and Tudor roses were brought to the tables. The wine flowed on, making the chatter brighter and louder, and the laughter freer. Even Rosamund felt herself growing easier.

She almost forgot to wonder if Anton Gustavson still watched her. Almost. She peeked back at him once, only to find he was talking quietly with a lady in tawny-and-gold silk. The woman watched him very closely, her lips parted, as if his every word was vital to her.

Unaccountably disappointed, Rosamund swung back to face forward again. She certainly hoped that life at Court would never make *her* behave like that.

As the last of the sweets was cleared away, the Queen rose to her feet, her hands lifted as her jewelled rings flashed in the firelight. The loud conversation fell into silence.

'My dear friends,' she said. 'I thank you for joining me this eve to honour these guests to our Court. This has only been a small taste of the Christmas revels that await us in the days to come. But the evening is yet new, and I hope Master Vernerson will honour us with a dance.'

Nils Vernerson bowed in agreement, and everyone

rose from their places to wait along the walls as servants pushed back the tables, benches and chairs and more musicians filed in to join the lutenists. Anton stood across the room, the attentive lady still at his elbow, but Rosamund turned away.

'I do hope you know the newest dances from Italy, Lady Rosamund,' said Mary Howard, all wide-eyed concern. 'A graceful turn on the dance floor is so very important to the Queen.'

'It is kind of you to worry about me, Mistress Howard,' Rosamund answered sweetly. 'But I did have a dancing master at my home, as well as lessons in the lute and the virginals. And a tutor for Latin, Spanish, Italian and French.'

Mary Howard's lips thinned. 'It is unfortunate your studies did not include Swedish. It is all the rage at Court this season.'

'As if she knows anything beyond *"ja"* and *"nej"*,' Anne whispered to Rosamund. 'Mostly *ja*—in case she gets the chance to use it with Master Gustavson! It is very sad he has not even looked at her.'

Rosamund started to laugh, but quickly stifled her giggles and stood up straighter as she saw the Queen sweeping towards them on the arm of the Scottish Secretary Maitland.

'Mistress Percy,' the Queen said. 'Secretary Maitland has asked if you will be his partner in this galliard.'

'Of course, Your Grace,' Anne said, curtsying.

'And Lady Rosamund,' Queen Elizabeth said, turning her bright, dark gaze onto Rosamund. 'I hope you have come to my Court prepared to dance as well?'

'Yes, Your Grace,' Rosamund answered, echoing Anne with a curtsy. 'I very much enjoy dancing.'

'Then I hope you will be Master Macintosh's partner. He has already proven to be quite light on his feet.'

A tall, broad-shouldered man with a mane of red hair and a close-trimmed red beard bowed to her and held out his arm.

Rosamund let him lead her into the forming dance-set, feeling confident for the first time since setting foot in Whitehall. Her dance lessons in preparation for coming to Court had been the one bright spot amid the quarrels with her parents, the tears over leaving Richard. For those moments of spinning, leaping and turning, she had been lost in the music and the movement, leaving herself entirely behind.

Her instructor had told her she had a natural gift for the dance—unlike conversation with people she did not know well! That often left her sadly tongue-tied. But dancing seldom required talk, witty or otherwise.

The dance, though, had not yet begun, and could not until the Queen took her place to head the figures. Her Grace was still strolling around the room, matching up couples who seemed reluctant to dance. Rosamund stood facing Master Macintosh, carefully smoothing her sleeves and trying to smile.

'Lady Rosamund Ramsay,' he said affably, as if he sensed her shyness. But there was something in his eyes she did not quite care for. 'Ramsay is a Scottish name too, I think?'

'Perhaps it was, many years ago,' Rosamund answered. 'My great-grandfather had an estate along the borders.' From which he had liked to conduct raids against his Scots neighbours, for which the Queen's grandfather had rewarded him with a more felicitous estate in the south and an earldom. But that did not seem a good thing to mention in polite converse with a Scotsman!

'Practically my countrywoman, then,' he said.

'I fear I have never seen Scotland. This is as far as I have ever been from home.'

'Ah, so you are new to Court. I was sure I would remember such a pretty face if we had met before.'

Rosamund laughed. 'You are very kind, Master Macintosh.'

'Nay, I only speak the truth. It's a Scots failing—we have little talent for courtly double-speak. You are quite the prettiest lady in this room, Lady Rosamund, and I must speak honestly.'

Rosamund laughed again, eyeing his fine saffron-and-black garments and the jewelled thistle pinned at the high collar of his doublet. The thistle, of course, signified his service to the Queen of Scots—a lady most gifted in 'courtly double-speak', from what Rosamund heard tell. 'You certainly would not be a disgrace to any court, Master Macintosh. Not even one as fine I hear as Queen Mary keeps at Edinburgh.'

He laughed too. 'Ah, now, Lady Rosamund, I see you learn flattery already. Queen Mary does indeed keep a merry Court, and we're all proud to serve her interests here.'

Interests such as matrimony? Rosamund noticed that Robert Dudley stood in the shadows with his friends, a

dark, sombre figure despite his bright-scarlet doublet.
He did not join the dance, though Rosamund had heard
before that he was always Queen Elizabeth's favourite
partner. He certainly did not look the eager prospective
bridegroom, to either queen.

'Is she as beautiful as they say, your Queen Mary?'
she asked.

Master Macintosh's gaze narrowed. 'Aye, she's
bonny as they come.'

Rosamund glanced at Queen Elizabeth, who fairly
glowed with an inner fire and energy, with a bright
laughter as she swept towards the dance floor with
Master Vernerson. 'As beautiful as Queen Elizabeth?'

'Ah, now, you will have to judge that for yourself, Lady
Rosamund. They say beauty is in the eye of the beholder.'

'Will I have that chance? Is Queen Mary coming
here on a state visit soon?'

'She has long been eager to meet her cousin Queen
Elizabeth, but I know of no such plans at present.
Perhaps Lord Leicester will let you study Queen Mary's
portrait, which hangs in his apartments. Then you must
tell me which you find fairer.'

Rosamund had no time to answer, for the musicians
started up a lively galliard, and the Queen launched off
the hopping patterns of the dance. Rosamund had no
idea what she could have said anyway. She had no
desire to be in the midst of complex doings of queens
and their courtiers. She liked her quiet country-life.

Even being at Court for a mere few hours was
making the world look strange, as if the old, comfortable, familiar patterns were cracking and peeling away

slowly, bit by bit. She could see glimpses of new colours, new shapes, but they were not yet clear.

She took Macintosh's hand and turned around him in a quick, skipping step, spinning lightly before they circled the next couple. In her conversation with him, she had forgotten to look for Anton Gustavson, to see where he was in the chamber. But as she hopped about for the next figure of the dance she was suddenly face to face with him.

He did not dance, just stood alongside the dance floor, his arms crossed over his chest as he watched their merriment. A small, unreadable smile touched his lips, and his eyes were dark as onyx in the flickering half-light.

Rosamund found she longed to run up to him, to demand to know what he was thinking, what he saw when he looked out over their gathering. When he looked at *her*.

As if he guessed something of her thoughts, he gave her a low, courtly bow.

She spun away, back into the centre of the dance, as they all spun faster and faster. That sense she had of shifting, of breaking, only increased as the chamber melted into a blur around her, a whirl of colour and light. When she at last slowed, swaying dizzily in the final steps of the pattern, Anton had vanished.

As the music ended Rosamund curtsied to Master Macintosh's bow. 'Are you quite certain you have never been to Court before, Lady Rosamund?' he asked laughingly, taking her hand to lead her back to the other maids.

'Oh yes,' Rosamund answered. 'I am certain I would remember such a long journey!'

'You dance as if you had been here a decade,' he said. His voice lowered to a whisper. 'Better even than your queen, my lady, though you must never tell I said so!'

With one more bow, he departed, leaving Rosamund standing with Anne Percy.

'Did you enjoy your dance with the Scotsman, Rosamund?' Anne asked.

'Yes, indeed,' Rosamund said.

'That is good. I wouldn't be *too* friendly with him, though.'

'Why is that, Anne?'

'They say he has been meeting often of late with Lady Lennox, Margaret Stewart.'

'The Queen's cousin?'

'Aye, the very one.' Anne gestured with her fan towards a stout, pale-faced lady clad in heavy black satin. She stood near the fireplace, watching the merry proceedings with a rather sour look on her face. 'She cares not for the Queen's scheme to marry Leicester to Queen Mary, and it is said that some of the Scots party agree with her.'

Rosamund eyed the dour woman suspiciously. 'Whose marital cause would they advance instead?'

'Why, that of Lady Lennox's own son, Lord Darnley, of course. I don't see his Lordship here tonight. He must be off chasing the maidservants—or the manservants—as his mood strikes him,' Anne said.

'I vow I will never remember who is who here,' Rosamund muttered. 'Or who is against who!'

Anne laughed. 'Oh, you will remember soon enough! They will all make sure you do.'

They could say no more, for Queen Elizabeth was hurrying towards them, the Austrians and Swedes with her. They looked like nothing so much as an eager flotilla drifting in the wake of a magnificent flagship.

Rosamund and Anne curtsied, and as Rosamund rose to her feet she found Anton Gustavson watching her again. He no longer smiled, and yet she had the distinct sense he was still strangely amused.

By her? she wondered. By the whole glittering scene? Or by some secret jest none could share?

How she wished he was a book, a text of Latin or Greek she could translate, if she only worked diligently enough. Books always revealed their mysteries, given time. But she feared the depths of Anton Gustavson would be too much for her to plumb.

Then again, perhaps she was too hasty, she thought, studying his lean, handsome body sheathed in the fine velvet. She had not even yet spoken to him.

'You are a good dancer, Lady Rosamund,' the Queen said. 'I see your lessons were not in vain. It was Master Geoffrey who went to Ramsay Castle, was it not?'

'Yes, Your Grace,' Rosamund answered, tearing her gaze from Anton to the Queen. Elizabeth's stare was so steady, so bright, that Rosamund was quite sure she could read every tiny, hidden secret. 'I enjoy dancing very much, though I fear I have much to learn.'

'You are too modest, Lady Rosamund. Surely you have not so much to learn as some at Court.' The Queen turned suddenly to Anton. 'Master Gustavson here claims he cannot dance at all.'

'Not at all, Your Grace?' Rosamund remembered how he had looked on the ice, all fluid grace and power. 'I cannot believe that to be so.'

'Exactly, Lady Rosamund. It is quite unthinkable for anyone *not* to dance at my Court, especially with the most festive of seasons upon us.'

Anton bowed. 'I fear I have never had the opportunity to learn, Your Grace. And I am a dismally clumsy oaf.'

Now, Rosamund knew *that* to be a falsehood! No one could possibly even have stood upright on the ice balanced on two thin, little blades, let alone spin about, if they'd been a 'clumsy oaf'.

'No one is entirely unable to learn to dance,' Elizabeth insisted. 'Perhaps they have not as much natural enjoyment of the exercise as I have, or as it seems Lady Rosamund has. But everyone can learn the steps and move in the correct direction in time to the music.'

Anton bowed. 'I fear I may prove the sad exception, Your Grace.'

The Queen's gaze narrowed, and she tapped one slender, white finger on her chin. 'Would you care to make a wager, Master Gustavson?'

He raised one dark brow, boldly meeting the Queen's challenging stare. 'What terms did Your Grace have in mind?'

'Only this—I wager that anyone can dance, even a Swede, given the proper teacher. To prove it, you must try and a dance a volta for us on Twelfth Night. That will give you time for a goodly number of lessons, I think.'

'But I fear I know of no teachers, Your Grace,' Anton said, that musical northern accent of his thick with laughter. *Why*, Rosamund realised, *he is actually enjoying this!* He was enjoying the wager with the Queen, the challenge of it.

Rosamund envied that boldness.

'There you are wrong, Master Gustavson.' Queen Elizabeth spun round to Rosamund. 'Lady Rosamund here has shown herself to be a most able dancer, and she has a patient and calm demeanour, which is quite rare here at Court. So, my lady, I give you your first task at my Court—teach Master Gustavson to dance.'

Rosamund went cold with sudden surprise. Teach him to dance, when in truth she barely knew the steps herself? She was quite certain she would not be able to focus on pavanes and complicated voltas when she had to stand close to Anton Gustavson, feel his hands at her waist, see his smile up-close. She was quite confused just looking at him—how would she ever speak? Her task for the Queen would surely end in disaster.

'Your Grace,' she finally dared to say, 'I am sure there are far more skilled dancers who could—'

'Nonsense,' the Queen interrupted. 'You will do the job admirably, Lady Rosamund. You shall have your first lesson after church on Christmas morning. The Waterside Gallery will be quiet then, I think. What say you, Master Gustavson?'

'I say, Your Grace, that I wish to please you in all things,' he answered with a bow.

'And you are also never one to back away from a challenge, eh?' the Queen said, her dark eyes sparkling with some mischief known only to her.

'Your Grace is indeed wise,' Anton answered.

'Then the terms are these—if I win, and you can indeed dance, you must pay me six shillings as well as a boon to be decided later to Lady Rosamund.'

'And if I win, Your Grace?'

Elizabeth laughed. 'I am sure we will find a suitable prize for you among our coffers, Master Gustavson. Now come, Ambassador von Zwetkovich, I crave another dance.'

The Queen swept away once again, and Anne followed her to dance with Johan Ulfson. She tossed back a glance at Rosamund that promised a plethora of questions later.

Rosamund turned to Anton in the sudden quiet of their little corner. It felt as if they were enclosed in their own cloud, an instant of murky, blurry silence that shut out the bustle of the rest of the room.

'I believe, Master Gustavson, that you are a sham,' Rosamund hissed.

'My lady!' He pressed one hand to his heart, his eyes wide with feigned hurt, but Rosamund was sure she heard laughter lurking in his voice. 'You do wound me. What have I done to cause such accusations?'

'I saw you skating on that pond. You are no *clumsy oaf.*'

'Skating and dancing are two different things.'

'Not so very different, I should think. They both require balance, grace and coordination.'

'Are you a skater yourself?'

'Nay. It is not so cold here as in your homeland, except this winter. I seldom have the chance of a frozen pond or river.'

'Then you cannot know if they are the same, *ja*?' A servant passed by with a tray of wine goblets, and Anton claimed two. He handed one to Rosamund, his long fingers sliding warmly against hers as he slowly withdrew them.

Rosamund shivered at the friction of skin against skin, feeling foolish at her girlish reaction. It was not as if she had never touched a man before. She and Richard had touched behind the hedgerows last summer. But somehow even the brush of Anton Gustavson's hand made her utterly flustered.

'I am sure they are not dissimilar. If you can skate, you can dance,' she said, taking a sip of wine to cover her confusion.

'And vice versa? Very well, then, Lady Rosamund, I propose a wager of my own.'

Rosamund studied him suspiciously over the silver rim of her goblet. 'What sort of wager, Master Gustavson?'

'They say your Thames is near frozen through,' he answered. 'For every dancing lesson you give me, I shall give you a skating lesson. Then we will see if they are the same or no.'

Rosamund remembered with a pang the way he had flown over the ice. What would it be like to feel so very free, to drift like that, above all earthly bonds? She was quite tempted. But… 'I could never do what you did. I would fall right over!'

He laughed, a deep, warm sound that rubbed against

her like fine silk-velvet. She longed to hear it again, to revel in that happy sound over and over. 'You need not go into a spin, Lady Rosamund, merely stay upright and move forward.'

That alone sounded difficult enough. 'On two thin little blades attached to my shoes.'

'I vow it is not as hard as it sounds.'

'And neither is dancing.'

'Then shall we prove it to ourselves? Just a small, harmless wager, my lady.'

Rosamund frowned. She thought he surely did not have a 'harmless' bone in his handsome body! 'I don't have any money of my own yet.'

'Nay, you have something far more precious.'

'And what is that?'

'A lock of your hair.'

'My hair?' Her hand flew up to touch her hair which was carefully looped and pinned under a narrow silver headdress and sheer veil. Her maid Jane had shoved in extra pins to hold the fine, slick strands tight, but Rosamund could feel them already slipping. 'Whatever for?'

Anton watched intently as her fingers moved along one loose strand. 'I think it must be made of moonbeams. It makes me think of nights in my homeland, of the way silver moonlight sparkles on the snow.'

'Why, Master Gustavson,' Rosamund breathed. 'I think you have missed your calling. You are no diplomat or skater, you are a poet.'

He laughed and that flash of seriousness dissipated like winter fog. 'No more than I am a dancer, I fear, my lady. 'Tis a great pity, for it seems both poetry and dancing are highly prized here in London.'

'Are they not in Stockholm?'

He shook his head. 'Warfare is prized in Stockholm, and not much else of late.'

'It *is* a pity, then. For I fear poetry would be more likely to win the Queen's hand for your king.'

'I think you are correct, Lady Rosamund. But I must still do my duty here.'

'Ah, yes. We all must do our duty,' Rosamund said ruefully, remembering her parents' words.

Anton smiled at her. 'But life is not all duty, my lady. We must have some merriment as well.'

'True. Especially now at Christmas.'

'Then we have a wager?'

Rosamund laughed. Perhaps it was the wine, the music, the fatigue from her journey and the late hour, but she suddenly felt deliciously reckless. 'Very well. If you cannot dance and I cannot skate, I will give you a lock of my hair.'

'And if it is the opposite? What prize do you claim for yourself?'

He leaned close to her, so close she could see the etched-glass lines of his face, the faint shadow of beard along his jaw. She could smell the summery lime of his cologne, the clean, warm winter-frost scent of him. *A kiss*, she almost blurted out, staring at the faint smile on his lips.

What would he kiss like? Quick, eager—almost overly eager, like Richard? Or slow, lazy, exploring every angle, every sensation? What would he taste like?

She gulped and took a step back, her gaze falling to his hand curled lightly around the goblet. On his smallest finger was a ring, a small ruby set in intricate gold filigree. 'That is a pretty bauble,' she said hoarsely, gesturing to the ring. 'Would you wager it?'

He held his hand up, staring at the ring as if he had forgotten it was there. 'If you wish it.'

Rosamund nodded. 'Then done. I will meet you in the Waterside Gallery on Christmas morning for a dance lesson.'

'And as soon as the Thames is frozen through we will go skating.'

'Until then, Master Gustavson.' Rosamund quickly curtsied, and hurried away to join the other maids where they had gathered near the door. It was nearly the Queen's hour to retire, and they had to accompany her.

Only once she was entirely across the room from Anton did she draw in a deep breath. She felt as if she had suddenly been dropped back to earth after spinning about in the sky, all unmoored and uncertain. Her head whirled.

'What were you and Master Gustavson talking of for so long?' Anne whispered.

'Dancing, of course,' Rosamund answered.

'If I had him to myself like that,' Anne said, 'I am certain I could think of better things than *dancing* to talk of! Do you think you will be able to win the Queen's wager?'

Rosamund shrugged, still feeling quite dazed. She feared she was quite unable to think at all any more.

* * *

Svordom! What had led him to promise her his mother's ring?

Anton curled his hand into a fist around the heavy goblet, the embossed silver pressing into the calluses along his palm as he watched her walk away. It seemed as if all the light in the chamber collected onto her, a silvery glow that carried her above the noisy fray.

He knew all too well what had made him agree to a ridiculous wager that didn't even make sense, to offer her that ring. It was her, Rosamund Ramsay, alone. That look in her large blue eyes.

She had not been at Court long enough to learn to conceal her feelings entirely. She had tried, but every once in a while they had flashed through those expressive eyes—glimpses of fear, nervousness, excitement, bravery, laughter—uncertainty.

He had lived so long among people who had worn masks all their lives. The concealment became a part of them, so that even *they* had no idea what they truly were, what they truly felt. Even he had his own masks, a supply of them for every occasion. They were better than any armour.

Yet when he looked at Rosamund Ramsay he felt the heavy weight of that concealment pressing down on him. He could not be free of it, but he could enjoy her freedom until she, too, learned to don masks. It would not be long, not here, and he felt unaccountably melancholy at the thought of those eyes, that lovely smile, turning brittle and false.

Aye, he would enjoy her company while he could.

His own task drew near, and he could not falter now. He unwound his fist, staring down at the ruby. It glowed blood-red in the torchlight, reminding him of his promises and dreams.

'Making wagers with the Queen?' Johan said, coming up to Anton to interrupt his dark thoughts. 'Is that wise, from all we have heard of her?'

Anton laughed, watching Queen Elizabeth as she talked with her chief advisor, Lord Burghley. Burghley was not terribly old, yet his face was lined with care, his hair and beard streaked with grey. Serving the English Queen could be a frustrating business, as they had learned to their own peril. She kept them cooling their heels at Court, dancing attendance on her as she vacillated at King Eric's proposal. Anton was certain she had no intention of marrying the king, or possibly anyone at all, but they could not depart until they had an official answer. Meanwhile, they danced and dined, and warily circled the Austrians and the Scots.

As for Anton's own matter, she gave no answer at all.

Maddening indeed. Battle was simple; the answer was won by the sword. Court politics were more slippery, more changeable, and far more time-consuming. But he was a patient man, a determined one. He could wait—for now.

At least there was Rosamund Ramsay to make the long days more palatable.

'I would not worry, Johan,' Anton said, tossing back the last of the wine. 'This wager is strictly for Her Grace's holiday amusement.'

'What is it, then? Are you to play the Christmas fool, the Lord of Misrule?'

Anton laughed. 'Something like it. I am to learn to dance.'

Chapter Five

Christmas Eve, December 24

'Holly and ivy, box and bay, put in the house for Christmas Day! Fa la la la…'

Rosamund smiled at hearing the notes of the familiar song, the tune always sung as the house was bedecked for Christmas. The Queen's gentlewomen of the Privy and Presence chambers, along with the maids of honour, had been assigned to festoon the Great Hall and the corridors for that night's feast. Tables were set up along the privy gallery, covered with holly, ivy, mistletoe, evergreen boughs, ribbons and spangles. Under the watchful eye of Mistress Eglionby, Mistress of the Maids, they were to turn them into bits of holiday artistry.

Rosamund sat there with Anne Percy, twisting together loops of ivy as they watched Mary Howard and Mary Radcliffe lay out long swags to measure them.

The Marys sang as they worked, sometimes pausing to leap about with ribbons like two morris dancers.

Rosamund laughed at their antics. For the first time in many days, she forgot her homesickness and uncertainty. She only thought of how much she loved this time of year, these twelve days when the gloom of winter was left behind, buried in music, wine and satin bows. She might be far from home, but the Queen kept a lively holiday. She should enjoy it as much as possible.

Rosamund reached for two bent hoops and tied them into a sphere for a kissing bough. She chose the darkest, greenest loops of holly and ivy from the table, twining them around and tying them with the red ribbons.

'Are you making a kissing bough, Rosamund?' Anne said teasingly. She tied together her own greenery into wreaths for the fireplace mantels.

Rosamund smiled. 'My maid Jane says if you stand beneath it and close your eyes you will have a vision of your future husband.'

'And if he comes up and kisses you whilst you stand there with your eyes closed, so much the better!' Anne said.

'That would help settle the question, I think.'

'But you need not resort to such tricks, I'm sure,' Anne whispered. 'What of your sweetheart at home?'

Rosamund frowned as she stared down at her half-finished bough; last Christmas, Richard had indeed kissed her under one very like it. That was when she had begun to think he cared for her, and she for him. But that seemed so long ago now, as if it had happened to someone else. 'He is not my sweetheart.'

'But you do wish him to be?'

Rosamund remembered Richard's kiss that Christmas Eve. 'That can't be.'

'Do your parents disapprove so much, then?'

Rosamund nodded, reaching for the green, red and white Tudor roses made of paper to add to her bough. 'They say his family is not our equal, even though their estate neighbours ours.'

'Is that their only objection?'

'Nay. They also say I would not be content with him. That his nature would not suit mine.' Rosamund felt a pang as she remembered those words of her father. She had cried and pleaded, sure her parents would give way as they always did. Her father had seemed sad as he'd refused her, but implacable. 'When you find the one you can truly love,' he said, 'you will know what your mother and I mean.'

'But you love him?' Anne asked softly.

Rosamund shrugged.

Anne sighed sadly. 'Our families should not have such say over our own hearts.'

'Is your family so very strict?' Rosamund asked.

'Nay. My parents died when I was a small child.'

'Oh, Anne!' Rosamund cried. Her own parents might be maddening, but before the business with Richard they had been affectionate with her, their only child, and she with them. 'I am so sorry.'

'I scarcely remember them,' Anne said, tying off her length of ribbon. 'I grew up with my grandmother, who is so deaf she hardly ever knew what I was up to. It wasn't so bad, and then my aunt came along and found me this position here at Court. They want me to marry, but only their own choice. Much like your own parents, I dare say!'

'Who is their choice?'

Anne shrugged. 'I don't know yet. Someone old and crabbed and toothless, I'm sure. Some crony of my aunt's husband. Perhaps he will at least be rich.'

'Oh, Anne, no!'

'It does not signify. We should concentrate on *your* romance. There must be a way we can smuggle a message to him. Oh, here, put mistletoe in your bough! It is the most important element, otherwise the magic won't work.'

Rosamund laughed, taking the thick bunch of glossy mistletoe from Anne and threading it through the centre of the bough. Surely there was some kind of magic floating about in the winter air. She felt lighter already with Christmas here.

Yet, strangely, it was not Richard's blond visage she saw as she gazed at the mistletoe but a pair of dark eyes. A lean, powerful body sheathed in close-fitting velvet and leather flying across the glistening ice.

'Holly and ivy, box and bay,' she whispered, 'put in the house for Christmas Day.'

There was a sudden commotion at the end of the gallery, a burst of activity as a group of men rushed inside, bringing in the cold of the day. Among them was the handsome young man who had winked at Anne the day before—and been soundly ignored.

And there was also Anton Gustavson, his skates slung over his shoulder, black waves of hair escaping from his fine velvet cap. They were full of loud laughter, noisy joviality.

The ladies all giggled, blushing prettily at the sight of them.

As Rosamund feared she did too. She felt her cheeks go warm, despite the sudden rush of cold wind. She ducked her head over her work, but there in the pearly mistletoe berries she still saw Anton's brown eyes, his teasing smile.

'Mistress Anne!' one of the men said. Rosamund peeked up to find it was the winker. He was even more good-looking up close, with long, waving golden-brown hair and emerald-green eyes. He smiled at Anne flirtatiously, but Rosamund thought she saw a strange tension at the edges of his mouth, a quickly veiled flash in his eyes. Perhaps she was not the only one harbouring secret romances. 'What do you do there?'

Anne would not look at him; instead she stared down at her hands as they fussed with the ribbons. 'Some of us must work, Lord Langley, and not go frolicking off ice-skating all day.'

'Oh aye, it looks arduous work indeed,' Lord Langley answered, merrily undeterred. He sat down at the end of the table, fiddling with a bit of ivy. On his index finger flashed a gold signet-ring embossed with the phoenix crest of the Knighton family.

Rosamund gasped. Anne's admirer was the Earl of Langley. And not old and crabbed at all.

She glanced at Anton, quite against her will; she didn't want to look at him, to remember their wager and her own foolish thoughts of kissing boughs and ice-skating. But she still felt compelled to look, to see what he was doing.

He stood by one of the windows, lounging casually against its carved frame as he watched his other companions laughing with the Marys. An amused half-smile curved his lips.

Rosamund's clasp tightened on her bough, and she had a sudden vision of standing with him beneath the green sphere, of gazing up at him, at those lips, longing to know what they would feel like on hers. She imagined touching his shoulders, heated, powerful muscles under fine velvet, sliding her hands down his chest as his lips lowered to hers…

And then his smile widened, as if he knew her very thoughts. Rosamund caught her breath and stared back down at the table, her cheeks flaming even hotter.

'We were not merely skating, Mistress Anne,' Anton said. 'We were sent by the Queen to search for the finest Yule log to be found.'

'And did you discover one?' Anne asked tartly, snatching the ivy from Lord Langley's hand.

He laughed, undeterred as he reached for a ribbon instead. 'Not as yet, but we are going out again this afternoon. Nothing but the very best will do for the Queen's Christmas—or that of her ladies.'

'You had best hurry, then, as Christmas Day is tomorrow.'

'Never fear, Mistress Anne,' Lord Langley said. 'I always succeed when I am determined on something.'

'Always?' said Anne. 'Oh, my lord, I do fear there is a first time for everything—even disappointment.'

Lord Langley's green eyes narrowed, but Anton laughed, strolling closer to the table. He leaned over Rosamund's shoulder, reaching out to pick up a sprig of holly.

Rosamund swallowed hard as his sleeve brushed the side of her neck, soft and alluring, warm and vital, yet snow-chilled at the same time.

'Ah, Lord Langley,' Anton said. 'I fear working with this holly has made the ladies just as prickly today. Perhaps we should retire before we get scratched.'

Lord Langley laughed too. 'Have they such thin skins in Sweden, Master Gustavson? We here have heavier armour against the ladies' barbs.'

'Is there armour heavy enough for such?' Anton asked.

Rosamund took the holly from his hand, careful not to let her fingers brush his. The ruby ring gleamed, reminding her of their wager. 'They say if the holly leaves are rounded the lady shall rule the house for the year. If barbed, the lord.'

'And which is this?' Anton took back the holly, running his thumb over the glossy green leaf. 'What does it signify if half the leaf is smooth, half barbed?'

'The impossible.' Lord Langley laughed. 'For each house can have only one ruler.'

'And in the Queen's house every leaf is smooth,' Anne said. 'Now, make yourselves of use and help us hang the greenery in the Great Hall.'

Anton tucked the holly into the loops of Rosamund's upswept hair, the edge of his hand brushing her cheek. 'There, Lady Rosamund,' he whispered. 'Now you are ready for the holiday.'

Rosamund gently touched the sprig, but did not draw it away. It rested there in her hair, a reminder. 'Best you beware my prickles, then, Master Gustavson. They may not be as obvious as this leaf, but they are there.'

'I am warned. But I am not a man to be frightened off by nettles, Lady Rosamund—not even thickets of them.' He laid his skates on the table, taking up a long swag of ivy and ribbon as he held out his hand to her. 'Will you show me where your decorations are to go? I should hate to ruin your decking of the halls.'

After a moment's hesitation, Rosamund nodded and took his hand, letting him help her rise. In her other hand she took up her kissing bough, and they followed the others from the gallery as a song rose up.

'So now is come our joyful feast, let every man be jolly!' they sang as they processed to the Great Hall, bearing their new decorations. 'Each room with ivy leaves is dressed, and every post with holly.'

Rosamund couldn't help being carried along by the song, by the happy anticipation of the season. She smiled up at Anton, surprised to find that he too sang along.

'Though some churls at our mirth repine, round your foreheads garlands twine, drown sorrow in a cup of wine and let us all be merry!'

'You know our English songs, Master Gustavson?' she asked as they came to the vast stone fireplace. He let go of her hand to fetch a stool, and Rosamund suddenly felt strangely bereft, cold, without him.

She flexed her fingers, watching as he set the stool

beneath the mantel. No fire blazed in the grate today, and they could stand close.

'My mother was English,' he said, climbing up on the stool. Rosamund handed him the end of the swag, which he attached to the elaborately carved wood. 'She taught everyone in our house her favourite old songs.'

'What else do you do at Christmas in Sweden?' she asked curiously. She followed along as he fastened the swag to the mantel, tying off the bows.

'Much the same as you do here, I suppose,' he said. 'Feasting, pageants and plays, gifting. And we have St Lucy's Day.'

'St Lucy's Day?'

'Aye, 'tis a very old tradition in Sweden, as St Lucy is one of our protectors. Every December we honour her with a procession led by a lady who portrays Lucy herself, who led Roman refugees into the catacombs with candles and then supplied them with food, until she was martyred for her efforts. The lady elected wears a white gown with red ribbons and a crown of candles on her head, and she distributes sweets and delicacies as everyone sings songs to St Lucy.'

Rosamund laughed, fascinated. 'It sounds delightful. We have no saints here now, though.'

'None in Sweden, either, except Lucy. And you would certainly be one of the ladies chosen to be St Lucy, Lady Rosamund.'

'Would I? I am sure my parents would say I am the least saint-like of females!'

Anton chuckled. 'You do seem rather stubborn, Lady Rosamund.'

'Oh, thank you very much!' Rosamund teased. 'Is another Swedish custom insulting ladies at Christmas time?'

'Not at all. Stubbornness is a trait that serves all of us well at a royal court.'

'True enough. I may not have been here long, but I do see that.'

'But you would surely be St Lucy because of your beauty. Lucy is always a lady with fair hair, blue eyes and the ability to convey sweetness and generosity. Those two attributes are surely not negated even by copious doses of stubbornness.'

Rosamund could feel that cursed blush creeping up again, making her face and throat hot in a way no one else's compliments could. He thought her beautiful? 'Perhaps, then, that is one tradition we could borrow from Sweden.'

'And so you should.' Anton stepped off the stool, examining their handiwork. 'Does it please you?'

'Does what please me?' she asked, still dazed. Pleased by him? She very much feared she might be. He was so different from Richard.

'The decorations.'

'Oh—aye. It looks most festive.'

'*Ganska nyttig.* Shall we find a place for that, then?'

He reached for the kissing bough Rosamund still held, half-forgotten. 'It is a silly thing,' she protested, stepping back. 'The Queen would surely not want it in her hall.'

'Why is that?' Anton persisted, moving closer until he could take the sphere of greenery from her hand. As he examined the mistletoe, the fluttering ribbons, a slow smile spread over his face. 'A kissing bough!'

Rosamund snatched it back. 'I told you it was silly.'

'My mother said when she was a girl she made kissing boughs at Christmas to divine who her future husband might be.'

'Well, that is not why I made it. I merely thought it looked pretty.'

Anton stepped even closer, leaning down to whisper in her ear. His cool breath stirred the curls at her temple, making her shiver. 'She also said if you kiss someone beneath it at midnight on Christmas Eve they will be your true love for the rest of the year.'

Rosamund closed her eyes, trying to ignore the way his voice whispered over her skin. 'I had best not hang it up, then. True love seems to wreak enough havoc here at Court.'

Anton laughed, taking the bough from her hand. 'Nay, it is much too pretty to hide. We will hang it over there, behind that tapestry. Only those who truly need it can find it there.'

Before she could protest, he carried it off. A tapestry depicting a bright scene of wine-making was looped up, revealing the gap between it and the panelled wall. Anton leaped up to attach the ribbon loop to a ripple in the carving.

The bough swayed there, all verdant-green and enticing. Anton unhooked the tapestry, letting it fall back into place before the little hidey-hole.

'There now, Lady Rosamund,' he said with a smile. 'Only we two know it is there.'

Their secret. Rosamund longed to run away as she had when she'd first seen him by the frozen pond. Yet she could not. It was as if she was bound to him, tied by loops of ivy and red ribbon. Caught by the dark glow of his eyes.

She touched the tip of her tongue to her dry lips, watching as his gaze narrowed on that tiny gesture.

'Is the Thames yet frozen through?' she queried softly.

'Very nearly,' he said roughly. 'They talk of a frost fair in the days to come.'

'A frost fair? There has not been one of those in many years, not since my mother was a child, I think.' Rosamund twined her hands in her velvet skirts, feeling suddenly bold. 'Then will you be able to teach me to skate, do you think?'

'You seem a quick enough learner to me, Lady Rosamund. And will I be able to dance at Twelfth Night?'

'That remains to be seen. Our first dancing lesson is not until tomorrow.'

'I very much look forward to it.'

Rosamund curtsied and hurried away. She too found she looked forward to their lessons. Lessons of *all* sorts.

Z'wounds! She had been so comfortable in her cozy life at Ramsay Castle. Now she felt so unsure of everything. She felt as if she balanced on the edge of some vast, unknown precipice, between her old self and a new self she did not yet see. Just one push would send her one way or the other.

Or she could jump. But that was probably for bolder souls than herself, much as she wished to.

She rushed out of the hall, turning towards the staircase that led back to the maids' apartment. But she went still as her foot touched the first step.

Anne stood in the darkness of the landing just above, deep in conversation with Lord Langley. Their voices were low and intense, as if they quarrelled. He reached for her hand, but she stepped back, shaking her head. Then she fled up the stairs, her footsteps clattering away.

Lord Langley swung round to come back down, and Rosamund shrank back against the wall, hoping he would not see her there in the dim light. He did not seem able to see anything. His handsome face, so alight with merriment earlier, was solemn, taut with anger.

'Bloody stubborn woman,' he muttered as he strode past her.

Rosamund lingered there for a moment, unsure what to do. Her own romantic life was so very confused, she was quite sure she could be of no help in anyone else's. But Anne was her friend, or as close as she had here at Court.

Feeling like she dove between Scylla and Charybdis, Rosamund climbed the stairs and made her way to the maids' dormitory.

Unlike last night, when the laughter and chatter had gone on for hours, the chamber was silent. All the other ladies were still decking the halls, and Anne lay alone on her bed, her back to the door.

She was very still, making no sound of tears or sighs. Rosamund tiptoed closer. 'Anne?' she said softly. 'Is something amiss?'

Anne rolled over to face her. Her eyes were dry but reddened, her hair escaping in dark curls from her headdress. 'Oh, Rosamund,' she said. 'Come, sit beside me.'

Rosamund perched on the edge of the bed, reaching into the embroidered pouch at her waist for a handkerchief in case it was needed.

'Tell me more about your sweetheart at home,' Anne said, sitting up against the bolsters. 'Is he very handsome?'

'Oh!' Rosamund said, startled by the request. She forced herself to remember Richard, the way he had smiled at her. A smile with no hidden depths and facets, unlike Anton Gustavson's.

'Aye,' she said slowly.

'Is he fair or dark? Tall?'

'Fair, and only middling tall.'

'But a fine kisser, I would wager.'

Rosamund laughed. 'Fine enough, I think.' Though she had little to compare him to.

'And he loves you. He wants to marry you and always has.'

Rosamund hesitated at that. 'He said he did, when last I saw him.' But then he had vanished, leaving her alone to argue their cause with her parents. The servants had said he had even quit the neighbourhood entirely in the autumn.

'You are fortunate, then,' Anne sighed.

'Does Lord Langley not want…?'

'I do not want to speak of him,' Anne interrupted. 'Not now. I would much rather hear of your love, Rosamund.'

Rosamund lay back with a sigh, staring up at the embroidered underside of the hangings as if she could read her answers in the looping flowers and vines. 'I have not heard from him in an age. I am not sure now I want to hear from him at all.'

'I would wager he has written to you but your parents intercepted the letters,' Anne said. 'That happened with my friend Penelope Leland when she wanted to marry Lord Pershing.'

'Truly?' Rosamund frowned. She had not thought of such a thing. 'How can I be sure?'

'Aye. We must find a way to contact him,' Anne said, her voice full of new excitement at coming up with a scheme. 'Once he knows where you are, he will surely come running to your side.'

Rosamund was not so certain. Her infatuation with Richard seemed to belong to someone else, a young girl with no knowledge of herself or of the world. But if it helped to distract Anne, and herself, she was willing to attempt it.

Perhaps then she would cease to drown in a pair of winter-dark eyes.

'Round your foreheads garlands twine, drown sorrow in a cup of wine, and let all be merry!'

Rosamund laughed helplessly as the entire Great Hall rang with song. It was quite obvious that the whole company had already drowned their sorrows copiously as the Christmas Eve banquet progressed. The long tables were littered with the remains of supper, with goblets that were emptied, and the musicians' songs were louder, faster than they'd been early in the evening.

The decorations of the hall, lit now by a blazing fire

and dozens of torches, fairly shimmered with rich reds, greens and golds, making the vast space a festive bower. Laughter was as loud as the song, and glances grew longer and bolder, ever more flirtatious, as the night went on.

Not everyone was happy, though, Rosamund noticed. The Austrians seemed rather ill at ease, though they tried gamely to enter into the spirit of the holiday. A few of the more Puritanical of the clergymen hovered at the edges of the bright throng, looking on with pinched expressions.

Surely they would be happier if everyone passed the holiday in solemn prayer, Rosamund thought, not frisking about with song and greenery, which echoed of the old days of popery. But Queen Elizabeth seemed not to notice at all; she sat on her dais, clapping in time to the song.

On the wall behind her was a large mural, an early Christmas gift from her minister, Walsingham. It was an allegory of the Tudor succession, centred on an en-throned Henry VIII, right here in the Great Hall of Whitehall, with a young Edward VI kneeling beside him. To his left was Queen Mary, with her Spanish husband King Phillip with Mars the god of war, all dark blacks, browns and muted yellows. To his right was Queen Elizabeth, with Peace trampling on a sword of discord, trailed by Plenty, spilling out her cornucopia. They gleamed in bright whites, silvers and golds.

Just as the Queen herself did tonight, presiding over her own feast of plenty and joy. She wore a gown of white satin, trimmed in white fur and sewn with pearls and tiny sapphire beads. She looked on the holiday she had wrought with a contented smile.

The others on the dais with her did not look so very sanguine. The Queen's cousin Lady Lennox, Margaret Stewart, sat to the Queen's left with her son, Lord Darnley, her ample frame once again swathed in black. He was handsome enough, Rosamund had to admit, with his pale-gold, poetic looks set off by his own fine black-velvet garments. But he looked most discontented, almost sulky, as if there was somewhere he would rather be. Chasing the servants into his bed, as Anne had said?

Next to them sat Lord Sussex and his wife, sworn enemies of Leicester, and thus united with Lady Lennox in their cause. On the Queen's other side was Lord Burghley and his serene wife Mildred, and the Queen's cousin, Lord Hunsdon, and his wife. The marital delegations were at their own tables tonight, just below the royal dais.

Rosamund peeked at Anton over the edge of her goblet, remembering the kissing bough that hung behind the tapestry, known only to the two of them. She remembered the warmth of his hand as it had touched hers, the brilliant light of his smile.

He smiled now as he listened to the song, his long fingers tapping out the time on the table. His ruby ring caught the light, gleaming like the holly berries. He saw her looking over and his smile widened.

Rosamund smiled back. She could not help herself. Despite her nervousness, her uncertainty of life at Court and what she should do, every time she looked at Anton Gustavson she felt lighter, freer.

There was still her family, her home, her duties—still

Richard out there somewhere, as Anne had reminded her. But when Anton smiled at her for just an instant she forgot all of that. He made her want to laugh at the wondrous surprise of life, the delightful mysteries of men.

But she only forgot for an instant. She turned away from him, and found Anne watching her quizzically. Rosamund just shrugged at her. She remembered Anne's red eyes all over Lord Langley and some mysterious romance gone sour. Rosamund wanted none of that for herself, or for her friend. Not now. Not when it was Christmas.

The large double doors of the hall burst open in a flurry of drums. Acrobats tumbled through, a blur of bright-coloured silks and spangles, tinkling bells and rattles. They somersaulted down the aisles between the tables, leaping up to flip backwards through the air.

As everyone applauded their antics, another figure appeared in the doorway, a broad-shouldered man swathed in a multi-coloured cloak and hood. His face was covered by a white leather Venetian mask painted in red-and-green swirls.

He rattled a staff of bells as the acrobats tumbled around him.

The Queen rose to her feet. 'What do you do here at our Court?' she demanded.

'I am the Lord of Misrule! I am the high and mighty Prince of Purpoole, Archduke of Stapulia, Duke of High and Nether Holborn, Knight of the Most Heroical Order of the Helmet and sovereign of the same,' the cloaked man announced, his voice amplified and distorted behind the mask. 'For this holiday season, I declare all kingdoms my dominion—the realm of merriment.'

The Queen laughed. 'The realm of chaos, I would vow! Very well, my Lord of Misrule—let your reign begin. But pay heed that it will only last until Twelfth Night.'

The Lord of Misrule bowed, and his tumbling minions dashed amongst the tables to claim partners for the dance. Anne, the Marys, Catherine Knyvett, even Mistress Eglionby, were all borne away into a wild, disorganised galliard.

Rosamund watched, astonished, as the Lord of Misrule himself came to her side, holding out his gloved hand to her. She stared up into that eerily masked face, searching for some clue to his identity, yet there was none at all. Even his eyes were shadowed, set deep behind that painted visage.

'Will you dance with me, my lady?' he asked, shaking those bells.

Rosamund slowly nodded, taking his gloved hand and letting him lead her to the centre of the dance. The steps were familiar, but the patterns disorganised, constantly shifting and reforming. The dancers lurched into each other and reeled away, laughing.

The Lord of Misrule twirled Rosamund around in an ever-growing circle, faster and faster, until the whole room spun in a wild blur. His hands held tightly to hers, in a grip that was almost painful, but she was pressed in on all sides by the other dancers and could not escape.

Her breath felt tight in her lungs, constricted by her tight bodice, and her heart pounded until she could scarcely hear the music. The brilliant lights of the banquet dimmed and she suddenly felt like a wild bird beating her wings against confining bars.

At last she was able to free her hands from her unseen partner and break away from the close patterns of the dance. Once out of the hot press of the crowd, she wasn't sure where to go. She just needed to breathe again.

She lifted the heavy hem of her skirt, dashing across the room past the knots of courtiers who did not dance. They were too busy with their own wine-soaked laughter to pay her any heed; even the Queen was occupied with watching the dance. Rosamund ducked behind one of the tapestries, wedging herself into the small, safe space between the heavy cloth and the wood-panelled wall.

She leaned back against the solid support of that wall, closing her eyes. The music and laughter was muffled, as if heard from under water, distorted by the thud of her heartbeat in her ears. Everything had changed so fast, the evening going from merry holiday-making to surreal strangeness in only a moment. Who *was* that man? He was indeed a Lord of Misrule.

She pressed her hand to her white silk bodice that was stiff with silver embroidery, willing her heart to slow, her breath to flow easily.

Suddenly, there was a rush of warm air, the scent of smoke, pine boughs and clean soap, as the tapestry was brushed aside. Rosamund gasped as she opened her eyes, afraid that the masked man had followed her into her sanctuary. She even went up on her toes in her velvet shoes, prepared to flee.

But it was not the Lord of Misrule who slid behind the tapestry with her. It was Anton. She had only a glimpse of his tall, lean figure, the dark-star gleam of his eyes, before the cloth dropped behind him. They were enclosed in their own little shadowed world.

Rosamund found she was not frightened, though. She felt no urge to run from him. Instead, she could at last breathe easily.

She was no longer alone.

'Rosamund?' he said quietly. 'Are you unwell?'

'I…' She swayed closer to him, drawn by the clean scent of him, by his warm, silent strength. 'I could not breathe out there.'

'I, too, mislike crowds,' he said. 'But we are safe here.'

His arms came around her, drawing her close, and she *did* feel safe. She rested her forehead against his velvet-covered chest, closing her eyes as she listened to his strong, steady heartbeat. It echoed her own heart, binding them together there in the dark.

She slid her arms around his waist, feeling the supple strength of him bonding to her. The chaotic dance outside vanished, and she had only this one moment in the eye of the storm.

She felt him kiss the top of her head, and she tilted her face up to his. His lips lightly touched her brow, her temple, the edge of her cheekbone, leaving tiny droplets of flame wherever he touched. Her breath caught again, and she shivered with the sudden force of her weakness, her desire for more of those kisses, more of *him*.

At last his lips touched hers with glancing, alluring

kisses—once, twice. And again, a slightly deeper
caress, a taste that made her moan for more. That small
sound against his lips made him groan, and he dragged
her even closer until their bodies were pressed tight
together. Every curve and angle fit perfectly, as if they
were meant to be just so.

She strained up on tiptoe, her lips parting beneath his.
His tongue, light and skilled, touched the tip of hers
before deepening the kiss, binding her to him even closer.

Rosamund twined her arms around his neck, her
fingers driving into the softness of his hair, holding him
to her as if she feared he would escape her. But he made
no move to leave her. Their kiss turned desperate,
heated, blurry, full of a primitive need she did not even
know was in her. Her whole body felt heavy and hot,
narrowed to the one perfect moment of their kiss.

He pressed her back to the wall, lifting her up until
her layers of skirts fell away and she wrapped her stock-
inged legs around his hips. He rocked into the curve of
her body, his velvet breeches abrading her bare thighs
above her garters. The friction was delicious, and she
moaned against his open mouth, wanting more of that
feeling, that wondrous oblivion.

His lips trailed wetly from hers, along her jaw and
the arch of her throat as she leaned her head back on
the wall, leaving herself open to him. His tongue
swirled lightly in the hollow of her throat, just where
her pulse pounded, before he nudged aside her sheer-
silk partlet to kiss the slope of her breasts.

'Oh!' she gasped. She rocked her hips into his,
clasping his hair even tighter as his teeth nipped at her

sensitive skin and his tongue soothed the tiny sting. His erection was heavy, taut as iron against her through layers of velvet and leather.

She opened her eyes, staring up at the kissing bough as it swayed above her head. It had worked its enchantment on her indeed, weaving a sensual spell that made her sure she would do anything, anything at all, to feel more of this. Of him.

She closed her eyes again, bending her head to kiss his tumbled hair. He rested his forehead against the wall beside her, his breath ragged in her ear. Slowly, slowly, she slid her feet back to the floor, feeling the earth solid beneath her again. She heard the music outside their haven, louder, more discordant than ever, the pounding thunder of dancing feet.

She tried to ease away from Anton. She was so close to him she could not think at all, could not stop all her senses from reeling crazily. But his hands tightened on her waist, holding her against him as their breath slowed.

'Nay,' he gasped, his accent heavy. 'Don't move. Not yet.'

Rosamund nodded, leaning against his shoulder. His entire body was rigid, perfectly still, as if he struggled to find his control.

''Twas the kissing bough,' she whispered.

He laughed tightly. 'Perhaps your Puritans are right in trying to ban them from the halls, then.'

It felt as if their wild kiss had released something inside Rosamund, some bold imp she had not even realised was a part of her. 'But where would be the merriness in that?'

'You are a most enticing winter-fairy, Lady Rosamund Ramsay,' he said, kissing her cheek quickly. 'But will the bough erase all memory of this madness tomorrow?'

Rosamund did not know. She half-hoped so; this had been a true moment of madness, one that made her understand the poet's sonnets after all. Passion was an unstoppable force, one that clouded all sense. But it would be a great pity to lose the sensation of his caress.

'We must all to church in the morning with the Queen,' she answered. 'And reflect on our mistakes.'

'I fear I would need more time than one Christmas morning for *that*,' he said wryly.

'Are your mistakes so many, then?'

'Oh, my winter fairy, they are myriad.'

And she had just added them, and to her own. She edged away from him, suddenly cold and very tired as she smoothed her gown and hair and straightened her partlet. What would tomorrow bring? She had no idea. It was as if Misrule had indeed taken control of the world, a world she had once thought so comfortable and ordered.

'I must go back to my duties before I'm missed,' she said.

He nodded, the movement a small flurry in the darkness. He swept aside the edge of the tapestry, and Rosamund eased past him back into the light and noise of the hall. The Lord of Misrule and his acrobats had vanished, but the dancing still went on. Queen Elizabeth sat at her dais, talking with a lady who stood just beside her.

Rosamund blinked in the sudden change from shadow to light. She could see only that the lady who talked with the Queen was tall and reed-thin, clad in purple velvet and black silk that went with her black hair drawn back tight from her pale, oval face. She was almost like a raven among bright-plumed peacocks.

Then Rosamund was startled to recognise her. She was Celia Sutton, the widow of Richard's elder brother. She had seldom been seen in the neighbourhood since the death of her husband, though she and Rosamund had once been friends of a sort. Yet here she suddenly was at Court, still clad in mourning for a husband who had died in the spring, leaving Richard heir to the estate. Whatever did she do here now?

'Celia!' Rosamund murmured aloud.

'Ah, Master Gustavson,' Queen Elizabeth called, gesturing to Anton. 'There you are. Your cousin, Mistress Sutton, has arrived at our Court just in time for Christmas. I am sure she is most eager to greet you.'

Rosamund's gaze flew to Anton. Celia was his cousin—the same one who disputed his English inheritance?

His jaw was tight, his eyes utterly opaque as he looked at the Queen and at Celia. She watched him too, her lips drawn close.

'My cousin Anton,' she said slowly. 'So, we meet at last.' Her gaze slid past Anton to Rosamund, and she finally smiled. 'Rosamund! You *are* here. We could scarcely credit that your parents would part with you.'

'Only to serve the Queen,' Rosamund said. 'How do you fare, Celia?'

'Well enough, now that I have come to petition for justice—' Celia answered.

'We will not talk of such solemn matters as petitions, not at Christmas,' Queen Elizabeth interrupted with a wave of her feathered fan. 'We will speak of this later, privily, Master Gustavson and Mistress Sutton. In the meantime, I hope the two of you might find time to converse in a civil manner. There is such resemblance between you. Family should not quarrel so, as I well know.'

Anton bowed. 'As Your Grace commands,' he said affably. Yet Rosamund heard tension laced within his polite words. What was his connection with Celia? What were his feelings as he stood there before all the Court?

'Very good,' the Queen said. 'Come! It is time we retired for the evening, I think.'

As she stepped from the dais on Lord Burghley's arm, Rosamund and the other maids falling into their place behind her, the doors to the hall flew open once again. But it was not the Lord of Misrule, it was Lord Leicester who stood there, his dark, curling hair mussed, his green-satin doublet torn and streaked with dust and his eyes full of flashing anger.

'My Lord Leicester,' the Queen said. 'How quickly you transform yourself!'

He gave her a low bow, his shoulders still held stiff, his fist opening and closing, as if he longed for a sword. 'Indeed I do not, Your Grace. I have worn this garb all evening, though not by my will.'

A small frown creased the Queen's white brow.

'What do you mean? Were you not the Lord of Misrule here, not an hour ago?'

'I was to be, by Your Grace's order,' Leicester answered. 'But some churl locked me in the stables, as I made sure all was in readiness for the hunt tomorrow. I have only just escaped. When I do discover the villain…'

The Queen's hand tightened on her fan, a flush spreading over her cheeks. 'Then who was in our hall?'

'Come, Your Grace!' Burghley suddenly urged, gesturing for the Queen's guard to surround her in a tight phalanx and escorting her quickly from the hall. 'We must get you securely to your chamber immediately, where you can be safe.'

Leicester snatched up a sword from one of the tables, brandishing it in the air. 'We will find this varlet, Your Grace, I vow to you!'

'Robin, no!' the Queen gasped, reaching out her hand to him as she was swept from the room. Rosamund hurried after them with the other ladies, suddenly cold with fear as she remembered the strange Lord of Misrule, that painfully tight clasp of his hands on hers.

Even the Queen seemed uncharacteristically flustered, glancing back at Leicester as she was pushed through the door, the room in disarray and confusion behind her.

Whatever would happen next? The whole Court seemed to have gone utterly mad.

Chapter Six

Christmas Day, December 25

Anton stared down at the garden from the window of the sitting room of the Swedish apartments. It was quite early yet; the walkways and flowerbeds were shrouded in curls of frosty morning fog blending with the smoke from the chimneys to form a thick, silver veil. No one was yet abroad except for one lady who strolled the paths.

Celia Sutton. She walked along slowly swathed in a black cloak, the hood thrown back to reveal her smooth, dark hair. Her head was bent, her hands clasped tightly together as if in deep spiritual contemplation on this Christmas Day—or, more likely, plotting her next move in their battle over Briony Manor.

He had never met her before, this cousin of his, the daughter of his mother's brother, yet he felt he knew her. They had exchanged letters for months, ever since their grandfather's will had been read and Briony had been revealed as Anton's. Letters that were full of a palpable anger he knew could not be assuaged while they remained strangers to each other.

The opportunity to travel to England with the marital delegation had been a most welcome one. King Eric had no chance of marrying Queen Elizabeth, everyone knew but him that after his last failed mission when the Queen had been new-crowned. If even the king's charming brother Duke John had not been able to finish the deal back then, none could. But it was perfect for Anton's personal business of claiming Briony Manor and making a new home there, a new start where he could right old wrongs.

And meeting his cousin, the only family he now possessed.

His lost family despised him as a stranger. He'd seen it in her eyes last night, those dark eyes so like his own and those of his mother. It would not be easy forging new links here in England. But he could not go back to Sweden.

Anton frowned as he watched Celia wend her way around hedges and fountains, her black cloak like a raven's wings in the cold mist. He thought of his home in Sweden, the ancient, chilly stone castle on the shores of a frozen lake, solitary and hard. Ruled over by an even colder father.

Roald Gustavson was a man of most uncertain temper, of no human emotion or feeling. Fortunately for Anton and his mother, he'd usually been away from home over the years, leaving them to their own devices. Anton's days had been spent studying with his tutors, skating on the lake and hunting in the forest that lurked behind the castle.

At night, his mother had told him tales of her English home, enticing stories of green woods and lanes, of people of learning and music; old stories of knights and quests; new stories of her own childhood visits to Briony Manor. Briony sounded like a magical place as the land of distant as Arthur and his knights. But his mother had insisted it was a real place, and one he would see some day. One day it would be his reality too, and the cold castle a memory.

And, when he was older and she'd been dying, she'd told him secrets too—secrets that had made him more determined to come to England, to Briony Manor. To find a new beginning.

His path had not been easy. It had been forged in battle against the Russians, in long days at the court of a king going mad. A knife's edge of a court, where there'd been none of the colour and merriment that surrounded the English queen's.

Much as he'd hated the place, he'd had to see to his father's castle too. After his father's death, before he'd gone off to battle, Anton had put his father's own cousin as steward of the place. Now he cared not if he ever saw it again.

Briony Manor was to be his new home. And, much as he hated to disoblige a lady, Celia Sutton would not stop him. She had dower property from her late husband; Briony was all he had now.

He watched as his newfound cousin turned back towards the palace, and he remembered how she had looked last night as she'd talked to the Queen: determined—just as determined as he was. There'd been no eager family reunion there!

And Rosamund Ramsay knew Celia. Were they friends, then? Co-conspirators of some sort?

If that was so, they were not very good at it, as Rosamund had obviously been surprised by Celia's appearance at Court. But that did not preclude them from being confidantes. And that meant he had to be very careful around Rosamund and not be drawn in by the warm, welcoming glow of her sky-blue eyes, the eager passion of her kiss.

Ah, yes—that kiss. Anton scowled as he remembered last night, the two of them wrapped around each other in the heated, secret darkness. The sudden rush of desire had taken him by surprise, but it had been no less potent for being unexpected. Indeed, it had been building between them like a spark grown to a roaring flame since he'd first glimpsed her by that pond.

The taste of her soft lips, the way her body felt pressed to his, the smell of her rose perfume—it was intoxicating, wondrous. He wanted more and yet more of her, wanted everything she could give. Her body, her smiles, her laughter—her secrets.

But she would surely demand the same of him in return, and that he could not give. Not when she knew Celia Sutton and when she was a loyal servant of Queen Elizabeth. His secrets were buried too deep, and they could cost him everything he wanted if he grew incautious. He had learned from his mother's mistake, and put the demands of his head above his heart. He had come here to find a sort of justice for his mother, to retrieve her estate and start a new life. He could not abandon that mission.

That left the question—what *could* he do about Rosamund Ramsay? He could not avoid her; there was the Queen's silly wager. The Court was too small, too intimate, to maintain distance from her for long.

There was yet one more consideration too—the mystery of the Lord of Misrule, the masked figure who had taken Leicester's place then disappeared. The plot was a strange one, and thick with the miasma of some sinister intent. The Queen was well guarded, but what of Rosamund? The villain had danced with her, after all, and she had seemed frightened of him. It made anger stir deep in Anton's heart, a burning desire to protect her from anything that could ever frighten her.

He folded his arms across his chest, frowning as he stared out at the empty garden. He had to be cautious, to be watchful. He could protect Rosamund from the Lord of Misrule and see what she knew of Celia's doings.

Without letting a lower part of his anatomy rule his brain again.

'I am no shivering coward, Cecil!' Queen Elizabeth cried. 'I will not let some misguided mischief ruin my Christmas.'

As Rosamund looked on, astonished, the Queen slammed her fist down on her dressing table, rattling Venetian-glass bottles and pots, upending her own jewel case. Pearl ropes and ruby brooches spilled out onto the floor, and maidservants scrambled to scoop them up.

William Cecil, Lord Burghley, leaned on his

walking stick, a look of long-suffering patience on his bearded face.

Rosamund stared at the scene—the Queen clad in her fur-trimmed bedrobe with her hair half-down as her ladies scrambled to ready her for the day, the bedchamber strewn with the results of her temper, tossed shoes, spilled pearl-powder, terrified faces.

She feared her own face might be one of them. Anne had told her the Queen had fits of pique at least once or twice a day, but they soon passed and she calmly turned to her business. The trick was to stay out of her way, as one would shelter from a rainstorm until the thunderclouds drifted away. So Rosamund stood half-hidden behind the looped-up bed curtains, clutching at a stack of prayer books as she watched the scene.

She doubted she could ever be as sanguine as Lord Burghley. No doubt he had witnessed such storms many times before and knew ways to persuade the Queen to do things for her own good. Today he tried to urge her to curtail the elaborate Christmas festivities in order to see to her safety. To stay guarded in her privy rooms until the mysterious Lord of Misrule was captured and questioned.

It would surely not be long, not with a furious Lord Leicester and his men tearing the palace apart. But the Queen would hear none of it.

'Your Grace,' Burghley said. 'None could ever accuse you of being a shivering coward. But it would not be wise to go among crowds when there is some plot at work.'

'Plot!' Elizabeth snorted. 'It was hardly a *plot*, just some holiday mischief against Leicester, who could certainly stand to be taken down a peg or two, anyway.'

'I cannot disagree with Your Grace about that,' Burghley said wryly. 'Yet we cannot know if it was solely a prank against Robert Dudley, or if deeper forces are at work. The fact that some villain was able to infiltrate your feast is most alarming. With the Spanish, the French and the Queen of Scots all in communication...'

'Do not speak to me of the Queen of Scots!' Elizabeth shouted. A maidservant who had cautiously begun to pin up her red hair hastily backed away. 'I am sick of the sound of her name. First Lady Lennox constantly beseeching me to let her useless son go to Edinburgh, and now you. Can I not enjoy my Christmas at least without *her* intervening?'

'I fear we cannot stop her from "intervening",' Burghley said. 'She is a constant threat, Your Grace, just over the border as she is and with France at her back. Her ambition has long been well-known.'

'If she would do as I say and marry Lord Leicester, her ambition would be curtailed,' the Queen muttered, reaching for a scent bottle. The smell of violets filled the chamber as she dabbed at it distractedly.

'Do you really think she will do that?' Burghley said.

Elizabeth shrugged. 'Not with Leicester distracted by some silly prank.'

'And what if it is not some silly prank, Your Grace?'

The Queen sighed. 'Very well. Add more guards to the chapel and the corridors. But that is all I agree to!'

'It would be best for you to stay here in your apartments.'

'Nay!' Elizabeth shook her head fiercely, dislodging

the pins that had just been eased into her hair. 'It is Christmas Day, probably dear Mistress Ashley's last, and I want her to enjoy it without worry. Time enough for doom and gloom later.'

'Very well, Your Grace.' Burghly bowed and departed, leaving the ladies to hover indecisively.

Until the Queen again pounded on her table, tumbling the jewels back to the floor. 'Why are you all standing about so slack-jawed? We must to church! And those sleeves will *not* do, fetch the gold ones.'

At last she was dressed in her fine green-and-gold garments, her hair bound up in a gold-net caul and jewelled band, her fur-lined cloak draped over her shoulders. She held out her beringed hand for her prayer book, which Rosamund hastened to give her.

'Thank you, Lady Rosamund,' the Queen said. 'Will you walk with me to the chapel?'

'Of course, Your Grace,' Rosamund said, surprised. Her allotted place was at the end of the procession with the other maids. But she could hardly protest with the Queen. She stayed by Elizabeth's side as they left the bedchamber and made their slow way through the Presence and Privy Chambers and along the gallery, where other courtiers joined the retinue.

'You danced with our unknown Lord of Misrule last night, did you not?' the Queen asked quietly, smiling and nodding at the crowds who made their obeisances to her.

'Yes, Your Grace,' Rosamund answered. She had been woken far too early that morning by Burghley to be questioned about it, too. She had no more to add, and was afraid of what might happen if they thought she did know more.

'You have no idea who he was?'

'None, Your Grace,' she said, giving the same answer she'd given Burghley—the only answer she had. 'He was masked, and I have not been at Court long enough to recognise anyone by their mannerisms.'

'It was probably not a courtier anyway,' the Queen said with a sigh. 'If you see anything else, anything at all, you will tell me immediately.'

'Of course, Your Grace.'

'In the meantime, I believe you know our newest arrival at Court, Mistress Celia Sutton?'

'Her family lives very near mine at Ramsay Castle, Your Grace. I do know her a little.'

'She has brought us a petition, one of dozens to be considered this holiday. Perhaps you will speak with her about it and tell me your thoughts.'

'Certainly, if Your Grace wishes it,' Rosamund said slowly. She had no idea what sort of petition Celia could be bringing to the Queen, or what she, Rosamund, could think of it. But if she helped the Queen then perhaps in turn the Queen could help her—and Richard.

If that was what she still wanted…

Rosamund remembered well the night before, kissing Anton Gustavson behind the tapestry. Nay, not just kissing, wrapping her bare legs around his hips, feeling his mouth on her breast, the hot, heady plunge down into desperate desire. A wild recklessness that was unlike her but could not be denied. She had wanted Anton, wanted him madly, beyond all reason.

She wanted him still.

She had been awake all night, pretending to sleep as

she'd listened to the whispers of the other maids. In reality, she thought of nothing but him, of his kiss, the way his hands had felt as they'd slid against her naked skin. Of all the things she wished he would do to her—naughty, wicked, delicious things she had never dared think of before. That she had never wished of Richard. And that was what really worried her. She had come here to serve the Queen, to prove herself to her family again, not get them into even more trouble.

Nay, she had to be very, very careful.

Her cheeks felt hot again as they turned onto yet another corridor, and she cursed her pale skin as she clutched at her prayer book until its leather edges bit into her hand. She was a most disloyal lover. Surely it was very wrong of her to think such things of the dark, dashing Swede, a man she had just met, when she had vowed to defy her parents for Richard?

Perhaps it was the romantic intrigues of Court invading her thoughts and emotions, turning her from herself, from her plans for the future. Aye, that was it. She needed to talk to Celia, to hear news of home.

Rosamund filed into the chapel, taking her seat on the bench behind the Queen's high-backed chair with the other maids. Even in the chapel—a long, vast space of soaring, ribbed ceilings, and marble columns draped with royal standards—there were gossiping whispers, but they were hushed. A breath of wind blew along the aisles between the cushioned benches.

Rosamund folded her hands atop the prayer book in her lap, staring up at the window high above the altar to the east of the chapel. But the reds and blues of the

Crucifixion and Resurrection scenes were muted in the grey day and gave little scope for contemplation or distraction.

Plus the nape of her neck prickled, as if someone watched her most intently. She rubbed at the tingling spot, peeking surreptitiously over her shoulder.

Anton grinned at her from his place in one of the galleries. Rosamund instinctively wanted to laugh in return, but she pressed her lips tightly, returning her stare to her hands.

She had been so busy with her own feelings about their kiss, about what it meant, but now she wondered what *he* thought. What he felt. Was he, too, moved by what had happened between them? Or was it a mere diversion to him, one of many? She remembered all the ladies who followed him about, and feared she was becoming one of them.

Just another reason to stay away from him. If she could.

She peeked at him again, to find that he still watched her. One of his dark brows arched, as if in question. But she had no answers, either for him or herself.

She faced forward again as Master Buckenridge, one of the Queen's chaplains, climbed into the pulpit. 'On this blessed day of the Nativity,' he began, 'we must always reflect on the Lord's many gifts to us for the year ahead…'

'What then doth make the element so bright? The heavens are come down upon earth to live!'

The Yule log was borne into the Great Hall, carried on the shoulders of a dozen strong men. Anton and

Lord Langley had indeed found a grand one, Rosamund thought, applauding with the rest of the company. As long and thick as a ceiling beam, the great, oak log was adorned with greenery and garlands tied up with ribbons. It would be lowered into the great fireplace, where it would burn until the end of the holiday on Twelfth Night.

And, as it burst into light, who knew what would happen?

Rosamund smiled as she watched the log being paraded around the hall, its streamers waving merrily. She remembered Christmases at Ramsay Castle; her father and his men had gone out to proudly carry back the largest, thickest Yule log from their own forest. Her mother had laughingly protested that it was too big even to come through the door. And the entire household would sing as the embers from last year's Christmas had set it alight.

Suddenly, she was engulfed by a cold wave of homesickness, of sadness that she was not there with her family to share their holiday. She felt terribly alone in the very midst of the noisy crowd, adrift.

Rosamund eased away from the others as they pressed towards the log until she could slip out of the doors and into the comparatively quiet corridor. There was no one there to see her as she hurried towards the Waterside Gallery. No one to see the sheen of tears in her eyes.

She furiously scrubbed at those tears, brushing them away as she dashed up a narrow staircase. She was a fool to cry, to miss something she'd never really had in the first place. Once, she had imagined her parents had truly cared for her and her happiness. She had envied their long marriage, their contented home, and had imagined she could have the same. It would never have been with Richard, though; she saw that now.

'It is only the holiday,' she muttered to herself as she tiptoed into the gallery. 'Everyone turns melancholy and sentimental at Christmas.'

She stopped by one of the high windows, leaning on the narrow sill as she peered outside. No one was in the gallery today; they were all in the Great Hall to watch the Yule log being brought in, and she had the echoing space to herself.

The gallery was narrow but very long, running along the Thames to afford a view of the life of the river, the boats and barges that constantly passed by. But now the great river was frozen over, a silver-blue expanse that sparkled under the weak sunlight. Only a small rivulet of slushy water ran along the centre.

Soon it would be frozen, through, solid enough to walk or ride on. Assuredly solid enough to skate on.

Rosamund wondered what it felt like, gliding along as if on glass, twirling through the cold air, her hand anchored in Anton's as he pulled her along. She knew his body now, the lean, flexible strength of it. He knew the ice; could he keep her safe on it too? Teach her his secrets?

'Rosamund?' she heard him say, as if her visions made him real. 'Is something amiss?'

She glanced over her shoulder to see him standing at the end of the gallery. He wore black as usual, fine velvet with an almost blue sheen set off with pewter-grey satin trim that made his dark hair gleam.

'Nay,' she said. 'It was just too warm in the hall. I needed some fresh air.'

'Very wise,' he said, walking slowly towards her. His movements had a powerful, cat-like grace, reminding her of her ice dreams. 'We should save our breath for dancing.'

Rosamund laughed. 'And you will need it. The volta is most challenging.'

He smiled at her, leaning against the window sill at her side. 'Do you think I am not equal to it?'

She took a deep, unsteady breath, remembering the strength of his hands as he'd grasped her waist, lifting her against him as she'd wound her legs around his hips. 'I think you have a fair chance of succeeding.'

'Only fair? You have not a high estimation of my skills, then.'

On the contrary, Rosamund thought wryly. His 'skills' were of a high calibre indeed. 'I am sure you will be able to dance by Twelfth Night. But when can we skate on the Thames?'

He peered out of the window, his dark eyes narrowed as he gauged the view of the river. 'Not long now, I think. But I should hate to try it too soon and run into danger. Not when you have not tried skating before.'

It is too soon; Rosamund remembered her father saying this about Richard. *You do not know him well enough to know your own mind. He is not the one for you.* She sensed, deep down, that Anton was not as Richard was, was not shallow. He was like the river under the ice, all hidden currents that promised escape and wondrous beauty such as she had never known. That was what made him so very dangerous.

'You look sad, Rosamund,' Anton said, turning his intent gaze onto her. 'You *are* unwell.'

She shook her head. 'I am not ill. I was just thinking of my family, my home. Christmas is a very merry time there.'

'And this is your first holiday away from them?'

'Nay. Sometimes, when I was a very small child, really before I can remember, my parents would come to Court. My father served the Queen's father and her brother. But in the last few years we have always been together. My father takes special pride in his Yule log, and my mother would always have me help her make wreaths and garlands to put all over the house. And, on Christmas night, all the neighbours come to a feast in our hall, and it is…'

Rosamund paused, the homesickness upon her again. 'But I will not be there tonight.'

Anton leaned closer to her, his shoulder brushing hers. Rosamund blinked up at him, startled to read understanding in his eyes. Sympathy. 'It is a difficult thing, to feel far from home. From where one belongs.'

'Aye,' she said. 'But your home is much farther than mine, I fear. You must think I am ridiculous, to be so sad when I am here at Court, surrounded by my own countrymen and all this festivity.'

'I do not miss Sweden,' he answered. 'But if I had a family like yours I would long for them, too.'

'A family like mine?'

''Tis obvious that you love them, Rosamund, as they

must love you. I've often wondered what it would feel like to have a home such as that. A place to truly belong, not just possess. A place where there are well-loved traditions, shared hopes, comfortable days.' He smiled at her. 'And feasts for the neighbours.'

'I…' Rosamund stared at him in astonishment. He described so exactly her own secret hopes, the dreams she had come to feel were impossible in an uncertain world such as theirs. 'That sounds wondrous indeed. Yet I fear it is an impossible dream.'

'Is it truly? And here I thought your England was a land of dreams. Of families like yours.'

'But what of your own family?'

His lips tightened. 'My family is dead, I fear. Yet my mother, she left me tales of her homeland here. Of, as you say, impossible dreams.'

Rosamund watched him, suddenly deeply curious. What was his family like—his home, his past? Where did he truly come from? What other dreams did he hold? She so wanted to know more of him, to know everything. To see what else they shared. 'What tales did she tell you, Anton?'

But the moment of quiet, intense intimacy was gone, vanished like a rare snowflake drifting towards earth. He gave her a careless smile.

'Far too many to tell now,' he said. 'Don't we have a great deal of work to do if I am to dance a volta on Twelfth Night?'

Rosamund sensed he would share no more glimpses of his soul now, and she should guard hers better. 'Quite right. Come, we will begin our lessons, then.'

'Just as you say, my lady,' he said, giving her an elaborate bow as he offered his hand with a flourish. 'I am yours to command.'

Rosamund laughed. She doubted he was anyone's to command at all, despite the fact that he was here on an errand for his king. But she would play along for the hour. She took his hand, leading him to the centre of the gallery.

As his fingers closed over hers, she had to remind herself that they were here to dance. To win—or, rather, lose—a wager, not to hide behind tapestries and kisses. To fall deep, deep into that blissful forgetfulness of passion. To leave behind the Court, the Queen, all she owed her family, all the careful balancing that life at Whitehall was. She wanted him, and that could not be. Not here, not now.

'Now,' she said sternly, as much to herself as him. 'We begin with a basic galliard. Imagine the music like this— one, *two*, one, *two*, three. Right, left, right, left, and jump, landing with one leg ahead of the other. Like so.'

She demonstrated, and he followed her smoothly, landing in a vigorous leap.

'Very good,' Rosamund said, laughing. 'Are you certain you do not know how to dance?'

'Nay. You are merely a fine teacher, Lady Rosamund.'

'We shall see, for now we come to the difficult part. We take two bars of music now to move into the volta position.' Rosamund drew in a deep breath, trying to brace herself for the next steps.

Her parents considered the volta a scandalous Italian sort of dance, and had only allowed her to learn it when Master Geoffrey had insisted it was essential at Court, the Queen's favourite dance. But Master Geoffrey was an older, mincing, exacting man who tended to have loud, ridiculous tantrums when frustrated by her slowness. She had a feeling that dancing the volta with Anton would be a rather different experience.

'Now, let go of my hand and face me, like so,' she said, trying to be stern and tutor-like.

'And what do I do now?' he said, smiling down at her as they stood close.

Rosamund swallowed hard. 'You—you place one hand on my waist, like this.' She took his right hand in hers, laying his fingers just where her stiff, satin bodice curved in. 'And your other hand goes on my back, above my…'

'Your—what?'

'Here.' She put his hand above her bottom, her whole body feeling taut and brittle, as if she might snap as soon as he moved his body against hers.

His smile flickered as if he, too, felt that crackling tension. 'And what do you do?'

Stand and stare like a simpleton, mayhap? Rosamund could hardly remember. 'I put my hand here, on your shoulder. Now, you face me thus, and I face to the side. We turn with a forward step, both with the same foot at the same time. One, two…'

But Anton got ahead of her, stepping forward before she did. His leg tangled in her skirts and she tilted off-balance, falling towards the floor.

'Oh!' she gasped, clutching at his shoulders. His balance from skating on the ice stood him in good stead, though, for he caught her swiftly in his arms, swinging her upright before she could drag both of them down.

'You see why I do not dance?' he muttered hoarsely, his gaze on her parted lips as he held her above him, suspended above time. 'Disaster always ensues.'

Rosamund shook her head. 'You give up too easily, Master Gustavson.'

'Me? I never give up. Not when something is of importance.'

'Then we should begin again,' she whispered, her mouth dry.

He nodded, slowly lowering her to her feet until they once again had themselves in position.

'After—after the step, which we take *together*,' she said, 'We turn with another step. Hop onto the outside foot—' she tapped at his foot with her toe '—and lift the inside foot ahead. See?'

They made the step and hop with no incident, and Anton grinned at her. 'Like thus? Perhaps this dancing business is not so very difficult.'

'Do not get *too* confident, Master Gustavson,' she warned. 'For now is the difficult part.'

'I am ready, Madame Tutor.'

'After the hop, there is a longer step on the second beat, close to the ground, thus. And that is when I bend my knees to spring upward.'

'What must I do?'

'You lift me up as I jump, like…' He suddenly swung her into the air as if she was a feather, his hands tight at her waist. Rosamund laughed in surprise. 'Aye, like that! Now, turn.'

He spun her around, both of them laughing giddily. The bright glass windows whirled around her, sparkling as diamonds. 'Not so fast!' she cried. 'We would knock over all the other dancers.'

He lowered her slowly to her feet, still holding her close. 'Then how do we turn properly?'

'We, well, it is a three-quarter turn at each measure. When the crowd cries out "volta!" we do it again. Then we return to the galliard position.'

'That does not sound so jolly,' Anton said, twirling her up into the air again. 'Is not our version much better?'

Rosamund laughed helplessly, laughed until her sides ached and tears prickled at her eyes. She couldn't remember ever laughing so much, or ever being with anyone who made her feel as Anton Gustavson did— as if she was carefree again, as if the world was all laughter and dancing.

'Our version is merrier,' she cried. 'But I do not think it would win the Queen's wager!'

He lowered her to her feet again, yet the gallery still spun around her. She clung to his shoulders, aching with laughter, her breath tight in her lungs. This, surely, was how all those ladies who got into trouble with the Queen for their amorous affairs felt right before they plunged down into ruin? It was intoxicating—and worrying.

'Why does it feel as if we have already won?' he whispered against her hair.

Rosamund stared up at him, startled by his words. He, too, looked startled; for a mere instant, it was as if his courtly mask had dropped. She saw surprise and a naked longing in his eyes that matched her own. And briefly a flash of loneliness, assuaged by their laughter.

Then it was gone; the armoured visor dropped back into place. He stepped back from her, giving her a quick, small bow.

They were separate again, as if the frozen Thames lay between them. And it felt even colder after the bright sun of their shared laughter.

'Excuse me, Lady Rosamund,' he said roughly, his accent heavy. 'I fear I have an appointment I have forgotten. Perhaps we can have another lesson tomorrow.'

Rosamund nodded. 'After the Queen's hunt.'

He bowed again and walked away, leaving her alone in the middle of the empty gallery. Rosamund was not sure what to do; the silence seemed to echo around her, the air suddenly chilled. She rubbed at her arms, wondering what had just happened.

Everything had been turned tip-over-tail ever since she'd arrived at Court. She hardly seemed to know herself any longer, and she did not know how to set it aright again. She seemed to be infected with the pervasive air of flirtation and romance all around at Whitehall, that danger and amorous passion all mixed up into one intoxicating brew.

Perhaps if she went home to Ramsay Castle? Yet, even as she thought it, Rosamund knew that would not be the cure. Even if she did go back, and everything there was just the same, *she* would be different. She was not the same as she had been before she'd come to Court and seen the wider world. Before she'd met Anton.

She left the gallery, walking down the stairs and turning back towards the long walk to the Privy Chambers and the Great Hall. She needed to be around people, to find some distraction.

But even in the crowded hall, where the Yule log at last smouldered in the vast stone grate, she found no respite from her restless thoughts. Anton stood near the fireplace, but he was not alone. Lettice Devereaux, Lady Essex, stood beside him; the two of them had their heads bent together in quiet conversation, her hand on his sleeve. The pretty countess's dark-red hair, laced with fine pearls, gleamed in the firelight.

So that was his urgent 'appointment', Rosamund thought, feeling some hot emotion like temper rise in her throat, choking and bitter. She suddenly wished she was the Queen, so she could throw her shoe at his too-handsome, too-infuriating head! She had been all in a quandary over him, while he'd merely had one of his many flirtations to see to.

First Richard had vanished, never writing to her, and now this. 'A pox on all men,' she muttered.

'I see you have at last settled into the ways of Court,' she heard Anne Percy say in a most smug tone.

Rosamund glanced over her shoulder to see her friend standing close behind her. Anne smiled at her. 'We must all be in either a passion or a pique over someone,' she said. 'It is not Court life otherwise.'

Rosamund had to laugh. 'I don't wish to be in either.'

Anne shrugged. 'You cannot escape it, I fear. There is only one cure, though I'm afraid it is only a temporary one.'

'What is it?'

'Shopping, of course. Catherine Knyvett tells me that Master Brown's mercer's shop in Lombard Street has some new silks from France. The Queen is with her Privy Council now and does not need us until this evening, we should go purchase a length or two before all the other ladies snatch them away. There is no better distraction from thoughts of dim-witted men than looking at silks.'

Rosamund nodded. She needed more than anything to cease thinking of men—one in particular. It had all gone much too far. 'Yes, let's. A temporary cure is surely better than none at all.'

'Here comes I, old Father Christmas!' proclaimed the player on the Great Hall's temporary stage, striding about in his green-velvet robes and long, white beard to much laughter from the audience. 'Christmas comes but once a year, but when it does it brings good cheer. Roast beef and plum pudding, and plenty of good English beer! Last Christmastide I turned the spit, I burnt my finger and can't find of it!'

The gathering burst into more helpless laughter as Father Christmas hopped and flailed around, but Anton found he could pay no attention to the stage antics. He could not look away from Rosamund's face.

He stood along one of the panelled walls, hidden in the shadows, while the rest of the company sat on tiered benches rising behind the Queen's tall-backed chair. The maids were on either side of her in their shining white-satin gowns, and Anton had a perfect view of Rosamund as she watched the mummers' play.

Her cheeks, usually winter-pale, glowed bright pink as she laughed. Every trace of the wariness that often lurked in her eyes was gone as she joined with the others in the holiday fun.

He could not turn away; he was utterly enraptured by her. Despite the way he had made himself leave her that afternoon, had made himself remember why he was in England—why there was no room for such a lady in his life—he had not been able to cut her from his emotions. From his thoughts, his heated imaginings.

She pressed her hand to her lips, her eyes shining with mirth, and he remembered too well what those lips felt like against his. How she tasted more intoxicating than any wine, sweet and tempting. How their bodies felt pressed together in the darkness. And how he wanted so much more, wanted to taste her breast against his lips, feel her naked skin, wanted to drive himself into her and feel that they were one.

Would nothing ever erase that raw need he knew whenever she was near? For one more smile from her, he would forget all he worked for here—and that could never be. He had promises to keep, to himself as much as his family, and he could not be lured from them by Rosamund Ramsay's kisses, by the softness of her white skin—as hard as it would be to resist! Perhaps harder than anything he had done before.

But his passion put Rosamund into danger, made her place at Court threatened. He could not do that to her.

'I'll show you the very best activity that's shown on the common stage,' said Father Christmas, sweeping his long sleeves to and fro. 'If you don't believe me what I say, step in, King George, and clear the way!'

A knight in clanking, shining armour leaped onto the stage, and for a moment a ripple of silent unease spread across the room as everyone remembered the strange Lord of Misrule at the Christmas Eve banquet. Leicester and his men gathered closer to the Queen, and Anton reached for the dagger sheathed at his waist. If that villain dared return, he would not again touch Rosamund!

But the knight threw back his helmet's visor, revealing the pretty face of Anne Percy. She bowed elaborately amid much applause and relieved laughter, the elaborate plumes of her helmet flourishing.

Anton noticed Lord Langley scowling as he watched the stage, watched Anne Percy swagger back and forth, brandishing her sword. For an instant, he almost looked as if he would snatch her off the stage, but then he just swung around, pushing his way out of the mirthful crowd.

Anton shook his head ruefully. So, he was not the only one infatuation had wreaked havoc with here at the English Court! Cupid played at Christmas too. Langley and Anne were bold indeed, and surely braver than Anton when it came to matters of the heart at Court.

'I am King George, this notable knight!' Mistress Percy proclaimed, waving her sword high. 'I shed my blood for England's right. England's right and glory for to maintain! If any should challenge me, I stand ready.'

As she swung the sword in a wide arc, another knight, clad in matte-black armour and a black-plumed helmet, leaped onstage.

'I am that gallant soldier, Bullslasher is my name,'

he announced, his voice deep and muffled behind the visor. 'Sword and buckle by my side, I mean to win the game! First I draw my sword—then thy precious blood.'

Anne Percy laughed. 'Don't thou be so hot, Bullslasher! Don't thou see in the room another man thou has got to fight?'

'Nay—a battle betwixt thee and me, to see which on the ground dead first shall be. Mind the lists and guard the blows—mind thy head and thy sword.'

Their swords met in a great clash; for a moment Anton—and, it appeared, everyone else—forgot it was a mere mock Christmas battle. The two players fought fiercely, first one then the other driven back to the very edge of the stage. The laughter in the hall faded, replaced by a taut tension, a breathless silence as the battle ground furiously on.

At last, King George was the one pushed back, falling to the stage as her sword skittered away. Bullslasher's blade pressed to her armoured breast, but she was undaunted, heaving up to push his helmet away.

Lord Langley's face was revealed, streaked with sweat, set in anger.

'You!' Anne cried. 'What have you done with Master Smithson? How dare you…?'

Queen Elizabeth rose abruptly to her feet, her emerald-green skirts swaying. 'Enough,' she said loudly. 'We are bored with this scene, bring back Father Christmas. Lord Leicester, perhaps you would escort the gallant King George from the hall so he can change his garb?'

In only a moment, Leicester had herded Anne Percy from the stage and Lord Langley had vanished, leaving a rather bewildered Father Christmas to resume the play with a doctor but no wounded King George. He managed it, though, helped by the Queen's loud laughter, and soon the rest of the company was laughing and clapping again.

Anton looked to Rosamund. She still sat in her place behind the Queen, but her rosy laughter had faded; her brow had creased with puzzlement. Her gaze suddenly met his, and she did not turn away. She just watched him, and the rest of the room faded into a dark silence.

The bright, shimmering cord that was *her*, that was the ephemeral bond between them, tightened around his heart. Suddenly he knew too well how Lord Langley felt—but fighting against desire only made it flame hotter.

Rosamund whispered something to Mary Radcliffe, who sat beside her, before hurrying out of the hall. Anton followed, needing to make sure she was well and safe. He would not let her see him; if they spoke, if she came close, he wouldn't be able to stop himself from kissing her. And more—much more.

She hurried up the stairs toward the maids' apartment, her gown a white beacon in the night. At the top she glanced back down, and he thought she glimpsed him there, that she would call out.

But she just shook her head, running back along the corridor out of sight. He stood there until he heard her door shut, a click in the distance. Even then he could not quite turn away, could not leave her.

He sat on the bottom step, resting his elbows on his knees as he listened to the laughter from the hall. His plans had been so carefully laid out when he'd left

Sweden for England; he'd known just what he wanted, what he had to do. Now it all seemed in complete disarray, like a pair of dice tossed up in the air and yet to land. What danger awaited when they came to earth?

'Good eve to you, cousin,' he heard a soft voice say.

He glanced up, cursing his distraction, to find Celia Sutton standing across the corridor as still as a marble sculpture. He rose to his feet, watching her warily.

If Rosamund Ramsay was a bright winter-fairy, Celia was a night bird, all glossy black hair and black-satin gown, her jewels onyx and dull diamonds. Her pale, pointed face was framed by a high, fur-trimmed collar. She, too, gazed at him with wariness in her eyes.

'I see you also needed a respite from false merriment,' she said.

'Is it false?' he said. Another burst of loud laughter drifted out of the hall. 'The pleasures of the holiday seem real enough here.'

'Of course it is false—as everything is here at Court.' She took a step towards him, her gown whispering over the stone floor. 'I will give you warning, cousin—I don't know how it is in Sweden, but here one must always beware the promises of princes. Of *all* men. For they are as hollow and changeable as Christmas cheer. And I will say this too—an English wife will not help you to Briony Manor, even a daughter of an earl.'

There was a chilly bleakness to her words, a flat hollowness in her eyes that made him half-raise his hand towards her. She was his family, after all, his own mother's niece, despite their rivalry, despite the fact that they were strangers to each other. Despite her warnings.

But she'd already turned away, vanishing down the corridor like a black wraith. He was alone again. Alone with the secrets of his own heart, and the yearnings that could prove his undoing at last.

Chapter Seven

St Stephen's Day, December 26

'Make way for the Queen! Make way for the Queen!'

The guards in the lead of the royal procession cried out as they made their slow way down the Strand, through Cheapside and towards London Bridge. Eventually they would make it to Greenwich Great Park for their hunt, but the Queen seemed in no hurry at all. From atop her prancing white horse, she waved and smiled at the crowds as they cheered for her and tossed bouquets of winter greenery.

Everyone seemed so happy they did not notice the extra number of guards, the way they suspiciously scanned the throngs of people, nor did they notice Leicester and his sword close by Elizabeth's side. The bitter winter and all it entailed was lost in the excitement of seeing their queen.

Rosamund also studied the scene from atop her own

horse, trying to keep the prancing, restive little mare from edging out of line. These were the same narrow, dirty, crowded streets she'd traversed on her way to Whitehall, yet they were transformed. The cobbles were scrubbed clean, covered by a new layer of snow and frost in the night that made the greys and browns of the city shimmer. Wreaths and swags of Christmas greenery draped from windows, where more people strained for a glimpse of their queen.

And the Queen rewarded them. Clad in a riding costume of red and dark-brown velvet, a tall-crowned, plumed hat on her head, she waved and laughed.

'Good people, pray do not remove your hats!' she called out. 'It is much too cold.'

But still they did remove their hats, brandishing them in the air as she passed by. A merry, excited gathering indeed.

Rosamund remembered her father's story of the Queen's first entrance to London after her accession to the throne. He had been there, witnessing the pageants and plays, the yards and yards of white satin and cloth-of-gold, the fountains running with wine; the ecstatic jubilation after years of fear and oppression under Queen Mary and her Spanish husband, the hope centred around the young, red-haired princess.

It seemed none of that had faded in six years. The crowds happily gathered in the bitter cold just to wave at Queen Elizabeth.

'Is it like this every year?' Rosamund asked Anne, who rode beside her.

'Oh, yes,' Anne said. 'Londoners wait all year for the

St Stephen's Day hunt, or for the Queen to leave on her summer progress. It takes hours to depart the city then, with all the baggage carts.'

Rosamund laughed, picturing the endless train of carts it would take to transport the contents of Whitehall, both humans and furnishings. 'I can imagine.'

'But you needn't worry about that, Rosamund! You will be married and settled in your own home before we go on progress again.'

Rosamund smiled, but in her heart she doubted that prospect. Ramsay Castle, Richard—it all seemed terribly far away, further with every day amid the sparkling distractions of Court. Richard's face faded in her mind, like a painting left too long in the sun—and other, more vivid images replaced it. Had her father been right? Yes, indeed, he had. For Anton was different from Richard, from anyone else she had ever known, and her feelings for him were richer and deeper than any she had ever known.

She shook her head. She could not think of all that now, with her horse frisking about and crowds pressing on all sides. She had to keep her place in the procession and not fall behind.

On London Bridge, that vast edifice lined on either side with looming structures of houses and shops, they stopped to listen to a children's chorus sing a Christmas tune for the Queen.

'Blessed be that maid Marie, born was he of her body! Very God ere time began, born in the time of Son of Man.' Their sweet, young voices rang out in the cold, clear air, like holiday angels soaring over the earth.

Their little round faces, scrubbed clean for this important moment, reflected nervousness, joy, terror and sheer pleasure.

Rosamund had to smile as she watched them, for she knew how they felt. It reflected her own emotions ever since she'd come to Whitehall and begun learning new, frightening things about herself: that she was not entirely the quiet, shy girl her family thought her; that she needed a man who could bring out those depths in her, could understand them. And someone whose own depths she could spend a lifetime discovering for herself.

She had grown up, and found her woman's heart.

She glanced back over her shoulder to where the Swedish party rode. Anton was in their midst, once again clad in black wool and leather riding-clothes. He almost looked like a centaur on his glossy black horse, a powerful warrior set to thunder into battle. His face was drawn in serious, thoughtful lines, his shoulders held taut under his short cloak, as if he planned his war strategy.

How endlessly interesting he was, she thought as she studied him. He was constantly revealing new facets, new contrasts of light and shadow. He could laugh and jest as if he hadn't a care in the world, could tease and flirt and play the courtier, the lover of ladies. Yet she could see the flash of granite-hard determination beneath the laughter. He hid secrets there, she was sure of it.

What was his life like in Sweden? What did he really hope to gain here in England—a disputed estate? Or something more?

Rosamund wished she knew how to find out.

Wished she had had more years at Court to learn subterfuge and intrigue.

Anton caught her watching him and grinned at her. Once again that secret solemnity vanished, like a cloud burned away by the sun. She smiled back, facing ahead as the song ended and a girl stepped forward to give a bouquet of herbs to the Queen.

Rosamund's gaze caught the heads displayed over the entrance to the bridge, a gruesome contrast to the music, the happy cheers. Their empty eye-sockets proclaimed silently that all was not entirely merry in the Queen's realm, even now at Christmas. Everyone had their secrets, and some led to pikes on the bridge.

They moved forward again, their long train snaking along the bridge and out of London proper. The congestion of narrow streets flowed to large estates along the river, and then to farms and fields. There were people to cheer even there, but they were fewer, and progress was quicker. Then they were on the road to Greenwich.

The tightly packed procession fanned out, still following the Queen and Lord Leicester, but more fluid. Conspirators and couples found each other, hoping for a quiet word before the rush of the hunt.

Anton drew up next to Rosamund just as Anne discreetly pulled away, falling back to ride with Catherine Knyvett. Rosamund smiled at him tentatively, not sure what to expect after he'd left their dance lesson so abruptly the day before.

'Good day to you, Master Gustavson,' she said.

'And to you, Lady Rosamund,' he answered. 'How do you fare this morning?'

'Quite well, thank you. Fortunately for me, it was Mary Howard who dropped the Queen's necklace and bore her temper today, so I escaped!'

She nearly clapped her hand to her mouth for joking about the Queen's temper in public, but Anton laughed. 'May you fare so well every day at Court.'

Rosamund smiled ruefully. 'We must all take our turn, I fear.'

'But you have had no more encounters with masked villains?' he asked in concern.

'Nay, thankfully.' Rosamund shivered, as much from remembering the Lord of Misrule and his tight grasp on her hands as from the sudden, sharp breeze. 'I have seen nothing at all suspicious, though I'm afraid I am not as observant as I should be here at Court.'

'We must all be vigilant,' Anton said. 'Her Grace does not seem worried, though.'

He gestured towards the head of the procession, where the Queen appeared to be teasing Lord Leicester about something. She leaned from her saddle towards him, laughing as he smiled reluctantly.

'Lord Burghley urged her to curtail the Christmas festivities,' Rosamund said. 'But she refused.'

'Hmm,' Anton muttered. 'She is probably wise. People who plot in the shadows thrive on fear and disruption.'

'So, to combat evil we must laugh and make merry?' Rosamund said. 'La, but I can do that!'

Anton laughed. 'I hope that will always be so, Lady Rosamund. The winter day looks brighter when you smile.'

Rosamund bit her lip, absurdly pleased at his compliment. 'I will smile even more when I win our wager. Should we have a dance lesson tomorrow?'

'I have a better idea,' he said. 'We should go skating.'

'Skating?' she said, startled. 'Already?' She had known that by the terms of their wager she would have to strap on skating blades eventually and launch herself out onto the ice. But not just yet.

'There is no better time,' he answered cheerfully. 'A few of us are going to the pond tomorrow, if you would care to join us once your duties to the Queen are finished?'

A few of us? Rosamund remembered the first time she'd seen him at that pond, when Lady Essex had held onto his arm. And then there was the lady in the gardens, and Lady Essex again yesterday, after he'd left their lesson so abruptly. Would *all* those ladies be there?

'Your friend Mistress Percy is to be one of the party, I believe,' he said, as if he read her doubts. 'It will be a fine respite from the Court. And I promise to be a very careful skating-teacher. I will not let you fall.'

The thought of escaping from the palace for a while, even if it was just a few hours, was very tempting. She missed quiet time to think, to just *be*, and this hunting excursion just whetted her appetite for more.

Not that she would be doing much thinking around Anton! When she was near him, all rationality seemed to fly away. She was just like all those passion-addled courtiers who ended in the Tower, and she surely did not want to be one of them. But there was not much trouble to get into in a large group, surely?

'Very well,' she said. 'The Queen always meets with her Privy Council in the afternoon and will not need us.'

'*Ganska myttig.*' They fell into a companionable silence for a moment as they rode along the country lane. The grime and noise of the city was left far behind, and there was only the rustle of hooves on the frosty earth, their own laughter and talk. Their harmony with each other.

'I am sorry, Lady Rosamund, for my sudden departure from our lesson,' Anton said slowly. 'You must think me ill-mannered indeed.'

Rosamund smiled at him. 'Perhaps manners are different in Stockholm?'

He smiled back wryly. 'We Swedes are rougher, I suppose, but I hope we are not so ungallant.'

'I don't think anyone could accuse you of lack of gallantry, Master Gustavson,' she said. Except perhaps Celia Sutton. But Rosamund had not been able to discover the exact nature of their family quarrel yet. It was yet another of Anton's facets, one of the things that drew her to him to the exclusion of all else.

The gates of Greenwich Palace stood open for them as they turned down a new lane. In the distance, the palace's red-brick towers stood against the pearl-grey sky, but they rode instead towards the waiting Great Park. The undulating hills and slopes, no doubt beautifully green in the summer, were brown and black, streaked with white veins of snow. The bare trees stood like bleak skeletons, frosted with ice at the tips. This would be the last hunt for a while.

But Rosamund did not mind the bare landscape at all. The rush of the cold, fresh wind against her face, the clean, country smells and wide, open spaces felt wondrous after long days indoors. She had not realised just how very much she missed it all, the freedom of the open fields. The horse pranced beneath her, as restless as she was to run.

Rosamund held tight to the reins, keeping the mare in check as they all came to a halt outside the head gamekeeper's cottage. The Queen's stewards had to greet her before the St Stephen's Day fox and the Queen's hounds could be set free and they could all take off in pursuit.

She glanced at Anton, who grinned at her again. In his expression, eager and excited, she saw some of her own exhilaration at the day. He was a wild creature, set free from his Court confines at last.

Then the fox was released, streaking away across the field in a russet blur, and the Queen and Leicester shot off after him. Everyone else galloped behind them, fanning out in pursuit to cover the extensive fields and woods. The horses thundered along, as thrilled as their riders to be set free at last.

Rosamund laughed as she urged her mount faster, the wind rushing through her hair, past her ears, in a high, whistling whine. 'I'll race you!' she shouted to Anton.

He also laughed, his horse gaining on hers. They leaped over a shallow ravine, and Rosamund felt as if she was flying. They skittered around a corner through a stand of trees, tumbling down a slope.

The hounds set up a howl in the distance, and the riders turned to follow the beckoning sound. Rosamund tightened her thighs, swinging her horse around, with Anton close behind her. Her horse galloped deeper into the woods, leaping lightly over fallen logs and ditches, veering around corners and off the pathway into the trees, excited by the chance to run. Rosamund laughed, just as excited. She felt free! Free of the stuffy rooms of the palace, of her worries and cares.

Perhaps a bit too excited, for suddenly up ahead of her was a low-hanging branch. She ducked her head, but she was just an instant too slow. The branch snagged at her hat, snatching it from her head. Laughing helplessly, she reined up her horse, leaning over its neck as her stomach ached from the laughter, from the pure wonderment of the chase.

Anton clattered to a halt beside her. His own hat was gone, his black hair rumpled over his brow. 'Rosamund! Are you hurt?'

She shook her head, quite unable to draw breath to speak. 'Only my dignity, I fear.'

He swung down from his saddle, reaching up to grasp her waist and lift her down beside him. She leaned against his shoulder, gasping for breath. His heart pounded in her ear, and he smelled delicious, of leather, soap, snow and honest sweat.

She wrapped her arms around his shoulders, holding him tight. How he seemed a part of this day, of the freedom and excitement. Of the wide outdoors and the wild, winter beauty.

'I am quite sure the Queen never loses her hat,' Rosamund murmured.

'The Queen would be fortunate to be half the rider you are, Rosamund,' he answered. 'You led me on a grand chase.'

She tilted back her head, staring up at him. His high cheekbones were stained a dull red with exercise and emotion, his eyes as black as midnight. A few tendrils of hair clung to his brow.

She had never seen anything so beautiful in her life.

'What will you do now that you have caught me?' she whispered.

In answer, he kissed her, his mouth taking hers hungrily as they clung together. His hands at her waist dragged her closer, until they were pressed together. She went up on tiptoe, wanting more, wanting to feel every inch of his body against hers.

His lips opened, welcoming the press of his tongue to hers, the wet, humid heat of desire that blotted out all else. The day wasn't cold now—it sizzled with a need so deep, so elemental, she could no longer deny it even to herself.

She twined her gloved fingers into his hair, holding him to her, half-fearing he would try to escape her. But he made no move to leave her; his kiss deepened even more, his lips slanting across hers.

Through the haze of her need, she felt one of his hands slide to her bodice, freeing the top button of her riding doublet, then the next and the next. As the cold wind bit through her thin chemise to touch her bare skin, Rosamund felt a shock shiver all through her. It was not frightening or surprising, though. It was just thrilling.

Their kiss seemed to *fit*, as if they had always been thus, had known each other's mouths and bodies for years and years. He knew just where to press, to feather lightly, to touch just where it would make her world spin.

She moaned against his lips. He drew back at the sound, as if he thought she protested, but Rosamund pulled him back to her, back into their kiss. She didn't want him to leave, didn't want to lose that glorious moment, the way he made her feel. The wondrous, hot forgetfulness.

His fingers fell away from her bodice, but she seized them, carrying them back to finish what they had begun. It was as if her small gesture freed something in him too. He groaned, his kiss deepening; their tongues entwined as his arms tightened around her and he tumbled them both back down to the ground.

Her thighs fell apart and his body cradled between them, hard against her heavy skirts. He leaned his hands on either side of her, their kiss rough and wild, born of the desire that had been simmering like embers from the very first moment they'd met. It burst into flame now, threatening to completely consume her.

Her hands slid down to his backside, taut in his tight leather riding-breeches, and pressed him even closer, wrapping her thighs around his hips as her skirts billowed around them.

'Alskling,' he muttered, his voice tight, as if he was in pain. His mouth moved from hers, kissing her jaw and the curve of her neck as she tilted her head back against the soft ground. He impatiently spread the fabric of her riding doublet, revealing her breasts, which were barely concealed in her thin chemise, pressed high over the edge of her light stays.

The cold wind rushed over her, but not for long. His hot kiss fell on the slope of her breast, making her gasp as his body covered hers.

'Anton,' she whispered, revelling in the delicious sensation of his caress. When Richard had tried such a thing with her, it had frightened her. Now, with Anton, she wanted more and more...

A scream suddenly rent the air. For a shocked instant, Rosamund feared it was her scream, that the wild excitement was breaking free. But Anton rolled off her, his body tense and alert as he peered through the trees.

Rosamund slowly sat up, drawing the gaping edges of her doublet together, hardly daring to breathe. Her heart pounded in her ears, an erratic pattern veering from sexual desire to sudden fear in only a second.

Another cry rang out, and then a clamour of loud, confused voices. The baying of the hounds carried over it all, a discordant madrigal.

Anton leaped lightly to his feet, reaching out to help her stand. Her boot caught on her skirt hem as she lurched to her feet, and he caught her against him, holding her protectively close. His body was taut as he listened as if, like some graceful, powerful forest creature, he could sense danger tightening all around.

Rosamund curled her hands in the open vee of his shirt, holding on as she too listened. She tried to decipher where the cacophony came from, but it seemed both very distant and impossibly close.

'What is it?' she whispered.

'Shh,' he murmured. He hastily buttoned her doublet and then smoothed his own clothes before taking her hand, leading her back to the horses. 'Stay very close to me,' he said as he lifted her into the saddle. 'I have to get you to the palace, behind sturdy walls.'

Rosamund nodded, enveloped in a haze of confusion. Everything felt unreal, as if she was caught in a bad dream where all was disjointed, out of place. The woods, so peaceful and private only a moment ago, were dark and menacing.

And the man she had kissed so ardently, so overcome with need for him that she'd forgotten all else, was now a cold-eyed stranger. Suddenly she recalled all too well how very little she really knew of him. She had once liked Richard too—how could she trust what she thought of a man, what she felt? Yet still those feelings were there. The attraction, the trust. The danger.

He swung up onto his own mount, flicking the reins into motion. 'Remember,' he said to her, looking at her through those black eyes that saw all and gave nothing away, 'Stay close to me, Rosamund. I promise I will keep you safe.'

Her throat felt dry, aching, but she merely nodded. She urged her horse onto the path behind his, listening to the distant hubbub. The wind whispered through her loose hair, tangling it around her shoulders, and she remembered her lost hat and caul, the hairpins scattered as she and Anton had tumbled to the ground. But it did not seem very timely to mention it.

They emerged from the shelter of the trees to find the rest of the party gathered a short distance away at the edge of the woods. It first appeared that it was merely the capture, the end of the day's hunt, but then

Rosamund noticed the pale fear on the ladies' faces, the fury on the men's. The horses pranced restively in a close pack, as if they sensed the confusion.

Anton reached out to grasp her mare's bridle, holding her close as they moved cautiously closer, coming to a halt just beyond the tangled edge of the crowd.

For a moment, Rosamund could see nothing; the knot of people and horses was too dense. But then it parted, and she saw the Queen and Lord Leicester, their horses drawn up beneath one of the bare winter trees. Leicester held his dagger unsheathed, bellowing something in furious tones, but Queen Elizabeth just stared straight ahead, white-faced.

Rosamund followed her stare—and gasped. Hanging from one of the lower branches was a poppet, with bright-red hair and a fine, white silk gown, streaked with what looked like blood. It was topped with a gold paper-crown, and pinned to the bodice was a sign proclaiming, 'thus to all usurpers'.

Leicester suddenly rose up in his stirrups, slashing out with his dagger to cut the horrible thing down. It tumbled to the frosty ground, landing in a white and red jumble. The hounds crept nearer to it, baying, but even they would not touch the thing. Surely it reeked too much of evil, of traitorous intentions.

A contingent of more guards came galloping over the crest of the hill. As they surrounded the Queen, Anne Percy edged her horse closer to Rosamund's.

'Rosamund!' she cried. 'Are you all right? You look as if you will be ill.'

Rosamund shook her head, sweeping her hair back

off her shoulder. 'I just fell behind,' she said. 'I fear my riding skills are poor. And then at last I caught up, only to find—this.' She shivered, staring at the crumpled doll.

Anne nodded grimly. 'The Queen has many enemies, indeed. It is easy to forget that on a fine day like this, but there is always danger for princes. Always black thoughts lurking behind smiles.'

And danger for those near to the princes, too? Rosamund looked back to find Anton again with his Swedish cohorts, who were listening as they whispered together intently. But he watched her closely, as if he could see her thoughts and feelings. Her suspicions.

Rosamund shivered again; the day was unbearably cold. Anne was right. It was all too easy to forget the realities of the world on a day like this. The fresh air, the wild ride—Anton and his touch, his kiss. It made her forget *everything* and want only him. Only those precious moments when he lifted her above the world.

But that was all an illusion. This was the world, with danger, secrets and hidden agendas all around.

Lord Langley drew near to them, his handsome face also solemn, watchful. Even Anne did not pull away from him today, but leaned infinitesimally towards him, as if she knew not what she did.

'Who has done this?' she asked him quietly.

'No one yet knows,' he answered tightly. 'Greenwich has only a small staff now, and they will be questioned, but it is doubtful they saw anything. The Queen will stay here until her safe transport back to Whitehall can be arranged.'

'It has been a strange Christmas,' Anne said.

'Strange indeed,' Lord Langley said, with a humourless little smile. He pushed the tangled length of his golden-brown hair back from his brow, reminding Rosamund of her own dishevelment—and how she had got that way.

Her enchanted-forest interlude with Anton seemed impossibly distant now.

'Come, ladies, let me see you to the palace,' Lord Langley said. 'A fire is being laid in one of the chambers for you.'

'You seem quite knowledgeable about our sudden change of arrangements,' Anne said, falling into step beside him as they turned towards the palace. The Queen, surrounded by her guards, had already disappeared through its doors.

'Ah, Anne,' he answered sadly. 'To know all is my constant task.'

The events of the hunt did not seem to greatly affect the maids, Rosamund thought as she lay in her bed at Whitehall late that night. Catherine Knyvett and the Marys were practising their dancing along the aisle between the two rows of beds, galloping and leaping in their chemises as they laughed and shouted.

Rosamund held her book tightly, sliding down against the pillows. How could they possibly dance after all that had happened? Her own mind was still spinning, filled with whirling images of Anton, shouts and screams, hanging dolls. And then the long afternoon in a half-bare chamber at Greenwich until they could be taken back to Whitehall by sleigh along the frozen river.

Queen Elizabeth had been silent as they'd waited, calm and serene. Rosamund could not even fathom her thoughts, her plans. The machinery was turning in the dark background of the Court to find the culprits.

Supper, too, had been quiet on their return to Whitehall, a quick repast in the Queen's privy apartments, but Elizabeth had vowed that the rest of Christmas would go on with no alterations. Feasts, dancing, plays—and foolish wagers—would go on.

'Rosamund?' Anne said softly. 'Are you asleep, or just hiding over there?'

Rosamund tugged down the bedclothes she had piled around herself, to find Anne watching her from her own bed. 'I'm reading,' she said.

'A great talent you have, then, for reading upside down.'

'What?' Rosamund stared down at her book, only to find that Boethius was indeed the wrong way round. 'Oh, bother. 'Tis true I haven't read a word since I opened it.'

'Better than listening to their shrieking,' Anne said, inclining her head towards the wild dancers.

'How can they be so carefree after what happened?'

'I suppose that is their way of forgetting. Such things occur all too often at Court. My uncle says it is all the foreigners who gather here.'

'The foreigners?'

'Aye. The foreign monarchs must send their delega-tions, even though many of them secretly think Mary of Scots is the *true* Queen of England. I suppose it is just surprising we don't see more such incidents.'

Rosamund frowned, thinking of Master Macintosh, the glowering Austrians. Of Anton, and all she knew of him—and did not know. 'Perhaps.'

'But if we thought too much of such things we would be frightened all the time,' Anne said. 'Better to get on with our business and forget it. However we can.'

Rosamund sighed. 'I'm sure you are right, Anne. But, still, must they forget by dancing so very *badly*?'

Anne laughed. 'Speaking of dancing,' she whispered, 'How do your lessons progress with the beauteous Master Gustavson?'

'Well enough,' Rosamund said cautiously. 'He has a great deal of natural grace, though perhaps some difficulty remembering the correct progression of the steps.'

'Which will require many more lessons, of course.'

Rosamund had to giggle. 'Mayhap.'

'Oh, Rosamund. Tell me—where were you really when you disappeared from the hunt? For I find it hard to believe you are any kind of poor horsewoman.'

Rosamund feared she could hide nothing from Anne. She surely had a long way to go before she became a true Court lady, jaded with plotting.

She slid down lower in the bed, whispering back, 'I was talking with Master Gustavson.'

'Talking?'

'Yes!' And a bit more—but secret-keeping had to start somewhere.

'Hmm. No wonder you were so flushed. And no wonder you have a little mark just there below your neck.'

Rosamund glanced down, drawing away the wide neckline of her chemise. 'Blast!' she muttered, yanking that neckline higher.

'Not that I blame you one bit. He is a luscious-looking gentleman indeed, all the ladies here are mad for him. But what of your old sweetheart? Do you no longer care for him?'

Rosamund was not sure she had ever cared for Richard, not really. There had only been her girlish dreams, which she had pinned onto him. 'Oh, Anne. I simply don't know. I thought I did once. But I haven't for a long time. Am I a faithless harlot, to be so easily distracted?'

Anne laughed. 'If you are a faithless harlot for a bit of flirting, Rosamund, then so are we all. It's easy to be distracted here at Court, especially if our lovers do not keep faith with *us*. But what think you, really, of Master Gustavson? Is he just a distraction for you?'

If he was, then he was a truly potent one. Rosamund could not think of anyone else when he was around. All the glimpses he gave her of his inner self, of a yearning for a home and place that matched her own, only increased his attraction. What did it mean?

Before she could answer, the door to their chamber burst open. Elderly Lord Pomfrey appeared there, clad in a nightcap tied over his unruly grey hair—and nothing else. His shrivelled, purplish member flapped about as he strode angrily down the aisle.

Rosamund sat straight up, staring in utter startlement as the dancing maids shrieked and dove into their beds.

'You cursed chits have kept me awake for the last time, I vow!' Lord Pomfrey thundered. 'You shout and frisk about all the night long, and it will end here! No more of your riots, I say. No more!'

As he continued his ranting and shouting—stopped only when a most indignant Mistress Eglionby appeared—Rosamund fell back onto her pillows, laughing helplessly. Anne was entirely right—one never knew what would happen at Court.

Chapter Eight

The cold air snapped at Rosamund's cheeks, whipping her cloak around her as she wondered if this was such a very good idea. The palace was warm, with plenty of fireplaces to huddle next to, and letters waiting to be written, mending to be done. Surely if she was sensible at all she would be back there?

But at the palace she would have to listen to the Marys gossiping and sniping. And there would be no Anton to look at.

She tucked her hands deeper into her fur muff, watching him as he built a fire with Master Ulfson and Lord Langley. He was a sight to see indeed, his close-fitting dark-brown doublet stretched taut over his lean shoulders as he stacked the wood. He had taken off his cap, and his hair gleamed like a raven's wing. He laughed at some jest of Lord Langley's, his smile as bright as any summer sun. It warmed Rosamund right down to the tips of her toes.

She was very glad indeed that she had ventured out today. Any danger, any doubt, seemed so far away.

That decides it, Rosamund thought cheerfully. *I am a faithless hussy!*

She had to face the fact that whatever had happened with Richard did mean what she'd once thought. That— horrors!—perhaps her parents had been right, that she would know the right person for her, the right situation, when she found it.

But her parents were not here now, and she was starting to enjoy the sensation of being a flirtatious Court lady, at least for a short time. At least for today, with Anton.

She went and sat next to Anne and Catherine Knyvett, where they perched on a fallen log covered by an old blanket. At their feet was a hamper, filled with purloined delicacies from the Queen's kitchen, which Anne was sorting through.

'Oh, marzipan!' she said. 'And cold beefpies, manchet bread. Even wine. Very well done, Catherine.'

Catherine laughed nervously. 'I did feel so terrible filching them. But no one seemed to notice, so I suppose all is well.'

'They are all too busy preparing for tomorrow night's feast to even notice one or two little things missing,' Anne said. 'And, even if they did, the Queen is too busy consulting with her Privy Council to listen to their complaints. Here, Rosamund, have something to drink. Wine will soon warm us.'

'Thank you,' Rosamund said, taking the pottery goblet from Anne. As she sipped at the rich, ruby-red liquid, she went back to studying Anton. The men had finished building the bonfire by the frozen pond, and it crackled and snapped merrily as they watched in smug self-satisfaction.

'Humph,' Anne scoffed. 'They act as if they were the first men to discover fire.'

Rosamund laughed. 'Better than letting us shiver here.'

'Quite right, Lady Rosamund,' Lord Langley said, turning to them with a grin. His gaze lingered on Anne, who did not look at him. 'What would you do without our fire-making skills?'

A reluctant little smile touched Anne's lips. 'Perhaps that is the *only* useful skill you possess, Lord Langley.'

'*Touché*, Mistress Percy,' Anton said. 'A palpable hit from the lady, Lord Langley. It seems we must work much harder to impress your fine English females.'

He sat down beside Rosamund on the log, unlooping his leather skate-straps from over his shoulder. Rosamund did not move away but stayed where she was, pressed to his side, feeling his body next to hers. They seemed wrapped in their own warm cocoon in the cold air, bound by invisible cords of memory and heady desire.

She remembered their kisses in the Greenwich woods, remembered falling heedlessly to the ground, their bodies entwined. She could hardly breathe.

He seemed to remember, too, staring down at her, at her parted lips.

'I doubt anything at all would impress such hard hearts,' Lord Langley said.

'Oh, we are not so immune as all that,' Rosamund said, glancing away from Anton. But even as she watched the red-gold ripple of the fire the spell held, and she was entirely aware of him beside her; their shoulders were touching. Through the thick wool and fur, her bare skin tingled. She worried for a moment they would cause gossip, but the Queen could not see them.

'We are impressed by diamonds and pearls,' Catherine said.

'And fine French silks!' said Anne.

'Furs are rather nice, too,' added Rosamund. 'Especially a nice sable on a day like today. And books! Lots of books.'

'I dare say we could also be impressed by great feats of strength,' said Catherine. 'It is a great pity there are no tourneys in winter.'

'We shall just have to make do with what we have, then,' Anton said, all mock-sadness. 'As, alas, we have no pearls, silks or tourneys to fight in. I challenge you to a race on the ice, then, Langley.'

Lord Langley laughed, pulling out his own skates from his saddlebags. 'Very well, Master Gustavson, I accept your challenge! If the ladies can provide a suitable prize, that is.'

'You shall have our undying admiration,' Rosamund said before Anne could venture something quarrelsome. 'And a share of our picnic.'

'A prize worth fighting for indeed,' Anton said. He bent to strap one of the skates to his boot, tying the leather thongs tight over his instep and calf until the thin, shining blade seemed a part of him.

'Will you gift me with your favour, Lady Rosamund?' he asked as he strapped on the other skate, raising his head to smile at her.

Rosamund smiled back, as she always did when he looked at her that way. His merriment was infectious; it chased away the doubts and fears that plagued her in the night. Until she was alone again, and it all came back.

But not now. Now, she just wanted to feel happy and young again, as she had not done in so long.

'I have never gifted a favour for a skating contest,' she said. 'Or for anything else, either, except country fairs.'

'Is that not what life is about, my lady?' he said. 'New experiences, new—sensations?'

Rosamund shivered, remembering all the new sensations he had shown her already. 'I am beginning to think so.'

She snapped one of the ribbons from her sleeve, a shining bit of creamy silk, and knotted it around his upper arm. It showed there, pale against the brown fabric, and for just a moment Rosamund felt some satisfaction at the mark. He wore *her* favour, fought for her, even if it was just here at this quiet pond with friends watching.

'And a kiss for good luck?' he said teasingly.

She laughed, shaking her head. 'When you have claimed victory, Sir Knight.'

'Ah, so you are right, Lord Langley—your English ladies *are* hard of heart,' Anton said. 'But I shall defeat all foes for you, my lady, and claim my prize ere long.'

He stood up from her side, launching himself onto the frozen pond in one long, smooth glide. As he waited for Lord Langley to finish putting on his skates, he looped around in long, lazy-seeming patterns, backward and forward again. He left smooth scores in the ice, unbroken lines and circles that showed the precision and grace of his movements.

Yet his hands were clasped behind his back, and he whistled a little madrigal as if it was all nothing.

When Lord Langley was ready, they stood side by side on the ice, poised to break into motion.

'Mistress Percy,' Johan Ulfson said as he and the three ladies gathered at the edge of the pond. 'Perhaps you would do the starter's honours? And help to keep count—three laps around the pond.'

Anne drew a handkerchief from inside her sleeve, waving it aloft. 'Gentlemen,' she cried. 'On your marks—one, two, three—go!'

The handkerchief fluttered to the ground and the men shot away. Lord Langley was good, powerful and fast, but not quite with the same easy, leonine grace as Anton. Lord Langley tried to push ahead with sheer, mute speed, but Anton bent lower to the ice, his feet a blur as his steps lengthened.

He truly seemed one with the ice, encircled by the same elegant, easy power, the same single-mindedness of purpose he showed on horseback or in dancing. The rest of the world seemed to vanish for him, and he was entirely, intently focused.

That was how he kissed, too, Rosamund thought as her cheeks turned warm. How he would make love to a woman—as if she was his entire focus, his whole world.

At the end of the pond, they twirled round and circled

back. Anton did not even seem out of breath, nor at all distracted from his task, his goal. The onlookers, including Rosamund, cheered as the racers dashed past, and Lord Langley looked up to wave. But Anton appeared not to even hear them.

Three laps was the agreed length of the race, and Rosamund watched, transfixed, as Anton circled around again. He bent closer to the ice, hands behind his back as he flew along faster than she would have thought humanly possible.

Lord Langley, though quite fast when starting out, expended his energy and fell behind. By the time they finished their final loop, and slid past Anne's fallen handkerchief for the last time, he was at least two steps behind Anton. He stumbled off the ice to fall onto the log, laughing and winded.

'I am defeated!' he declared. 'I cede all victory in ice-skating to the barbaric Northman for evermore.'

Anton grinned. He still stood on the ice, balanced lightly on his blades, but he leaned his hands on his knees. His shoulders lifted with the force of his expelled breath. 'You only cede in skating, Langley?'

'Aye. I challenge you to a horse-race next. We Englishmen are renowned for our horsemanship!'

'I would not be so quick to brag, Lord Langley,' Catherine said. 'Did you not see Master Gustavson at the hunt yesterday? It seems the Swedes do not neglect their equestrian education either.'

'And yet they *do* seem to neglect their dancing,' Lord Langley said. 'What say you, Lady Rosamund? How goes your tutelage?'

'Quite well,' Rosamund answered. 'I think he will surprise you on Twelfth Night, if he will apply himself to his lessons.'

'That will be no hardship, I think,' Anton said. 'Given the sternness of my teacher.'

''Tis true,' Rosamund said, pouring out a goblet of wine and finding a serviette in the hamper. 'I am a very stern teacher, indeed.'

As the others turned to the food and the fire, she went to the edge of the pond, watching as Anton removed his skates. When he finished, she held out the wine and cloth to him.

'They are poor spoils for the victorious hero, I fear,' she said.

Anton laughed, wiping at his damp brow. His dark hair clung to his temples, and a faint flush stained his high cheekbones, but those were the only signs of his athletic effort. He looked as if he had just finished a stroll in the garden.

'I would prefer that kiss for my prize,' he murmured.

Rosamund shook her head. 'Patience is another virtue heroes must possess, I fear.'

'And kisses are not so easily won?'

'Hercules, a hero if there ever was one, had *twelve* labours, did he not?'

'You will not make me clean a stable next, will you?'

She laughed. 'That remains to be seen!'

He laughed too, and took a long swallow of the wine. She watched the movement of his throat muscles, fascinated. 'Come, Lady Rosamund, walk with me for a while.'

'Should you not sit and rest?' she asked, glancing

over at Lord Langley, who lounged on the fallen log as Catherine fed him marzipan.

'Nay—he will be sorry when his muscles ache tonight,' Anton said. 'It's better to keep moving until the body is cooler.'

Rosamund shivered as another gust of wind swept around her. 'That should not take long.'

Anton left the empty goblet and his skates near the fire, taking her arm as they walked out of the clearing. They went through the narrow, wooded path where Rosamund had walked on her journey into London on that day she'd first seen Anton. Then the bare trees and tangled pathways had seemed somehow ominous, lonely, her heart full of trepidation.

Today, with him by her side, they were beautiful, a Christmas marvel of glass-like icicles and glittering frost. She did not even fear masked Lords of Misrule and dark warnings, not when she was with Anton. She had never met anyone she trusted more to keep her safe; he was so steady, so firm of purpose. So determined.

'I remember when I first saw you,' he said. 'You suddenly appeared there by that very pond, like a ghost or a fairy. I thought you an illusion at first.'

'And I you,' she admitted. 'I didn't know people could perform such feats on the ice. I am sorry I ran away so quickly.'

'Ah, yes. When you vanished, I was *convinced* you were an illusion!' he said. 'That I imagined a winter-fairy. No human woman could be so very beautiful.'

Rosamund's breath caught in her throat at his words, at the force of them. Anton thought her beautiful! Other men had said so—Richard, men of the Court. Yet they had seemed empty words, polite conventions that they said to every lady. Perhaps that was all it was with Anton, too—but his tone, his gentle smile, had the soft ring of sincerity. And the lure of all she had ever really wanted, despite the danger of reaching out to grasp it.

She had never thought herself beautiful at all, despite the gift of her fashionable pale hair. Next to vibrant women like Anne Percy, Lady Essex, and even Celia Sutton's dark mystery, she was a milk-faced mouse. But with Anton, she felt transformed, like a rosebud under the summer sun. Or a winter-fairy in the ice.

Would she shrink back inward again, when he was gone, back to Sweden?

'Perhaps I never should have spoken to you, then,' she said. 'I like the idea of being a beautiful winter-fairy.'

'*Nej,*' he answered. He suddenly faced her, taking both her hands in his. Holding them tightly, he pressed them to his chest. His heart thrummed against her gloved hands, flowing through her whole body, meeting her own heartbeat, joining their life forces as one.

'A warm, human woman with a kind heart is far better than a cold fairy,' he said. 'You have been a gift in these English days, Rosamund, one I could never have expected.'

'And so have you,' she said, leaning into his body, into the hot protection of his strength. She rested her forehead on his chest, sliding her arms around to wrap all about him, as if by holding tightly she could keep him from flying away. 'I was so sad, so frightened when I came to Court. But that is all gone when I'm with you.'

'*Alskling,*' he whispered, and lowered his head to kiss her.

Their kiss was slow, gentle, as if they had all the time they wanted. As if there were long hours to come to know one another, not the mere stolen moments they really had together.

He framed her face between his hands, softly pressing tastes to her lips as if she was the finest of wines, the most delectable of delicacies. Rosamund revelled in his tenderness, in being close to him. She wanted to memorise every moment, every sensation, store them up for that time when their moments ran out. She flattened her palms against his chest, the fine fabric of his doublet rubbing against her soft skin. She stared, fascinated, at the pulse throbbing at his throat, feeling the rise and fall of his breath under her touch.

Rosamund slid her hands up to curl over his shoulders, holding on tightly as the earth seemed to tilt under her. She felt so giddy, dizzy, with wild anticipation. She went up on tiptoe, leaning against him as he deepened their kiss. His tongue pressed hungrily, roughly, between her lips, suddenly greedy as if he, too, felt that knife-edge of need.

She wanted everything—*all* of him! And she wanted to give him everything of herself. Their tongues mated, clashing, unable to find enough of each other.

But then he drew slowly back from their kiss, from the fireworks building up between them, before they could explode in an uncontrollable conflagration. He rested his forehead against hers, his breath heavy, as if he was in pain.

Rosamund closed her eyes tightly, clinging to Anton as if he would vanish from her, as he well could very soon. He was from Sweden, and surely his errand here would end soon enough. He could gain his English estate, but, even then, persuading her parents as to the prudence of the match would be difficult—as would persuading the Queen, who so hated for her ladies to marry.

And, also, he had not talked to her of any tender feelings, any real intentions. Any plans or hopes for the future. She was a foolish romantic indeed. A romantic who put her love before all else.

Yet this moment, alone with him in the cold winter silence, felt right. Right in a way her hurried meetings with Richard never had been. The deep, dark passion was so very different, the urge to be with him, to know him. She had to absorb every tiny sensation of the now, of how he smelled, how his body felt under her touch. The wind swirled around them as if to bind them together.

This moment might be all she had. She had to make it count, make it a memory she could hold onto for the years ahead.

She tilted back her head to stare up at him. His face was etched in shadows, his smile as bittersweet as the feelings in her own heart. She smoothed back the wind-tossed waves of his black hair from his brow, framing his face in her hands. His skin was warm through the thin leather of her gloves, and with her fingertips she traced the line of his high cheekbones, his nose, the chiselled edge of his jaw. A muscle tensed under her caress.

She wanted to memorise every detail. 'Some day, when I am an old woman huddled by my fire,' she murmured, 'I will remember this moment. I'll remember a young, strong, handsome man who held me in his arms like this. I'll remember everything he made me feel, and made me know about myself.'

He reached up to take her hands in his, holding them tightly. 'What do you feel?' he said roughly, his accent heavy. Usually his English was nearly impeccable, she thought wonderingly, but in moments of emotion the edge of his words turned lilting, musical.

'I feel alive,' she said. 'When I'm with you, Anton, I feel all warm and tingling with life. As if I could fly higher and higher like a bird, above these trees, above Whitehall and London and everything. Fly until I find my own place, where there is safety and happiness always.'

'Oh, *alskling*,' he said, pressing her open palm to his cheek as he smiled sadly. 'There is no place with happiness always.'

'There is when you find your true home, your real place,' she insisted. 'I have always believed that. It is just not easy to find, I fear.'

'And what should one do when it *is* found?'

'Hold onto it with all your might, of course. Fight for it. Never let it go.'

In answer, he kissed her again, pulling her up on tiptoe as their bodies pressed together. Their kiss was swift, hard, a deep caress that tasted of promise. Of hope.

'Rosamund,' he murmured, hugging her close. 'We will meet tomorrow, yes? I think we have much to speak of.'

And more kisses to share? Rosamund could only hope. Feeling absurdly happy, she nodded. 'Tomorrow.'

* * *

Rosamund paused at the top of the stairs leading to the maids' apartment, peering down over the carved balustrade before she turned down the corridor after Anne and Catherine, who had already disappeared. Anton still stood down in the foyer with Lord Langley, laughing over some jest.

How she did love it when he laughed! When he looked so young and happy. It made the whole room seem to blaze with the light of a thousand torches, and warmed her own heart more than any fire could.

If only it could be thus all the time.

He glanced up to find her watching him, and his smile widened. Rosamund waved, laughing, and ducked away.

Perhaps it would not last long, she thought, but surely it would be glorious while it did. She saw now what drove people like Katherine Grey and her secret husband to dive headfirst into foolish passion—it was a force impossible to resist. It was like a sonnet, brought to vivid, unruly life. She did not want to put her reputation, her family's opinion of her, in danger again. But she could not seem to help herself.

She drew off her gloves, holding them carefully as she remembered how she'd touched Anton's face. How she'd felt the heat of him through the leather. Then she laughed at her silliness. Soon she would be pilfering his cap-feather or eating-knife, making a treasure of them!

'Lady Rosamund,' she heard someone say, startling her from her giddy romantic fantasies.

She looked up to find Celia Sutton emerging from one of the chambers. She still wore her mourning colours, a black-velvet surcoat trimmed in dark fur over a violet and black gown. She smiled, yet it seemed tense, unsure, as if she did not often use it.

'Mistress Sutton,' Rosamund answered. At home, they had sometimes called each other Rosamund and Celia when they'd met, but now that felt too strange. 'How do you do this day?'

'As well as one can be, in this crowded, cold city,' Celia answered. 'I look forward to the day I can return to the country, as I'm sure you do too. You must miss Ramsay Castle.'

'Of course,' Rosamund answered. 'But Court has its own attractions, I'm finding.'

Celia's smile stretched tauter. 'Like the Court gentlemen, perhaps?'

'They are handsome, I believe. And fashionable.'

'And clever? Unlike our men of the countryside.'

Rosamund remembered Celia's late husband, Richard's elder brother, who had seemed to be a man who'd enjoyed hunting and hawking and not much else. His conversation at local weddings and banquets had always revolved around how many stags he'd killed on his last outing, how many pheasants bagged, or the new hounds in his kennel. A good-looking man, but a dull one.

Everyone had been secretly surprised when he'd married Celia, the granddaughter of Sir Walter Leonard, a landowner of old and distinguished family from another county. It seemed an uneven match, especially once they met Celia and found she was a dark beauty, well-educated for a lady and very elegant.

It had proved to be a match that did not last long, as the husband had died in a hunting accident a few months later, leaving Richard heir to the family's lands. But it seemed Celia still mourned her husband.

And, Rosamund suddenly remembered, Sir Walter Leonard must also be Anton's grandfather. How strange to think the two of them related. They were so very different—both mysterious, yes, but there was a light edge to Anton that was missing in Celia.

'Court is not *better* than the country,' Rosamund said. 'Merely different. I am finding the experience— educational.'

'Will you stay here, then, and continue that education?'

'I will stay as long as Her Grace requires me. Or until I am needed at home.'

'Home?' Celia said quietly, and Rosamund remembered why she was here at Whitehall—the dispute over the estate.

She also remembered that the Queen had asked her to speak with Celia about the matter.

'I am surprised you travelled all this way in the winter,' Rosamund said. 'Especially when you are still in mourning.'

'I had not the time to have new Court clothes made,' Celia answered. 'But I did not mind the journey. It was a chance to be quiet with my thoughts, away from my husband's parents.'

Rosamund knew the feeling, the inexpressible ache to be alone, to be able to think clearly again. Her own journey to London had taught her so much. 'And will you stay here long?'

'As long as it takes for my petition to be addressed,' Celia said. 'Do you know if the Queen has yet read it?'

'I fear I don't know. She never talks to her ladies of state matters. But she has been quite distracted of late.'

'Oh, yes.' A tiny, humourless smile just touched the corner of Celia's lips. 'The Lord of Misrule and the hanging poppet. What will happen next this Christmas, one wonders?'

'Nothing at all, I hope,' Rosamund said sharply. Only fine things could happen this Christmas; if only there was not that edge of worry constantly hanging over her, over the whole Court.

'Well, what can one expect with a Court full of Scotsmen? Not to mention Austrians—and Swedes. They all have their own scores to settle, their own interests to serve.'

'Just as you have yours?'

'And you yours, Lady Rosamund.' Celia's dark eyes, so like Anton's, narrowed. 'You seem to enjoy my foreign cousin's company.'

Rosamund frowned, slapping her gloves against her palm. 'He is quite charming. I am sure if you came to know him…'

Celia cut her off with a wave. 'I do not *wish* to know him. My grandfather sought to cause a great family mischief in leaving him Briony Manor, but I will soon see things set right. Even if I have to fight here at Court, on my own, to do so.'

'Oh, Celia, he *is* your family. Perhaps you need not be on your own here! If you would talk to him, perhaps an accord could be reached.' Families should surely always be united, whether they were Anton's or her own?

Celia shook her head. 'Lady Rosamund, you cannot understand. You have always had the protection of your family. But I have always been on my own, have always had to fight for my very place in the world. My own father sold me in marriage, and he is now dead. My husband's family cares naught for me now that I am a widow and they owe me my dower rights. My brother-in-law has not even been seen in months—he is probably spending the last of my dowry!

'I will not now throw myself on the uncertain mercies of some foreign cousin. I am not so foolish as that.'

Rosamund knew not what to say. After the sweet delight of her afternoon with Anton, to be faced with Celia's bitterness was saddening. It reminded her too much of the clouds hanging over her own life.

But surely now, at Christmas, anything was possible.

'I am sorry, Celia,' she said gently. 'Yet surely there is time for matters to come aright?'

'Only if the Queen grants me my estate,' Celia answered. 'You will tell me if she mentions the matter?'

'Yes, though I doubt she will to me.'

'Because she keeps her ladies free of serious matters— or because you think my cousin so *charming*?'

Before Rosamund could answer, Celia turned and hurried away down the corridor, her dark garments blending into the late-afternoon shadows. But she left that palpable air of sadness behind her. A sadness that infected everything, and reminded Rosamund of the true danger of her life at Court, her feelings for Anton.

It was only when Rosamund was changing her clothes for the evening's pageant that she remembered something. When they'd met in that corridor, Celia had been emerging from the Scottish delegation's rooms. What business could she have there?

Chapter Nine

Holy Innocents' Day, December 28

The leather tennis-ball smacked against the black-painted walls of the Queen's court, rebounding like a clap of thunder as Anton and Lord Langley raced to defeat each other in their game. Langley was ahead at the moment, but Anton was intent on gaining the winning point by hitting the ball through the opening in the dedans penthouse high above their heads. It was hot work, and neither of them ever seemed to get far enough ahead.

But Anton relished the burn of his muscles, the sweat that dampened his brow. It gave him something to focus on besides Rosamund, something to take the knife-edge from his hunger for her. He gave a fierce swing of his racket, smacking the leather ball back to Lord Langley. Langley dove for it, but missed, falling onto the court floor with a curse. Anton finally hit the ball through the opening, gaining his winning point.

Anton swiped his damp shirt-sleeve over his face, calling out, 'Do you concede then, Lord Langley?'

Langley rolled to his feet, laughing. 'I concede—for now! But this can't go on, Gustavson. First skating, now tennis. I shall have to best you at *something* soon.'

'Such as? It is too cold for a tourney, and everyone is told to stay at the palace for the rest of Christmas.'

'Thus no horse races, fortunately for you,' Langley said. They went to the end of the tennis court, where pages waited with linen towels and warm, velvet jackets to keep away the cold chill from damp skin. 'I am sure I could best you there. For don't you Swedes just skate everywhere?'

Anton laughed, roughly running the towel over his hair. 'Skates are of little use in battle, I fear, so we are sometimes forced to the primitive transport of horse-back.'

'Not so very primitive as all that, I hope. Equestrian feats do seem to impress the ladies.'

'As much as they are impressed by a lofty title?'

Langley grinned wryly. 'Alas, that is only too true. I could have a hunchback and a squint, and there would still be ladies to flatter and fawn.' He accepted a goblet of ale from one of the pages, drinking deeply before he added, 'And then there are ladies who are impressed by nothing at all.'

'Sadly, that only makes us want them more, does it not?'

'I see you learn the ways of courtly romance, Master Gustavson.'

'Your English ways, you mean?' Anton drank his

own ale, but there was no forgetfulness in its heady, spiced blend. He still saw Rosamund's blue eyes in his mind, felt the touch of her hand on his skin. Her sweetness—the innocent, heedless force of her passion—they were addictive, and he feared he came to need them more and more as the days went on. He could not stay away from her.

The more he saw her, the greater her charms. The more he wanted to know. And that craving was dangerous. It distracted him from his work here, from the careful plans he had held so long. It made him dare to think things he never could have before. If he gained possession of Briony Manor, if he was able to settle in England, his mother's homeland, if he could take an English wife...

It was too many 'if's, and Anton preferred to work in certainties. In what *was*, and how he had to work to achieve his goals. Rosamund did not seem like a logical goal. There were too many dreams of her own that she harboured in her heart; he could see that when he looked in her eyes.

His cousin Celia accused him of seeking an English wife to aid his petition for Briony Manor. But she was wrong. Rosamund was one of the Queen's ladies, and the Queen did not easily relinquish those in her household to marriage. Such a wife could only harm him in his errand.

And it would not do her any good, either, even if Rosamund would have him, which he did not think she would. He could never do anything to harm her, his beautiful winter-fairy, even as he fantasised about making love to her. Of seeing her pale, perfect body in his bed, her hair spread over his pillows as she held out her arms to him, smiled at him in welcome.

'*Svordom,*' he muttered, and tossed back the rest of his ale.

'Our English ways of romance can be labyrinthine indeed,' Lord Langley said. 'English ladies insist on being properly wooed, but each of them seems to have a different notion of what that means. What works for one repels another.'

Anton thought of Langley's efforts to impress Anne Percy, and laughed. 'I thought the ladies claimed to be impressed by pearls and silks.'

'Ah, that is another thing you must learn about our English females,' Langley said. 'What they desire changes day by day. And, also, they sometimes lie, just to confound us. Are the Swedish ladies so contrary? Or is it merely here, because we are ruled by a queen?'

'Nay, the Swedish ladies are every bit as demanding,' Anton answered. 'Perhaps they are affected by what they hear of the English, and insist on poetry and gifts. But matters of marriage are much simpler—it is arranged willy-nilly, and everyone does as they must, poetry or no.'

'So it often is here as well,' Langley muttered.

'Have you a betrothed, then? Someone chosen by your family?'

Langley shook his head. 'Not as yet, though my mother has taken to writing insistent letters every fortnight, suggesting this lady or that. She and her friends have played matchmaker for years, ever since I attained my majority. But I have not yet found the one who meets my family's requirements *and* my own inclination.'

Anton knew how he felt. His duty and his inclinations were decidedly at odds. 'The two are seldom reconciled.'

'How is it that you are not married, Gustavson?' Langley asked. 'You seem to have collected enough female attention here in London. Surely there is some lady in Sweden?'

'I have been too occupied of late with my own family matters to think of marrying. Perhaps once I have settled into a proper home, a place that needs a chatelaine...' And could that chatelaine be Rosamund? She would grace any house. But the Queen, and her family, would have to let her go first, and he feared they never would. He would not put her in danger by spiriting her away from them.

'Fortunately for us, we don't have to marry every lady who catches our eye,' Langley said, laughing.

'True. But there are some who would insist on it!'

Langley sighed. 'You are correct. But come, enough of this solemn talk! I fear we will never solve the mysteries of women today. Let us go out and see how the frost-fair preparations progress.'

Anton nodded, glad of the distraction. But even then his thoughts were of how much Rosamund would surely enjoy the delights of the frost fair...

'Tidings I bring for you to tell, what in wild forest me befell, when I in with a wild beast fell, with a boar so fierce...'

Rosamund smiled as she passed by the chamber where the chapel choir rehearsed, pausing for a moment to listen to the old tune of the boar's head.

Since tonight's traditional Feast of Fools had been changed to a mere banquet, with the mummer's antics cancelled, everyone had to work just a bit harder to make things festive. Everyone looked forward to the feast of Bringing in the Boar two night's hence.

She did not linger long, though. She had been sent across the palace to fetch some books for the Queen, and still had a distance to go. She didn't mind the errand. It was difficult to sit still in the Queen's chamber, to concentrate on her sewing and the other maids' chatter, when all she could think about was Anton.

She wondered what he was doing today, as Queen Elizabeth had not been receiving any official business and they hadn't seen anyone all morning. Was he off skating again? Walking in the garden, where so many flirtatious ladies waited to besiege him? Or perhaps he was closeted away on his own business, that disputed estate.

Rosamund remembered Celia emerging from the Scottish apartments. It seemed she looked for her allies, no matter how unlikely. Who would stand with Anton? She could, if he would let her. If they could forget the danger of it for only an hour.

She hurried on to find the books where the Queen had left them, and turned back towards the Waterside Gallery. Anne said they were setting up the frost fair on the frozen river, and Rosamund hoped for a glimpse to distract herself, to take a moment to think how she herself could broach the estate matter to Queen Elizabeth.

She leaned against a window sill, staring out at the river scene. It was indeed crawling with activity; from this distance it looked something like a chilly anthill with every ant set to some vital task.

They were building booths for the frost fair, places to sell hot cider and candied almonds, ribbons and lace. Icy avenues were laid out between the sledding and skating. Bright streamers were being tied to the booths, loops of greenery that added to the holiday excitement.

The prospect of the fair was a merry one in the midst of a tense Court. Everyone seemed to walk on a dagger's edge, afraid of what might happen next, even as they tried to hide it beneath Christmas cheer.

Rosamund too felt on edge, but Anton was the largest part of that—not knowing his feelings for her, or even the true nature of hers for him, was difficult. And, too, the fact that she was always daydreaming about him. Surely her distraction would soon earn her a slap from the Queen? Or more, if the Queen ever discovered what was between her and Anton!

But she could not be late with the books. Rosamund took one more peek at the frozen river and hurried away back towards the Queen's chamber.

As she turned through a narrow corridor leading from the gallery to the wing connecting the Privy apartments, she saw a small group headed her way. They were led by Lady Lennox, the Queen's cousin, her stout figure swathed in her usual black satin. She looked even more pinched and unhappy than usual. Probably her petition to the Queen to let her son Darnley go to Scotland, ostensibly to visit his father, was still not progressing well.

Rosamund shrank back into a curtained alcove, having no desire to be the focus of one of the countess's gimlet stares. Or, worse, to be urged to speak to the Queen on her behalf! She was trying to avoid notice and trouble, not court it.

She peeked past the edge of the velvet drape as they drew nearer, their voices a low murmur. With Lady Lennox was the Scotsman Melville—and also Celia. She walked at the countess's side, listening closely as the countess whispered furiously to Melville.

Rosamund could make out none of their words, and they quickly passed onwards, moving out of the corridor. She waited until they were certainly gone before slipping out of her hiding place and away in the opposite direction.

She thought of what Anne's uncle had said, about how the Queen's Court was filled with dangerous foreigners and their intrigues. Yet it seemed even the Queen's own family was not averse to intrigues of their own.

She was so intent on her path that she swung swiftly around a corner, not seeing the man standing there until she collided with him. Strong hands shot out to steady her as she reeled backwards, the books tumbling to the floor.

'Rosamund!' Anton said. 'Where are you off to in such a great hurry?'

Of course it would be him, she thought with a strange mixture of delight and chagrin. He always did seem to see her at her most awkward, her most unguarded! She held onto his arms to keep herself upright, smiling at him.

He looked as if he just came from some exercise, his hair smoothed back damply from his face and his dark eyes shining like polished onyx. He wore a simple black-velvet jacket over his shirt, which was loosely laced to reveal a smooth vee of glistening skin.

Rosamund could not stop staring at that skin, she feared to her great embarrassment. Staring at it—and longing to touch it, to discover exactly what it felt like. To trace a light pattern just there with her fingertips…

'Rosamund?' he said, bemused.

She shook her head, stepping back until her hands fell away from his arms. 'I—I was just fetching some books for Her Grace,' she said, staring over his shoulder at a patch of panelled wall. 'She does hate to be kept waiting.'

'I have certainly been here at Court long enough to know the truth of *that*,' he answered. 'I will not keep you. But should we have a dance lesson tonight?'

'A dance lesson?' she said, her head still whirling.

'Aye. Our time grows short until Twelfth Night. I was playing tennis with Lord Langley this morning, he told me of a chamber near the chapel we could use. It is assigned to his cousin, who is in the country, and thus it is empty. No one would be there to see me make a fool of myself.'

They would be alone? In a chamber, after the banquet? Rosamund was quite sure that under those too-tempting circumstances, *he* would not be the one acting foolish! But she felt as if she had already leaped down into a precipice, tumbling into a dark world she didn't recognise at all and could not stop. Falling, falling, down into peril.

'Very well,' she answered. 'Your dancing could certainly use a great deal of polishing before Twelfth Night.'

He grinned at her and bowed. 'Until then, my lady.'

Rosamund started to turn away, but then swung back, remembering what she had just seen. 'Anton!' she called.

He glanced back at her. 'Aye, Rosamund?'

'Did you…?' She looked around to be sure no one was near, then tiptoed closer to whisper, 'Did you know your cousin has made friends with the Scots delegation?'

His eyes narrowed, but other than that he showed no reaction. 'Friends?'

'I saw her yesterday, coming out of their apartments,' she said. 'And just now walking with Lady Lennox and Melville. Has she some Scottish connection?'

'Not that I know of, but then I know so little of my English family.'

'Could she…?'

'Rosamund.' He took her hand in his, holding it tightly. 'I thank you for telling me this, but pray be very careful in these matters. I know not what game Celia is playing, but with all that has been happening here of late it cannot be good. I will look into it.'

'But then *you* will not be safe!'

He raised her hand to his lips, kissing her bare fingers warmly, lingeringly. 'I have been taking care of myself for a very long time. But if anything happened to you I don't think I could bear it. Promise me you will stay far away from Celia and her—friends.'

Rosamund nodded, curling her fingers around his. He kissed them once more before he let her go. 'Until tonight, then, my lady.'

'Aye,' she murmured. 'Until tonight.'

* * *

'One, *two,* three! One, *two,* three! And—jump.'

At Rosamund's words, Anton tried the cadence but landed wrongly, dragging her down with him. She fell to the floor in a tangle of silk skirts, arms and legs—again.

'Oh!' she said, laughing. 'Perhaps it is time for a rest.'

'Rosamund, I am so sorry,' Anton cried, helping her sit up. 'I knew you would come to rue the day you agreed to teach me to dance.'

'I am not quite ruing it yet,' she said, smoothing down her skirts. 'You are getting better, I think. The volta is a very difficult dance.'

'And you are much too kind,' he said, sitting down beside her on the floor, stretching his long legs out before him. 'I can only hope not to cause complete chaos when we dance before the Queen—or injure you before that.'

'As for that, I am sure I'm safer here than in the maids' apartments,' Rosamund answered. 'The Marys leap about, shouting and quarrelling all night long.'

She leaned back on her palms, studying the tapestry-lined walls around them. It was nice in here, in Lord Langley's cousin's room, quiet and peaceful, far from the maids and the rest of the Court as they went to their late-night card parties and then stumbled home drunkenly. There was no fire, but those rich tapestries, the fine rugs on the floor and the exercise kept it warm.

She wished she could just stay there with Anton, cocooned in their own little peaceful place, for the rest of the night. For days and days.

Or at least until the Scots went home, and old Lord Pomfrey ceased to burst in on the maids in the altogether.

'It is not so tumultuous in your own home, I'm sure,' Anton said. He lay down on his side next to her, propping his hand on his palm. His hair was rumpled from their dance, falling in unruly waves over his brow. His fine satin doublet was unbuttoned, revealing his white shirt dampened by their exercise. The candle-light played over the planes and angles of his handsome face.

It all felt so wondrously intimate, just to be so close to him. To feel his warm body next to her, keeping the cold night at bay as they talked. She felt she could tell him anything, share anything with him.

'Ramsay Castle is very peaceful,' she said. 'I have no brothers or sisters, and so have always had my own chamber. I could read there in the evenings with none to disrupt me. But it can be lonely too.'

'I, too, have no siblings,' he said. 'At our home, my father was often away and it was only my mother and me. And the snow and ice!'

'No wonder you are such a fine skater, then.' She wished he would tell her more, tell her all about his life. His past, his hopes, his wishes.

'Aye, for there was little else to do.' He smiled at her, but there was a melancholy tinge to it. A whisper of memories and regrets. 'It was not like a true home.'

'And that is why you want to dance well for the Queen?' Rosamund asked. 'In hopes it will persuade her to grant your petition for the estate?'

'I doubt a fine leg on the dance floor will do that,' he said ruefully. 'At least, not on its own. But to gain her attention at every opportunity can only help, don't you think?'

Rosamund laughed. 'Her Grace does seem to admire an athletic gentleman.'

'And my pretty face?' Anton teased. 'Will that help too?'

'You are pretty indeed, Master Gustavson, though I hate to inflate your pride to even greater heights by saying so. And I am not the only one to notice,' she said. 'You can't fail but gain her attention. As for your petition—if right is with you, you definitely can't fail. The Queen is just.'

'My grandfather left it to me in his will,' he said. 'Surely that means right is with me?'

'If the will is proper and legal. He must have meant you to have it. Yet you never met him?'

He shook his head, lying down flat beside her. 'Nay, though my mother spoke of him so often I felt I knew him. They used to go to Briony Manor in the summer when she was a girl, and she would ride with him and her brother over the fields and meadows. She loved it there.'

'And that is why he left it to her—to you? It was her special place?'

'I think so, and because her brother and his sons inherited their other properties and had no need of a smaller place like Briony.' He reached out to stroke the edge of her white silk skirt between his fingers, studying it closely as if some secret was writ in the fine fabric. 'Also, my mother and grandfather quarrelled about her marriage before she left England. She always regretted it, and hoped that they could reconcile. Perhaps this was his way of doing so.'

'Oh, Anton.' Rosamund slid down to lie on her side

next to him, facing him. Her heart ached at his tale, at the thought of families broken apart by quarrels, by disagreements over romances and marriages. At a lonely boy growing up in the midst of ice and snow, longing for the green warmth of a land he knew only in his mother's stories.

Always searching, as she was, for a place to belong.

He turned his head to watch her, his eyes so dark, so full of swirling depths. She felt she could fall into them and be lost, like plunging beneath the winter ice to find a whole new world. A place of unimaginable beauty, worth the danger of obtaining it.

He rolled to his side, his palm reaching out to touch her face. His long fingers slid into her hair, loosened as it was by their dance, caressing, binding them together. Slowly, slowly, as if in a dream, he cupped his hand to the back of her head, drawing her closer.

Her eyes closed tightly as he kissed her, as his lips touched hers, seeking her out hungrily. As if he had longed for her, only her, for so long, a starving man granted his one life-giving wish.

Rosamund moaned softly, her lips parting as his tongue pressed forward, seeking hers. She touched the tip of hers to his lips, licking gently to taste the wine and sugared wafers from the banquet. To taste that dark bittersweetness that was Anton alone and was more intoxicating, more needful, than anything she had ever known. He tasted of the essence of life itself.

Their tongues tangled, all artifice melting away in a torrent of sheer need, of primitive desire that washed away all before it. Come what may, ruin or wonder, none of it mattered when they kissed, when they touched.

Through the shimmering, blurry haze of lust and tenderness she felt his fingers in her hair, combing free the last of the pins as he spread the pale strands over her shoulders. With a groan, his lips slid wetly from hers, and he buried his face in her hair, in the curve where her shoulder met her neck.

'Rosamund, *hjarta*,' he whispered against her bare skin. 'You are so beautiful.'

'Not as beautiful as you,' she whispered back. She reached out for him, pulling him on top of her so she could kiss him again, could press her open, hungry mouth to his jaw, his throat, to the smooth skin revealed between the laces of his shirt. He tasted of salt, of sunshine, winter ice, candle-smoke and mint. She held onto him so tightly, closing her eyes to absorb all of him, his heartbeat, his breath, the wondrous, vibrant, young strength of him.

He was beautiful, she thought, every part of him, body and soul. And she wanted him beyond all words, all rational thought. Beyond any realisation of danger or risk.

'Alskling,' he muttered hoarsely. His lips trailed down her bare neck, his tongue swirling in the hollow at its base where his life-blood beat. He kissed the soft edge of her breasts, pushed high by the beaded neckline of her bodice. She gasped at the waves of pleasure that followed his mouth, the touch of his hands on her bare skin.

She drove her fingers into his hair, holding him close as he licked at the line of her cleavage, nipped at her breast then soothed the sting with the tip of his tongue.

'I want to see you,' he said.

Rosamund nodded, mutely arching her back so he could loosen her bodice-lacing. The stiffened silk fell away with her thin chemise, and he drew it down until her breasts were revealed to him.

For a moment, as he stared at her avidly, she held her breath. Were they not right? Too small? Not small enough? She had not bared herself thus to another person, not even Richard when he had pleaded with her. It had never felt right, safe, as it did now with Anton. But suddenly she was unsure.

'So beautiful,' he said roughly. 'Rosamund, you are perfect, perfect.'

She laughed, tightening her fingers in his hair and drawing him back down to her. His lips closed over her aching nipple, drawing and licking until she moaned in delight.

Her eyes closed. She pushed his unfastened doublet off his shoulders until he shrugged it away. She closed her arms around him, her palms sliding along the groove of his spine, feeling the muscled tension of his shoulders beneath the clinging shirt. Yet still it was not nearly enough.

She wanted him in every way there could be, every way she had read about, heard whispers of. She wanted only him, and it burned inside her like a bonfire.

'Please, Anton,' she whispered, throwing every caution to the four winter winds. 'Make love to me.'

He stared up at her, raising himself to his elbows on either side of her. His eyes were shadowed with a flaming desire that matched hers, a lust that was out of control. But there was also a flash of caution, and that she did *not* want. Not now. Not when she finally knew exactly what she wanted: him.

'Rosamund,' he said hoarsely, his accent heavy. 'Have you been with a man before?'

She shook her head, swallowing hard. 'There was a—a gentleman at home. A neighbour. We kissed, and he—he wanted to do more. But I did not. I didn't trust him, not really. I didn't want him, as I do you.' Richard had been a bluff boy; Anton was a darkly mysterious, alluring man, and her desire for him was that of a woman. She saw that now.

'*Hjarta,*' he said. He rolled away to sit beside her, but he still held her hand. They were still connected in that magical moment of growing certitude and undeniable need. 'It will hurt the first time. And there could be— consequences. There are ways we can prevent it, but they are not certain.'

Consequences, as with Katherine Grey and Lord Hertford? That was chilling indeed. But Rosamund was not the Queen's cousin, and Anton was not an indiscreet fool. 'I know,' she said simply. 'But I want you, Anton. Do you not want me?'

'Want you?' He ran his hand roughly over his face. 'I burn for you, *hjarta*. I need you.'

'Then it is right.' She stood up, filled with the sure knowledge that this *was* right, that she and Anton were meant to be together, even if just for this one night. She reached for the tapes at her waist, intending to shed her heavy skirts, but her fingers fumbled at them. She was trembling too much.

'Here, my lady, let me,' he said softly. He rose to her

side, his long fingers reaching out to deftly unknot the tapes. Her overskirt, her embroidered petticoat and the cage of her farthingale fell away. He finished unlacing her bodice too, and cast it away along with her sleeves.

She stood before him in only her chemise, stockings and her heeled shoes.

Anton slid down her body until he knelt at her feet. Gently, he removed first one shoe then the other, running his thumb caressingly over her instep, the sensitive curve of her ankle. His palm flattened and slid along her calf, the bend of her knee, slowly, slowly, until she could barely breathe.

He reached the hem of her chemise, lifting it up, dragging it over her silk stockings until he revealed her garters, the bare skin of her thighs above. His fingertips just traced that line where skin met knitted silk, and Rosamund thought she might snap from the tension, the anticipation. Her womanhood felt damp, aching with heavy need.

And then, at last, he touched her *there*. His fingers combed through the wet curls then pressed forward to circle one aching, throbbing point.

Rosamund cried out, her knees buckling beneath her with the jolt of lightning-hot pleasure. Anton caught her up in his arms, carrying her to the alcove bed waiting in the darkness.

He reached down to draw back the bedclothes before he laid her down amid the linens. As she pushed herself back against the bolsters, propped on her elbows, he pulled off his shirt, revealing his bare chest to her at last.

The candlelight on the wall outlined him in a contrast of shadows and golden glow, his bare, damp skin glistening.

He was well-muscled and lean from exercise, from a life lived outdoors, and his skin had a smooth, olive cast to it, roughened by a sprinkling of coarse dark hair. It arrowed down towards his hose, as if to draw her gaze.

And she did stare. She had to; she could not look away. He was a truly wondrous sight, powerful and beautiful, like a god from his Norse homeland.

He leaned onto the bed, bracing his palms on the mattress either side of her, holding her a willing captive. His head lowered, his mouth capturing hers in a passionate kiss. A kiss that blotted out everything else. There was no doubt or fear, only the knowledge that, tonight, she was his. And he was hers.

He broke their kiss only to draw her chemise over her head and toss it away with his shirt. Her legs fell apart, and he eased between them, his body pressed to hers. Through the rough velvet of his hose, his penis was heavy and hard against her.

She almost giggled hysterically as she thought surely he would not look like old Lord Pomfrey! Then he kissed her again and any need to laugh, or even think, fled.

She wrapped her thighs around his hips, arching up against him, trying to feel yet more of him. His naked skin against her breasts made her cry out with need.

His moans answered hers, his mouth trailing away to press the hollow just below her ear. His hot breath against her made her shiver, mindless with desire.

'*Ledsen, hjarta,*' he whispered. 'I'm so sorry. I need you *now*.'

Rosamund nodded, closing her eyes as she felt him reach between their bodies to unfasten his hose. His penis, long and thick, sprang out against her thigh. She was surprised at how it felt on her bare skin, like velvet over iron, at how hot it was, and how thickly veined.

He gently pressed her legs further apart, and she braced her feet flat to the mattress as his fingers slid inside her.

Then his manhood followed, sliding slowly, ever so slowly, against her damp flesh. She tightened her jaw against the stretching, burning sensation, her shoulders tensing.

'I'm sorry,' he whispered against her cheek, his whole body held taut above her. 'I'm sorry.'

Then he drove forward and she felt a tearing deep inside, a flash of lightning-quick pain. She tried to hold back her cry but it escaped her lips.

'Shh,' he murmured. His body went perfectly still against hers. His breath rushed against her skin, as if he held his power tightly leashed. 'It will fade now, *hjarta*, I promise,' he soothed. 'I will make it better.'

He was right. As he lay still, their bodies joined, Rosamund felt the pain slowly fade away, leaving only a tiny curl of pleasure low in her belly.

She ran her hands down his back, feeling the hot, sweat-damp skin over his lean muscles pressing him closer to her.

He pulled slowly back and drove forward again, a bit deeper, and pleasure unfurled. Every thrust, every movement of his body against hers, every moan and sigh, drove the pleasure to greater heights. It was like a brilliant strand of sunshine unravelling inside her, blinding her with its brilliant light, its hot sparks of pure joy.

He suddenly arched above her, shouting out involuntarily as he pulled out of her.

Rosamund hardly noticed. Those sparks had blown into an enormous explosion of blue, red and white flames that threatened to consume her from within.

Then everything fell into darkness. When she opened her eyes, she found herself collapsed back onto the rumpled sheets, Anton stretched out beside her.

His arm was around her waist, holding her close. She turned her head to see that he lay on his side, his eyes closed, his breath laboured as if he too had felt the same wondrous, devastating pleasure as she.

'Anton…' she said.

'Shh,' he whispered, not opening his eyes. He just pulled her closer until their bodies were curled together. 'Just sleep for a moment, *alskling.*'

Rosamund closed her eyes again, resting her head on his shoulder as she felt the cold night air brush over her skin. She would happily sleep for a moment, happily stay just here, in his arms, for all the moments to come.

Anton held Rosamund as she slept, listening to her soft breath, feeling her stir against him as the night slipped away from them. The candles sputtered low, and the light at the window was edging from black into pale grey.

Soon, all too soon, he would have to let her go; their magical hours would end.

But they had been magical indeed. Women had

always been a large part of his life. He liked them, liked to talk with them, laugh with them and, yes, make love with them. Their minds worked in such wondrously subtle, fascinating ways. He loved to listen to their voices as they sang, loved their perfume, their laughter, their elegance. And they often seemed to like him in return.

Yet never had he met a lady who made him respond as Rosamund did. He found himself so completely fixated on her, wanting to be with her all the time. When she laughed at his jests, his spirits soared. And when they kissed…

He had never imagined he could feel this way about a woman, about anything. Yet Rosamund could not have come into his life at a more complicated moment.

Even with all that faced him—his uncertain circumstances, her position, the dangers at Court—he could never regret finding her. Could never regret the night they had just shared. But he would have to find a way to keep her safe.

He drew her closer, pressing a gentle kiss to her brow. She murmured, her soft skin wrinkling in a frown as if she resented the interruption of her dreams.

'It grows late,' he whispered.

''Tis too cold,' she answered, burrowing closer to him. She laid her freezing feet against his bare leg, giggling when he jumped.

'I would like nothing more than to stay hidden here with you all night,' he said, and he found he did. More than anything he just wanted to lie there with her in his arms for ever. 'And then all day, and all night again.'

'That sounds a wondrous prospect,' she answered.

'But I don't think I could find enough excuses for such an absence!'

'Will you be missed for these last few hours?' Anton asked in concern. Would she be caught, just from this one night, because of him and his carelessness?

'Nay,' she said, shaking her head. Her hair flowed over his chest, a skein of fine silk. 'Almost all the maids vanish mysteriously at one time or another. And I'm sure Anne will tell some tale for me. She is such a romantic—or maybe just a mischief-maker!'

'Nevertheless, I never want you to find any kind of trouble,' he said, kissing her forehead. 'I'm sorry, Rosamund, I should have thought of it before time got away from us.'

Rosamund laughed. 'We were rather distracted. But I cannot be sorry.' She sat up in their bed, leaning down to kiss him. Her lips were soft, tasting of wine and their night together. 'Can you?'

Anton wrapped his arms around her waist, pulling her down on top of him as he kissed her again. 'Sorry for being with you? Never, my lady Rosamund. You are surely the greatest gift I have ever known.'

She touched his cheek gently, tracing over his skin lightly with her fingertips. Her touch feathered over his brow, his nose, his lips, studying him carefully as if to memorise him. He caught the tip of her finger between his lips, nipping and suckling at the soft skin until she gasped, and he felt his body harden again.

'I should take you back to your chamber,' he said hoarsely, reluctant to let her go even as he knew he must.

Rosamund nodded silently. She rolled off him,

sitting on the edge of the bed as she reached down for her discarded chemise. The curve of her back was wondrously beautiful, so pale and elegant as the length of her silvery hair fell forward over her shoulders.

He did not resist. He sat up behind her, kissing the soft, vulnerable nape of her neck. She shivered and curled back against him as he wrapped his arms and legs around her, holding her close.

They sat there, bound together in silence, in that one perfect moment that was out of time and belonged only to them. Where there was no duty, no danger, just them—for ever.

Chapter Ten

''Tidings true there be come new, sent from the Trinity by Gabriel to Nazareth, city of Galilee! Noel, Noel…'

Rosamund bent her head over her sewing, unable to contain her smile as she listened to the other ladies singing. She feared she must look like an utter imbecile, the way she kept smiling that morning, smiling and laughing at every tiny jest. Yet she could not help herself. That small, warm knot of happiness deep down inside would not be suppressed.

She'd had little sleep last night. By the time she'd crept into her own bed, Anton's cloak wrapped over her half-laced bodice, the other maids had been asleep. Even after she had shed her garments, carefully folding the cloak into her clothes chest, and slid under the blankets she'd not been able to sleep. She kept remembering, going over every little detail, every delicious sensation, in her mind.

She was a wicked woman now, surely? But being wicked seemed entirely worth it! Perhaps she would not feel this way come tomorrow, but for today it seemed she floated on a cloud of delight, of close-held secrets.

Unfortunately, that bright cloud obscured her stitchery. She glanced down to find that her seams were all puckered and uneven. She reached for her scissors, trimming away the thread before anyone could notice.

The Queen sat by her window, a book open in her hands. Yet she did not seem to be reading, for she merely stared out through the diamond-shaped panes of glass. The other ladies, the ones who did not sing, also read and sewed or played quiet card-games, like Anne and Catherine Knyvett.

It was a slow, silent day; the moments ticked away by the crackling flames in the grate. Too much time to be lost in lustful daydreams.

As Rosamund reached into her sewing box for a skein of thread, her gaze met the painted black eyes of the Queen's mother. She seemed to warn of the dangers of being wicked, even over the years. The dangers of trusting men, of putting one's heart above one's head and duty.

But it still felt so very good.

'God's breath!' Queen Elizabeth suddenly cried, tossing her book across the room. It narrowly missed one of the Privy Chamber ladies, who ducked out of the way before going back to her tapestry.

'I am bored,' the Queen said. 'I cannot stay in this

room another moment. Come, help me dress! We are going down to the frost fair, and perhaps a sleigh ride.'

'Your Grace,' Mistress Parry said, her voice tinged with alarm. 'Lord Burghley says…'

'Forget Burghley,' the Queen said. 'Staying cloistered in here will achieve naught. I must be out among my people.' She threw open one of her clothes chests, tossing about piles of sleeves and petticoats as her ladies rushed to help her.

'Your Grace, please,' Mistress Parry begged. 'If you must go out, let us find your warmest garments for you.'

The Queen plumped herself back down in her chair, arms crossed. 'Be quick about it, then! Lady Rosamund?'

'Your Grace?' Rosamund cried, startled to hear her name. She leaped to her feet, dropping her sewing. Was she in trouble? Her secrets discovered?

'Lady Rosamund, go to the stables and instruct them to ready my sleighs. We will depart in an hour.'

'Yes, Your Grace.' Rosamund made a quick curtsy, hurrying out of the bedchamber.

The Privy Chamber and corridors were crowded with courtiers milling about gossiping, hoping for a glimpse of the Queen, a chance to speak to her, to catch her eye. But Rosamund was accustomed to them now, and dodged swiftly around the shifting groups to make her way down the stairs.

Amid all the people gathered there, between the swirling patterns of bright silks, glowing pearls and the wind-like rush of whispers, she caught a glimpse of Anton.

Her stomach lurched in a sudden jolt of excitement.

Everything in her cried out to run to him, to throw her arms around him and kiss him. But everyone was watching, always watching, hoping for a new titbit of gossip about someone. Anyone.

Rosamund bit her lip to keep from smiling, and slowed her steps as she passed him, hoping he would see her and come to speak to her, give her some sign that he, too, remembered last night. That it had truly meant something.

He *did* see her and smile, an exuberant grin that transformed his solemnly watchful face to youthful radiance. Her heart seemed to skip a beat at the sight, then pounded in her breast.

He excused himself from his Swedish friends, making his way past the crowds to her side. At first, his hand reached out for hers, as if he too longed for their touch. But then he seemed to recall that they were not alone, and just smiled down at her.

He looked so very handsome in the light of day, his dark waves of hair smoothed back to reveal the amethyst drop in his ear. The gold-embroidered high collar of his purple-velvet doublet set off his olive-complected skin perfectly, and he was every inch the consummate, cosmopolitan courtier.

Yet she recalled how he had looked last night as they'd kissed goodbye outside her door—his rumpled hair and sleepy, heavy-lidded eyes. The way their lips had lingered, their hands clinging together. How wonderfully beautiful he was.

'Lady Rosamund,' he said, his voice low, caressing. That voice, with its faint touch of a musical accent, its velvety texture, seemed to touch her as his hands could not. 'How do you fare this morning?'

'Very well indeed,' she answered. She gazed into his eyes, trying to send him her thoughts, her feelings. To convey all that last night truly meant. 'I hope that you are the same?'

'I have not seen a finer day yet in England,' he said. 'Perfect in every way.'

Rosamund laughed happily. 'I think Her Grace agrees. We are to visit the frost fair, then go for a sleigh ride along the river.'

'Indeed? A sleigh ride sounds most delightful on a such a perfect day.'

'But perhaps commonplace to you? You must use such conveyances often in Sweden.'

'And a taste of home would be welcome.'

'Then I am sure the Queen would be happy to see you there. Perhaps we will meet you at the frost fair?'

'Perhaps you will, Lady Rosamund.'

She curtsied as he bowed, still trying to hold back her exuberant smile, her laughter. She hurried on her errand, but could not help glancing back over her shoulder.

He still watched her.

The frost fair was truly an amazing sight. As Rosamund walked with the other maids between the booths, she feared she was gawking like a silly country-maid. But it was all too easy to be continually distracted by the sights and smells.

The booths, peddling everything from ribbons, embroidered stockings, gloves, spiced cider and warm gingerbread, were hung with bright pennants. The streamers of red, green and white snapped in the cold breeze, blending with the cries of the merchants, the laughter of the shoppers.

On the wide lanes between the booths people skated past, dodging around the strollers and gawkers. Beyond were sleds and sleighs, even people on horseback using the frozen river as a new kind of road.

It was very crowded, noisy with merriment that was a welcome respite from the hardships of such a cold winter. No one even seemed to notice the weather, especially as Queen Elizabeth came among them.

One would never have guessed that there had been any danger of late, any darkness hanging over the Queen's holiday celebrations. She went into the crowd of her subjects with a warm smile and happy words. She accepted bouquets of fresh greenery, a goblet of warm cider, kneeling down to speak to one shy little girl.

Rosamund observed the faces of the people who gathered around, all of them shining with joy to see their Queen, awestruck, hopeful, thrilled. As if Elizabeth was made of some winter magic. It was inconceivable in that moment that anyone could want to hurt her, want to mar that golden aura that surrounded her and touched all who looked on her.

No one even seemed to notice the extra guards who surrounded their little procession, who kept such close watch on the exuberant crowds and held their pikes and swords ready. Lord Leicester, especially, stayed close to the Queen's side, scowling at any who dared edge too near.

At one moment Elizabeth turned to him with a smile, tucking a sprig of holly into the fastening of his doublet. 'Do not frown so, Robin,' she murmured. 'It is Christmas!'

He smiled back at her, and in that moment Rosamund glimpsed something profound. The Queen looked at Leicester as she herself looked at Anton. There was such tenderness and longing in their smiles. How could she be trying to marry him off to the Scottish queen?

Master Macintosh seemed to feel the same. He fell into step with Rosamund as they continued on their way, and she saw that he too watched the Queen and Leicester, frowning.

But he just said, ''Tis a fine day, is it not, Lady Rosamund?'

She gave him a polite smile, not entirely trusting his sudden friendliness. 'If you like ice and chilly winds, Master Macintosh.'

'In Scotland, my lady, this would be a balmy summer's day!'

'Then I am glad I don't live in Scotland.'

'You do not enjoy the winter, then?'

Rosamund remembered Anton skating on the ice, and their warming kisses amid the frosty woods. 'Winter does have its own pleasures, I think. But spring has many more. Sunshine, green things growing…'

'Ach! You English are a delicate lot,' Macintosh scoffed.

'Not all of us, I think,' she said. 'Some of us seem most eager to travel to your windswept country, Master Macintosh. Lord Darnley, for instance.'

Macintosh's expression seemed to close, even as he still smiled at her. 'I understand he wishes to visit his father, who is in Edinburgh.'

'So I hear. It is very touching that family affection can overcome even the rough weather you speak of.'

'Indeed so, my lady.'

Rosamund remembered Celia emerging from the Scots' apartments, walking with Lady Lennox. Perhaps she was also intrigued by the Scottish weather. 'And surely there must be others among us frail English you have found to be hardy souls?'

'Well, there is you, Lady Rosamund.'

'Me?' She shook her head. 'I fear I am the least hardy among us.'

'Oh, I do not believe that, my lady,' Macintosh said. 'You seem filled with many—hidden depths.'

'Yes?' Rosamund said warily. 'My family would disagree with you. They think I am as shallow as can be.'

'Nay. I would say you are more like what lies beneath this ice under our feet,' he said, tapping at the bluish-silver ice with his boot. 'Swirling winter tides.'

'I am a simple female, Master Macintosh. I want only what everyone wants—a home, a family.' And freedom to gain what she desired with no danger.

'And you think to find that here at your Queen's fancy Court?'

'I think to do my duty here, until I am needed at home again. It is an honour to be asked to wait on the Queen,' Rosamund said, even as she knew very well that was no longer true. She did not want to go home. She wanted to stay close to Anton for as long as possible. No matter the perils.

'So, Lady Rosamund of home and hearth,' Macintosh said, again all teasing smiles. 'What do you think of Court life?'

'I like the fashions very much indeed,' Rosamund answered lightly, holding out her velvet skirt. 'And I have heard that your Queen Mary is most stylish. Tell me, Master Macintosh, is she as tall as they say?'

They went on to speak of inconsequential matters of fashion, but still Rosamund could not quite erase the sensation that Master Macintosh wanted something from her, some nugget of information about Queen Elizabeth and her matrimonial intentions for Queen Mary. She would have to be even more careful of everything she said in the future, to be always cautious. It was easy to forget that, but she could not afford to.

Once they had walked round the whole fair, stopping to admire the wares at the various booths and watch the skaters, they all made their way back to their transport. The Queen's sleighs waited for them, piled high with blankets and furs, the horses' bridles jingling with silver bells.

As Rosamund watched Leicester hand the Queen into the grandest sleigh, the one at the head of the procession, Anton appeared at her side. She did not see him at first, but she knew he was there. His warmth seemed to surround her; his clean scent carried to her on the cold breeze like a spell.

She smiled, closing her eyes to imagine that she hugged his very presence close to her.

'My lady,' he said. 'Will you join me?'

'Of course,' she answered, turning to face him. She was quite sure she would join him wherever he cared to lead her, come what may. He held out his arm, and she slid her hand atop his woollen sleeve, resisting the urge to cling, to run her fingers up his arm to his shoulder and plunge them into his hair, to pull him close for a kiss. She had to remember her resolve to be careful, to be wary of the eyes of others.

He seemed to divine her thoughts, for his eyes darkened. He led her to the end of the line of sleighs, where one just big enough for two people waited along with a pair of beautiful white horses.

Only one vehicle was behind it, another small sleigh already occupied by Anne and Lord Langley. They seemed to have declared some sort of truce, for they were laughing together over some jest.

Rosamund glanced ahead. All the other sleighs were larger, crowded with jostling courtiers. 'How did you procure this vehicle, Master Gustavson?' she asked.

'By my wondrous charm, of course, Lady Rosamund,' he answered, giving her a jaunty grin. 'And a little bribe never hurts, either.'

She laughed, taking his hand as he helped her up onto the cushioned seat. He settled blankets and fur robes around her, tucking them close against the cold.

And, under the cover of those robes, he pressed a quick kiss to her wrist above the edge of her glove. His lips were warm, ardent, against her skin.

But his kiss was as fleeting as it was sweet. He leaped up onto the seat beside her, taking the reins from the groom. 'Are you warm enough?' he asked roughly.

Rosamund nodded mutely. She tucked her hands into her muff, trying to hold onto his kiss as he set their sleigh into motion behind the others. The bells on all the harnesses rang out merrily, a high, silvery song in the cold air, and some of the people burst into song along with them.

'Love and joy come to you, and to you, your wassail, too! And God bless you and send you a happy new year...'

Rosamund smiled, leaning against Anton's shoulder as they lurched into movement. A few lacy snowflakes drifted from the pearly-grey sky, clinging to her eyelashes, to the fur trim of the blanket around her.

She laughed aloud, tasting the crisp snow on her lips. 'Now it truly feels like Christmas!' she said.

Anton laughed. 'You do not see snow so often, then?'

'Rarely,' she said. 'It must seem foolish to you, me getting so very excited about these tiny flurries, after the great blizzards of Sweden.'

'Oh, no,' he answered. 'I love anything that makes you smile.'

Under the cover of the robes, she linked her arm through his, feeling the tension of his lean muscles as he drove, the strong heat of him. It held her up, made her strong. Strong enough to face any danger.

'This day makes me smile,' she said. 'But what do you think of our puny English winter?'

'I think that I hope to see many more of them just like this,' he said.

They fell into a companionable silence as they flew along on the ice as if the sleigh had wings. They went under London Bridge, waving at the people above, and past the Tower. In the haze of snow and laughter, even its dark, ominous roof-lines, its thick walls, seemed muted. They rushed past Traitor's Gate, where once the Queen herself had passed through as a princess, and it was behind them.

At the docks, they went around the curve of the river and were released into the countryside. The trees along the river, thick enough to hide the fine country estates, were heavy with ice. They sparkled and glinted, like massive clusters of diamonds.

They passed a set of broad water-steps, a gate crusted with more ice, and in the distance Rosamund could see the square battlements of an old red-brick manor house. For just a moment she allowed herself a distant, impossible dream: that it was *her* house, hers and Anton's. That they would stroll along those battlements in the evening, arm in arm, looking out over their gardens before they went inside to sit by their fire.

In her dream, her parents came to dine with them, to play with their grandchildren, all quarrels forgotten, a true family once again. But then the fantasy house was past; the dream burst like a shimmering ice-bauble. Like the delicate moments she had with Anton.

'Did your mother truly quarrel with her father before she married?' Rosamund asked wistfully.

Anton glanced down at her, his brow arched in surprise. 'Indeed she did. He did not approve her choice of a Swedish diplomat she met at Court, and protested that she would go too far from home. That she would be lonely and unprotected. Sadly, he proved correct in the end.'

Rosamund bit her lip, staring out at the countryside as it flew past, a grey blur. 'It is sad when families are torn apart by disagreements. We all have so little time together as it is.'

'Rosamund, *kar*,' Anton said gently. He shifted the reins to one hand, putting his other arm around her shoulders to draw her closer. 'This is not a day for melancholy! I do so hate to see you sad.'

Rosamund smiled, resting her head on his shoulder. 'How can I be sad when I'm here with you? It's only…'

'Only what?'

'It is so difficult to admit when one is wrong and one's parents are *right*!' she said, laughing. 'Your own grandfather was surely right in a terrible way, but I admit I am glad now of my father's advice.'

'And what was his advice to you?'

Rosamund remembered her father's words: *when you find the one you truly love, you will know what your mother and I mean.* Then, it had made her so angry, so confused. Now she saw the great foresight of it. Her feelings for Richard had been nothing but a girlish infatuation, a candle flame next to the bright sunlight of Anton.

How long could their time last? A fortnight, a month? Rosamund feared it could not be long, not in such a world of uncertainty. She just had to make the most of every moment.

'My father said I would one day find my own place, the place that is right for me, and I should never settle for less,' she said.

'And have you found it at Court?'

Rosamund laughed. 'Nay, not at Court! I am not clever enough to survive long there. But I think I am close. What of you, Anton?'

He hugged her closer against him. 'I think I might just be close myself.'

The sleigh swung around a curve in the frozen river and up over a rise, and a magical scene was revealed before them.

On the banks a flat space had been cleared and open-sided pavilions of green and white erected. The Queen's banners snapped from the poles, bright streamers of green, white, red and gold embroidered with Tudor roses. Bonfires were blazing with rising orange flames that sent out tendrils of welcome warmth even from that distance.

Under the pavilions, liveried servants rushed to and fro, bearing laden platters and jugs of wine.

'A snow banquet!' Rosamund said happily. 'How lovely. You are quite right, Anton.'

'I know I am,' he answered. 'But what am I right about just now?'

'That this is not a day for sadness. It is Christmas, after all. We must make merry.'

'Oh, yes. I am quite sure I can do *that*,' he said. He bent his head, kissing her quickly before they could be seen. His lips were warm on hers, sweet and perfect. Rosamund longed to wrap her arms around him, holding onto him tightly, but he was suddenly gone from her side.

He leaped down from the sleigh, reaching under the seat and drawing out a knapsack.

'I brought you a gift too,' he said. 'In honour of the holiday.'

'A gift?' Rosamund cried in delight. 'What is it?'

'Open it and see,' he said, grinning.

She pulled aside the sack, wondering what it could be. Jewels? Silks? Books? But out tumbled a shining pair of new skates, just like Anton's, only in miniature.

'Skates?' she said slowly, holding them up to the light.

'Made especially for you, my lady. It took a great deal of searching in London to find a blacksmith who could make them,' he answered. 'I did say I would teach you to skate.'

Rosamund smiled down at them, cradling them in her lap. 'They are beautiful,' she said. 'Thank you, Anton.'

'You will be a veritable Swede in no time at all,' he said.

She laughed. 'But I fear I have no gift for you!'

'On the contrary,' he whispered. 'You gave me a most wondrous gift last night.'

Rosamund felt her cheeks burn, but Anton just kissed her again and took the skates from her hands, tucking them back under the seat. He lifted her down from the sleigh, leading her to their place in the procession into the pavilion. Once there, they were separated, Anton seated with the other Swedes and Rosamund with the maids at the table just below the Queen's.

'Your cheeks are all red, Rosamund,' Anne whispered.

'Are they? It must be the cold wind,' Rosamund answered, reaching for a goblet of wine to cover her silly urge to giggle.

'Oh, aye. The cold,' Anne said. 'We will have to start calling you "Rosie".'

'But what of you?' Rosamund said. 'You and Lord

Langley seem to have mended your quarrel, whatever it was.'

Anne shrugged. 'I would not say mended. But if he makes proper amends...'

Rosamund longed to ask what was really going on between Anne and Lord Langley, longed to see her friend as happy as she was herself. But it was obvious Anne was not in a confiding mood, so she turned her attention to the food, to the fine tapestries draped around the pavilion walls to keep the wind out.

To trying not to stare at Anton like a love-sick school-girl. That was a great challenge indeed.

Anton walked along the bank of the frozen river, listening to the hum of laughter and music from the pavilion behind him. The merriment grew louder as the wine flowed, and he had found he desperately needed a breath of fresh air. A moment alone to try and break the spell he seemed to have fallen under.

The cold wind cleared his head of the music and the wine, but not of the one thing he most needed to banish. The sight of Rosamund's wide, sky-blue eyes gazing up at him as they'd dashed over the ice. Of her smile, so full of sweetness. The sweetness that was so much more alluring than any practised flirtation could ever be.

It drew him in, closer and closer, until Rosamund was all he could see, all he cared about. It was so dangerous for both of them.

Anton raked his fingers through his hair, cursing at how complicated everything had become since he'd arrived in London. He'd thought to gain his estate, start a new life free and clear—not tumble into infatuation with one of the Queen's ladies!

Anton, my dearest, he suddenly heard his mother say, the memory like a whisper on the wind. In his mind he saw her face, white with illness as she clutched at his hand. *Anton, you are so dutiful, so ambitious. But I beg you—do not let your head always rule your heart. Do not let what is really important slip by you. I regret nothing in my life, nothing I did, because I followed my heart.*

He had not understood her then, as she'd lain on her deathbed. What could be more important than duty, than bringing honour to his name? His mother had followed love and it had brought her unhappiness.

But now when he heard Rosamund laugh, when she looked at him with those eyes, he saw what his mother meant. The demands of the heart could be just as strong as those of the mind, twice as clamorous. Could he afford to listen to them?

Were they telling him what was really important in life?

Anton shook his head; he wasn't sure he knew any longer. His old, stone-solid certainty, the certainty that had carried him through battle and all the way to England, was turned to ice, liable to crack at any moment.

He turned to look back at the pavilion. Rosamund stood in the doorway, rubbing her arms against the chill as she glanced around the bleak landscape. Then she saw him and smiled.

Even from that distance it was as if the summer sun emerged from the grey cold of winter.

She waved to him, beckoning him to return to the party. Anton took one more long look at the frozen river before making his way back to her.

Surely that cracking sound he heard was his own heart, breaking open to let her peek inside for one instant before it froze up again for ever.

Chapter Eleven

Bringing in the Boar Day, December 30

'The boar's head in hand bear I, bedecked with bays and rosemary! I pray you all now, be merry, be merry, be merry…'

The gathered company in the Great Hall applauded as the roasted boar was carried in, borne aloft on a silver platter. It was a large boar, adorned with garlands of herbs and surrounded by candied fruits, a whole apple in its mouth. It was presented to Queen Elizabeth, who received it on her dais, and then paraded around the chamber.

More delicacies followed—roasted meats of all kinds, including deer and capons brought in from the Queen's hunt, pies, stewed broths and even a few fish dishes, carefully prepared with spices and sauces. These were doubly precious with the river frozen. On the multi-tiered buffets the sweets were displayed—gold-leafed gingerbread, cakes topped with candied flowers, the Queen's favourite fruit-suckets with their long-handled sucket spoons. The centrepiece was an elaborate subtlety of Whitehall itself, complete with windows, cornices, brickwork and even a blue-sugar river rippling alongside with tiny boats and barges.

Rosamund applauded along with everyone else, laughing as the Queen's jesters tumbled and gambolled between the tables. It was yet another lavish Christmas display, with everyone happily flushed with the fine malmsey wine, with flirtation and with the reckless joy of the holiday.

Yet underneath all the loud merriment there was a knife's edge of tension, of some darkness, some desperation, lurking underneath. There was always that heated blade under everything at Court, waiting for the unwary to fall onto it and destroy themselves.

Rosamund peeked over her shoulder, searching for Anton in the crowd. He sat with his Swedish friends, observing the gathering with quiet, watchful eyes. *He must feel it too,* she thought. That taut sense that something was just on the verge of happening.

What that something was, none could say. But the foreign delegations seemed the most tense of all, as if the usual perils of manoeuvring through a foreign monarch's Court were increased, even darker and deeper than usual. Like the hidden, swirling depths beneath the ice outside.

Her gaze slid along the wall, over the extra guards placed about the hall by Lord Leicester. At least no enemy could invade tonight. The merriment was safe for one more banquet.

She turned back to Anton, finding him watching her. He grinned at her, and she laughed into her serviette. She could not help it; whenever he smiled at her thus it was as if the bright sun emerged from the winter clouds. As if she soared free above any danger or worry.

That was foolish, of course, because nothing could change their tenuous circumstances. But for one moment she could forget, could dream.

'You seem happy tonight, Rosamund,' Anne said, sipping at her wine.

'And you seem pensive,' Rosamund answered. Anne had certainly seemed happy enough on their sleigh-ride along the river, but she had received a letter on their return and was now quiet. 'I hope you did not have sad news from home?'

'Certainly not. Merely more lectures from my aunt,' Anne said. 'What of you? Have you lately heard from your parents, or your lost suitor?'

Rosamund was startled. She had almost forgotten Richard in all that had happened here at Court. He seemed almost a dream now, a ghost of sorts who had drifted into and out of her life, leaving only a mist of memories. Memories of the girl she had once been.

'Nay, to either,' she said. 'My father sends my allowance, but I have had no other word. I'm sure they want me to think only of my work here.'

'And do you?' Anne asked. 'Have you found new distractions here to make you forget the old?'

Rosamund laughed, thinking of Anton's kiss—his smile, his eyes, the way his body felt against hers as they made love. Aye, she had found ample distractions in the present to make her forget the past. Or forget the dangers of the present.

Would it break her heart all over again in the end, far worse than the smaller pain Richard's desertion had caused? She feared it would, for her feelings for Anton were a hundred times whatever the infatuation she had felt for Richard had been.

'I have enjoyed my time here,' she said. 'Haven't you, Anne?'

Anne shrugged. ''Tis better than cooling my heels at home, I dare say! At least there is dancing and music.'

And handsome men such as Lord Langley? But Rosamund said nothing, and soon the remains of the food were cleared away and the tables moved for the dancing. The Queen and Leicester led the figures for the galliard.

Anne joined the dance with one of her admirers, but Rosamund retreated into a quiet corner to watch. She was suddenly weary—weary of the feasting, the loud holiday-gaiety, the music and laughter. She longed for a warm fire to curl up next to in her dressing gown, for a book to read, a goblet of warm cider—and Anton beside her to laugh with, to kiss. To keep the endless cold winter away.

Could such dreams ever truly happen? Or was she merely fooling herself again? Perhaps Anton would go back to Sweden and disappear from her life, as Richard had. What would become of her dreams then?

Suddenly she felt a gentle touch on her arm, warm through the thin silk of her sleeve. She spun round to find Anton standing there, his eyes dark and fathomless as he watched her. As if he divined something of her strange, sad mood. He, too, seemed in a strange mood tonight.

'Are you well, my lady?' he asked quietly.

'Quite well, I thank you, Master Gustavson,' she said. 'Merely a bit tired from all the feasting.'

'It would be enough to make anyone out of sorts,' he said. 'But you seem rather melancholy.'

'Perhaps I am a bit.'

'Is it because…?' His words broke off as a rowdy crowd passed near to them, jostling and laughing drunkenly. Anton's hand tightened protectively on her arm, drawing her away from them. 'Follow me.'

He led her around the edge of the crowded hall, keeping close to the wall where the flickering shadows hid them from view. Everyone was far too busy with their own flirtations and quarrels to notice them anyway as they ducked behind one of the tapestries.

It was the same one where they had first kissed, Rosamund saw, with her kissing bough still hung high above. The heavy cloth muffled the raucous noise of the dance, and the only light was a thin line of torch flame at their feet.

Anton held her lightly by the waist, and she wrapped her arms around his shoulders. At last that tension she had felt all night began to ebb away, like a tight cord unwinding, and she sensed a slow peace stealing over her. Perhaps he might be gone from her soon, but they were together tonight. As alone as they could be at Whitehall, closed around by their own shelter of quiet.

'Tell me why you are sad, Rosamund,' he said.

'I am not sad,' she answered. 'How could I be, when you have rescued me yet again?'

Yet he seemed unconvinced, drawing her closer in the darkness. 'Is it because of what happened between us?'

Because of their love-making? How could that be, when it had been the finest, most glorious thing that had ever happened to her? 'Nay! I could never regret *that*. Why? Do you?'

Anton laughed, kissing her brow. 'Regret being with the most beautiful woman in all of England? Oh, *alskling*, never. I *am* a man, after all.'

Rosamund grinned. 'That fact did not escape my notice.'

'I truly hope not! But there must be something that has you melancholy tonight.'

'I was just thinking of my home,' she said with a sigh. 'Of how I have not heard from my family for a while.'

'And you miss them?'

'Yes. That is it.' She did not want to speak of her fears for the future, of what would happen when he left. Not now, not yet. Not when every moment they were alone, like this one, was so precious.

'Well, we shall just have to make a merry holiday here ourselves,' he said, drawing her closer and closer until they were pressed against each other in the shadows.

Rosamund slid her hands around his neck, twining his hair over her fingers, tickling the nape of his neck. 'Oh? And how do you propose we do that?'

'Well, we start with this…' He softly kissed her brow and each of her eyelids as her eyes closed, and a sharp breath escaped her at the sudden, fiery rush of excitement. 'Or this.' His lips slid to her cheek, to the hollow just below her ear. 'Or—this.'

At last his lips met hers, his tongue touching hers as she shivered. It felt as if years had passed since their last kiss, as if she had been waiting, longing, for this for such a long time, fearful it would never come again. Yet it also seemed they had spent all their lives together just so, and that their kiss was a sweet homecoming.

He tasted of wine and sweet fruit, of Anton, of her lover. Rosamund held him tightly, straining up on her toes to be closer, ever closer, to him. To hold onto this moment for ever.

He groaned, his arms sliding to her hips as he pressed her back to the wall. He lifted her up as her legs wrapped around his waist, her heavy skirts falling back. As he held her there, braced against the wood panelling, she felt his hand slide to her thigh, caressing the bare skin above her stocking.

Every place he touched left like a trail of fire, of burning need and deep delight. Slowly, teasingly, his fingers trailed up then back again, ever closer to her aching, damp womanhood but never quite touching.

Only when she moaned, arching her hips toward him, did he at last give her what she longed for.

One finger delved inside her, pressing to that one sensitive spot. Pleasure shot through her like lightning, burning but icy-cold. He kissed the side of her neck, his breath hot, heavy, enticing against her skin.

'Rosamund,' he groaned.

She forgot where they were, forgot the world that waited just beyond their hiding place. She wanted only him, knew only him.

She reached between them, her hand fumbling under

his doublet until she found the iron-heavy press of his erection straining against the lacings of his hose. If she could only free him, if they could only be joined…

A blast of trumpets stilled her hand, like a sudden rush of cold water. Anton also went still against her; he pressed his forehead to her shoulder, his fingers sliding from inside her to brace against the wall.

He drew back and they stared at each other in the shadows, as if shocked at how quickly they forgot everything when they were together.

Shocked at how disappointed they were to have their lustful moment ended.

Slowly, carefully, he eased her back to her feet, arranging her skirts around her again. She smoothed her hair up under her pearl-trimmed cap, but she feared she could do nothing about her flushed cheeks. 'Rosie', indeed!

'I'm sorry, *alskling*,' Anton whispered, kissing her hand. She smelled herself on his skin, and it made her shiver all over again.

'I'm not,' she whispered back, feeling wondrously wanton, feeling marvellously unlike herself. Or perhaps more herself than she'd ever been before she'd found him.

Once they were able to stand, to walk without shaking, Anton held aside the tapestry to let her pass by him. Her legs were still weak, but she could not cease smiling.

She blinked at the sudden rush of torchlight, the dazzle of flame and noise after the sultry darkness. For an instant she could see only a blur, then the scene grew clearer. The trumpets had signalled a new arrival, and the dancing paused as everyone gathered around to see.

A new arrival in such an insular world as the Court was always an occasion of great interest. But not to Rosamund. She found the only thing of interest to her was Anton, the prospect of hiding behind the tapestry with him again, hiding all night, forever in his arms.

She glanced back, trying to be discreet, to find that he stood several feet away, watching her with that intense light in his dark eyes that always made her tremble. Now it made her want to grab his hand and drag him away from the crowd, make him hers alone. He gave her a secret smile, and she smiled back, trying to put all she thought and felt into that one little gesture.

But that was all she could do. The other ladies were gathering with Queen Elizabeth near the vast fireplace, and Rosamund's absence would be noticed. She couldn't afford trouble now, not for herself, and certainly not for Anton. If they were caught, he would surely be sent back to Sweden without his English estate, and she would be sent home in disgrace. Then she would never see Anton again, never even have the chance of a future with him.

She turned away from him, hastily straightening her bodice before she went to stand beside Anne.

Anne gave her a questioning glance, but they had no time to speak. The Queen's new guests had entered the hall.

The page that led the party bore Queen Mary's standard of a red lion-rampant on a gold background, so they were new representatives sent from Edinburgh. Behind the standard came a stern-faced man in black, and two finer-dressed young men carrying boxes that were surely Christmas gifts to Queen Elizabeth from her cousin.

And behind them…

Rosamund gasped, pressing her hand to her mouth. Nay, surely it could not be? But she rubbed at her eyes and he was still there.

It was Richard, unmistakably. His skin was less ruddy than it had been in the summer, and he wore a closer-trimmed beard. He wore fine new clothes too, of sky-blue and silver satin. But his tall, burly chested countryman's physique was the same, as was his shining cap of blond hair, the ever-watchful way his gaze darted about.

After all the months without any word, any appearance, here he was at Court—with a party of Scots! Rosamund was utterly bewildered. It was like the months had slid away and she was back in the past again. Only with all the new knowledge she possessed.

She glanced across the room to where Celia stood with Lady Lennox. Richard's sister-in-law did not seem surprised, but then she never did. Celia just watched the proceedings with her lips pressed together, while Lady Lennox smiled smugly, and her son Darnley just seemed drunk. As usual.

Rosamund's gaze flew back to Richard. He had not yet seen her; what would happen when he did? Would he smile at her, speak to her? Did he even remember what had happened between them last summer? For herself, she had no idea what she felt. She felt numb, frozen, by the sudden intrusion of the forgotten past into the present. By the sudden reminder of the girl she had been and the woman she had become.

'Rosamund?' Anne whispered, gently touching her sleeve. 'What is amiss?'

Rosamund shook her head, watching as the new Scots party, including Richard, bowed to the Queen.

'Your Grace,' the older man in black said. 'I am Lord Eggerton. We are happy to bear Christmas greetings from your cousin, Queen Mary, as well as dispatches from her and her hopes that you may soon meet in amity and family unity.'

'We wish the same, and we welcome you to our Court,' Elizabeth answered. 'Queen Mary is most generous to spare so many of her own Court at such a time of year!'

'We are most happy to attend on you, Your Grace, and to serve Queen Mary,' Lord Eggerton answered. 'May I present Lord Glasgow and Master Macdonald? And this is Master Richard Sutton, one of your own subjects, who brings word of your many friends in Edinburgh.'

'You are all most welcome,' the Queen said. 'I look forward to reading your dispatches tomorrow. Right now, though, you must be hungry after your journey. Please, partake of our banquet. My ladies will fetch wine.'

And it was then that Richard saw her; his eyes widened. A slow smile spread across his face, and he veered away from his group to grab her hand in his.

Startled, Rosamund fell back a step. His skin seemed rough on hers, his palm clammy. It gave her no sudden thrill, as Anton's touch always did. She had changed truly. The past had no hold on her at all now.

But he held on tightly, not letting her go.

'Rosamund!' he said. 'Here you are at last, my dear little neighbor. And looking prettier than ever. London life agrees with you.' He raised her hand to his lips, pressing a damp kiss to her knuckles as he smiled up into her eyes.

Nay, there was none of that old feeling left, of the old illusions.

She felt ridiculously foolish, admitting to herself that her parents *had* been right all along. And where exactly had Richard been all those months? What had he been doing in Scotland?

'So this is where you have been hiding,' he said. 'Here at the Queen's Court!'

'I have not been *hiding*,' Rosamund said, taking back her hand. She tucked it in the satin folds of her skirt. 'One is never more out in the open than in London, surely?'

'And yet your parents claimed they could not disclose your location!' said Richard. 'We thought you had been sent to some Continental nunnery.'

Rosamund had to laugh at the thought of her staunchly Protestant parents packing her off to a nunnery. Though perhaps they would prefer it to seeing her make a foolish and unhappy marriage. 'If anyone has been hiding, it is surely you. No one has had a glimpse of you since the summer.'

'And I am heartily sorry for that, Rosamund,' he said solemnly. 'I have thought of you so often.'

Somehow she doubted that. Their summer flirtation been nothing more than a passing breeze for them both, she knew that now. 'But you had important business in Edinburgh, it would seem?'

'I have. I want to tell you—'

'Lady Rosamund!' Queen Elizabeth called sharply. 'Come along.'

Rosamund backed away from Richard, not liking the glow in his eyes, the desperation she saw there. 'I must go,' she said.

Richard's hand shot out to grab hers again, holding on tightly. 'Rosamund, I must talk with you. Explain things.'

Rosamund shook her head. That was all done now. 'Explain what? I assure you, Master Sutton, there is no need…'

'Rosamund, please! Please, meet with me. Hear me out,' he begged. His hand held onto hers, and she could see he would not let her go until she agreed.

'Very well,' she murmured, knowing it would be the only thing that would make him let her leave. 'I will meet with you tomorrow.'

'Thank you, Rosamund. Beautiful, sweet Rosamund.' He kissed her hand again before letting her go at last. 'You will not regret it.'

And yet she already did. She regretted being a young, romantic fool, for fancying herself in love with the first man who had ever looked at her. A man she saw now played at some game between the Scots and English. Some game with her heart.

A man not like Anton at all. Or was he? Anton was such a mystery to her.

As she joined the Queen her gaze frantically scoured the crowd for a glimpse of Anton. She suddenly had a desperate need to see him, to know he was still there, that he was real.

But at the same time she hoped he had not seen her— had not seen Richard kiss her hand.

When she found him, though, she saw that her hopes and fears were in vain. He stood near the doorway with Lord Langley, his arms crossed over his chest as he watched her with narrowed eyes.

She could read nothing of him at all.

Anton saw the blond, bearded man kiss Rosamund's hand and hold that hand tightly in his as he talked to her. It was no polite greeting; their hands were bent close, their eyes meeting as they spoke intimately, almost as if no one else was near.

Rosamund knew him; Anton could see that. She had looked shocked when he had walked past, her face suddenly as pale as if she had seen a spectre. And the man knew Rosamund, enough to boldly take her hand and whisper in her ear.

Where had the cursed man come from? What was he to Rosamund?

A wave of bitter jealousy rose up in him, and his hands tightened into fists he longed to drive into the man's blond, English face. He had never known such a fury before, and he wasn't sure he liked it. But it all could not be denied. He detested this man he had never met, because he had dared kiss Rosamund's hand, dared to be known to her in some way.

And Anton detested him for the smug smile he exchanged with his Scottish cohorts. He was up to something, and Anton determined to discover what it was—and what exactly he was to Rosamund, even as he knew he had no right to feel that way about her.

Anne Percy joined Lord Langley and him by the doorway.

'Nothing like a surprise appearance, yes?' she said, watching the new Scots delegates as they sat down to their repast. 'Too bad they are not more handsome. But then Queen Mary probably keeps the best of them at her own Court.'

'You do not think them handsome?' Lord Langley asked, striving to sound disinterested, but not quite achieving it.

'Not like our own Court gentlemen,' Anne teased. 'Though that blond-haired Englishman is not so very bad. But I fear his heart seems to be already claimed.'

Claimed by Rosamund? 'Do you know him, then, Mistress Percy?' Anton asked.

She gave him a shrewd glance. 'I know only his name—Richard Sutton. He seems to be some kinsman of Celia Sutton. And he also seems to admire Lady Rosamund—which I am sure *you* can understand, Master Gustavson.'

'Is she already known to him?' Anton asked, compelled to know, even as he did not want to know, not really.

Anne hesitated. 'I am not entirely sure yet, but I think…'

'Think what?' Anton urged.

'Rosamund told me once she had a suitor back at home,' Anne said. 'Someone her parents did not approve of, though she did not name him to me.'

'But you suspect this Richard Sutton is he?' Anton asked.

'Perhaps. He did seem rather closely acquainted with her,' said Anne. 'And she went quite pale when she saw him.'

'I see,' Anton said tightly. 'An ardent suitor.'

Anne suddenly laid her hand on his sleeve. 'Master Gustavson,' she said quietly. 'I am quite certain that whatever was between them is in the past.'

'Or *was* in the past,' Anton said, giving her a smile. Anne Percy loved to seem the careless Court flirt, sophisticated, knowing. But underneath she was a hopeful romantic.

Much like himself, fool that he was. It seemed he had too much of his mother in him, was too inclined to follow the demands of his heart even against duty and danger.

'Shall I set my men to discover why he is here?' Lord Langley said. 'To be mixed up with the Scots—it cannot be good.'

'Set your spies on him, you mean?' Anton said. 'There is no need, Lord Langley.'

Anton would find out what he needed to know all on his own. He would not see Rosamund hurt, no matter how 'ardent' the suitor. And no matter that he himself would most probably hurt her in the end…

Chapter Twelve

New Year's Eve, December 31

'Your Grace, I fear I must heartily disagree with these plans,' Lord Burghley said, thumping his walking stick against the parquet floor for emphasis.

'My dear Cecil,' answered the Queen, pounding her fist on her desk to make her own emphasis. 'I fear *I* must then remind you who is master here! This is *my* Court, and I shall order my own Christmas.'

'But your safety…'

'My safety? From what? A few paltry threats, that are as nothing compared to what I have faced in the past,' the Queen said. 'My father always had a masquerade ball to mark New Year's Day, and so shall I.'

Rosamund bent her head over her sewing, trying to pretend she was not there in the Queen's chamber, was not hearing her quarrel with Lord Burghley—again. There was always a quarrel between them.

Even in her short time at Court Rosamund felt she had heard this before—Queen Elizabeth insisting she would do something, and Lord Burghley arguing she should not for her own sake. Today it was the Queen's insistence that she would have a masked ball tomorrow night. Next week it would surely be something else.

It put Rosamund in mind of her own father. Did her father know Richard was here in London? Had he heard any rumours at Ramsay Castle as he and her mother celebrated their own holiday? If he had, he would surely summon her home in haste. But she knew she could not go now, not when Anton was still here. Not while she was still learning him.

Rosamund bit her lip, remembering Anton's face as he had watched her with Richard. What would he think of the way Richard had kissed her hand, had spoken to her so familiarly? What if Anton thought she did not care for him even after everything?

She had lain awake in her bed all night thinking of it, even as she feigned sleep to keep Anne from questioning her. She had to speak to Anton, and to Richard, too, to find out what he was doing at Court. Yet there was no time, as they all had to attend on the Queen.

Oh, how did all these Court ladies manage all their tangled love affairs? she thought as she stabbed at the linen with her needle. It was confusing enough with only two!

'Rosamund,' Anne whispered. 'Are you quite well?'

'Of course I am,' Rosamund whispered back. 'Why do you ask?'

'Because you have sewn that linen to your skirt.'

Rosamund looked down, startled to see that she had indeed firmly attached her embroidery to her velvet skirt. 'Oh, blast,' she muttered, reaching for her scissors.

'Here, let me,' Anne said, taking the scissors away. 'You would cut your gown to ribbons in your distracted state.'

Rosamund sat very still, watching as Anne snipped loose the threads. 'Tell me, my friend,' Anne said, under cover of the task, 'Is the new arrival your swain from back home?'

'Aye,' Rosamund muttered. 'Richard. I have not seen him since the summer, and I thought that was all ended.'

'But it is not?'

'He wants me to meet with him,' Rosamund said. 'He wishes to explain, he said.'

'Hmm. It did not appear *his* feelings were dimmed, not with the eager way he held your hand,' said Anne. 'But what of you?'

'I fear I do not feel as I once did towards him,' Rosamund admitted. And she had not for a very long time. Maybe not ever.

'Because of Anton Gustavson?'

'Perhaps. Or perhaps I have changed.' She knew she had. Anton had helped her change.

Anne snipped away the last of the threads. 'Will you meet with him?'

'I do not know. I feel as if I owe it to him to at least hear him out.'

'I don't think you owe him anything at all! Not with the way he deserted you. But you must do as you see fit.' Anne handed her the scissors. 'Just be careful, Rosamund, I beg you.'

'Of course I will be careful,' Rosamund said, straightening her sewing box. 'I hope I have learned *some* caution here at Court.'

Anne laughed. 'Not from me, I fear.'

'Mistress Percy! Lady Rosamund!' the Queen called. 'What are the two of you whispering about, pray?'

Anne sat up straight as Rosamund tried to stifle her giggles. 'Of our costumes for your masquerade, Your Grace,' Anne said.

'Ah. There, you see, Cecil?' Queen Elizabeth said. 'Everyone plans for the masquerade already. We cannot disappoint them.'

'As you wish, Your Grace,' Lord Burghley said reluctantly.

'And I must make my own plans,' Elizabeth said. 'Lady Rosamund, fetch Mistress Parry to me. She is in the Great Hall.'

'Yes, Your Grace.' Rosamund abandoned her ruined sewing and hurried out of the chamber, grateful for some task. For the chance to look for Anton.

Yet she did not see him in the crowds in the Presence and Privy chambers, or in the corridors. Nor was he in the gallery, where the choir was again rehearsing. This time it was for the wassail carols that traditionally accompanied the New Year's gift-giving that would commence at that night's banquet. The strain of that gift-giving showed on courtiers' faces. Would their gift impress the Queen? Would it bring them favour?

'Wassail, wassail, all over the town, our toast it is

white and our ale it is brown! Our bowl it is made of
the white maple-tree, and a wassailing bowl we'll drink
unto thee!'

Rosamund listened to their wassail song, stopping to
peer out of the window at the gardens below. She did
not see Anton there, either, among the many people
strolling the pathways under the weak, watery sunshine.

As Rosamund stared down at the garden she did not
see the paths, the people bundled up in their furred
cloaks or the winter greenery under the dusting of
sparkling snow. She only saw Anton, saw his smile as
he held her, his laughter as he twirled over the ice.

She saw the dark look in his eyes as he watched her
with Richard. The danger that was already around them
all the time.

She spun away from the window, only to come face
to face with Richard himself.

He smiled at her, reaching for her hand.
'Rosamund! At last we meet. I have been looking for
you all morning.'

'Indeed, M-Master Sutton?' Rosamund stammered,
trying to take back her hand. He held it too tightly,
though, and she worried people were watching. 'I have
been with the Queen, as usual.'

His smile widened, his blue eyes crinkling in a way
she had once found so attractive. 'You are very busy
with your tasks here at Court. I see the Queen shows
you much favour.'

'No more than any of her other ladies,' Rosamund
said quickly. But then she relented a bit, drawn in by
his eyes, by the memory they evoked of summer and

home, the times they had shared. 'But it is true she has
not thrown anything at me yet!'

Richard laughed. 'And that is quite an accomplish-
ment, from what I have heard.' He raised her hand for
a quick kiss, then he released her at last. 'Rosamund,
will you walk with me? Just for a while?'

'I…' She glanced around the crowded gallery. 'I am
meant to fetch Mistress Parry for the Queen. She is in
the Great Hall.'

'Then I will walk with you there,' he said. 'Please,
Rosamund. I must speak with you.'

'Very well, then. I would be glad of the company,'
she answered. She would also be glad of the chance to
find out where he had been all those months. Why he
had left her. Why he had returned now.

They fell into step together as they made their way
through the crowds, but he did not try to touch her again.
It was as if he, too, sensed the new gulf between them,
the distance of time and reflection. The distance of new
pursuits and affections. A new truth, a new way of life.

Or perhaps it was only she herself who felt that,
Rosamund thought wryly. Even as Richard smiled at
her, as she felt the tug of home and memories, he seemed
a stranger to her. What they had once been to each other
seemed strange and foolish now. The emotions were of
someone she scarcely even knew, a girl.

'You do look lovely, Rosamund,' he said quietly.
'Court life agrees with you.'

'You mean I look better in my fine gown than I did
at home with loose hair and simple garments that can't
be mussed by the country mud?'

His eyes crinkled again, and he leaned towards her, as if to find something of their old connection. 'You looked lovely then, too. Yet there is some new elegance about you here. You seem—changed.'

'As do you, Richard. But then, it has been a long time since last we met.'

'Not so long as all that.' He paused. 'I thought of you often, Rosamund. Did you think of me?'

'Of course I did. There was much speculation in the neighbourhood about where you had gone.'

'But did *you* think of *me*?'

She stilled her steps, facing him squarely. This had to be ended now. 'For a time. When I did not hear from you, though, I had to turn to other matters. To listen to the counsel of my family.'

'I wanted to write, but I fear I was not able to. Not from where I was.'

'And where were you?' she asked, not sure she wanted to know. Richard had secrets; she could tell. She needed no more secrets in her life.

'On an errand for my own family,' he said. But Rosamund noticed he would not quite meet her gaze. Mysteries, always mysteries; there were so many of them at Whitehall. 'I moved about too often, I fear. Yet I thought of you every day, remembered our declarations to each other.'

'The declarations of foolish children. My parents were right—I was too young to know my own mind.' She started to turn away, but he caught her arm in a tight clasp, crumpling the fine satin of her sleeve.

'Rosamund, that isn't true!' he insisted. 'I had work

to do, for *us*. So I could support you as you deserve, to show your parents I was worthy.'

'I thought you worthy,' Rosamund said. She tugged at her arm, trying to free herself. There was a glow to Richard's eyes, a hard set to his jaw she did not like. It was as if the mask of the laughing summer-time Richard had fallen away, showing her the stony anger and resentment underneath. His hand tightened on her arm, painful enough to bruise.

'Let me go!' she cried, twisting her wrist. A few courtiers glanced their way, hoping for new distraction, new scandal.

The mask fell back into place, leaving a repentant visage behind. Yet there was still a red flush of anger in his cheeks. Rosamund suddenly remembered more than their sunlit kisses, remembered things she had once ignored, excused: the temper when a groom had fumbled with his horse; his railing against her parents, against the injustice of society. His unkind words about Celia, disguised as concern for his brother. Those memories only made Rosamund feel doubly foolish, especially as she rubbed at her sore arm.

'I am sorry, dear Rosamund,' he said repentantly. 'Forgive me. I just have thought of you, longed to see you, for so long...'

She shook her head. 'Please, Richard, do not. Our flirtation was sweet, but it seems so long ago. It is over,' she said, trying to be firm. Even if there had not been Anton, anything she had once felt for Richard was entirely over.

His lips tightened into a flat line. 'You *have* changed.

Living here at Court, amid all these riches, these grand courtiers, has changed you.'

Aye, she had changed; Rosamund knew that. Yet it was not the glitter of Court that had changed her. It was knowing what a truly good man was like; it was Anton. A man who tried to do his duty, to protect her, even as their passion drew them closer and closer together.

'I am older now, that is all,' she said. 'Please, Richard. Can we not part as friends?'

'Part?' He looked as if he would very much like to argue, perhaps to reach for her, grab her again. But a laughing group passed close to them, jostling, and he stepped away. 'Yet we still have so much more to speak of together.'

'Nay, Richard,' she said. 'My life is here now, and yours is—wherever you have made it in these last months when I did not hear from you. We must part now.'

She took a step back, only to be brought up short when he snatched her hand again. That laughing knot of courtiers was still nearby, so she had no fear. Yet she did not like the way he looked at her now, the way he held onto her.

He jerked her to his side, whispering roughly, 'You and your parents think you are so great, so high above my family that you would refuse my suit. But soon, when I have made my fortune and great events have come to pass, you will be sorry.'

Rosamund twisted her hand away from him, hurrying down the gallery as fast as she dared. She longed to run, to dash to her chamber and wash her hands until the feel of him was erased. Until all her old memories, good and bad, were gone too.

She turned down another corridor, and at its end glimpsed Anton. He still wore his cap and cloak, and his skates were slung over his shoulder as if he'd just come in from the cold day. He saw her too, and a smile of welcome lit his face. But then a wariness took its place, dimming, dampening, as the grey clouds outside.

Rosamund did not care, though. She had to be near him, to lean into him, to feel that calm strength of his and know she was safe. Know that the past was gone, and Richard held no threat.

She hurried towards him, dodging around the ever-present crowds until she stood before him. She reached out and lightly touched his hand, tracing the little gold-and-ruby ring on his finger. His skin was cold, the frost still lingering on his woollen sleeve.

His smile returned, warmer than any fire, any sun.

'You were skating on the river?' she said, taking her hand back before anyone could notice her bold touch. Her fingers still tingled, though.

'Aye. 'Tis a fine day, Lady Rosamund, you should join me later and try those new skates.'

'I should like nothing better,' she answered. 'Yet I fear I will be busy with the Queen this afternoon. She is finishing preparations for the gift-giving tonight.'

'Then I shall not keep you from your tasks,' he said. He glanced over her shoulder and his eyes narrowed.

Rosamund looked back to see that Richard stood at the other end of the corridor, watching them. She leaned closer to Anton, seeking his strength.

'Or perhaps you are also busy with your old friends from home?' he said slowly.

Her gaze flew back to his. He knew of Richard? Ah, but then of course he would. Everyone knew everything at Court. There were no secrets.

Almost.

'I—nay,' she said. 'That is, yes, Richard's family's estate neighbours ours, and I have known him a long time. I begin to think I was quite mistaken in his character, though. Too long a time has passed since I last saw him.'

'He seems quite pleased to see *you*,' Anton said. 'But then, who would not be?'

'Anton,' she whispered. 'Can we meet later?'

His hand brushed hers under cover of his cloak. 'When?' he said, his voice reluctant but deep with the knowledge that he could not resist. Just as she felt.

'There will be fireworks tonight after the gifts. Everyone will surely be distracted.'

'Lord Langley's cousin's chamber again?'

'Aye.' Rosamund longed to kiss him, to feel his lips on hers, and she saw from the intent look in his eyes that he must feel the same. Or was she imagining things again? She wanted to stay, to talk to him.

Yet she had her errand, and had to be content with one more quick touch, a smile. 'I will see you there.'

Then she hurried on her way, glad her path did not again take her past Richard.

Anton watched Rosamund dash out of the corridor, her velvet skirts twirling, before he turned his attention to the man: Richard Sutton.

Anne Percy had said he was a 'suitor' of Rosamund. Yet obviously he was not one her parents approved of, for she had been sent to Court rather than married to him. Was he now some danger to her?

When Rosamund had run up to Anton and taken his hand, he'd seen a flash of fear in her eyes, like that of the St Stephen's Day fox going to earth. He was glad indeed she felt she could run to him, but there was a fury that anyone should frighten her at all.

He leaned back against the wall, his arms crossed over his chest as he watched Richard Sutton. The man talked with Celia Sutton now, and she looked angry as well. Her usually solemn, stone-serene face was tense. She shook her head at whatever he was saying to her, and he flushed a dark, furious red.

The man did appear to be burlier than he, Anton had to admit—thick-chested and broad-shouldered; an English tavern-brawler. But he also showed signs of running to fat, where Anton was lean and quick from skating and sword-play. Surely he could best this harasser of ladies in a duel?

And a harasser he seemed indeed. He grabbed Celia's wrist, his fingers tightening as she shook her head again. Anton had seen enough. He pushed away from the wall, striding towards the arguing pair.

'Excuse me,' he said, sliding smoothly between them. He took the man's thick hand in a firm grip, peeling his tight clasp back from Celia's thin wrist. With his other hand he took her arm, drawing her a few steps away.

For once, she did not protest. She hardly seemed to

notice who held her arm, so occupied was she in glaring at Richard Sutton.

So, Anton thought, he was not the only one she quarrelled with. 'I beg your pardon for interrupting such a cozy *tête-à-tête*,' he said. 'But I have an appointment with my fair cousin. I am sure you will excuse us, Master…?'

'This is my brother-in-law, Richard Sutton,' Celia said. 'He and I have nothing left to say to each other.'

'On the contrary, Celia,' Richard said, all false, bluff heartiness. 'We have a great deal to say to each other! And who is this foreigner, anyway?'

'He told you,' Celia said. 'He is my cousin. And also a *foreigner* who is much admired and favoured here at Court. Just ask Lady Rosamund Ramsay.'

She swung away suddenly, pulling Anton with her as he still held her arm. But he looked back at Richard, holding her still for just a moment longer.

'And also a foreigner well-educated in gallantry and courtesy to ladies,' he said lightly, but with an unmistakable threat of steel laced underneath. 'In my country, we tend to become very angry indeed when we see a woman treated with less than proper respect.'

The flush on Richard's florid face deepened. Celia smiled at him sweetly, and added, 'And that is why the ladies here are so appreciative of you, Anton. Our rough Englishmen from the countryside have little knowledge of such gallantry and fine manners.'

'Nay, for we have knowledge of far more useful matters,' Richard said. 'Such as warfare. Dispatching our enemies.'

'Tsk, tsk, brother,' Celia said. 'Such martial tendencies will never win you a fair maiden like Lady Rosamund.'

Anton arched his brow and gave Richard a mocking bow before walking away with Celia on his arm. He could feel the burn of the man's glare on the back of his neck all the way down the corridor, and it made him itch to draw his dagger.

But there were too many people about, and Celia's clasp was tight on his sleeve.

'So, that interesting person is your brother-in-law,' he said.

Celia snorted contemptuously, her steps so quick he had to pay close attention to keep up with her. They passed the open doors to the Great Hall, where much activity went on to prepare the tables meant to display that night's New Year's gifts.

'He *was* my brother-in-law, until my husband died,' she said. 'Now that family seeks to deny me my dower rights.'

As he sought to deny her her rights to Briony Manor? But he did not seem to be the focus of her ire today.

'They are a greedy lot, the Suttons,' she said. 'I would never have married into their midst if I had a choice. Lady Rosamund is most fortunate.'

'Lady Rosamund?'

'Ah, yes. I forgot you, too, admire her. Perhaps your suit will fare better with her parents than Richard's.' A tiny, cat-like smile touched her lips. 'I would like to see Richard's face if *that* happened.'

'They objected to his offer?' Anton asked, even as he cursed his curiosity, his damnable need to know everything about Rosamund.

'It never came to a formal offer. Richard and his family are quite ambitious, and they schemed for the match. I believe he even tried to woo her in secret, but I knew it would come to naught.'

'Why is that?'

'Why, cousin,' Celia said slyly. 'Who knew you would be so interested in provincial gossip?'

Anton laughed. 'I am a man of many interests.'

'Indeed you are. Foremost among them Lady Rosamund, perhaps?'

'Anyone may know my regard for her.'

'I would advise you to be sure of her affections, then, before you brave the Queen. Or the Ramsays. She is their only child, their treasure, and they quite dote on her. I knew they would never let her go to a clod like Richard.'

'Or to a foreigner?' They must know what a treasure they had, then, and would not easily let her go.

'That remains to be seen, does it not?' She abruptly came to a halt, staring up at him with those brown eyes so like his mother's. And his own. His only family, so very angry at him.

'I will say this, cousin,' she said. 'We have been rivals, but I am not entirely a fool. I can see that you are made of finer stuff than the Suttons, and that Lady Rosamund cares for you. But you should not underestimate Richard. He looks bluff and hearty, an empty-headed farmer sort of man, but he is ambitious. He hides and creeps like a snake, and he detests to be thwarted.'

'I have no fear of a man like him.' It was not Richard Sutton who kept him from Rosamund but his own duty.

'I know you do not. In truth, you remind me much of my own father. He feared nothing at all, for everyone seemed charmed by him, yet that was his undoing in the end. Just watch for Richard, that is all. Especially if you somehow succeed in gaining Lady Rosamund's hand.'

'Mistress Sutton!' a woman called. Anton looked up to find the Queen's cousin, Lady Lennox, beckoning to Celia.

'I must go now,' Celia said, turning away.

'Cousin, wait,' Anton said, catching her hand. 'Perhaps I am not the only one who needs must beware. What business do you have with Lady Lennox and the Scots?'

Celia gave him a crooked little smile. 'We all have to make our way here at Court, yes? Find what friends we may. Just remember what I said.'

Anton watched her go, frowning, as the day seemed to darken. It was true that he did not fear Richard Sutton, or any man. He had faced villains aplenty in battle, and in the austere court of the temperamental King Eric, and he had bested them all.

Yet he had only had to be concerned with himself then. Now there was Rosamund, and Celia too. And nothing made him angrier than threats to a lady.

That anger was also a sign that his own connection to Rosamund grew too great. He had told himself he was careful, that his heart would not rule his sense, that they would not get into trouble for their affair. That he could protect her.

But that had been foolish; he saw that now. He had to end it, once and for all.

* * *

All the courtiers crowded around the open windows of the Waterside Gallery, bundled in cloaks and furs against the cold. But no one seemed to notice the sharp night wind, for there was too much excited laughter, too much exultation over the success of their gifts to Queen Elizabeth, and the fineness of hers to them. The long tables of the Great Hall were piled high with jewels, lengths of velvet and brocade, feathered fans, exotic food and wines and all manner of lovely things, including the pearl-encrusted satin sleeves Rosamund's own parents had sent.

Not everyone was filled with happiness, of course. A few thought their gifts had been overlooked, or they were slighted by what the Queen had presented to them, and they thus sulked at the edges of the room. But they were few indeed. Everyone else was content with the warm, spiced wine passed among them by the royal pages, and with waiting for the fireworks Lord Leicester had so painstakingly planned to usher in 1565.

Rosamund felt all overcome with excitement, though not for the same reasons. Soon she would meet Anton again in their secret place, and they would be alone at last. She craved those moments in their secret world far too much, it was a bright moment of hope.

Yet some of that brightness dimmed when she glimpsed Richard across the gallery, watching her. At first she surprised him, and the expression on his face was darkly scowling, heavy with some discontent— perhaps that she had not answered the note he'd sent her via one of the pages? Then he smiled broadly and seemed something of the old Richard again. But she no longer trusted that smile. She turned away from him, hurrying over to the windows to stare out at the river.

The frost fair was still in force, full of activity under the glow of torches and the moon. Sleds glided along the frozen grooves of the Thames between the booths and she could hear the distant hum of music, wassail carols to bring in the New Year.

What would the year bring? she wondered. Everything she hoped for? Or heartbreak and trouble?

The night sky suddenly exploded above them, a crackling, glittering shower of red-and-white fireworks. A flare of green followed, and a long waterfall of blue stars. It was wondrously beautiful, and Rosamund stared up, open-mouthed with delight. It reflected the hope in her own heart, the hope that dared shine its tiny light even in the midst of danger.

Everyone out on the river stopped to stare, too, exclaiming at the beauty of it all. The sparks glistened on the ice, turning it all to a fantasy land far from the harsh realities of winter.

Rosamund eased away from the crowd as their attention was absorbed by the spectacle. Holding her silk skirts close to her sides, she tiptoed out of the gallery into the silent corridor. Once she was certain she wasn't followed, she dashed headlong towards her rendezvous.

The apartment was quiet and dark, yet she remembered well where everything was. The chairs and tables, the fine carpets—the bed. She felt her way to the window, pushing back the heavy curtains to let in the glow of the moon, the sparkle of the fireworks. They illuminated the space that had become such a haven against the world to her.

Dear; how cold! She rubbed at her arms in their embroidered sleeves, wishing for a cloak. But soon enough Anton's arms would be around her, and she could forget the cold, and everything else, for a time.

As she stood there, staring out at the night, she heard the door open behind her. Footsteps hurried across the floor, heavy and muffled by the carpet, and strong arms did indeed slide around her, drawing her back against a hard, velvet-covered chest.

For an instant, she remembered Richard staring at her, and she stiffened, half-fearful he might have followed her. But then she smelled Anton's scent—clean soap winter greenery—and felt his familiar caress at her waist, and she knew she was safe.

She relaxed against him, resting her head back on his shoulder as they watched the fireworks.

He softly kissed her cheek. 'Happy New Year, *alskling*,' he whispered.

Rosamund smiled. 'And Happy New Year to *you*, Master Gustavson. What is your wish for the next year?'

'Is this an English custom, then? Making a wish for the New Year?'

'Of course. Oh—but I forgot. You mustn't tell it, or it might not come true.'

She spun around in his arms, going up on tiptoe as their lips met in the first kiss of the new year. She tried to put all she wished for in that kiss, all she felt for him and hoped for in the future. That fear was left entirely behind.

He seemed to feel it, too. He groaned against her

mouth, his tongue touching the tip of hers, tasting her as if she was the finest, sweetest of wines. His hands combed through her hair, discarding the pins and pearl combs as it tumbled over her shoulders.

'*Hjarta,*' he muttered, burying his face in her hair, kissing the side of her neck and the curve of her shoulder as he eased away her bodice.

Rosamund's eyes drifted closed, her head falling back as she lost herself in the delicious sensations of his caress, his kiss, the feel of his lips on her bare skin. But she wanted more, wanted to feel him too. To be closer, ever closer.

She fumbled eagerly for the fastenings of his doublet, but suddenly his hands grasped hers tightly, holding her away.

Rosamund stared up at him, bewildered. His jaw was tight, his eyes hooded, hidden from her. 'What— what?' she stammered. 'What is amiss?'

'I'm sorry,' he said hoarsely. 'I'm sorry, *alskling*, I should never have met you here tonight. Never let things go so far.'

Rosamund shook her head in puzzlement. Anton still held her hands, they still stood close together, but she felt him slipping away from her. It was as if a cold wind rushed between them, pushing them further and further apart.

'Things have gone—so far before,' she whispered.

He kissed her hand, his hair falling over his brow as he bent over her fingers. How handsome he was, she thought numbly. Like a dark Norse god. Other ladies thought so, too; they all sought him out, flirted with him. Yet she had been foolish enough to join their ranks, to think he cared for her, only her.

Had she been wrong? Had she entirely misread what was between them?

Rosamund stepped back, drawing away her hands. She could not think when he touched her. Her mind raced, going over every kiss, every glance and word. Nay; she had not been mistaken, surely? No man was such a fine actor.

Why, then, did he turn from her now?

'I know we have gone thus far before,' he said roughly, raking his hair back with his fingers. It fell into even greater disarray, and Rosamund longed to smooth it back, to feel the warm satin of his hair under her touch.

She tucked her hands into her skirts, forcing them to stay still.

'I was wrong, very wrong, to behave thus,' he continued. 'I put you in danger, and that was inexcusable. I'm sorry, Rosamund.'

'Nay, we both wanted this!' Rosamund cried. She took a stumbling step towards him, but he backed away. He was so distant from her. 'We could not help ourselves, no matter the danger.'

'Nonetheless, it was a mistake. It must end here.'

'End?' She felt an icy finger creep down her spine, making her feel suddenly numb, removed from the scene, as if she watched a scene in a mummer's play. If only it was not so terribly real, the end of her hopes.

'I have work to do here in England, work I have been too long distracted from,' he said implacably. 'And you have your own duties. I would not bring you trouble with the Queen, Rosamund.'

'I care not for work and duties! Not beside what we have, Anton, what we could have.' That numbness faded, and Rosamund felt instead the hot prickle of tears. Sad, angry, confused tears that she impatiently dashed away.

She had thought—nay, known!—he felt the same. But now he watched her with such cold distance in his dark eyes. He would not turn away from her, from what they had between them, out of sudden duty. Unless…

'You prefer someone else,' she whispered. 'Lady Essex? One of the other maids?' Someone prettier, more flirtatious. More careless with their emotions.

Anton frowned, looking away from her, but he did not deny it. 'I am sorry,' he said again. 'Sorry for all the trouble I have caused you.'

Trouble? Oh, that was not the half of all he had caused her! She had given herself, body and heart, to him and now he turned from her. What was wrong with her?

Rosamund spun around, dashing out of the chamber before those dreadful tears could fall. She would not give him the satisfaction of seeing them, of seeing the terrible pain he caused her with his strange words.

'This will be the last time I cry,' she vowed as she hurried down the dark, abandoned corridor. Men were not worth it in the least.

Anton listened to Rosamund's footsteps fade until there was only silence, only the faint scent of her perfume still in the air. Then he doubled over, falling to the floor at the pain in his stomach.

At the agony of hurting his sweet Rosamund.

It had had to be done, even as he let himself steal one more kiss, one more caress, had let himself feel her in his arms again. Things had gone too far between them already. He could not let them fall into the dangerous whirlpool and be lost for ever. They had this one opportunity to draw away from the precipice, to turn back to their lives of duty, and he had taken it.

He had done what was right, at last. Why, then, was it such agony?

Anton straightened to his feet, tugging his doublet into place, smoothing back his hair. He had to be himself again, as he'd been before he'd met Rosamund and let himself be tempted by her sweetness and goodness, her angelic beauty. It should not be so difficult to do.

Yet it felt terribly as if some vital part of him was torn away and bleeding.

Chapter Thirteen

New Year's Day, January 1

'You were out very late last night, Rosamund,' Anne Percy said, brushing out Rosamund's hair as they prepared for the Queen's masquerade ball.

'Was I indeed?' Rosamund answered, feeling that heat creeping up in her cheeks again. Everyone had seemed soundly asleep when she'd tiptoed in before dawn, so hurt and confused she could only curl up in her bed and pray for the pain to leave her. But she should have known Anne would miss nothing.

'Did anyone else notice?' she whispered.

'Nay,' Anne said, reaching for the bowl of hairpins on the bedside table. 'I told them you were on an errand for the Queen. They were so full of wine they would not have noticed if the roof collapsed on them, anyway.'

'Thank you, Anne. You are a fine friend,' Rosamund said, sitting very still as Anne fastened her hair up tightly. Anne *was* a good friend, a comfort, even if she did not know it. 'If I can ever help you and Lord Langley to a secret meeting…'

Anne snorted. 'I doubt that shall ever happen! I may one day hold you to your promise of assistance, Rosamund, even if I must be with someone else. But are you sure naught is amiss? You seem distracted today.'

Rosamund had certainly seen the way Anne looked at Langley, and the way he looked at her. The air between them fairly crackled. But she said nothing; she was done with romance. It caused such numb hurt; Anne was well out of it. 'Nay, I am just tired.'

'And no wonder, we have been so busy with holiday festivities! Tell me something, though,' Anne said. 'When you returned, did you see anyone lurking about in the corridor?'

'Nay, I saw nothing,' Rosamund said, glad of the distraction of a change in topic. 'It was quite dark, though. Why?'

Anne shrugged, pushing in the last pin. 'When I came up here with Catherine and the Marys after the dancing, I thought we were followed. I just had that sense of being watched.'

'Oh, yes, I know that feeling,' Rosamund said, with a shiver of dangerous intimation.

'But when I looked there was no one. Only shadows.'

'Who would be lurking about so near the Queen's own chambers?' Rosamund said, still feeling that disquiet. She did remember well that sense of being watched, observed, even in the midst of a crowd. There had been that strange Lord of Misrule. 'The guards would be sure to send them off.'

'If they saw them. I think the guards had too much spiced wine too. Ah, well, it was likely naught. Now, which wig do you like? The red or the black?'

'It doesn't signify,' Rosamund said. Gowns and wigs were far from her mind. 'You choose.'

'You wear the red, then, and I will take the black. I shall be a sorceress of the night!' Anne said, combing out the wigs as she watched Rosamund sort through her jewels until she found her emerald-drop earrings. 'Those are very pretty.'

'Do you not think them too old-fashioned?' Rosamund said, looping one through her ear lobe. Their familiarity gave her some comfort, even as she was sad thinking of home and all she had lost. 'They were my grandmother's.'

'Nay, they will do well for an autumn spirit, I think.' They crowded together near the precious looking-glass, pushing Mary Howard out of the way so they could fit on their wigs, borrowed from the Queen's players for the masquerade. Rosamund laughed as Anne jostled her, trying to enter into the festive spirit of the night. She would not be the ghost at the banquet.

Once they were dressed, Anne in black-and-silver satin and Rosamund in deep-green velvet bound at the waist with a gold-and-emerald kirtle, they took out their jewelled masks and tied them over their faces. It felt excellent to hide behind it, Rosamund thought, as if she could be someone else for a while, and hide even from herself.

'Do we look suitably mysterious?' Anne said, twirling around.

'Surely no one will know us?' Rosamund declared.

'Oh, I think at least one person will know you!' Anne teased, laughing as she twined pearls around her throat. 'But, come, we will be late, and even masked the Queen will surely notice.'

They dashed down the privy stairs, joining the flow of people moving towards the Great Hall. It seemed a glittering, shining river of bright silks, sparkling jewels, masked visages. There were cats and stags, pale Venetians, parti-coloured jesters, solemn black veils and cloaks. No one knew each other, or at least pretended not to know, which led to much flirtatious laughter and guessing games.

Perhaps the Queen had been right to keep to the old tradition of the New Year's masquerade, Rosamund thought, despite Lord Burghley's misgivings. All the trepidations and uncertainties of the last few days seemed melted away in giddy excitement—except for her.

They all spilled into the Great Hall, which was also transformed for the night. Vast swaths of red-and-black satin draped from the gilded ceiling down the walls, like an exotic pavilion. The tables, benches and dais were removed, and the multi-tiered buffets were laden with delicacies, pyramids of sweets, platters of roast meats and even bowls of rare candied-fruits. The servants who offered wine were also masked, adding to the dark air of mystery and possibility.

'Look at that man there,' Anne said, taking two

goblets of wine and handing one to Rosamund. 'The one who looks like a peacock. Do you suppose that to be Lord Leicester?'

Rosamund sipped at her wine below the edge of her mask. It was stronger than usual, richly spiced, deep enough to help her forget. 'Perhaps. He does seem fond of blue. I would think that man there more likely, though.' She gestured towards a tall, broad-shouldered man with dark hair, dressed like a knight of a hundred years ago. He whispered intently to a veiled lady.

'Quite so. But who does he speak with? The Queen incognito, do you think?' But it was not the Queen, as they soon found when the doors to the Great Hall opened again and a hush fell over the noisy crowd.

A golden chariot appeared, drawn by six tall footmen clad in white satin. And riding the chariot was the goddess Diana, a golden half-moon crowning her long, red hair. She wore a gown as green as the forest, a white fur-cloak over her shoulders and a gold bow in her hand. A quiver of arrows hung over her shoulder.

She wore a white-and-gold mask, but it could be no one but Queen Elizabeth. As the chariot came to a halt, a man dressed as a huntsman in green-and-brown wool stepped forward to offer his hand. She took it, stepping down as hidden musicians struck up a pavane. The huntsman led Diana to the dance, everyone else following.

'If that is not Leicester, then he must be perishing of jealousy!' Anne whispered.

Rosamund shook her head. 'But if the woodsman is Leicester, then who is the knight? And the veiled lady?'

'Just one of tonight's many mysteries, my friend,'

Anne said as one of the Venetians claimed her hand for the dance.

Rosamund had not seen the one man she once wanted to dance with. She went instead to one of the heavy-laden buffets, inspecting the marzipan flowers and the gold-leafed cakes.

As she nibbled at a bit of candied fruit, a man enveloped in a black cloak embroidered with stars, his face hidden by a spangled, black mask, came to stand beside her. He was silent for a long moment, completely covered in that enveloping disguise, yet she could feel the heat of his intense regard. It made her most uneasy. But as she tried to edge away she found her path blocked by a knot of revellers.

'You do not dance, fair lady?' he asked, his voice hoarse and muffled.

'Nay,' Rosamund answered firmly, trying to shake away shivers of sudden fear. She had had enough of dancing with strange masked men. 'Not tonight.'

'Such a great loss. But then, surely there are other, finer pleasures to be had on such a night as this? Perhaps you would care to see the moon in the garden…'

Rosamund finally saw a gap in the crowd and broke through it, just as the importunate man reached for her hand. His laughter followed her.

The dance floor was even more crowded now, the couples twirling and leaping in a wild Italian *passamiente*. Despite the cold night outside, the room was hot, close packed, filled with smoke from the vast fireplace and the torches, and the heavy scent of expensive perfumes and fine fabrics packed in lavender. All the voices and the music blended in one loud, shrill madrigal set off by the drumbeat of dancing feet.

Rosamund suddenly could not breathe. Her chest felt tight in her closely laced bodice, and the red-and-black hangings seemed to be closing inward. Surely they would fall, enveloping them all in their suffocating folds.

Her stomach felt queasy with the wine and sweets, the heat. The sadness amidst the revelry was too overwhelming. She wanted to leave, to curl up somewhere and be alone. But as she turned away her path was blocked.

'Lady Rosamund?' the man said.

Rosamund was startled; for an instant she saw the man wore a black cloak, and she stiffened. But then she noticed that this man's cloak was plain, not embroidered with stars, and that it could be none but Lord Burghley. His only nod to a disguise was a small black mask and a knot of ribbons on his walking stick. Over his arm he held the Queen's fine white fur-cloak.

Rosamund smiled at him. 'La, my lord, but you are not meant to recognise me! Is that not the point of a masquerade?'

He smiled back. 'You must forgive me, then. Your disguise is most complete, and indeed I should never have known you. I am no good at masquerades at all. But Her Grace described your attire to me when she sent me to find you.'

'She knows my costume?'

'Oh, Lady Rosamund, but she knows everything!'

Not quite *everything*, she hoped. 'That she does, thanks to you. Does she need me for an errand?'

'She asks if you will be so kind as to fetch some documents to her. They are most urgent, and I fear she failed to sign them earlier as she meant to. They are in her bedchamber, on the table by the window. She said you would know where to find them.'

'Of course, Lord Burghley, I shall go at once,' Rosamund answered, glad of the distraction, the chance to leave the ball.

'She also sent this,' he said, holding out the fur cloak. 'She feared the corridors would be chilled after the heat of the dance.'

'That is most kind of Her Grace,' Rosamund said, letting him slide the soft fur over her shoulders. 'I will return directly.'

'Thank you, Lady Rosamund. She waits in the small library just through that door.'

As Burghley left her, she glanced around for Anne, finding her arguing with Lord Langley, who was clad in huntsman's garb. She hurried over to her, tugging on her black-velvet sleeve.

'Anne,' she whispered. 'I must run on a quick errand for the Queen.'

'Of course,' Anne said. 'Shall I come with you?'·

Rosamund glanced at Lord Langley. 'Nay, you seem—occupied. I won't be gone long, the papers I'm to fetch are in Her Grace's bedchamber.'

She hurried out of the hall, drawing the Queen's cloak close around her. The corridors were indeed chilly, with no fires and only a few torches to light the way. They were silent, too, echoing with solitude after the great cacophony of the hall. Outside the windows, the frosty wind rushed by, sounding like ghostly whispers and moans.

Rosamund shivered, rushing even faster up the privy stairs and through the Privy and Presence Chambers. Those spaces, usually so crowded with attention-seekers, were empty except for shifting shadows. She found she wanted only to be gone from there.

In the bedchamber, candles were already lit, anticipating the Queen's return. The bedclothes were folded back, and a fire had been lit in the grate.

Rosamund eased back the fur hood, searching quickly through the documents on the table by the window. The only papers not locked away in the chests were piled up, waiting for the Queen's signature and seal.

'These must be them,' she muttered, catching them up. As she folded them, she could not help noticing Lord Darnley's name. A travel pass, for him to proceed to Edinburgh? But why would Queen Elizabeth suddenly give in to Lady Lennox's petitions, giving up pressing Lord Leicester's suit on Queen Mary?

Rosamund glanced up, meeting the painted dark eyes of Anne Boleyn. The Queen's mother seemed to laugh knowingly. *For love, of course,* she seemed to say. *She could no more part with him than you could your Anton.*

Yet sometimes life held other plans for people. The Queen, and her mother, knew that well. And Rosamund knew it now, too.

She hastily stuffed the folded papers into her sleeve, raising the hood as she dashed out of the silent chamber. She had suddenly had quite enough of ghosts. She wanted, needed, to see Anton again.

As she turned the corner out of the Presence Chamber, an arm suddenly curled out of the darkness, wrapping around her waist and jerking her off her feet. A gloved hand clapped hard over her mouth.

Rosamund twisted about, panic rising up inside her like an engulfing wave. She tasted the metallic tang of it in her mouth, thick and suffocating.

She twisted again, screaming silently, but it was as if she was bound in iron chains.

'Well, this is a lucky chance,' her captor whispered hoarsely. A black, hazy cloud obscured her vision, even her thoughts, and she could see nothing. 'Most obliging of the lady to come to us. I hope we did not interrupt an important assignation?'

'And no guards or anything,' another man said gloatingly. 'It must be Providence, aiding us in our cause.'

Rosamund managed to part her lips, biting down hard on her captor's palm so hard she tore away a piece of leather glove. She tasted the tang of blood.

'Z'wounds!' the man growled. 'She is a wild vixen.'

'I'd expect no less. Here, hold her down so we can bind her. There's no time to waste.'

The two men bore her down to the floor, Rosamund kicking and flailing. The heavy cloak and her velvet gown weighed her down, wrapping around her limbs, but she managed to kick one of the villains squarely on the chest as he tried to tie her feet.

'That is enough of that,' he cried, and she saw a fist descending towards her head.

Then there was a sharp, terrible pain—and nothing at all but darkness.

* * *

Anton glanced around the bacchanal of Queen Elizabeth's masquerade without much interest. The bright swirl of rich costumes and wine-soaked laughter could hold no appeal for him right now. Since he'd parted with Rosamund last night, it was as if the world had turned to shades of grey and drab brown. All colour and light was gone.

He had vowed to focus only on his work now, had told himself that in staying away from her he was keeping her safe. Letting her go on with her life. But whenever he glimpsed her from a distance it was as if the sun emerged again, if only for a fleeting moment.

Had he been wrong, then? Doubt was not a sensation he was familiar with, and yet it plagued him now. In trying to do the right thing, had he irrevocably wounded them both?

He studied each passing face, each lady's smile, but he saw no one who looked like Rosamund. The ball had started long ago; surely she should be there? After all that had happened...

Across the room, he saw Langley and a black-wigged lady in dark velvet. Most likely, Anne Percy, who was Rosamund's friend. Surely Anne would know where she was? He made his way through the crowd towards them, needing to know she was at least somewhere safe.

'Have you seen Lady Rosamund?' Anton asked Anne Percy.

'Aye, the Queen sent her on an errand,' Anne answered, giving him a searching, suspicious glance. 'I have not seen her since, though she should have returned long ere since.'

Anton frowned, a tiny, cold prickle of unease forming in his mind. It seemed ridiculous, of course—Rosamund could be in any number of places, perfectly safe. Yet he could not quite shake away the feeling that all was not right, a sense that had once served him well on the battlefield.

'Is something amiss, Master Gustavson?' Anne asked. 'Shall Lord Langley and I help you to look for her?'

'Yes, I thank you, Mistress Percy,' Anton said. 'You know better where she might have gone on this errand.'

Anne nodded, leading him out of the Great Hall, dodging around drunken revellers who would draw them back into the dance. They traversed the long, shadowy corridors which grew quieter, emptier, the further they went. The only sound was the click of their shoes, the howl of the wind outside the windows.

Anton scowled as he noticed the lack of guards, even as they entered the Queen's own chambers. Had they been given the hour's respite, perhaps a ration of ale to celebrate the New Year? Or had something more sinister sent them away?

The darkened rooms certainly felt strangely ominous, as if ghosts hovered above them, harbingers of some wicked deed. Even Anne and Lord Langley, who usually were never quiet when they were together, were silent.

'The papers Rosamund was sent to fetch were in the bedchamber,' Anne whispered, pushing back her mask. 'In here.'

Even the Queen's own chamber was empty, a few flickering candles and a low-burning fire in the grate illuminating the dark, carved furniture and the soft cushions where the ladies usually sat. There were no papers on the table by the window.

'She must have gone back to the hall already,' Anne said. 'But how did we miss her?'

Anton was quite sure they had not missed seeing Rosamund there. The battle instinct was suddenly very strong in him, that taut, ominous feeling that came before the clash of war when the enemy's armies gathered on the horizon. Something was surely amiss with Rosamund.

Anne seemed to feel it, too. She leaned her palms on the table, shaking her head as Lord Langley laid his hand on her arm. 'I did think someone was lurking outside our apartment last night,' she murmured. 'I thought it was just one of Mary Howard's suitors—she does have such terrible judgement in men. But what if it was not?'

Lord Langley took her hand in his. 'There is always someone lurking about here, Anne. I'm sure it was not a villain lying in wait for Lady Rosamund.'

She slammed her free hand down, the crash echoing in the silence. 'But if it was? She is pretty and rich, and too trusting—valuable commodities here at Court. And that country suitor of hers…'

Anton glanced at her sharply. 'Master Sutton?'

'Aye, the very one. He certainly did not seem happy to have lost his prize.'

'Was she frightened of him?' Anton asked.

'She said he was not what she once thought,' Anne said. 'And I did not like the look of him.'

Did not like the look of him. Anton did not like the sound of that. He carefully studied the room, searching for any sign that things were not as they should be, that there had been a disturbance in the jewelled façade of the palace.

He found it in the corridor just outside the bedchamber—a glint of green fire in the darkness. He knelt down, reaching out for it, pushing back his mask to examine it more closely.

It was an earring, an emerald drop set in gold filigree.

'That's Rosamund's!' Anne gasped. 'She said they were her grandmother's. She wore them with her costume, a green gown and wig of red.'

Anton closed his fist around the earring, searching the floor for more clues. Crumpled up by the wall was a roughly torn scrap of glove leather, stiff with dried blood. Not Rosamund's—she had not worn gloves—but blood was never a good sign.

'I think she has been seized,' he said, his mind hardening, clarifying on one point—finding Rosamund as quickly as possible. And killing whoever had dared hurt her.

He showed the crumpled bit of leather to Lord Langley and Anne, who cried out.

'The stables,' Lord Langley said, holding onto her hand. 'They will have to get her away from the palace.'

'Should we tell the Queen?' Anne asked. 'Or Lord Burghley, or Leicester?'

'Not just yet,' Anton answered. 'If it is Rosamund's disappointed suitor, or some villain seeking ransom, we do not want to startle them into doing something rash. I will find them.'

Lord Langley nodded grimly. 'We will help you. I

have men of my own household. They will be discreet in their search until we must tell Her Grace.'

'Thank you, Langley,' Anton said. 'Mistress Percy, if you will search the Great Hall again, and look wherever you know of hiding spots within the palace. But do not go alone!'

Anne nodded, her face pale, before she dashed out of the corridor. Anton and Lord Langley headed for the stables.

It had been quiet there all evening, the servants told them, with everyone at the Queen's revels. But one of the grooms had prepared a sleigh and horses earlier in the evening.

It was for Master Macintosh of the Scottish delegation.

'He wanted to be quiet about it, my lords,' the groom said. 'I thought he had a meeting with a lady.'

'And did he bring a lady with him when he departed?' Anton asked.

'Aye, that he did. He carried her. She was all bundled up in a white fur-cloak. And there were two other men, though one left in a different direction.'

'And Master Macintosh? Which way did he go?' Anton said.

'Towards Greenwich, I think, along the river. They were in a hurry. Eloping, were they?'

A lady in a white fur, carried off towards Greenwich. The cold, crystalline fury in Anton hardened into steel.

He turned on his heel, striding back towards the palace. He needed his skates—and his sword.

Chapter Fourteen

Snow Day, January 2

Rosamund slowly came awake, feeling as if she struggled up from some black underground cave towards a distant, tiny spot of light. Her limbs ached; they did not want to drag her one more step, and yet she struggled onward. She knew only that it was vital she reach that light, that she not sink back into darkness.

She forced her gritty eyes to open, her head aching as if it would split open. At first, she thought she was indeed in a cave, bound around by stone walls. She could see nothing, feel nothing, but a painful jolting beneath her.

Then she realised it was a cloak wrapped around her, the hood over her head. A soft fur hood, shutting out the world. And then she remembered.

She had been snatched as she'd left the Queen's chamber, grabbed by a man who had muffled her with his gloved hand. Who had knocked her unconscious when she'd kicked him. But where was she now? What did he want of her?

The hard surface beneath her jolted again, sending a wave of pain through her aching body. A cold, metallic-tasting panic rose up in her throat.

Nay, she told herself, pushing that panic back down before she could scream out with it. She would not give in to whoever had done this, would not let them hurt her. Not when she had so much to fight for. Not when she had to get back to Anton.

Slowly, her headache ebbed away a bit and she could hear the hum of voices above her, the clatter of horses' hooves moving swiftly. So, she was in some kind of conveyance being carried further and further from the palace with each second.

She eased back the hood a bit, carefully, slowly, so her captors would think her still unconscious. Fortunately, they had failed to tie her as they'd threatened.

'…a bloody great fool!' one man growled, his voice thick with a Scots burr. 'That's what comes of paying an Englishman to do something. They muck it up every time.'

'How was I to know this was not the Queen?' another man said, muffled by the piercing howl of the wind. 'She had red hair and a green gown, she's wearing the Queen's cloak. And she was coming out of the Queen's own bedchamber!'

'And how often do you see Queen Elizabeth wandering about alone? She may be a usurper of thrones, but the woman is not stupid.'

'Perhaps she had an assignation with that rogue, Leicester.'

'Who she would betroth to Queen Mary?' the Scotsman said. 'Aye, she's a lusty whore. But, still— not stupid. Unlike you. This woman, whoever she is, is too short to be the Queen.'

Rosamund frowned. She was *not* short. Just delicate! But the Scotsman was right; the other man was a foolish knave indeed not to be sure of his quarry. It was an audacious scheme, seeking to kidnap Queen Elizabeth, and would require sharp, deft timing, as well as steely nerves.

What would they do with her now, since they had realised their terrible failure?

She felt the press of a sheet of parchment against her skin, the travel visa for Lord Darnley, tucked into her sleeve what seemed like days ago. Were they in the pay of Darnley and his mother, then? Or someone else entirely?

Her head pounded as she tried to make sense of it, as she thought of Melville, Lady Lennox and Celia Sutton. Of the Queen's scheme to marry Queen Mary to Lord Leicester. Of the poppet hanging from the tree—*thus to all usurpers.*

And she thought of Anton, of how she had to return to him. To set things right, to find out why he said what he did, and how they could go forward.

'What do we do with his girl, then?' the other man said. He sounded strangely distant, as if masked. 'She bit me!'

'And you deserve no less,' the Scotsman said wryly. 'These English females usually lack the spirit of our

Scottish lasses, though. I wonder who she is. I suppose we should discover that before we decide how to correct your foolish error.'

Before Rosamund could brace herself, her hood was thrown back and her mask roughly untied and pulled away. Her wig was also hastily removed, and her own hair tumbled free of its pins.

'Well, well,' the Scotsman murmured. 'Lady Rosamund Ramsay.'

It was Master Macintosh, Rosamund realised in shock, wrapped in the black, star-dotted cloak. She remembered those prickles of mistrust she had felt when he'd talked to her at the frost fair, and wished she had heeded their warnings.

She scrambled to sit up, sliding as far away from him as she could. She found she lay in the bottom of a sleigh, gliding swiftly along the frozen river. Macintosh knelt beside her and the other man held the reins, urging the horses to even greater speeds as the ice flew past in a sparkling silver blur. He glanced at her, and even though his face was half-wrapped in a knitted scarf she could see it was Richard. Richard—the man she had once thought she could care for!

Even through her shock, it made a sort of sense: his disappearance from home for months with no word; his sudden reappearance at Court; the hard desperation in his eyes whenever they met. The tension between him and Celia, who had her own dealings with the Scots. But why, *why*, would he involve himself in some treasonous conspiracy?

But, whatever his plot, it seemed clear he had not

intended her to be a part of it. His eyes widened with surprise.

'Rosamund!' he cried. 'What are you doing here?'

White-hot anger burned away the cold shock, and Rosamund actually shouted, 'What am I doing here? I was foully kidnapped by *you*, of course. What would your parents say if they knew of this shame? You are a villain!'

Macintosh laughed, reaching out to grab Rosamund's wrist and pull her roughly towards him. 'Your Scots blood is showing, Lady Ramsay! She certainly re-minded you of what is important, Richard—what your parents would say.'

'And I would bleed myself dry of every drop of Scots blood, if this is what it means,' Rosamund said, snatch-ing back her hand. 'Treason, threats—not to mention imbecility.'

Macintosh scowled, grabbing her by the shoulders and shaking her until her teeth rattled. Her head felt like it would explode under the onslaught, but she twisted hard under his grasp, wrenching herself away.

'"Twas English imbecility brought us to this,' he said. 'Your ardent suitor here was the one who mistakenly grabbed you. You weren't meant to be involved at all.'

'Then I am glad his stupidity led him to take me and not the Queen,' she declared. 'She is safe from your evil intent.'

'We never intended evil towards her, Lady Rosamund,' Macintosh said. Somehow she could not quite believe him, with his bruising clasp digging into her shoulder. 'We merely sought to help her to a meeting with her cousin. Queen Mary is most eager to see her, and yet your Queen Elizabeth keeps delaying. Surely if she saw my Queen's regal and dignified nature, her great charm and beauty, she would give up the notion of marrying her to that stable boy, Leicester.'

'So you were going to carry her in secret all the way to Edinburgh?' Rosamund asked incredulously. It seemed there was plenty of imbecility all around.

''Tis true, it is a long voyage,' Macintosh said. 'And accidents do happen when one travels. These are perilous times.'

Then he did intend to kill Queen Elizabeth. And probably now her, as well, for getting in his way. Furious, Rosamund lunged towards him, arcing her fingernails toward his smirking face.

Macintosh ducked away, even as her nails left an angry red scratch down his cheek.

'Bloody hell!' he shouted. As he dragged her against him, his body fell into Richard, causing him to jerk hard on the reins. Confused the horses cried out and veered off their course towards the river bank. They crashed through the drifts of ice-crusted snow, coming to a halt wedged at an angle.

The cries of the horses, Macintosh's furious shouts and Rosamund's own screams tore the peace of the winter night. She elbowed him as hard as she could in the chest, and he slapped her across the face. Her head snapped back on her neck, her ears ringing.

Suddenly, burly arms seized her around the waist, dragging her from the listing sleigh. Richard held onto her even as she fought to be free, pulling her through the snow up the river bank.

Macintosh, still cursing, knelt by the river, pressing a handful of snow to his scratched cheek. 'Tie up the English witch, and don't let her out of your sight,' he growled. 'She'll pay for this foolishness.'

'Richard, what are you about?' Rosamund said as he plunked her down beneath a tree. Her thick cloak kept away some of the cold, but the wind still bit at her bruised skin. It was a terrible cold, dark night here in these unknown woods, and she couldn't shake away the nightmare quality of it all.

'They offered me money,' he muttered, leaning his palms on his knees as if he struggled to catch his breath. 'A great deal of money, and land to come. With so much, your parents could surely no longer disrespect me. They would be sorry for what they said.'

'They did *not disrespect* you! They merely thought we were a poor match, and it is obvious they were correct.' More than correct. They had seen things in Richard she could not then, but now saw so clearly. He was not Anton, he was nothing like a man she could love.

'This was for *you*, Rosamund!'

She shook her head, sad beyond anything. 'Treason cannot be for me. Only for yourself, your own greed.'

'It was not greed! If seeing the rightful queen put on the throne could help us to be together...'

'I would not be with you for all the gold in Europe. I am loyal to Queen Elizabeth. And I love someone else. Someone who is honourable, kind, strong—a thousand times the man you are.' Rosamund slumped back against the tree, feeling heartily foolish that she had ever been deluded by Richard.

'So, you are like your parents now,' he said, straightening to glare down at her. Even through the milky moonlight she could see, feel, the force of his anger. The fury that she would dare reject him. It frightened her, and she pressed herself hard against the tree, gathering her legs under her.

'You think yourself above me, after all I've done for you, risked for you,' he said. 'You will not be so haughty when I am done with you!'

He grabbed for her, but Rosamund was ready. She leaped to her feet, ignoring her cramped muscles; her painfully cold feet in their thin shoes. She shed her cloak and ran as fast as she could through the snow, her path lit only by the moon shining on the ice. She lifted her skirts, dodging around the black, bare hulks of the winter trees.

Her breath ached in her lungs, her stomach lurching with fear. Her heart pounded in her ears, so she could barely hear Richard stumbling behind her. She did not know where to go, only that she had to get away.

She leaped over a rotten fallen log, and Richard tripped on it, landing hard on the snow.

'Witch!' he shouted.

Rosamund, panicked, suddenly remembered how she would climb trees as a child, how she could go higher and higher—until her mother had found out and put a stop to it.

She saw a tree just ahead with a low, thick branch and launched herself at it. Tucking her skirts into her gold kirtle, she jumped onto the branch, reaching up, straining until she could clasp the next branch up. Her palms slid on the rough, frosty wood, her soft skin scraping. She ignored the pain, pulling herself up.

Up and up she went, not daring to look down, to listen to Richard's shouted threats. At last she reached a vee in the trunk and wrapped her arms tightly around the tree as the wind tore at her hair, battered at her numb skin. She remembered golden moments with Anton, moments where they had kissed and made love, and she knew they were meant to be together.

She held onto the thought of him tightly now.

Help me, she thought, closing her eyes as she held on for her life. *Find me!*

Anton glided swiftly along the river, the dark countryside to either side of him flying along in a shadowed blur as he found his rhythm. The rhythm that always came as he skated, made of motion and speed, the knife-like sound of blades against ice. The cold meant nothing, nor did the darkness.

He had to find Rosamund, and soon. That was all that mattered. He loved her. He saw that so clearly now. He loved her, and nothing mattered beside that. Not his estate, not her parents, not the Queen, only their feelings for each other. He had to tell her that, to tell her how sorry he was for ever sending her away.

He followed the grooved tracks left in the ice by the runners of a sleigh. The vehicle had been heavy enough to leave a pathway, but it was already freezing over.

The thought of Rosamund out there in the cold night,

shivering, frightened, alone, made him angrier than he had ever been. A flaming fury burned away all else, or surely would if he'd let it. But he knew that such fury, out of control, boundless, would not serve him well now. He needed sharp, cold focus. The anger would come later, when Rosamund was safe.

He remembered how he had felt on the battlefield, enclosed by an invisible shield of ice that distanced him from the death and horror. Such a feeling kept fear away, so he could fight on and stay alive.

Now it would help him find his Rosamund.

He leaned further forward, remembering her smile, the way she curled against him in bed, so trusting and loving. His beautiful, sweet winter-fairy. She was all he had thought could not exist in the bleak world, a bright spirit of hope and joy. She made him dare to think of the future as he had never done before. Made him think dreams of home and family could even be real, that loneliness could be banished from his life for ever.

And now she was gone, snatched away from the Queen's own palace with nary a trace. But he would find her, he was determined on it. Find her—and see that her kidnappers paid. That was the only thing that mattered. He listened to his heart now, as his mother had urged him to do, and it pressed him onward.

At last he noticed something, a break in the endless snowy riverbank. As he came closer, he saw it was a sleigh driven into the snow at an angle. It was empty, and for a moment Anton thought the only living things near were the horses, standing quietly in their traces. No Rosamund, no people at all. Only silence.

But then he heard a faint noise, like a muffled, muttered curse. Anton crouched low as he crept closer, drawing his short sword from its sheath.

A man in a black cloak knelt on the other side of the sleigh, scooping up handfuls of snow and pressing them to his bearded face. He half-turned towards a beam of chalky moonlight, and Anton saw it was the Scotsman, Macintosh.

A Scottish conspiracy, then. Somehow he was not surprised. The concerns of Queen Mary seemed to have permeated every corner of Whitehall of late. Now they had absorbed Rosamund, too, ensnaring her in that sticky web.

But not for long. Anton carefully slipped off his skate straps, inching closer to Macintosh in his leather-soled boots. Silently, carefully, like a cat, he came up behind the Scotsman and caught him a hard hold about the neck. He dragged him backward, pressing the blade of his sword to the man's treacherous neck.

Macintosh tensed as if to fight, but went very still at that cold touch of steel.

'Where is Lady Rosamund?' Anton demanded.

'She ran off, the stupid wench,' Macintosh said in a strangled voice. 'We never meant to grab *her*, anyway, she just got in the way.'

'You thought she was Queen Elizabeth,' Anton said, thinking of Rosamund's red wig, the fur cloak.

'I didn't want to hurt the lass, even after she clawed me,' Macintosh said. 'Not that it matters now. She'll probably freeze out there, and our errand is all undone.'

Anton's arm tightened, and Macintosh gurgled,

clawing at his sleeve. 'You let a helpless lady go off into the snow and did not even follow her?'

'That fool Sutton ran after her, wretch that he is. He's the one that took her in the first place. He was in a fury. If he catches her, she'll likely wish she froze to death first.'

So Richard Sutton was involved, determined to take some revenge on Rosamund for her rejection. A man like him, with primitive emotions and urges, would be capable of anything when angered. Anton twisted his sword closer to Macintosh's neck.

'Are you going to kill me?' the man gasped.

'Nay,' Anton answered. 'I'll leave that to the Queen. I'm sure she will have much to ask you, once you're taken to the Tower.'

'Nay!' Macintosh began frantically. He had no time to say more, for Anton brought down the hilt of his sword hard on the back of his head. He collapsed in an unconscious heap in the snow.

In the bottom of the sleigh were some thick coils of rope, no doubt meant for the Queen—or Rosamund. They served now to bind Macintosh. Anton made short work of the task, depositing the Scotsman in the bottom of the sleigh to wait for the Queen's men, before cutting the horses free so the man could not escape.

Surely Lord Langley and Anne Percy would have alerted Leicester to what had happened by now? Anton had to find Rosamund quickly. He scanned the woods just beyond the river bank, turning his sword in his hand.

At last those beams of moonlight caught on a set of

blurred footprints leading into the trees. Large, booted prints, heavy, as if they dragged—or dragged something with them.

He followed their erratic pathway until he discovered a small clearing, a smudged spot just beneath a tree where perhaps someone had sat for a time. And, just beyond, a crumpled white fur-cloak, lightly covered by new snow.

He knelt down, lifting up the soft, cold fur. It still smelled of Rosamund's roses, and the Queen's richer violet-amber scent. Along its edge were a few flecks of dried blood. Macintosh's—or Rosamund's? His heart froze at the thought of her bleeding, hurt, alone.

Slowly, he stood up, examining the tracks leading away from the clearing—small, dainty feet, blurred as if she ran, zigzagging. Followed by those heavy boots. Dropping the cloak, he trailed those tracks, every sense heightened, fully aware of every sound and motion of wind in the bare branches.

Rosamund gave a good chase, he thought with pride, veering around trees, over fallen logs. Then, at last, he heard a noise breaking through that eerie, glass-like night: a man's hoarse shout, a woman's scream.

Holding his sword firmly, Anton followed the sound, running lightly through the snow until he found them. It was an astonishing sight—Rosamund was high up in a tree, balanced on the split trunk, her skirts tucked up and her white stockings glowing in the moonlight. Richard Sutton was at the base of the tree, shouting and waving his sword at her, even though she was too high for the reach of the blade.

Rosamund tottered on her perch, grabbing harder onto the trunk. The freezing wind had to be numbing her bare hands—yet another thing to kill Sutton for.

'Sutton!' Anton shouted, advancing on the man with his sword held out in challenge. 'Why don't you face someone your own size, rather than bully defenceless females?'

Richard swung towards him, waving his own sword about erratically. The steel fairly hummed in the frosty air. 'Defenceless? You are deluded, foreigner. The witch has defences aplenty, as well as a cold, fickle heart. She will desert you as sure as she did me.'

'Anton,' Rosamund sobbed, her fingers slipping on the bark.

'Hold on very tightly, Rosamund,' Anton called, struggling to hold onto his icy distance. The sight of her pale, frightened face, her tangled hair and torn gown, threatened to tear away that chilly remove as nothing else could.

But it also made him determined to protect her at all costs.

'You will never be worthy of her, not in her haughty eyes,' Richard cried. 'Nor with her family. None are good enough for the mighty Ramsays.'

'Ah, but I have something *you* will never possess,' Anton said, tossing his sword lightly from hand to hand as he advanced on his quarry.

'What might that be? Money? Land?'

'Nay. I have the lady's love.' Or he had once—and he would fight for it again for the rest of his life.

With a furious shout, Richard dived towards Anton,

swinging his blade wildly. Anton brought his own sword arm-up, and the blades met with a ringing clang. He felt it reverberate down his whole arm, but he recovered swiftly, twirling his sword about to parry Richard's blows.

At first he merely defended himself, deflecting Richard's wild attacks, fighting to keep his balance on the frozen ground. But his opponent's burning fury quickly wore him down, while Anton was still fresh, still fortified with his quiet, cold anger. When Richard faltered, Anton pressed his advantage, moving forward with a series of light strikes.

He drove Richard back towards one of the looming trees, until the man clumsily lost his footing and stumbled against the trunk. With a roar, he tried to shove his sword up into Anton's chest, unprotected by armour or padding. But Anton was too quick for him, and drove his own blade through Richard's sleeve, pinning him to the tree.

'It seems I have something else you lack,' Anton said. 'A gentleman's skill with the sword.'

'Foreign whoreson!' Richard shouted. He ripped his sleeve free, driving forward again, catching Anton on the shoulder with the tip of his blade. Startled by the sting, Anton was even more shocked by what happened next. Richard took off, running through the woods, crashing like a wounded boar.

Anton ran after him, following his twisted, half-blind path as they headed back towards the river. His shoulder ached and he felt the stickiness of blood seeping through his doublet. The sweat seemed to freeze on his skin, but he hardly noticed. He ran on, chasing after Richard as the coward fled.

Richard broke free of the trees, sliding down the steep, snowy banks towards the sleigh as if he meant to drive away and escape. But the horses were gone now, broken from their traces, and Macintosh, still unconscious, lay bound in the bottom of their sleigh.

Richard, though, kept running, straight out onto the river itself. Anton pursued him, but skidded to a halt as he heard an ominous cracking sound, one he heard all too often in Swedish spring-times. He eased back up onto the bank, watching in shock as a thin patch of the river cracked beneath Richard's heavy weight. Screaming with horror, a terrible sound indeed, Richard fell down into the water below.

His head surfaced briefly, a pale dot above the jagged, diamond-like ice.

'I can't swim!' he cried. 'I can't…'

Carefully, Anton crept out onto the ice, watching for tell-tale fissures. But he was lighter than Richard, leaner, and he knew the ways of the ice. It held for him. Near the edge of the hole, he held out his sword towards the flailing man.

'Catch onto the blade!' he called. 'I can pull you out.'

Richard's hand grasped for the lifeline, but he just kept sinking down. Creeping closer, crouching down, Anton managed to grab Richard by the collar of his sodden doublet, yanking him upward. But his hands were cold, his muscles tired from the sword fight, and Richard fought against him. He tore away from Anton's grasp, sinking below the water one last time.

Anton braced his palms on the ice, exhausted, horrified, saddened. It seemed the Queen's river had exacted justice for her, before he could.

But his own task was far from finished. He made his careful way back to the bank, though it seemed the river was done with violence now, and the ice held beneath him. Once back on solid land again, he ran for Rosamund's tree.

She met him on the forest path, sobbing as she stumbled into his arms. 'I knew you would come,' she cried. 'I knew you did not mean it when you sent me away.'

Anton held her close, kissing her hair, her cheek, over and over, all quarrels forgotten, the past gone. She was alive, safe and warm and vital in his embrace. *'Alskling,'* he muttered, over and over. 'I was so scared I would not find you in time. My love, my brave, brave love.'

'Brave? Nay! I was frightened as could be. I was sure Richard would catch me, and would—oh. Richard!'

'Never fear, he won't hurt you now.'

Rosamund drew back, staring up at him with wide eyes. 'You—killed him?'

'I would have. But in the end, I did not have to. The ice did it for me.'

'How terrible.' She leaned her forehead against his chest, trembling. 'But you are hurt, Anton! Look, your shoulder.'

In truth, he had quite forgotten the wound. The cold numbed it; finding Rosamund had made it completely unimportant. ''Tis just a scratch. I cannot feel it at all. Come, my love, you will catch a terrible chill. We should find one of the horses and make our way back to the palace.'

'I *am* cold,' she murmured. 'I didn't even notice when I was in that tree, but now I'm frozen to the core. Isn't that odd?'

She was also worryingly pale, he saw. He lifted her in his arms, holding her against his unhurt shoulder as he carried her hastily out of the woods. He retrieved the Queen's cloak, wrapping it tightly around her as a meager shelter against the biting wind.

'We'll have you in your own chamber very soon,' he said. 'With a warm fire, spiced wine and plenty of blankets. Just hold on a bit longer, my love.'

'I'm not frightened now,' she responded, resting her head on his chest as her eyes drifted closed. 'I'm not even cold now. Not with you.'

'I'm sorry, my love,' he whispered. 'I'm so very sorry.'

She grew heavier in his arms, as if she sank into a chilled stupor. For the first time, he was truly, deeply afraid. She could not be ill! Not when they were together at last.

Where were those cursed horses? He had been a fool to set them free!

At the river's edge, he saw a flicker of light in the distance—torches breaking through the darkness. It was a procession of horses, led by Lord Leicester.

'You see, *alskling*?' Anton said with a wry laugh. 'We are both rescued.'

Chapter Fifteen

January 4

Rosamund lay on her side in bed, staring out of the window at the river far below. The private bedchamber the Queen had given her was a palatial one, with fine tapestries on the walls to shut out the cold and velvet bed-hangings and blankets. A fire crackled merrily in the grate.

Yet she saw none of it. She thought only of Anton, of the way he had held her so close there in the dark, cold woods. How he had kissed her as if she was precious to him, how his words had erased all the hurt of before.

He did love her, she was so sure of it. He'd come after her because he could not live without her, as she could not live without him. And the fear of the kidnapping had been worth it, as it had brought him back to her. They could face anything to be together now.

But she had not seen him since they'd returned to the

palace. She had not even had a note. She wished with all her strength she knew his thoughts now. Knew what happened in the world outside her chamber.

'Rosamund? Are you awake?' Anne Percy whispered from the doorway.

Rosamund rolled over and smiled at her friend. 'Of course I am awake. I'm not an invalid any longer, to be slumbering away at noontime.'

'Even if you are not, you should pretend to be. Being an invalid in the Queen's service has such fine concessions!' Anne teased, hurrying into the chamber Rosamund had occupied since Anton had brought her back from the forest. 'A room of your own, far away from that chattering magpie Mary Howard. Nourishing wines and meat stews. Even furs!'

She gestured towards the glossy sable wrap at the foot of the bed, as Rosamund laughed and sat up against the bolsters. 'That is all very well, but I am quite recovered now, and it is very dull to be alone here so near Twelfth Night.'

'You have books, also sent by Her Grace,' Anne said. 'And gifts such as these, which I am bid bring to you.' She put down a basket full of jellies and sweets on Rosamund's table, next to the stack of books from the Queen's library.

'Her Grace is very kind,' Rosamund said. 'But I am allowed so few guests. It is lonely.'

'The physicians say you must be quiet for at least one more day to allow your blood to warm sufficiently,' Anne said. She straightened the velvet coverlet before perching on the edge of the bed. 'You are not missing a great deal, I declare! There have been no scandalous elopements or duels at all. Things are especially quiet today, as the Queen is hunting again. Everyone feels safe again, now that you have caught the villains and foiled their wicked plot.'

'Have they all been caught, then?' Rosamund asked. 'I am sure Richard and Macintosh did not conceive such an idea themselves.'

'Secretary Melville disavows all knowledge of such a scheme, and Queen Mary has sent word of her shock and sympathy. But Macintosh is in the Tower, and Lord Burghley is on the trail. You are acclaimed the heroine of the Court!'

Rosamund shivered, remembering Richard as he'd chased her through the snow in such a fury. Picturing him sinking beneath the ice. That terrible, bitter fear, the feeling of being so cold she could never be warm again, never feel again.

But Anton had come for her, saved her—and then had not seen her again after he had left her safe at the palace. Would they quarrel again, then? Better that than be apart, surely?

'I should not be called a heroine,' she said, sinking deeper under the bedclothes. 'I did naught but run away and climb up a tree to wait.'

'You saved the Queen from being abducted!' Anne protested. 'And I should have been far too terrified to have the presence of mind to run away.'

'I doubt you have ever been terrified of anything in your life, Anne Percy! I have never known anyone bolder.'

'There is a difference between boldness and bravery.'

'Not at all. Daring to join the mummers' play and fight with Lord Langley in front of the Queen and everyone—that is bravery indeed. No other lady I know would dare such a thing.'

Anne laughed humourlessly. 'Foolishness is more like. And that act gained me naught in the end.'

'Do you and Lord Langley…' Rosamund began tentatively.

Anne shook her head. 'We are a dull subject indeed. Not like you and your swain, the brave young Swede! Since he so daringly effected your rescue, the Court ladies are even more in love with him.'

Of course they were. How could they help it? Rosamund was no different. 'So, that is why I have not seen him of late.'

'He has been with the Queen in private council,' Anne said. 'But I think you need not fear. When he is not with Her Grace, he is hanging about in the corridor here, questioning all the physicians and servants about your health.'

A tiny light of hope flickered to life deep in Rosamund's heart. He had been there, she just had not seen him! Surely that was a good thing? 'But why has he not come in to see me?'

'You are not yet allowed visitors, remember? I am quite sure he has not forgotten you, Rosamund, nor does he pay attention to any other lady.'

Before Rosamund could question Anne further, her maid, Jane, entered the room with a curtsy. 'I beg your pardon, my lady, but you have a caller.'

'I thought I was not allowed visitors,' Rosamund said.

'They could hardly refuse *me*,' a man said, sweeping through the door. He was tall, silver-haired, and blue-eyed, still clad in a travel cloak and boots. He smiled, but his bearded face was creased with worry and tiredness.

'Father!' Rosamund cried in a rush of happiness. It was so long since she had seen her family. To see him there now was like a rush of warm, summer sunshine. She started to push back the blankets, but he rushed over to hold her there.

'Rosie, dearest, you should not exert yourself.'

Rosamund threw her arms around her father, hugging him close as she buried her face against his shoulder, her eyes shut as she inhaled his familiar scent. He smelled of home. 'Father, you're here.'

'Of course I am,' he said, kissing the top of her head. 'I set out as soon as the Queen's messenger arrived at Ramsay Castle. Your mother is beside herself with worry. She follows in the litter, but I rode ahead as quickly as I could. We could not be easy until we had seen you ourselves.'

'I have missed you so very much,' Rosamund said, drawing back to study him closer. From the corner of her eye, she glimpsed Anne easing towards the door. 'Oh no, Anne, do not go! Come, meet my father. Father, this is Mistress Anne Percy, who has been my best friend here at Court. I could never have made my way without her.'

He stood to bow to Anne, who curtsied to him. 'You are Mildred Percy's niece, I think?' he said. 'We have heard much of you.'

'I am her niece indeed, my lord,' she answered. 'But I hope you have not heard *too* much.'

Rosamund's father laughed. 'Well, I am most grateful for your friendship to my daughter. And for looking after her in her illness.'

'She has been a great friend to me as well,' Anne said. 'I will look in on you after supper, Rosamund.'

She departed, leaving Rosamund alone again with her father. She held onto his hand, still not sure he was really there. And he held very tightly to her in turn.

'You need not worry, Father. I am quite recovered,' she said. 'And the Queen has been very attentive.'

He shook his head. 'Your mother and I thought you would be safe here at Court. What fools we were.'

'Not nearly as foolish as I was. You were quite right about Richard, Father,' Rosamund admitted.

'We had not thought him as wicked as all this. The son of our own neighbours, in a plot against the Queen!' he said sadly. 'I did not expect such a thing.'

'It was not a very well-thought-out plot, truly. But you thought him somewhat wicked, even then?'

'We heard tales of debts, of other bad behaviour that could not be acceptable in your husband. Even aside from that, his personality was not suited to yours. We knew you would not be happy with him, as your mother and I have been happy together all these years. We never imagined treason, though.'

'Nor did I,' Rosamund answered. 'Though I have to admit, Father, that even before his terrible actions I came to see Richard was not the man for me at all. You and Mama were right to send me here to Court.'

'Were we, daughter? In truth, we began to regret it as soon as you departed Ramsay Castle. Home is quiet without you there.'

'It is true that I prefer the peace of home,' she said with a laugh. 'But I have learned so much here.'

'And perhaps even found someone to replace Richard Sutton?'

She glanced at him sharply. Did he already know, then, even as her mind tumbled with ways to tell him of Anton? To persuade him that this time she had found her right match? 'You have heard tales?'

'I saw my old friend Lord Ledsen as I arrived. He told me the Court is all a-buzz with the romantic story of a handsome young Swede skating to your rescue.'

Rosamund felt her cheeks grow warm, but she pressed ahead. 'It is true, Anton did rescue me. I would surely be dead without him—or—or dishonoured by Richard.'

Her father's lips tightened, as if in deep anger. Over Richard's threats—or her feelings for Anton? 'It seems we owe him much, then.'

'We do. And I have to tell you, Father, that even before this happened I had developed the most tender of feelings for him.' As he had for her, she hoped. Her heart had given her uncertainties before. Did it now, as well?

'Ledsen did say he has a fine reputation here at Court. But, Rosie, he is Swedish. He would take you far away from here, to a rough and cold land where you would have none of the comforts you are accustomed to,' her father said sternly.

'Perhaps he would not!' Rosamund hastened to tell

him of Anton's English connections, of his estate and hopes. 'And, Father, I do care for him. You were correct when you said one day I would meet the right man for me and I would know it. Just as you and Mama knew.'

'But I did not take your mother away from everything she knew,' her father said gently, implacably. 'He does not yet have this English estate, I think.'

'Nay,' Rosamund admitted. Nor was she entirely sure he wanted her, either. 'But I am quite sure that now the Queen will...'

'Enough now, my dear.' He kissed her cheek, gently urging her to lie back against the cushions. 'I fear I have tired you, after I promised the Queen's physicians I would do no such thing. You should sleep now. I will consider what you have told me.'

Rosamund knew well enough when arguing with her father would do no good. He had to be left to do his considering, and she had to go on waiting. 'I am most glad to see you, Father. I have missed you.'

'And we have missed you. We will talk more later.'

She nodded, watching her father depart. A few moments later, Anne returned. Her friend knelt down by the bed to whisper, 'Did you tell your father of Anton, Rosie? What did he say?'

Rosamund frowned, punching at the bolster with her fist. 'He said he would consider what I have told him.'

'Consider? Is that good or ill?'

'I hardly know.'

Anton paced the corridor outside the Queen's chamber, listening closely for any word, any sound, behind that door. There was only silence. And yet he knew his entire future was in that room.

He raked his fingers through his hair impatiently, restraining the urge to curse. He had tried to see Rosamund, yet she was closely guarded in the Queen's keeping, tucked away as she regained her health. His bribes to the physicians had gained him the knowledge that she recovered, but nothing could tell him of her heart.

Had she forgiven him for ever hurting her? Did she care for him still? She had declared she did when he'd found her in the woods, but matters had been emotional then. Would she change her mind now, back at the centre of the Court?

And what would they do if the Queen denied his suit? Could he dare to ask Rosamund to go to Sweden with him, leaving behind all she knew? Or could he find the strength to leave her once more, for ever?

Suddenly the door opened, and Lord Burghley hobbled out with his walking stick. 'You may go in now, Master Gustavson,' he said. Anton searched his lined face, but there was no hint there of his fate.

Anton smoothed his hair again, and walked into the room. It was empty of the usual gaggle of ladies, the hum of constant conversation. Queen Elizabeth sat alone at her desk, busily writing on a sheet of parchment spread before her. Anton knelt, waiting for her to speak.

At last, he heard the scratching of the quill cease and the rustle as she folded her hands on the desk, her draped sleeves falling back.

'Arise, Master Gustavson,' she said, laughing as he

bowed to her. 'La, but you look as if you are being sent to the Tower! Why the great frown?'

Anton smiled reluctantly. The Queen's laughter was infectious, even as his hopes hung in the balance. 'A man cannot help but have concerns, Your Grace, when he is summoned so urgently.'

'Ah, but you are not just *any* man, Master Gustavson. You are the hero of the day. All my courtiers talk of your daring midnight ride to rescue Lady Rosamund and vanquish the villains who plotted against me.'

'I did what anyone would do in the circumstances, Your Grace.'

'Anyone? Somehow I doubt that. Many men speak of loyalty unto death, but not many have the actions to prove such poetic words.' Queen Elizabeth sat back in her chair, watching him thoughtfully. 'I am in your debt, Master Gustavson. What do you desire? Money? Jewels?'

Anton stiffened. She offered him a *reward*? Would she be willing to replace one of her ladies for the money and jewels? Or did the Queen's largesse go only so far, as everyone whispered?

Before he could answer, she smiled slyly, tapping at her chin with one long, white finger. 'Nay. I know what you truly desire. I have been reading over your petition for Briony Manor.' She gestured towards the parchment on her desk. 'I have been reading Celia Sutton's letters, as well.'

'And has Your Grace reached a conclusion?' he asked tightly.

'I do not rush into such things,' she said. 'Haste so

often leads to regret, as my father and my sister often learned to their detriment. Would you crave this manor as your reward, then?'

'Of course, Your Grace.'

'Of course,' she echoed. 'But—I sense you crave another boon as well, Master Gustavson.'

Anton hardly dared move. 'Your Grace has been most generous already.'

'Indeed I have. Yet it did not escape my notice that you were in great haste to rescue Lady Rosamund—or that she is a pretty girl indeed.'

Anton's eyes narrowed as he steadily returned the Queen's stare. 'I cannot deny that she is pretty, Your Grace.'

'I do not like my ladies to leave me,' she said, reaching again for her quill as if she dismissed him. 'I must think on this a bit longer, Master Gustavson. You may go now.'

He bowed again, restraining himself from arguing as he earlier had from cursing. Quarrelling with the Queen would gain him nothing at all in this delicate, perilous dance. He played for the greatest stakes of his life, for Rosamund's love, and his every move had to be calculated to that one end.

He had to plan his next step carefully indeed, or he, like the volta he practised with Rosamund, would fall into ruin.

Chapter Sixteen

Twelfth Night, January 5

'Are you quite sure you want to do this, Rosamund?' Anne asked, fastening Rosamund's pearl necklace for her. 'You still look rather pale.'

Rosamund shook out the folds of her white-satin gown trimmed with silvery fox-fur and embroidered with twining silver flowers. Her best gown, saved for Twelfth Night. 'I could hardly miss the festivities, could I? It is the most important night of Christmas. Besides, I could not stay in bed another moment.'

All that time alone had left too much time to think. To think about Anton, and the fact that she had not seen him since their icy adventure. To think about their future, and how she would feel if she lost him for ever. Would she be able to move forward again? To forget all that he had taught her, all they had together?

Tonight felt like the end of something. But would it be a beginning, too—or a step into dark uncertainty?

She quickly pinched her cheeks, hoping to look less pale. She had to be completely well, or risk being sent back to bed by the Queen and her infernal physicians. 'How do I look?' she asked.

'Lovely, as always,' Anne answered. 'And me?'

'Beautiful, of course,' Rosamund said, examining her friend's sable-trimmed red-velvet gown.

'Mary Howard will faint of envy when she sees us!'

'And Lord Langley will fall even more in love with you.'

'Pooh,' Anne scoffed. 'He is not in love with me, and even if he was I care not. I have found there are far grander men here at Court.'

Grander than a young, handsome, rich earl who was clearly in love with Anne? Rosamund thought not, but she knew better than to argue. Things were not always as they seemed. 'We should go down, then, and start inciting that envy.'

Anne laughed, and she and Rosamund linked arms as they hurried down the stairs and along the corridors to the Great Hall. Unlike the dark, mysterious scarlet and black of the ill-fated masquerade ball, the vast chamber was now a wintry paradise. Hangings of white and silver draped from the gilded ceiling, and the walls were lined with trees in silver pots hung with garlands of spangled-white satin to resemble ice. Silver urns held chilled white wines, and musicians in their gallery high above played soft madrigals of love.

But, unlike the real ice-wrapped forest, it was warm

from the crackling fire and from the well-dressed crowds of courtiers packed all around. They all flocked to surround Rosamund when she appeared, exclaiming over her adventure.

Anton, though, was not among them, and nor was her father, who she had not seen since they had broken their fast together that morning. She smiled and chatted, but their absence, and all the uncertainty, made her feel nervous and unhappy deep down inside. She did like to have a purpose, to know what would happen next and what her actions should be. Where she belonged.

I am not cut out for Court life, then, she thought wryly. Uncertainty was an everyday matter here. But she accepted a goblet of wine and went on with her conversation as if she had not a care in the world.

Suddenly, there was a herald of trumpets from the gallery and Queen Elizabeth appeared in the doorway, dazzling in black velvet and cloth-of-gold, her red hair entwined with a wreath of wrought-gold flowers. On her arm was the head of the Swedish delegation, Master Vernerson.

And in the procession behind her was Anton. Rosamund's breath caught at the sight of him, so very handsome in his tawny-coloured doublet sewn with black ribbons in a fashionable lattice pattern, a topaz earring in his ear. He seemed none the worse for their adventure. Indeed he seemed more hale and hearty than ever, radiating youth and life.

The Queen mounted her dais with the Swedish party, her golden train rippling behind her. Rosamund's father came to her side as they watched Queen Elizabeth, taking Rosamund's hand in his.

'You look lovely tonight, daughter,' he said with a smile. 'So much like your mother, at a Court much like this one.'

'You look fine yourself, Father,' she answered, examining his purple velvet and black-satin garments. 'I haven't seen you so well clad in ages!'

He laughed. 'There is no need for such finery at home! Hopefully we shall be back there soon, sitting by our own fire. I am too old for this.'

The Queen raised her hand, and silence fell over the hall. 'Welcome all to our Twelfth Night celebration! We have much to celebrate, methinks, after weathering many hardships in these last days. It is cold beyond our walls, but here we have a good fire, fine food—and the best of friends.'

A cheer went up, and only as it faded did Queen Elizabeth continue. 'Some friends will remain with us,' she said, smiling at Lord Leicester who would not, after all, be travelling to Edinburgh. 'Yet we must say farewell to others. Master Vernerson and his Swedish party will be returning to King Eric, bearing our everlasting friendship. And Master Von Zwetkovich will return to Vienna. Our Court will soon be much less merry, I fear.'

Rosamund glanced frantically at Anton, who stood behind the Queen's shoulder. The Swedes were departing so very soon? That left them little time to make their plans. Very little time for her to persuade her father that this time she was very, very certain. That she was willing to do anything for her love.

The Queen continued. 'One of our new friends will remain with us, though, or so we hope. In thanks for his efforts to save us from a most wicked plot, and in honour of his grandfather's long service to my own father, I grant the deed of Briony Manor to Master Anton Gustavson, along with the rank of baronet.' She half-turned, holding out her hand to Anton. 'Come, then, *Sir* Anton.'

He knelt before her as she laid her bejewelled hand on his glossy dark head. 'Your Grace,' he said, 'You have my deepest thanks.'

'It is only your due, Sir Anton. Your family has long served mine, and indeed continues to do so, as Mistress Celia Sutton is going on an errand for us to Edinburgh, bearing my greetings to my cousin there. I hope I may rely on you in the future?'

'Indeed you may, Your Grace.'

Rosamund nearly laughed aloud with the sudden bright rush of joy, and she clapped her hand over her mouth. Anton was given his manor, and a title! A place in England. But what did it all mean for her, for them?

'We think you have one more task to perform, though,' the Queen said, raising Anton to his feet. 'Was there not a wager made, one concerning dancing?'

Anton smiled. 'I believe that is true, Your Grace.'

'Then we must determine a winner. Lady Rosamund Ramsay, come forward!'

The crowd parted, letting Rosamund pass. Her stomach fluttered, and she feared she could not breathe. She walked slowly, carefully, to the base of the dais, dropping into a low curtsy. 'Your Grace.'

'Lady Rosamund, are you recovered enough to dance for us?'

'I hope I am, Your Grace, thanks to your fine physicians.'

'And do you think your pupil is ready for his test?'

Rosamund laughed, daring to peek at Anton. 'We can only hope so, Your Grace.'

'Play a volta!' the Queen commanded the musicians, as Anton came to take Rosamund's hand in his. He bowed low, kissing her fingers lingeringly.

'You look well, my lady,' he murmured.

'I *feel* well,' she answered. 'Now.'

'But shall we impress the Queen with our dancing? Or were we too distracted in our lessons?'

'Do you need to impress her?' Rosamund teased. 'Are you so in need of yet more prizes?'

'Only one, I think.' He led her to the centre of the hall, where the other courtiers had made space for them and gathered around to watch.

Rosamund held tightly to Anton's hand as they took up their opening pose, smiling as if she was tranquil and happy—not quaking with fear inside. She wanted so very much for them to do well before her father and the Queen, to show that she and Anton could be truly united. But there was always the memory of the many falls they had taken in rehearsing—and the way those rehearsals had always been interrupted by kisses!

The music started, a lively tune, quicker than they were used to. Rosamund squeezed his hand and they stepped off—right, left, right, left, and jump.

To her joy, the leaping cadence went off perfectly, and they landed lightly with one foot before the other. After that, the dance went as if by magic. They jumped and twirled and spun, then whirled into the volta, facing each other.

Anton held her by the waist as they turned, Rosamund shifting onto her inside foot as she bent her knees to spring upward.

'La volta!' the crowd shouted, and Anton lifted her high, twirling her around and around as she laughed in utter joy.

Anton spun her about one last time as she laughed merrily. It had been a grand dance, perfect in every way. She hated to see it end, but it did end so splendidly, with her held tightly in Anton's arms.

He slowly lowered her to her feet, her head spinning giddily.

'Did I do that properly, then, Mistress Teacher?' he whispered.

'You are a fine pupil indeed,' she answered.

They gazed at each other, the rest of the room fading away into a mere bright blur. They seemed the only two people in all the world. All the danger, the worry, faded away, and she was sure this was where she was meant to be all along.

But they were not alone for long. Queen Elizabeth applauded, drawing them back to her. 'Very well done, Sir Anton. I think you must now concede that anyone can dance.'

'Indeed, Your Grace,' Anton said. 'If even *I* can, it is true anyone may—with a good teacher.'

'I believe you owe Lady Rosamund a boon, then,' the Queen said. 'Was that not the agreement?'

'I will give Lady Rosamund anything in my power,' he said.

'Yes? Then we have a suggestion, in which we are seconded by the lady's excellent father,' said the Queen. 'You should marry Lady Rosamund, and make her mistress of your fine new estate. Are you content with this?'

Rosamund's hand tightened on Anton's, and his fingers folded around hers. It could not be real, she thought in a daze. She had just been given all she desired, all she had hoped for so ardently. Was she dreaming?

She glanced back at her father, who smiled at her. Then she turned back to Anton and saw her own joy reflected in his beautiful dark eyes.

'I am most content with this, Your Grace,' he said.

'And you, Lady Rosamund?' the Queen said. 'Do you accept this as your wager's prize?'

'I do, Your Grace,' Rosamund whispered, sure she must be dreaming those words. 'Most heartily.'

'I do hate to lose the company of my ladies, but surely a wedding is a cause for celebration. We must all have a dance! Master Vernerson, will you partner me?' the Queen said, holding out her hand to the bowing Swede as the musicians launched into a galliard. 'It is not every day we look forward to a wedding.'

Laughing, Rosamund and Anton joined the line of dancers, twirling and leaping until they reached the end of the hall and could slip out of the doors.

There, hidden in the shadows, they were truly alone at long last.

'Is it true, then?' she whispered, holding close to his hands so he could not escape her. Not now, not so close to their dream's realisation. 'We may marry and live at our own home here in England?'

'It seems so,' Anton said, laughing. 'But do you want to marry me, Rosamund, after everything we have been through? After my foolish behaviour in letting you go? Will you be content as Lady Gustavson, far away from this grand, courtly life?'

'I will be the most content lady in all the land!' Rosamund cried. 'I only ever wanted your love, Anton.'

'And you have it, my lady. For ever.' He took the gold-and-ruby ring from his finger, sliding it onto hers. 'As you cannot yet skate, I believe you won this fairly.'

Rosamund laid her hand flat against his fine doublet, admiring the gleam of her new ring, the shining promise of it. 'And your heart?' she teased.

'You have certainly won that as well. From the first moment I saw you, it has been entirely yours.' Anton gazed down at her, his face more solemn and serious than she had ever seen it.

'As mine is yours. For ever.'

With the music of Twelfth Night in their ears, and the promise of the new year to come before them, they kissed and held each other close, knowing at last that it was truly for ever and always.

Epilogue

Briony Manor, Christmas Day, 1565

'Do you see it, Bess?' Rosamund whispered. She gently waved the newly made kissing bough above her daughter's cradle, laughing in delight as tiny Bess reached for it with her chubby rosebud hand.

Rosamund kissed those pink little fingers, marvelling at their perfection. Bess laughed, kicking her feet under the hem of her long gown. Behind them the fire crackled in the grate of the great hall, flickering on the greenery and red ribbons of the holiday.

'You know it is Christmas, don't you, my darling?' Rosamund said, swinging the bough back and forth before her daughter's fascinated gaze. The baby's eyes were dark, like her father's, but a fluff of pale-blonde hair crowned her perfect little head.

''Twas a year ago I found your father, on the coldest Christmas that ever was seen. And now this year I have you.' Her heart truly overflowed with joy, Rosamund thought. 'Christmas is the finest time of year.'

'I agree most heartily to *that*,' Anton said, bounding into the hall. He still wore his riding boots, and bore the chill of the outdoors, the crispness of green and smoke of the winter's day. But Rosamund cared naught for the dust on his boots as he kissed her.

'How are my ladies this fine afternoon?' he said, reaching for the baby's hand. Her fingers curled tight around his as she laughed and cooed.

'Quite well with our decorating, and hoping your hunt was successful,' Rosamund said, marvelling at the sight of her husband and child together—her two great loves.

'Indeed! We will have a fine feast to welcome your parents tomorrow.'

'They don't care about that. They only want to see Bess.'

'I hope you told them she is the most perfect baby in all the world.'

'In every letter since she was born. Mama writes she expects no less from *her* grandchild, and Father says we must betroth her to a duke at the very least.'

Anton laughed. 'Perhaps we should wait for her betrothal until she is walking.'

Rosamund tucked the fur-lined blanket around Bess, handing her a toy lamb to play with. 'I saw there was a letter this morning from Celia. Will we see her back in England for the holiday? She has been away on the Queen's business for so long.'

Anton shook his head. 'My cousin says her work is not yet done in Scotland. Perhaps next year.'

'Then our table will be complete. But for now we must make certain Bess's first Christmas is wondrous.'

'Just as ours is now?' he said, catching her in his arms for a long, passionate kiss. Even after a year of marriage, his kiss thrilled her to her very toes, making the cold day as warm as July.

She wrapped her arms around him, holding him close as their baby cooed and laughed. 'Oh, my dearest. There could *never* be a finer Christmas than this one!'

Author's Note

I *love* Christmas, so was very excited to dive into Rosamund and Anton's story! The history of Christmas traditions in the Renaissance is a rich—and fun!—one, especially in the reign of Elizabeth I, who certainly knew how to put on a party. Despite the lack of trees and stockings, we would be very familiar with many aspects of the holiday in the sixteenth century—the music, the feasting—though not many of us have peacock and boar's head on our tables!—the greenery and ribbon used in decoration. And the possibility of romance under the mistletoe…

I also enjoyed weaving real Elizabethan history into the story. The winter of 1564 was indeed so terribly cold that the Thames froze through and a frost fair was set up on the ice. Mary, Queen of Scots, as always for Elizabeth, was a great concern and nuisance. Her disastrous marriage to Lord Darnley was just over the horizon, despite Elizabeth's suggestion that her cousin marry Lord Leicester.

While Anton and Rosamund, as well as their families, friends and enemies, are fictional, a few real-life historical figures play a role in their story. Among them are Lord Burghley, Lord Leicester, Blanche Parry, Mistress Eglionby—who had the unenviable task of corralling the young maids of honour!—the Scots Melville and Maitland, the Austrian Adam von Zwetkovich, and the Maids Mary Howard, Mary Radcliffe and Catherine Knyvett. I also used much of Queen Elizabeth's complicated courtship politics in the story, including King Eric of Sweden—who a few years later went mad and was deposed by his brother—and Archduke Charles.

A few resources I found useful and interesting are:

Maria Hubert's *Christmas in Shakespeare's England*

Simon Thurley's *Whitehall Palace: The Official Illustrated History*. Most of Whitehall is gone now, of course, except for the Banquet Hall, but this book has old floor-plans and descriptions of the grand old palace.

Alison Sims's *Food and Feast in Tudor England*

Liza Picard's *Elizabeth's London*

Anne Somerset's *Ladies in Waiting: From the Tudors to the Present Day*

Janet Arnold's *Queen Elizabeth's Wardrobe Unlock'd* and *Patterns of Fashion 1560-1620*

Josephine Ross's *The Men Who Would Be King*, about Queen Elizabeth's many political courtships.

There are many good general biographies of Elizabeth I out there, but two I like are Alison Weir's *The Life of Elizabeth I* and Anne Somerset's *Elizabeth I.*

The manuscript of the traditional mummers' play used in Anne Percy and Lord Langley's scene came from one performed annually at the town of Chudlington in Oxfordshire, which was first written down in 1893, but which is said to have been performed in this form for hundreds of years before that!

I hope you enjoyed Anton and Rosamund's Christmas romance! Be sure and visit my website at *http://ammandamccabe.tripod.com*, where I'll be posting lots more fun research-titbits…

* * * * *

Regency

HIGH-SOCIETY AFFAIRS

Rakes and rogues in the ballrooms – and the bedrooms – of Regency England!

Volume 8 – 2nd October 2009
Sparhawk's Angel by Miranda Jarrett
The Proper Wife by Julia Justiss

Volume 9 – 6th November 2009
The Disgraced Marchioness by Anne O'Brien
The Reluctant Escort by Mary Nichols

Volume 10 – 4th December 2009
The Outrageous Debutante by Anne O'Brien
A Damnable Rogue by Anne Herries

Volume 11 – 8th January 2010
The Enigmatic Rake by Anne O'Brien
The Lord and the Mystery Lady by Georgina Devon

Volume 12 – 5th February 2010
The Wagering Widow by Diane Gaston
An Unconventional Widow by Georgina Devon

Volume 13 – 5th March 2010
A Reputable Rake by Diane Gaston
The Heart's Wager by Gayle Wilson

Volume 14 – 2nd April 2010
The Venetian's Mistress by Ann Elizabeth Cree
The Gambler's Heart by Gayle Wilson

NOW 14 VOLUMES IN ALL TO COLLECT!

millsandboon.co.uk Community

Join Us!

The Community is the perfect place to meet and chat to kindred spirits who love books and reading as much as you do, but it's also the place to:

- Get the inside scoop from authors about their latest books
- Learn how to write a romance book with advice from our editors
- Help us to continue publishing the best in women's fiction
- Share your thoughts on the books we publish
- Befriend other users

Forums: Interact with each other as well as authors, editors and a whole host of other users worldwide.

Blogs: Every registered community member has their own blog to tell the world what they're up to and what's on their mind.

Book Challenge: We're aiming to read 5,000 books and have joined forces with The Reading Agency in our inaugural Book Challenge.

Profile Page: Showcase yourself and keep a record of your recent community activity.

Social Networking: We've added buttons at the end of every post to share via digg, Facebook, Google, Yahoo, technorati and de.licio.us.

www.millsandboon.co.uk

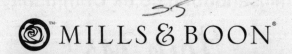